UNDUE INFLUENCES

DEBRA E. BLAINE, MD

ISBN: 979-8-9866211-2-8 (paperback)

ISBN: 979-8-9866211-3-5 (ebook)

Blaine, Debra

Edited by Erika Nein

Cover design by Joe Montgomery

Published by Very Indie Press

Melville, NY

VeryIndiePress.com

Printed in the United States

ALSO BY DEBRA E. BLAINE, MD

Beyond the Pillars of Salt

CODE BLUE: The Other End of the Stethoscope

"Move over Michael Crichton, Nelson DeMille and Patricia Cornwell, I have a new favorite author for my library and so will you.
Debra Blaine's book is brilliant. Filled with fascinating characters woven into an intriguing plot demonstrating how the genuine passion of the most well-meaning people can turn to extremism when influenced and manipulated by powerful forces. Stripped from the social and political headlines of today, there are so many twists and turns you won't want to stop reading."

—*Berry Fowler, Founder Sylvan Learning Centers and Fowler International Academy*

"Debra Blaine, a physician turned author, has created *Undue Influences*, a new kind of intriguing thriller that goes beyond front page news and takes the reader on a quest to fight against everyday manipulation from our government and media sources.

This Pinnacle Book Achievement Winner will keep you enthralled from beginning to end."

—*Al Galasso, National Association of Book Entrepreneurs*

"*Undue Influences* is a chilling story with unexpected twists and turns. A medical mystery that is an edge of your seat, timely novel that speaks to the events of our present day. A page-turner that you can't put down."

—*Lynne Hinton, author of "The Beekeeper's Wife"*

For my grandfather, *Lazer Gutman*

1902 – 1971

For his courage to see the world as it was, and respond in kind.

"Our normal waking consciousness, rational consciousness as we call it, is but one special type of consciousness, whilst all about it, parted from it by the filmiest of screens, there lie potential forms of consciousness entirely different. We may go through life without suspecting their existence; but apply the requisite stimulus, and at a touch they are there in all their completeness...."

—William James
Gifford Lectures at the University of Edinburgh, 1902

———

"As far as the Laws of Mathematics refer to reality, they are not certain; and as far as they are certain, they do not refer to reality."

—Albert Einstein
Address to the Prussian Academy of Sciences, 1921

CHAPTER 1

Joshua stumbled through the door to the building. Somehow *this* door felt like the right one. Even if he were wrong, he had to get off the street. The summer sunlight was blinding him like a dagger slicing through his eyes until his head felt like it was splitting open. He pushed at the revolving door and leaned on it wearily as it circled slowly inward, depositing him in a vast open space about thirty feet from a long counter that extended fifty feet across the back of the room. The counter barred entry to the rest of the building except at the security stops on either side, each guarded by an armed man in uniform. He felt like he had just run a marathon and very nearly fell to his knees.

The light inside didn't feel much better on his eyes. The wall behind him where he had come in extended up at least twenty feet, composed of either windows or mirrors—he couldn't be sure—and even the smooth, slate, gray-tile floor seemed to reflect light directly into his brain. Some voice in his head reassured him that this was normal for New York City. *What is New York City? Where am I?*

"Whoa, there, son!" The voice of the man in uniform who was suddenly by his side was vaguely familiar, and Joshua wondered if he should know him from somewhere. "What happened to you, Joshua?"

So, obviously the man knew *him*. About the only thing that was clear right then was that his name was Joshua. Everything else was a blur. An exquisitely painful blur.

The other guard came over and spoke to the first. "Frank, get him a chair." He then shouted over his shoulder to the woman at the counter. "Call 911!" He turned back to Joshua. "What happened to you, man? Are you okay? Are you hurt? What happened?"

Joshua looked at him slowly, his eyes trying hard to focus. "Who... who are you? Do I know you?" His words sounded impressively clear despite how muddled his brain felt.

"Liam! It's Liam. Of course you know me, man. Geez, you must have hit your head. You're bleeding—like—everywhere. Were you hit by a car?"

Bleeding... Joshua looked down. Yes, there was blood on him, everywhere on him. Why hadn't he noticed?

The man Liam had called Frank was back with a chair, and Joshua gratefully sank into it. "I called upstairs," Frank told Liam. "Mr. Vaderman is coming right down."

Frank turned to Joshua and said, "Your Uncle Russell is on his way, and so is the ambulance. You're going to be okay. Just take it easy."

Joshua's ears started ringing, and he felt like he might faint. He gripped the sides of the chair and shut his eyes. It felt like he was spinning. The noise in his head grew louder. "Make it stop," he whispered. Then he screamed, "Make it stop!"

"Make what stop, sweetie?" A gentle woman's voice reached out to him. "Joshie, honey, what happened? It's Aunt Maya, sweetheart. Talk to me."

Joshua opened his eyes a crack. The entryway was now

flooding with people. The loud ringing was suddenly right behind him and then ceased, but lights were flashing from a truck. He felt like he was going to vomit and clutched the hand belonging to the gentle woman's voice who called herself Aunt Maya. He wasn't sure who she was, but he felt safe with her. Then the world went black.

————

When he came to, paramedics were swarming all over Joshua, pulling his arms and his body in all different ways. They took his blood pressure, put some small piece of plastic on his left index finger, and cut his clothes away to attach sticky leads to his chest.

"My name is Micky," the EMT said. "Can you tell me your name?"

Joshua knew his name was Joshua, but he couldn't say it. The more he tried, the harder it was to speak. He started struggling and grabbing at Micky. He opened his mouth, but he couldn't say his name; his mouth was completely dry.

"His name is Joshua Plessman," Liam offered. "This is his aunt, Maya Vaderman, and his uncle—oh, there he is! Mr. Vaderman, he's over here."

Russell Vaderman walked quickly, but somehow he always conveyed the sense that he was never in a rush, even if he was running. He was in his mid-forties, stood about six-feet, one-inch, and was trim and muscular without looking like a gym rat. He had thick, dark, wavy hair that was full on top but cropped close at the neck. His fingers were long and tapered, presaging his extensive talents as an artist and a pianist. His blue eyes were piercing, and he always spoke with quiet authority.

"Does anyone know what happened to him?" Russell asked Liam and Frank. He looked expectantly at Maya.

When he saw his uncle, Joshua became even more agitated.

He started squirming and struggled to break free of the EMTs and their equipment, but they held him fast.

"Easy there, Joshua," Micky said. "Does it hurt anywhere? Where are you bleeding from?" Joshua quieted as his uncle stepped out of his field of vision as if Russell instinctively recognized his presence was causing some mysterious distress in his nephew. The EMT examined Joshua's head with gloved hands. Then he held Joshua's head still while he shined a penlight in his eyes. The light hurt.

The EMT dictated to his partner. "Altered mental status but he responds to stimuli, pupils are dilated; heart rate is 120, but he's otherwise stable, sinus tachycardia; O_2 sat is 99 percent, BP 102/60. I can't find the source of his bleeding, but it seems to have stopped. There's no fresh blood," he said to his partner who was entering the notes on a tablet. "Actually, this blood is all dry. Let's get him to New York-Presby, they'll take a closer look." He looked at Maya and Russell. "You can meet us at the hospital."

Joshua was laid on the stretcher, but he would not allow the stretcher straps to be attached until the EMTs lifted the back to put him in a sitting position. They wheeled him out the door and across the crowded, sun-drenched city sidewalk to the waiting ambulance.

———

The ground floor of Vaderman Ventures was chaotic. Onlookers tried to maneuver into a position to stare. Bloody sneaker prints had been smeared on the floor, where some escaped fluid flushed from the IV line had mixed with the dried blood from Joshua's clothes, and there was discarded trash from EKG leads and a small strip of the bloody, button-down cotton shirt remained. Russell Vaderman took a measured look around, signaled to the custodian, Vinny, to come over and clean up, but an NYPD officer stepped up first.

"I'm Officer Callan. This is potentially part of a crime scene, so we are going to rope it off and process it. We'll let you know when you can clean up."

Great, Russell thought. Just what they needed, to have police milling about a bloody scene in the middle of the lobby on a busy day. What had Joshua gotten himself into? The kid had a good heart, sweet disposition, and was well-intentioned, although, for a time, he had proven to be quite prone to attracting trouble—not nearly as much as Joshua's mother was, and of late, he seemed to have put most of that behind him.

Russell realized he was not overly concerned with Joshua's health. He *knew,* with a certitude he could never have explained, that Joshua was going to be fine. Physically, anyway.

Joshua wasn't the brightest kid. He was a C minus student in high school and not college material by far, but Joshua could learn well enough; it just took him many times longer than an average student, so, he had never qualified for extra services. He was one of those borderline pupils who fell through the cracks. Russell had always thought, if given a chance and proper guidance, Joshua could make it; so, he had taken his nephew under his wing, hired him, and started giving him easy challenges to build his confidence.

A couple of years ago, Russell's wife, Maya, had come to Russell enthusiastically suggesting they enroll Joshua in a new program called Cingulate Services. It was an up-and-coming learning center for mildly challenged individuals, and seemed tailor-made for Joshua. It was specifically for kids and adults who, like Joshua, had never qualified for personal services in school, because they weren't truly learning disabled or "on the spectrum." They were just barely average achievers who weren't going far in life. These clients were precisely *not* trying to study for tests or pass courses in academia, but they wanted to improve their basic intelligence to increase their workplace value and earnings and make a better life for themselves.

Cingulate Services was fairly experimental and Russell had mixed feelings about it, especially since his sister, Joshua's mother, was strongly opposed. But Braelyn would not give Russell any reason for her aversion; she rarely made constructive suggestions about her son or even seemed to engage in his life, whereas Maya kept pushing it, presenting the case that she and not his mother had basically raised Joshua. Russell researched the program and found it had rave reviews and seemed harmless enough. It was government funded for low-income individuals, but Russell paid them a little extra to take special care of Joshua, and it looked like his nephew was making great progress.

Maya appeared at his side as the EMTs left. "We have to call Braelyn. She needs to know her son is in the hospital with a concussion—he didn't know who I was, Russell!" Maya started wringing her hands and fidgeting with her wedding ring, something she always did when she was nervous. "I'm going to head over to Presby now, he shouldn't be alone. My God, he had blood all over him! The poor boy."

"Yes, do that," Russell said. "I'll stay until the police are finished." He sighed heavily. "I don't know how easy it will be to reach my sister in Colombia right now. I'm not even sure where she is exactly. Ugh. I wish Braelyn didn't have such a fascination with that place. It's not safe. And I get that she didn't think the kid needed that much looking after; he is twenty-four years old and divides his time between our households now anyway, but seriously, she should have given us a way to reach her in case of an emergency."

"I guess it doesn't matter," Maya said. "It's not like she's ever been all that attentive to Joshie. Fortunately, I love the boy, and he's always welcome, but what *is* it about Colombia that makes her so hell-bent to go there all the time? I never get a reasonable answer from her, and you are always so elusive about it." Maya peered sidelong at her husband. "She once said it was a 'family thing,' and that you'd been there as a child too, but you've never breathed a word about wanting to go there as an adult."

"Now's not the time, Maya, and no, I have no inclination to visit that part of the world. I was only a toddler when I was there. I'll meet you at the hospital as soon as I can. Call me if they find out anything."

Maya hailed an Uber and was off to New York-Presbyterian Hospital.

Now definitely wasn't the time, Russell thought. Perhaps never was the time to talk about Colombia. Or Peru. Or wherever it was. If not for his aging father's phone call four years ago, begging to reconnect after forty years, he would never have been the wiser. Sure, it was nice to understand the forces that had affected him as a child and why his parents divorced when he was little more than three years old, but he could have lived just as well not knowing. Except for the dreams, of course. But he had learned to live with those.

Russell was an enormously successful architect and engineer in New York City, with his own brand of art. He was commissioned all over the world to create functional structures of supreme splendor. Who cared where he had gotten this talent? It was his. He sighed and called upstairs to Rosalee, his secretary, and told her to reschedule his afternoon appointments. It was money potentially lost that his business would miss right now. These last few years, the trend was to build cheap and flimsy, and Russell would never compromise on quality and beauty. But he wouldn't let Maya worry about that, and Joshua was apparently the closest thing to a son he would ever have. Family first.

CHAPTER 2

Maya paced the floor on the other side of the curtain from where the doctor examined her nephew. She'd been told Joshua had abruptly "woken up" en route to the emergency department and started recognizing his surroundings, but he still had no idea at all what had happened to him. At least he should recognize Maya now. He told the EMTs the last thing he remembered was heading to a Thai restaurant to meet a friend from his learning center for dinner, but strangely, he couldn't say who the friend was. He'd made several loose connections with other clients at Cingulate and had started to socialize with them, but Maya had never met any of his new acquaintances.

Over time, Maya had begun to instinctively distrust the organization, even though she was the one to endorse it in the beginning. She wondered now if Cingulate Services had anything to do with Joshua's current state. It wasn't that Maya had changed her mind about the program as a whole, but she was getting a slimy feeling from the new chapter director, Mark Wheeler, who had come on board nine months ago. There was something about him she instinctively didn't like. She'd been extremely impressed with his predecessor, who had served them tea and cookies (can you imagine!) and then invited her to serve on their consultation council. Russell was so highly regarded, she frequently *met* leadership in various organizations, but she'd never been encouraged to contribute at so high a level. Although Russell wasn't a huge fan of the company, he'd had no concrete objections, and Maya knew he would never get in the way of her achieving success on her own. He just wasn't that type of guy. For herself, Maya was enthralled to be part of such a grassroots service at the upper levels.

So, Maya and her Undivided group had gotten briefly involved with the New York Cingulate Services chapter, hoping it would serve as a means of leveling the job opportunities available to all. Cingulate Services made a lot of promises about how they could increase the IQ of average people. The program was presented as a human resource aiming to compensate for the fact that so much of the wealth was in so few hands.

But on closer look, despite its success in improving cognition, the curriculum seemed designed more for producing citizens who favored the Cingulate agenda. The students definitely learned to work out math problems that were directly applicable to daily business needs and to comprehend literature from all sources, but once Joshua started evaluating issues, presumably for himself, Maya could see he was definitely being steered to promote the Cingulate party line, which was overly conservative for Maya's taste.

Recently, Joshua had come home and announced that the only way President Ganaffe would lose the upcoming election was if it were rigged, because he was just that popular. Maya was beside herself—she despised the current president—but she could not convince her nephew otherwise. It wasn't until Russell came home, and in his calm, rational way explained to Joshua that the election was still nearly four months away and nobody could predict what would happen between now and then, that Joshua let it go. Joshua's idolization of Russell and his craving to be in agreement with everything his uncle believed seemed to take precedence over the way he was being steered to think at the center. Maya kept Joshua in the program because his reasoning skills and aptitude for learning new things were undeniably improving, but free thinking of any sort was definitely not encouraged at Cingulate.

Abruptly, the curtain pulled back from Joshua's bed and Dr. Alexander motioned for Maya to step up.

"Joshua would like you to come in," he said. "So… I've done a full exam, and none of this blood appears to be Joshua's. There's not a mark on him—except the blood itself, which appears to be mostly dry. Do you have any idea whose blood this could be?"

Maya took a step back. "Why, no. I haven't seen Joshie for three days, not since came over for dinner Saturday night. He's been staying at his mother's apartment; she's in Colombia on vacation right now." She looked at Joshua. "Sweetie, don't you know what happened to you?"

"Aunt Maya, I swear, I don't." His face was a mix of honest bewilderment and near panic. "I don't remember anything! I barely remember getting into the office, that part feels like a dream. I just remember the pain in my head was excruciating. It's better now, but it still hurts." He rubbed his right temple.

Maya felt immensely relieved that at least Joshie really did know who *she* was now. She looked at Dr. Alexander. "Why can't he remember? Was he hit in the head? Is that why he can't remember?"

"I don't know," the doctor replied. "We sent a toxicology screen, and he will be going in for a CT scan of his brain in just a few minutes. Just so you know, the police have been notified; it's protocol, since the blood is not his own. They'll have questions for you both."

"Oh my God," Maya whispered.

"Doctor, can I *please* have a drink of water?" Joshua asked. "My mouth feels like glue. I can barely swallow."

"Yes, I'll have someone bring it now that we know you don't need surgery of any sort. But really, with the IV running, you shouldn't feel so parched." The doctor laughed. "You'll probably be running to the bathroom soon enough with all this fluid."

"That's the other thing," Joshua said. "My bladder feels so full, but I could barely go when you asked me to pee in the cup."

"Hmm." Dr. Alexander looked at Joshua sideways for a second. "Well, let's get you into that CT scanner."

By the time Joshua was back from radiology, two New York City police officers were chomping at the bit to speak to him. Officer Ronald Greenstone was dark skinned, muscular, and handsome, in his mid-thirties with a quick wit. He was a favorite among the female staff. Detective James Rodriguez was older and a no-nonsense sort. He picked up Joshua's chart and started scrolling casually through it.

"Hey, you can't look at that," the radiology technician said as he brought Joshua back to his ED bed in a wheelchair. "That's private information."

Detective Rodriguez looked at Joshua. "You have any problem with my looking at your medical records, son? You don't have anything to hide, do you?"

Joshua squirmed, uncertain, and looked toward his aunt; she had seen the police descend on her nephew and was marching over from the waiting area.

"What's the problem?" she demanded.

The rad tech looked pointedly at the detective as he helped Joshua into bed. "Unless the patient or a legal guardian gives consent, no one but Joshua's immediate medical providers should have access to his records. Unless you have a warrant."

Detective Rodriguez scowled, and Officer Greenstone broke

in with a charming smile. "Now, Joshua, would it be okay with you if we peeked in your chart? I'm sure you want information as much as we do." He ran his index finger over the edge of the clipboard.

Maya stepped between the officers and Joshua and grabbed the chart. "I think Joshua has the right to know what's in there before he gives you access," she said. "Why are you so interested in his medical information? Is he under arrest?"

Officer Greenstone looked at her with his most beguiling smile. "No, no, of course not. I'm sorry, we didn't introduce ourselves." The officers flashed their badges briefly. "And who are you?"

"My name is Maya Vaderman, and this is my nephew, Joshua Plessman." Maya walked over to stand protectively next to Joshua. She kept his chart tucked firmly beneath her arm.

"Joshua looks to be of age to make this decision himself, aren't you, Joshua?" Greenstone ducked his head and tilted it sidewise as he asked, trying to make eye contact.

Joshua averted his eyes. "I—I agree with my aunt. She should decide. Until my mother gets back from Colombia," he said.

The two officers looked at each other, then back at Joshua. "Now, what might your mother be doing in Colombia, young man?" Detective Rodriguez asked.

"Never you mind," Maya broke in. "His mother has nothing to do with any of this. She went on vacation, is all, and Joshie is twenty-four years old. He can make decisions without his mother."

Dr. Alexander walked over. He glared at the police officers and asked, "Is there a problem here?" After a moment, the officers took a few steps back and out of earshot.

"How are you feeling, Joshua?" the doctor asked quietly as Maya handed him the medical chart.

"Okay, I guess. Just still really thirsty, and I have a headache.

And I was barely able to, um, pee again on the way back from the x-ray place."

"Probably just nerves. All your lab work is basically normal, your tox screen is negative, and the head CT looks fine. And you said you have no history of seizures, right?"

Both Joshua and Maya nodded in agreement.

"Since there are no apparent injuries that need to be treated," the doctor continued, "if you're feeling okay, I can discharge you, as long as you have somewhere to go where you will be with a responsible adult. We're going to give you a follow up appointment with a neurologist for next week, unless you already have someone else you'd like to see. It's important that you keep this appointment, even though I expect your memory will start to return in the next few days. Do you understand?"

Joshua nodded.

"I'll take him home with me, of course," Maya said, and started gathering his clothes. She handed them to Joshua and closed the curtain so he could take off the hospital gown and get dressed.

The doctor walked over to the detectives. "Unless you are charging Joshua with something, you need to let him leave," he told them. "I understand you have questions, but he won't be able to answer them now, and interrogating him will only aggravate his psychological trauma. Give him a few days. He's obviously been through quite an ordeal; luckily, outside of the memory lapse, he seems to be no worse for wear. I think you'll get further after he's had a chance to go home and relax."

———

Greenstone and Rodriguez sat in their car outside the hospital. "If none of the blood covering Plessman is his own, whose blood is it?" Rodriguez asked. "Callan sent the sample from Vaderman Ventures over to CODIS, right? Any matches yet?"

"Nothing has shown up," Greenstone said, "and no one has filed a complaint against a mid-twenties Caucasian attacker meeting this kid's description."

"Any dead bodies turn up?" Rodriguez asked with one eyebrow raised. "That was a hell of a lot of blood from the little bit I saw."

"Nope, nothing." Greenstone sighed.

"Okay, let's get back to the station," Rodriguez said.

CHAPTER 3

Maya hugged Joshua tight while they waited for their ride. Why hadn't Russell called? Why did business always seem more important to him than family? Once again, she rued the fact that they couldn't have their own children. The doctors had determined it was *her* fault, something about her eggs not releasing from her ovaries. Russell must have thought he was making it better to tell her it didn't matter, that she was all he needed. But of course, he'd already been covering for his sister's escapades since Joshua was ten.

To be fair, Russell *had* wholeheartedly embraced his nephew when his sister Braelyn went off the deep end fourteen years ago. Joshie had called them one evening because the refrigerator was empty and he was hungry; he'd been on his own for three days. Braelyn had gone off on some drug adventure and forgotten she had a little boy at home. From that day on, he lived with Russell and Maya, and Russell had forced Braelyn to sign papers giving them guardianship. If she had refused, he would have reported her to Child Protective Services, and she would have lost Joshie anyway.

So, Russell felt like he was already raising a child. And Joshie was always so cuddly; what he lacked in intelligence, he made up for in affection. His mother never would consistently take the bipolar medication she was given, and Joshie seemed to understand clearly that Braelyn was entirely unable to care for him.

The universe was so unkind. Maya would have been such a strong, nurturing mother, but she was infertile, and Russell's sister was such a flake, yet she'd had three pregnancies. Braelyn aborted the last two, saying that between her medications and the street drugs and alcohol, it wasn't safe to carry them. Each time, Maya begged her to get clean for nine months and give Maya and Russell the child to raise, but to no avail. Braelyn was always a selfish one.

Russell would have sent a private company car to pick up Joshie and her from the hospital, but

Maya wasn't having that. Right then, Lyft was even faster than Uber when she checked the apps. Maya helped her nephew into the back seat, and Joshie laid his head on her shoulder, something he hadn't done in years. He was asleep in less than a minute. *Maybe when he wakes up, he will remember what happened to him*, she thought.

They had cleaned him up in the hospital, but there were still bloodstains on his clothing. The whole thing was shocking to Maya; she could barely imagine how horrible it was to wake up as the one covered in blood.

She tried to put together what she could remember about the last few days. Joshie had his usual learning session at Cingulate Services on Friday, and on Saturday he said he was meeting a friend from the group for dinner Sunday night. That would have been nearly forty-eight hours ago. She hadn't heard from him all day Sunday, Monday, or today until he stumbled into their midtown office on Sixth Avenue around 1:00 p.m. That wasn't unusual. Joshie was pretty independent. He made his own money and liked to go to local meetups and out to dinner with his friends, even if it was just for pizza. He was a very likable kid. And Russell had him working autonomously on various projects, so Joshua didn't have to check in every day, as long as he got his work done, which he always did. Maya was quite proud of him. These days, he often stayed at his mother's apartment in the Village, unless he wanted to come home for a warm meal. Braelyn never cooked. Maya had just assumed he was hanging out in lower Manhattan since he had the apartment all to himself while his mother was away.

Maya started to berate herself for not keeping closer tabs on him, but then reminded herself that he was twenty-four, for God's sake, and hadn't given them reasons to worry since he used to get drunk in high school. That seemed so long ago, and she had come to trust him as he grew up. He seemed perfectly fine when he came to dinner the other night. He really seemed to have put the booze behind him, especially seeing what it did to his mother.

CHAPTER 4

Thomas Brunner tossed the bloody gloves into the incinerator and washed his hands carefully. Why did *he* have to be the one to get his hands dirty? He wished he'd had the guts to object to the whole operation at the time; now it was way too late. It was the story of his life: He always seemed to get his courage up long *after* he needed it. He sighed and walked back into the office where his immediate superior, Mark Wheeler, was pacing the floor.

"Well, that couldn't have been much riskier," Wheeler nearly snarled. "What the hell were you thinking?"

Brunner pushed his hair back, his tell that he was nervous, revealing dark sweat patches under his armpits. The question pissed him off. It wasn't like any of this had been his idea; they'd totally shared the responsibility, and no one needed to tell *him* they'd made a mess.

"The Plessman kid was *not* supposed to be there. It was just supposed to be Donny and Jackson. Two nobodies who wouldn't raise an eyebrow," Brunner said.

Wheeler's eyes were shooting daggers. "Joshua Plessman is hardly a *nobody*, not with one of the richest and most influential people in the city for an uncle, *and* he's a primary subject all on his own! What do we say now? 'Sorry, he was collateral damage, showed up in the wrong place at the wrong time'? Is that the story we're going with? Geez, we need to figure out a way to explain this. Did we even learn anything useful that we can offer as solace?" Wheeler always gesticulated when he was stressed, and now his hands were shaking wildly.

"Maybe so," Brunner said slowly, scratching his temple. Wheeler was raising his ire, trying to blame it on him, but Brunner could always think more clearly when he was angry. "This was potentially an even better 'trial run' than we had planned. They want to know if the effects can be expanded to last over time, right? We just weren't going to use Plessman for that. And there was only supposed to be one DB." Brunner couldn't bring himself to say "dead body;" the whole thing made him crazy uncomfortable.

Wheeler's face brightened somewhat. "That's true. It *was* a success, wasn't it? We just have to make sure it is perceived that way. As long as the kid's memory doesn't push through the veil we created, or Vaderman isn't satisfied with his nephew's lack of a story. *That* could get us screwed. Russell Vaderman is a man you don't poke at. He is unrelenting when provoked."

———

Russell arrived home at 6:15 p.m., just as Maya was cleaning up the dinner dishes. "You're home early." Maya couldn't quite keep the sarcasm out of her voice. "You never showed at the hospital."

"I called you twice and texted you, Maya. Then I called Jim Werner, and he checked for me. Joshua was unharmed except for the memory loss and set to be discharged. What was the point of going over there?" Jim Werner, MD, MBA, was the president and CEO of the hospital, and a good friend of Russell's.

Maya checked her phone. "I'm sorry, I didn't see the text; I wasn't really looking at my phone, and cell service must have been patchy. I never got a call." The sarcasm was turned down a decibel, but still present.

"Where is he? Does he remember *anything*?" Russell asked.

"After a shower and dinner, I sent him off to bed, Russ. The kid was exhausted. Such a nightmare! And he feels terrible, not remembering anything. I'm worried about him. And the police were there, and they looked like vultures. You've got to call the commissioner and tell them to lay off. Joshie doesn't know anything, and no one got hurt, so they should just leave him be."

"Well, that's the thing, right? We don't know if anyone got hurt. But unless they find a victim…."

Maya looked carefully at her husband. After eighteen years of marriage, she knew his moods like she knew the inside of Barney's. "What happened, Russ? I mean, what *else* happened? What aren't you telling me?"

Russell looked up and frowned. He was busted. "Braelyn called this afternoon. Bad timing."

"And…?"

"And she was stopped at JFK customs with two kilos of cocaine."

Maya put a hand to her mouth. "And what does she want you to do about it?"

"What do you think? She wants bail money. Half a million dollars." Russell made himself a plate of chicken and pasta with broccoli before it made it into the fridge as leftovers and sat down at the kitchen table to eat.

Maya blanched. "And…?" she asked again.

"And nothing. I told her to cool her jets and I'll have a lawyer see her in the morning."

"I bet that didn't make her happy."

"Nothing makes my sister happy."

———

The next morning, Joshua woke up having had the most bizarre and disturbing dreams full of painfully bright lights that obscured terrors without shapes. It was after 11:00 a.m., and while he could believe he had overslept—he had never been a morning person—the fact that no one had woken him to get to work was the strangest thing of all. Especially since he was apparently in his aunt's and uncle's home on East 59th Street, when he was sure he had been staying in the Village this past week.

Joshua had the loft bedroom in midtown. It was the smallest room in the otherwise huge co-op apartment, but it was his choice, and he was very attached to it. It felt like having his own little hidey-hole, both protected by and separate from his aunt and uncle who'd been parents to him for so long.

He found himself a little unsteady as he headed downstairs for breakfast and wondered if he'd been drinking last night. That would be weird, since he'd given that up after high school, when he realized how his mother's alcoholism had played into her bipolar illness and general craziness. Everyone said if she'd just stop drinking and take her meds, she would be "normal." Sometimes he'd have a single beer, nothing more, but he didn't think that was it because he couldn't remember anything except being in the hospital and being poked and prodded and scanned. In fact, he couldn't clearly remember the last several days at all.

Aunt Maya was downstairs, another strange thing. Unless

maybe it was Saturday? She rushed over to him as he got to the bottom step. "Joshie! How are you feeling?"

"I don't know. What's today? How come I slept here last night? I thought I was staying at Mom's?" He gripped the railing, and his knuckles turned white.

Aunt Maya stroked his wavy hair like she used to do when he was very young. "Don't you remember anything from yesterday, sweetie?" she asked.

Joshua stopped. So it wasn't *all* a dream. The hospital and the sharpness of the light that seemed to cut his brain open, and before that… no, no, no. He couldn't look at before that. His face must have taken on an expression of complete distress, because Aunt Maya clucked at him and led him to the kitchen without asking him again to answer.

"Aunt Maya…" His tongue felt thick and weird in his mouth. "Something horrible happened."

Maya sat him down at the kitchen table. She sat down next to him and took his hand. He saw French toast on the counter and knew it was for him, but he wasn't hungry.

"Tell me about it, Joshie."

Joshua's head started to hurt again, and he remembered his mammoth headache from yesterday. His mouth felt dry, but not like it had been, and he realized he'd been able to pee this morning without the problem he was having in the hospital. He started shaking and realized that trying to remember was bringing back all that pain in his head.

"That's the thing, Aunt Maya, I can hardly remember. I remember finding my way into the office, and the knife in my eyes and in my head… and then Liam telling me I was bleeding. Did I cut myself? I didn't follow everything going on in the hospital, that's kind of a blur, too. Where did the blood come from?"

"Well, my dear, that's the sixty-four-thousand-dollar question. It didn't come from you, thank God, but there will be a lot of people asking you about it. We managed to put the police off yesterday because the doctor told them you couldn't remember yet, but he also said it should come back to you. Don't you worry. Come, sweetie, have some breakfast." She put the plate of French toast in front of him.

But every time Joshua tried to figure it out, he was sure of only one thing: that he really didn't want to know.

CHAPTER 5

Russell's intercom buzzed. "Yes, Rosalee?"

"Sorry to disturb you, Mr. Vaderman. There are two police officers downstairs who are looking for Joshua."

Russell nodded to himself and frowned. *It starts.* "Send them up," he said.

It took ten minutes for them to get upstairs, and Russell chuckled to himself, knowing Liam and Frank would have made them go through full security and validated their credentials before letting them come upstairs armed.

Officer Greenstone and Detective Rodriguez were shown in looking slightly annoyed and introduced themselves. Russell offered them chairs, but they preferred to stand.

"What can I do for you gentlemen?" Russell asked as he sat back in his ergonomic office chair.

Detective Rodriguez started. "We're looking for your nephew, Joshua Plessman. He was not at his home in the East Village, so we thought he may have come in to work today."

"He's not here."

Officer Greenstone shifted uneasily from foot to foot.

Rodriguez seemed undeterred and asked, "Do you know where he is?"

"Why do you want to speak to him?" Russell asked. He sat forward and pointedly started shuffling some papers on his desk to indicate he had other business to attend to.

Rodriguez's expression looked forbidding, and he stood tall and straight. He would have been intimidating to most other people. "In connection with an assault, possible murder. I know you are aware, Mr. Vaderman. Plessman came here yesterday to this office covered in blood." He put his hands on his hips.

Russell looked up. "Really. Assault? Murder? Who was the victim?"

"We don't know who the victim was yet," Rodriguez said. "But the blood has to have come from somewhere."

"Indeed. Well, if you don't have a victim, you don't have a crime. And if you don't have a crime, you do not need to speak with my nephew, who is recovering from yesterday's ordeal and needs some peace and quiet right now." Russell stood up to dismiss them.

Detective Rodriguez did not move. "Even if he doesn't remember anything yet, we want to look at his cell phone to see where he was and what calls he might have made over the last few days. That would be a good place to start." He raised an eyebrow and cocked his head at Russell. "I would think it would be in your best interest to cooperate with us."

"Do you have a warrant?" Russell asked Rodriguez.

"No."

"Do you have an actual crime?"

"No."

"Really. Then I think this conversation is over. I will, however, be sure to give a call to my good friend, Police Commissioner Harrows, and tell him what an excellent job you are doing. And if anything comes to light, we can speak again. One thing I can tell you, Joshua is one of the gentlest souls you'll meet on this earth. He can't bring himself to harm a cricket. Now, let me show you out." Russell guided the officers to the door and opened it. He turned to the side and then looked back as if it were an afterthought. "Oh, and Detectives… If you do harass my nephew in any way, I will be sure to pass that along to the commissioner as well."

Russell drummed his fingers on the desk after they left. It was going to be an irksome week. He had already asked a defense lawyer, Jeremy Southpine, to see to Braelyn. Posting bail wasn't on Russell's agenda, although he didn't think she'd skip town, and, of course, they'd take her passport. He was just so tired of extricating her from the myriad of personal disasters in her life. And since the "talk" their father had had with each of them four years ago right before he died, everything wrong in Braelyn's life was apparently Russell's fault, even though Russell was only three years old at the time of the whole South American experience. Russell thought again how he would have happily lived his whole life without knowing why his father had abandoned them when they were only tiny children.

And Joshua. Russell shook his head. He was telling the police the truth when he said Josh was the gentlest soul on the planet. Joshua was totally incapable of hurting anyone. He must have seen something that he was blocking out. After a brief spell in high school, Joshua never used any mind-altering drugs or alcohol; besides, the hospital had run a full toxicology screen, which showed nothing. Russell wanted to know what had happened as much as anyone, but a boy like Joshua would not respond to interrogation. That would just frighten him, and he'd recede into his shell like a tortoise. He'd been through so much over the years with his mother's antics, it wasn't even a question. Thankfully, Josh was safe at home with Maya, who would nurture and mother him, and if he were not already sleeping when Russell got home tonight, they could talk. The cell phone was actually a great place to start.

Maya had dinner coming out of the oven, and Joshua was setting the pale gray acacia wood dining table when Russell got home. Maya came over for a quick hug and kiss and said quietly in Russell's ear, "Thank you for getting in early tonight, dear. I was hoping you would."

Russell took her face gently in his hand. "I'm as worried about him as you are," he whispered. He kissed her again, more passionately, and they went into the kitchen.

"Hi, Josh, how are you feeling?" Russell asked.

Joshua saw his uncle and started to tremble involuntarily. "Hi, Uncle Russell. I'm sorry I put you through all that mess yesterday. I didn't mean to bother you. I really didn't even know I was going to the office until I got there. Actually, I wasn't sure where I was...." His voice trailed off.

Russell walked over to his nephew and put his hand on his shoulder. "Look at me, Josh. There's nothing to apologize for. We're family. If you're in some kind of trouble, of course you should come to me." As Russell said these heartfelt words, the room shifted in a feeling of *déjà vu*, and he remembered saying something similar to his sister Braelyn many years ago. Look where that had gone.

Maya took Joshua's favorite dinner out of the oven and put it down on a trivet on the Italian Calacatta white marble countertop. She'd made lasagna, but being the health-conscious woman she was, hers was made half with organic pasta and half with zucchini linguini, and instead of meat, she filled it with ricotta cheese, spinach, carrots, and butternut squash between the layers of her homemade marinara sauce. It smelled heavenly.

They ate dinner peacefully. Russell saw no reason to trouble Joshua with news of his mother's return and subsequent arrest, and Joshua seemed happy for the quietude. His still tousled hair fell in long dark bangs over his forehead, and it was cut short in the back. He was obviously trying to emulate his uncle, whom he revered. He had showered the night before when he got home from the hospital and was wearing a blue T-shirt that said "Think About It" with a light bulb on the front. Another promo from Cingulate Services.

After he finished his lasagna, Russell methodically took the napkin from his lap, folded it, and put it onto his empty plate. He turned to his nephew. "Josh," he began gently, "do you remember anything, anything at all? Whatever happened, it'll be okay. Tell me if you can, and I'll help you."

Joshua started to shake, and he rubbed the sides of his head. "I can't remember, Uncle; honestly, I can't. Except, something tells me I'm not supposed to tell *you* what happened. But I don't remember what it is I'm not supposed to tell you… or why." He rubbed his head harder and faster. "I'm not supposed to tell anyone, but especially not *Russell Vaderman*." When he said his uncle's name, his tone dropped and sounded scripted, almost like he was mimicking someone else's voice. "I'm supposed to forget it ever happened, that's what I was told. When I try to think about it, it's all a blur of blinding white light. There are shapes underneath the light, but I can't make them out. And it hurts. It hurts my head and my eyes, and I just want to scream. It was something *bad*, Uncle Russell, that's all I know. It was *real bad*, and I'm afraid of it. I don't even *want* to know what happened!"

Russell was looking at him intensely now. "Who told you to forget?"

Joshua shook his head, and his eyes looked wild with panic. "I don't know, I don't know!" He started crying and covered his face with his hands.

Maya put her arms around him and crooned at him. "It's all right, Joshie, it's gonna be all right." She looked at Russell with wide, terrified eyes.

"Josh, we have to find out before the police find out. That's the only way I can protect you—if you need protection," Russell said gently. "Perhaps you made calls to your friends who might know where you'd been? May I look at your cell phone?" Russell's voice was calm and steady, as it always was, and Joshua quieted.

Joshua was sniffling. "Okay, but I have to get it; I left it upstairs." Josh went up to retrieve his phone, and Maya and Russell looked at each other in puzzlement. Josh never went anywhere without his phone in his pocket.

Joshua came down and handed Russell his phone. "It might help, Uncle. I sometimes put things in my calendar. I try to be like you, you know, and you keep all kinds of important things in your calendar, so I put stuff in my phone calendar too."

The three of them pored over the phone together. The last time Maya and Joshua had spoken on the phone was Saturday afternoon at 4:15 p.m., before he came over for dinner. "You told me you were meeting a friend for Thai food on Sunday," Maya said.

Sure enough, the calendar entry on Sunday read, "Dinner with Donny."

"Who's Donny?" Russell asked.

Joshua smiled. "Yeah, my friend Donny! I told you about him, remember Aunt Maya? He's from the learning center. We used to get pizza every week, but we were going to get Thai food this time, you know, just to change it up a little."

"And… did you get Thai food on Sunday night?" Russell asked.

"I… I don't remember." Joshua looked distressed again. "Maybe. I think so."

Russell checked the recent calls. "Someone called you on Monday night. Whose number is this? You only spoke for forty-three seconds."

"I don't know," Joshua whispered. "Maybe Donny… but that's not his number."

Maya brightened up. "How about you call Donny and ask him if he knows anything?"

Joshua's face darkened. "No, no, no, no, no! I'm not calling Donny. Never call Donny again. He… we… we can't be friends anymore." Joshua stood up and started tearing at his hair.

"Why not, Joshua?" Russell stood up too, pulling Joshua's hands away from his head and raising his voice. "What happened with Donny?" Maya backed up and leaned against the counter with her hands over her mouth.

"No, no! No more Donny! No!" Joshua shouted, and he abruptly turned and ran up the stairs and slammed the door shut.

Russell and Maya stared at each other.

Russell sat back down again slowly, staring at the dirty dishes as Maya started cleaning up. Normally he helped her, but he felt frozen, quite an uncommon feeling for him, and Maya kept looking over at him as she walked from the table, to the sink, to the fridge.

For all the world, it sounded to Russell like Joshua had been drugged. And not just any drug. Something that wouldn't show on a toxicology screen. Something that could be used to make someone forget… and maybe to ply that someone to another's will? It couldn't be. How would Joshua get mixed up in anything like that? It was absolutely illegal in the free world. Briefly, Russell wondered if Braelyn's escapades to Colombia played a part, if maybe the cocaine was just a front. She was clear off her rocker and hugely resentful, but would she use her own son in criminal dealings? Was she *that* angry? The timing was suspicious.

Over the last year, Braelyn had tried more and more fervently to engage Russell in discussions about their history and what she was convinced had been done to them. As kids, Russell had always looked to her to explain everything. She was four years his senior, and he had relied on her to make sense of a shared experience he could barely remember from when he was three years old. But as he got older, he began to realize her experience was far different from his, and perhaps far more frightening. She used to tease him about the "Monster in The Hut," as Braelyn referred to him, and they played children's games of tag and hide and seek revolving around that. But Russell's "monster" had not been terrifying like Braelyn's was. Russell's monster was all strangeness and he had been drawn to it as to an irresistible magnet, but it felt like a curiosity more than a threat.

At forty-four years old, there was still so much Russell did not recall. He had been having the dream since he could remember, and it was always the same. Misty, murky, heavy air in the dense, sodden woods, the strange bamboo hut that seemed small and large at the same time, the smoke inside the hut and the smell of the incense that had made Russell's eyes tear. He could barely see beyond the smoke. And the "monster's" eyes. White eyes that were obviously blind yet could see right through him. The "monster" seemed to know everything about him, and Russell was sure the apparition—or whatever it was—had spoken wordlessly to him in some other language, directly into his mind, but Russell could not grasp what was said. In the dream, Russell would walk slowly, inexorably closer to those sightless, all-seeing eyes, with a chill up his spine, unable to stop moving forward until he was within a couple of feet of the Hollow Man—which is how Russell had sometimes come to think of him. Then he would suddenly wake up, disoriented despite how familiar it was. The dream was always the same. It never progressed; it never varied.

As an adult, Russell had decided that *if* the dream represented an actual person who existed, the white pupils were probably from cataracts and that was what had been confusing to a child of three and perhaps terrifying to his sister at seven, but he had no answers to what the rest of it meant. He had convinced himself that the details weren't important, and since the dream was more odd than scary, he tried to let it go. Mostly, what was so disturbing was that the image seemed to always be there, even when he was awake, hovering at the limit of his awareness and not quite accessible, not even in the dream. Over the years, he had learned to ignore it.

Russell shrugged off the thought. A fine time to be thinking along this channel. He felt Maya glaring at him from where she had sat down across the table, the kitchen now tidied up and back in order.

"What is it, Russell? What are you thinking? You know *something*, that's obvious. Tell me!"

"It couldn't be what I'm thinking, Maya. I've just... I've seen unconscious wakefulness before. Or, I was told I have. I know about it. But how Joshua could fall victim to something like that...." He looked up at her. "How could Joshua get mixed up in something like *that*?"

"Something like what?"

"I... I don't know. Let me talk to Jim Werner at New York-Presby. I'm sure they still have his blood. Maybe he'll humor me and test it." Russell abruptly got up and walked out of the kitchen, leaving an open-mouthed Maya gazing after him.

CHAPTER 6

I t was dark by the time Fezzie dragged himself down the deserted subway station steps. Thievery was tiring business, but it was his livelihood. While other city dwellers were ticked off by the construction that was closing subway stations, Fezzie saw it as an opportune place for privacy, to eat and tally up the day's take. The 57th Street station on the Sixth Avenue line should have been as good a place to pass the night as anywhere, except that it smelled hellishly rotten tonight. Nevertheless, he took his stolen sandwich into the darkness, his pockets heavy with little trinkets he'd surreptitiously snatched, and sat down to eat in peace, cursing the wet concrete he sat on. How does rain manage to get underground? Someone else must have been down here and spilled their drink. Was there no quiet, dry place for a simple vagrant and thief?

He moved over, pushing himself out of the black puddle, and took a bite of his sandwich. Just a ham and cheese he'd pilfered from a truck stand. The pale light from a single bulb barely illuminated him in the darkness as he munched. It tasted funny, metallic somehow, and his hand was sticky, and dark. No wonder the food truck owner just let him go; the sandwich was old, and he probably knew he couldn't sell it anyway. Finally, Fezzie got up and went to look under the faint bulb. Instantly, he started to retch. There was blood on his hands, which had transferred to the sandwich he had been eating.

———

Matthew Trenaman looked at his underlings from Cingulate Services with incredulity. They were in their usual meeting place on the West Side. "Tell me you did not let that happen. Tell me you are not that *stupid*," Trenaman snapped. He shifted his weight with a limp that emphasized his displeasure and slid off the edge of the small desk he had been sitting on to sit in the chair. Ironically, Trenaman's lameness served to make him appear more threatening than vulnerable. Like he'd been through hell and was still a survivor, and nothing and no one was ever going to change that.

Thomas Brunner and Mark Wheeler exchanged nervous glances. They were standing in the small office cubby that was being rented as part of co-working space under the name of a company that did not exist, since they needed a cheap but private place to meet. The walls were lined with a clear sound-proofing film and a white noise generator was placed at the doorway. The walls were cream-colored behind the plastic film and the furniture was sparse, just a couple of desks and chairs, with little tensor lamps on each desk. It was designed to be bare bones. There was a single picture of the New York City skyline hanging slightly off-kilter that looked decidedly out of place.

"It wasn't supposed to go down that way," Wheeler said.

"*It wasn't supposed to go down that way,*" Trenaman repeated. "Why don't you start from the beginning and tell me what you were doing and how it ended up like this. With Vaderman's nephew, for God's sake! We need to study that kid in a controlled manner. We have *plans* for him. He's the biological son of…. You morons, you may have just bungled one of the most important parts of this project."

Brunner swallowed hard and looked to Wheeler.

"We gave the class their usual dose in the cookies," Wheeler began with feigned confidence. "Each kid had their one cookie, and we let them mingle, and then we did our customary meditation with a hypnosuggestion to improve memory and cognitive ability half an hour later; that's been working incredibly well, and their thought processes have been improving tremendously. Then we did assignments and review of the week and current events; after class, we asked Donny Anderson to stay back."

Trenaman just stared at Wheeler until he continued. "We gave Donny the fast-acting milkshake with the high dose as a reward for the great strides he was making and told him we wanted to celebrate with him personally and see how he felt about moving up to the next level. He was quite pleased by the acknowledgment. We asked him to fill out a survey while the drug was taking effect, and then we gave the clear instruction: He was to leave his phone at home, find the addict named Jackson at his usual corner on Monday evening, bring him to the subway station under construction at 57th and Sixth with an offer of drugs, and then slice him and dice him. Simple."

"And…?" Trenaman growled with impatience.

"And nothing. He gave us a fleeting blank stare, but just nodded his head, and he left. It looked like it would work perfectly," Wheeler said.

"But of course, you found and followed him on Monday." Trenaman's words were not a question.

Brunner took a step forward. "Of course." He looked over at Wheeler. "We went together and stayed a safe distance back. Donny didn't see us." Brunner licked his lips, like he was suddenly sorry he'd joined the conversation.

"So, what happened?" Trenaman asked. He stood up again and started pacing. Every step looked agonizing, but he stubbornly refused to stay seated.

Wheeler cleared his throat and answered. "He slashed Jackson, all right. Killed him in a couple of seconds. But that's where it went off script. Donny got the blood all over himself, and we hadn't really thought about that. He came out of it as soon as the proscribed task was done, and when he saw the blood, he freaked out."

"Well, what did you expect him to do?" Trenaman was screaming now. "Did you not give any follow up instructions before he was allowed to break out of the drug effects?"

Wheeler and Brunner said nothing.

"How did the Plessman kid get involved?"

"Apparently, Donny and Joshua were friends, like not just in the learning institute; they socialized," Wheeler said. "I mean, we encourage that. Before we could get to him, Donny grabbed Jackson's phone and called Joshua. He was hysterical and pleaded with Joshua to meet him in the subway right away. The drug did work; Donny had no idea what he had done—just as we planned—but he found himself bloody next to a dead body. It turned out the Plessman kid was only a couple of blocks away...."

"How did this kid Donny even *know* Plessman's phone number? These guys are virtual morons, aren't they?" Trenaman was seething.

"You don't understand how successful the program is," Wheeler said. "They *are* getting smarter. And one of their exercises is memorizing their friends' phone numbers. It makes it more fun and relevant for them. We just hadn't counted on that being a problem because we had instructed Donny to leave his cell phone at home; we didn't want him tracked that way."

Brunner picked up the story. "We couldn't get Donny out of there cleanly in such a short period of time. When Joshua showed up, Donny threw himself on him in a great big panic, and next thing you knew, Joshua was covered in blood too. Donny pulled Joshua over to show him the DB and Joshua slipped in the blood and was completely drenched in it."

Wheeler interrupted. "But it's okay. I had some of the powder in my pocket, it had just come in. I covered my face with my handkerchief and blew it at the two of them through the one-way straw, and that was it. They were ours. First we separated them, and we molded Joshua *quite* carefully.

"We told Joshua he was not to use his phone," Wheeler continued, ticking off on his fingers the instructions they gave him. "He was to stay underground and sleep until morning. We told him he will not remember anything about the last couple of days; he will no longer have any interest in Donny; and he will not tell anyone where he was that night, *especially* not his uncle, Russell Vaderman." Wheeler looked at Brunner for reassurance.

Trenaman stared at them both, waiting for the rest.

Wheeler continued. "First, we tied a cinder block around Donny's waist and bound his hands to it, and we covered the block and his hands with his jacket to make it look like he was just carrying his coat, and then we instructed him to forget everything that happened, walk to the East River, and when no one was watching, throw himself in."

Brunner licked his lips and picked up the story. "The DB we wrapped in a sack and threw in the chest we'd brought. We put that in the trunk and threw that in the river too, also weighted down with cinder blocks. It was dark and no one saw us, we're certain of that," Brunner said. "With no DB, they'll lose interest quickly. Jackson has no record, so his DNA won't show up anywhere, and anyway, the river will wash the blood off of Donny, and it will look like a suicide if he surfaces."

"You mean *when* he surfaces," Trenaman said stiffly.

"We knew we shouldn't eliminate Plessman," Wheeler said. He kicked at the wastepaper basket, unable to look up. "He'd be missed too much, and the search would be tenacious. But," he continued, looking for the silver lining, "we have made a dry run with success. We hadn't planned to use the raw Devil's Breath yet, but we improvised when Joshua showed up because it's the fastest acting delivery system." Suddenly, Wheeler couldn't keep the excitement from his voice. "It was something to see, Mr. Trenaman; it worked immediately—like, in seconds!" He looked up hopefully, like a puppy begging for praise.

Trenaman frowned. "We'll see if it worked. Plessman is part of a different and bigger mission, and you may have just blown the lid off it. We've been watching that kid for years. Some very powerful people are going to be *very angry*." Trenaman gave them each a withering look and stormed out, his awkward gait making him appear more robot than human.

Brunner and Wheeler relaxed only slightly after Trenaman left. Finally, Brunner spoke up, his voice shaking, and he smacked his hand on the desk as he sat down. "This has become more than I signed on for. I thought it was an amazing tool that we should investigate, but I never thought he wanted to commit murder. I thought it was just to 'influence' certain outcomes for investment purposes. A sniff here, a 'cookie' there. Make our stocks a certainty, like that. And, we were doing some good for these kids who might not otherwise ever earn more than minimum wage, so I figured, you know, payback. Give a little, take a little. And, of course, the remuneration is good."

"More than good, and you're in it for the long haul now," Wheeler said. "The murder was to test the extreme scenario, but that is not the major intended application, at least, not as I understand it. Of course, it is important to know that we can eliminate resistance if we need to."

"Well, I don't like it. Murder is a whole different thing. Who does Trenaman need to eliminate?" Brunner asked. "Wait, never mind." Brunner raised his hand above his head in a stop signal. "I don't want to know. The less I know, the better."

"No idea," Wheeler said, "but this is much bigger than Trenaman, he just admitted that. He's been hired by someone whose name is above my pay grade. And if I were you, I wouldn't be too vocal about wanting out. We already know how easily they can make us disappear."

"So, you mean we're stuck in this now?" Brunner was sweating.

"Could be. Don't worry, you'll be well paid. And as long as you do your job and keep your mouth shut, you'll be fine. You didn't balk when he told us we were going to murder some street junkie." He turned off the white noise generator. "Ready to go?"

Thomas Brunner walked in the other direction as soon as they hit the street. He turned into a Starbucks to get off the highly visible avenue but had no stomach for coffee or food. He stood by the window and hailed an Uber on his phone.

Easy for Wheeler to say, he thought, just "do my job." He actually hadn't realized Wheeler was serious when he'd said they were going to murder someone. Wheeler had such a snarky sense of humor; it would have been just like him to joke about something like that.

Now Thomas would have to look at those kids every week and know what he'd done. Especially the Plessman kid. If the Devil's Breath really worked, he should be back next Friday as if nothing had happened. Which would be weird. And what if it didn't work? They had no experience with the drug at this dosage; what if Plessman took one look at Thomas and remembered everything? What if he had already gone to the police? Or his uncle, which was tantamount to the same. Geez, Thomas thought, what was he going to do? He wanted to flee, buy a plane ticket to—anywhere! Just leave. Could they find him?

The sweat had soaked his shirt under his arms, and he found himself hyperventilating. He kept looking around, sure that someone must notice how panicked he was, but thankfully, no one was paying any attention to him. Nevertheless, he nearly missed the second Uber text that said his ride was out front and he had only two more minutes before it would leave and he would be charged anyway. He pushed his way through the crowd to the door.

CHAPTER 7

Braelyn Plessman sat in her cell, still waiting for whichever lawyer Russell might have sent. She was not alone. There was a young woman in her early twenties with dark blonde, tangled hair and tattoos on every visible surface of her skin. The tattoos included multiple toothy animals, a heart pierced by three arrows, and a black chain inked around her throat. Her lips were red and inflamed with blisters, and her teeth looked black and rotten. The woman desperately needed a shower, and Braelyn thought sharing a cell with someone who smelled this bad should have been enough to expiate her for a lifetime of sins.

No one is coming. She didn't want to acknowledge that, but it was 6:30 p.m. already. Maybe he's busy. "Mr. Successful," aka "Mr. Preferential," aka her brother, was always busy. Too busy for her anyway. He had reaped the blessings of their mother's stint in South America, while she, Braelyn, had been cursed.

She shifted her weight on the hard metal bench and listened absently to a conversation down the hall. She was both hungry and thirsty, but the thought of putting anything from this place in her mouth nauseated her. Three sets of footsteps were coming down the hallway and stopped on the other side of the cold bars. Two guards and a man in a dark suit.

The man in the suit spoke first. "Ms. Plessman? I'm Jeremy Southpine. I'm a defense attorney. Your brother asked me to come talk to you."

"Took you damn long enough! I already gave up on seeing anyone today. Don't you work from nine to five?"

One guard was unlocking the cell door. The other hand-cuffed Braelyn and led her out of the holding area while the first guard watched Tattoo Lady warily and relocked the cell. Braelyn was escorted into a private room where her right handcuff was removed and locked into a chain attached to a metal table that was solidly attached to the floor. How humiliating. There were about ten inches of play in the chain holding her left wrist. At least the air was fresher.

Jeremy did not respond to Braelyn's comment, but put a bag containing a sandwich from Panera's and a diet Coke on the table. She smelled it and her stomach growled. She glared at him in silence for a full minute, then dove into the bag and pulled out a Chipotle Chicken Avocado Melt. Russell had at least asked him to bring her favorite. She wolfed it down without a word, not caring that she looked like an animal. They had taken her as she walked through customs, so she'd had nothing to eat or drink for fourteen hours. She had refused what passed for food at the detention center.

Jeremy waited until the last chunk of sandwich was in her mouth. "You're being charged with drug trafficking. You had two kilos of cocaine in your possession. Tell me what happened," he said.

"Not mine," Braelyn said, her mouth still full with the last large bite. She wiped her mouth on the back of her hand despite the napkins in the bag.

"How did they get in your suitcase?"

"I have no idea," Braelyn said. "I'm sure my brother told you I had a habit—on and off—but it's off right now, has been for the last few years. But anyway, I'm not a dealer, and I wouldn't ever be stupid enough to try to bring that stuff through customs. That's just ridiculous. I have had some problems, yes, and I may not be as intelligent and… and *charmed* as my brother, but I'm not a complete fool."

"Maybe you packed the drugs in your bag and you forgot?" Jeremy asked her.

Braelyn stopped chewing to stare at him. There were daggers in her eyes.

"Okay," Jeremy said. "Tell me what happened."

"There's nothing to tell. It's not mine. Someone must've put the cocaine in my suitcase at the airport. Or before. Definitely after I finished packing. I had no idea there was anything in there. You know, I saw the dogs, and I even put my hand down to call one over to pet; why would I call the drug-sniffing dog over if I had something in my suitcase?"

"So… you think it was planted." Jeremy made it a statement.

"It *had* to be planted! It. Was. Not. Mine." Braelyn slammed the nearly empty diet Coke down on the table for emphasis.

It was clear to Braelyn that Jeremy had not expected this. Maybe he'd waited until after office hours thinking this would be a quick plea-down case. Now Jeremy's stomach was heard growling, and Braelyn took some sick satisfaction in that.

"Who would have planted it?" Jeremy asked her evenly as he loosened his tie. "It would have to be someone who either had solid expectations of being able to retrieve it later or someone who has a grudge against you and wanted to get you in trouble. Do you know anyone who would fit in either category?"

Braelyn shook her head slowly while wiping her hands on the previously ignored napkins. Lots of people didn't like her, but no one hated her, as far as she knew. And she hadn't known anyone flying home with her. "When is Russell posting bail so I can get out of this dump and get a shower?"

"He didn't mention anything to me about bail," Jeremy said.

Braelyn was floored. "So, what, I have to stay in this God-forsaken place?"

"If he doesn't post bail, you'll be held until your arraignment. I think we both expected you would admit to trying to smuggle in the cocaine. You really want me to enter a plea of not guilty? It was found in your luggage; it's going to be very hard to defend against that."

"That's just what my brother would love, isn't it? For me to rot in this place while he thrives out there as the 'enchanted child.' Did he ever tell you why he is so fortunate and I am so cursed? Did he? I bet he never told you how Mother always praised and pampered him and I was always scolded and could do no right!" Braelyn felt herself catapulting toward a rage state and struggled to keep it together. As much as she hated the idea, she did need this guy's help.

"To be honest, Ms. Plessman, I am not close with your brother like that. I don't know anything about your childhood or your parents. Our relationship is strictly professional."

Braelyn slumped down in her chair, her anger suddenly dissipating like a balloon pierced by a pin. Figures, she thought. He didn't even send his best lawyer.

Jeremy sat back in his chair with a posture of surrender. "Why don't you start from the beginning," he said. "What were you doing in Colombia?"

She peered at him over her diet Coke and slurped the last sip through the straw. "Colombia and South America have always been important to me—to us, really. Except Russell doesn't talk about it. He doesn't need to, he was so young, he barely remembers, and it all worked out *well* for him." She stared at Jeremy with her most challenging attitude, but he said nothing. Braelyn heard his stomach growling again in the silence. Good, she thought. Let him know how I felt.

"Look," she said, "it's not something I talk about, okay? Truth is, I didn't remember all that much myself until our father thought to tell us about our 'legacy' a few years ago, right before he died. Said we had a right to know. Mother never did divulge anything, so we never even knew why they split up."

Jeremy continued to look at her blankly. He had loosened his tie even more and opened the first button of his yellow Joseph A. Bank shirt. His deep brown Armani suit looked disheveled from the day. At that moment, he seemed more like a shrink than a lawyer to Braelyn, who found herself sweating.

She plunged ahead. "So, when I was seven and Russell was three, we went as a family to Peru. I think it was Peru, it was somewhere in South America. Peru, Ecuador, Colombia, I'm not sure. Daddy wasn't even sure anymore, or he was confused, I don't know. Anyway, Mother had this terrible arthritis, I think she'd had it since she was a teenager, and sometimes she'd get these skin things. They were ugly, and they itched her. She met someone in a little café who was raving about some doctor he had seen, and how he had been cured of the 'rot' and the 'lame.' Daddy said he didn't want any part of it, but Mother insisted, because her condition was getting worse every few months. She said some days, every step was agony. So, we went. Somewhere high up in the mountains. I don't know exactly where."

Braelyn took a deep breath. She supposed lawyers were used to hearing all kinds of tales and were obligated not to judge, but she was sure they formed their opinions behind their masked faces. She didn't know why she cared, but she wanted Jeremy to believe her. Maybe because she was telling her story to another human besides her brother for the first time. Except for shrinks, of course, and she'd mostly given up telling it to them. They labeled her bipolar, schizoid, ADHD, and they threw medicines at her. All except the new one.... Braelyn shook herself and fought to refocus on the moment. Jeremy's face was lined with fatigue but otherwise remained impassive.

"Daddy said it turned out not to be a doctor. Some primitive medicine man, who called himself *El Curandero Grande*. We had to stay for a week while he mixed some stupid plants and tied them to parts of Mother's body. She wasn't allowed to wash or look at sunlight or water for five days, and she could only eat certain stuff. It was gross. Daddy wanted to leave, but Mother said since she could barely walk anymore without pain, this remedy had better work or she'd be stuck there forever." Braelyn looked up. "I remember that part clearly. I remember how scared I was that we might *never* go home."

Jeremy scratched behind his neck and eyed her through narrowed lids. Maybe she was boring him and he was fighting off sleep. "I don't understand what this has to do with your recent trip to Colombia or the cocaine in your suitcase," he said.

Braelyn's frustration exploded and she screamed at him. "I'm getting to that! You said to start from the beginning, so that's what I'm doing. It all started in Peru. Or Colombia. I don't know how to explain any of it, so maybe that's the only way to do it!" The chain holding her left hand to the table clanged menacingly.

Jeremy sat up straight, as if he expected her to hit him; he was wide awake now. A guard appeared at the door.

"Everything all right in here?" the guard asked.

Jeremy was still staring at Braelyn, muscles tense and on full alert. After a minute, he said, "Yes, thank you. We're fine." He nodded to Braelyn to continue. "You better keep your voice down," he said.

Braelyn collected herself as best she could and stumbled on in her tale. "So, there we were, stuck in some crazy place in the Northern Andes, in the mountains, in the middle of nowhere. There was no plumbing and we could only get water from the stream. I felt sick there and I couldn't run and play without getting out of breath. Not for a few days, anyway, and Daddy said it was because we were so high in the mountains. I was bored to death, and frightened, and I just wanted to go home. I was seven! And I guess I wasn't *behaving* all that well—as usual —and the medicine man, or whoever he was, took me aside to 'treat' my misbehavior. I mean, I was just being a kid, for God's sake!"

"And what did he do for you?" Jeremy asked.

Braelyn could tell he was struggling to pay attention. She could tell in the way she could sometimes *see* someone, like she could look right into them, the way the *Curandero* had looked into her. She knew Russell got these flashes too, but he wouldn't talk about them. It was happening now.

"You mean what did he do *to* me?" she continued. "He took me to this little hut. It smelled funny and it was smoky, like incense. Then he took some liquid from a little flask and dabbed it in my nostrils. It burned a little in my nose. That's all I remember. Except that I was… it was… it was really scary. I was frightened, and I wasn't allowed to go back to Daddy for a long time."

Jeremy was still staring at her, waiting for the connection. "And this is about your recent trip to Colombia… how?"

"You know," Braelyn snapped, suddenly out of patience entirely, "how about I finish telling you tomorrow? Or you can ask my high and mighty brother, the 'Great Russell Vaderman.' Just ask him to post bail for me. He has it. I'm not going anywhere. I can go home with an ankle bracelet. I can't believe he would up and leave me in this place! Tell him I didn't do it. *I* didn't bring cocaine back here, not that I knew about, anyway."

Braelyn turned around and faced the wall. She was done talking. Her brain, sometimes with such crystal clarity, could suddenly switch and get all muddled like this, and she couldn't put two words together. Her father had explained it that one day they had talked, but it wasn't clear in her memory. She had been so young to be exposed… the effects on her little seven-year-old brain not predictable… and then something about her being immune, but she wasn't sure if that was immune *to* the shaman's treatment or immune *from* the shaman's treatment, like as if now because of it, she was immune to… something else…. Apparently, she had resisted the effects quite successfully, since she was such a "difficult" child. Or… did the resistance come later? In some manner, the story made perfect sense to her, since she never was one to *behave*, not on the mountain, not in school, and not at home.

That conversation was four years ago. She should have written it down, but it took her completely by surprise that Daddy was even alive—she hadn't heard from him in decades. She didn't think to write it down. She thought she'd have another chance to see him. But after he met with Russell separately the very next day, he had a stroke and then was gone forever. And Russell never would discuss whatever he learned from Daddy.

Jeremy looked at his watch. It was 8:00 p.m. "Okay," he said and stood up abruptly. "I'll tell your brother." He called for the guard and left the cell.

CHAPTER 8

At 9:00 a.m., Jeremy Southpine was shown into Russell Vaderman's office. Russell was dictating a note and held up one finger as he finished, so Jeremy sat down quietly and waited.

The office was sleek and elegant. Mostly white with clean architectural lines, with a few deep chocolate brown accents. Russell's sizable desk was neat and tidy, with everything in its place. There was a five-foot-tall Madagascar Dragon Tree standing by the side of the window, simple and elegant and well-cared for, drinking in the sunlight that cascaded into the room. A bookshelf was just below the expansive picture window directly behind Russell's seat, which sported a view of all of midtown from the fortieth floor, and the large white table off to the side of the office was strewn with architectural plans that Jeremy would never be able to read.

On the walls, pictures of beautiful buildings with arches that blended smoothly into glass side panels and perfect upper cascades hung handsomely. They were all Russell's creations, established in various places around the globe; their effects were of such beauty they took your breath away. Jeremy knew they were designed to withstand powerful earthquakes and hurricanes, and yet these spectacular structures made you want to just sit and gaze at them. And when those structures were built to scale, well, it was no wonder Russell Vaderman commanded such respect in his field and had been so incredibly successful. It was pure genius combined with the most inspired artistic finesse. Jeremy understood why the struggling sister, who was barely able to hold a job, could have such feelings of resentment.

Russell stopped his dictation and stood up. "So sorry, Jeremy," he said, and put out his hand. "Good to see you. Thanks for the crisis intervention last night. What can you tell me?"

"Oh, right," Jeremy came back to himself. He shook Russell's hand and sat back down. "Yeah, she says she didn't do it."

"What? I thought the cocaine was found in her possession."

Jeremy held up his hands and shrugged. "It was. She says she has no idea how it got in her suitcase. Says she's been clean for a couple of years and she doesn't deal, so she must have been set up. That will be hard to prove under any circumstance, but she won't even tell me what was going on before she got on the plane. She started telling me about your father and mother, in Peru or somewhere when you guys were kids...." Jeremy's voice trailed off. "I mean, I don't even know how that's relevant. And then she just shut down. I'll go back again today and see if she will elucidate further, but if she can't, I'm fresh out of ideas."

Russell's forehead was furrowed. "Did she not want to talk about the arrest, or did she say she couldn't remember anything?"

Jeremy marveled at how Russell managed to keep his cool, even in outrageous circumstances. "I'm not even sure," Jeremy said. "For someone who wants out of her cell and says she's not guilty, she was exceptionally uncooperative. She did ask for you to post bail."

The office was quiet long enough to get uncomfortable. Then

Russell straightened up, decision made. "How much is her bail?"

"It's half a mil," Jeremy said.

"Okay," Russell frowned. "Let's post it. They'll no doubt put her on house arrest with a bracelet. Please tell her I'll go talk to her when she gets home."

Jeremy raised his eyebrow at that but tried not to show any other surprise. He supposed Russell knew his sister and knew what he was doing. It wasn't Jeremy's place to get in the middle of family matters on that level. After another moment of silence, he nodded, and left the office.

CHAPTER 9

Russell was scheduled to spend most of the day mentoring an architect intern. Her name was Analise, and she showed great promise, but this young woman seemed to behave a bit too familiar for his comfort. He didn't want to say anything and bring attention to it, but she stood just a step too close, wore her skirt just a shade too high, and was a tad too touchy-feely. He tried his best to keep the design table between them, but she kept coming over to see what he was doing from "his" point of view, even when he turned the plans upside down so they were facing her.

Russell could process information independent of its orientation in space. When he looked at designs, they almost seemed to step off the paper and float into the air, where he could rotate and manipulate them geometrically in his mind. It was how he could simultaneously look at their artistic appeal and make sure all the structural boxes were checked. He prided himself that his buildings were able to withstand a category 5 hurricane or an earthquake up to 8.0 on the Richter Scale. He would create it all in his head and then have his junior architects spend weeks checking numbers and stresses to make 100 percent sure his edifice was sound. They always were. And each one was a thing of beauty to behold.

None of his colleagues understood how he did this—Russell didn't really understand it either. It was the natural course his mind would take, and while he recognized that he was apparently unique in his mental functions, it was just his innate way of looking at the world; for him, there was nothing unusual about it at all.

Russell was also an accomplished pianist and composer, and music did the same thing for him. He would "see" the sound, as if in three-dimensional space, and then manipulate what he wanted to play in his head before he even touched the keyboard, which he played with tenderness and passion. He never forgot a single piece of music either.

The woman brushed against him this time, and Russell sighed. He had mentioned several times to Analise that he needed to get home early to *his wife*, but she seemed not to notice. Her perfume was starting to choke him, and finally he suggested they call it a day. Geez, the last thing he needed was for Maya to smell Analise's fragrance on him. He had never cheated on her, and she had never accused him, but you never knew what a woman might focus on if she was in a bad mood. Maya had a tendency to become insecure at times, for no sensible cause that Russell could discern, and he saw no reason to encourage that.

———

Russell sniffed at his sleeve as he left the office and was glad he wasn't going directly home; it would give his clothes more time to air out. He kept smelling Analise's perfume even after she had gone, but then he had always had a sensitive nose. He texted Maya as he left the office and told her why he'd be late, and headed over to Braelyn's apartment in the East Village.

Russell wished he could escape feeling so responsible for his sister. She was the older sibling, but even before he'd hit his teens, it had become clear that he was the dependable and resourceful one. Crazy, since she had practically raised him, their mother having been sickly through all of Russell's memory. Except when it came to her little brother, Braelyn was an oppositional child, and when she hit puberty, it all erupted. She was drawn to alcohol and drugs and marginal relationships, and as she got older, she could not hold a job. She was married for half a year when she conceived Joshua, and then her shifty husband was murdered by someone in the drug cartel.

By contrast, Russell was brilliant, always unflappable, rational, and immensely creative. He was playing Beethoven at the age of eight, and he played it well, with skill and finesse. By the time Russell turned fifteen, their roles had reversed, and he started taking care of Braelyn. But throughout his childhood years, it was Braelyn he ran to when he needed love and reassurance, and she had never let him down. Now she resented him so much, it broke his heart.

For all that, he found Braelyn seldom lied to anyone. She'd tell you to your face what mischief she was up to and dare you to do something about it. If she had meant to bring cocaine back to the States, it would be more in her character to own up to it and demand exemption.

He stepped off the elevator and walked to her apartment door. It was open about an inch.

"Braelyn?"

His sleepy sister was lying on the knock-off Natuzzi couch against the far wall. She was showered and dressed in jeans and a loose, pale blue shirt, and she stared at him as he came in. He closed and locked the door behind him.

"Brae, you really should lock the door. It's not safe."

"Are you really so worried about me, little brother? Wouldn't it just solve *all* your problems if I conveniently 'went away'?" She swung her legs around to sit up. "Good of you to come visit. Thanks for posting bail. I didn't think you were going to."

"How could your 'going away' solve my problems, Brae? I love you; I never want you to be hurt. I just want you to find a little peace and happiness."

Braelyn snorted.

Russell set down the bag he was carrying. "I brought you sushi."

Braelyn glanced at it hungrily. "Where's Josh?" she asked. "Did you tell him his *criminal* mother was no person to be associating with? How come I haven't heard from him—like, nothing? I thought he'd be home when I got home, and he's not answering his phone, either."

Russell sat down quietly and measured his response. "I haven't told Joshua you're back, or that you were arrested. He… he had a mishap, and we haven't completely sorted it all out yet. He's been staying with us right now."

"My Josh? What happened? I'm his mother, Russell, I have a right to know—is he okay? Was he hurt?"

"He was not hurt, Brae, he's just a little shaken up. Maya is home with him right now, and he'll be fine. Tell me what happened to you. Jeremy Southpine tells me you did not intend to smuggle cocaine in from Colombia. Then how did it get in your suitcase? And why were you even there this time? I thought you'd had all your questions answered last time and did not want to set foot in that country again."

Braelyn stared at him for a full minute, as if trying to decide if she could get him to talk about Josh if she pushed him. She knew him better than anyone, and Russell sensed she itched to understand how his mind worked, how he sifted through the torrents of information and stayed steady all the time. She seemed to have many of the same challenges he did; he *felt* it, and he wished he knew how to help her.

She continued to stare at him, and finally seemed to give up and she broke down.

"I know I've been a horrible mother, Russ, and Josh is very, *very* lucky to have you and Maya. You're obviously not going to tell me... but I'm so sorry I haven't been there for him. I wanted to be... I will never understand why life is so hard for me and so easy for you." She rubbed her eyes with her hands, trying unsuccessfully to hold back tears.

Russell softened. "Life isn't easy for anyone; I just manage it better. Look, Brae, you're exhausted, you're in trouble, you're probably scared. Talk to me. Why are you still going to Colombia? It's the largest producer of cocaine in the world. It's not a safe place. Do you have a friend you visit there? Why do you go there?"

"You really don't know?" Braelyn asked.

She stood up and started pacing the room. "It must have all happened in Peru, in the Northern Andes; even if Daddy doesn't remember exactly, I've been researching it. There's a site in Piura that is still sacred land, but no one is letting me, a forty-eight-year-old, sometimes-addicted misfit into a place like that. But you can also buy it from the Indians in Sibundoy Valley in south Colombia. They grow it there too. Actually, it's grown all over Colombia, but I can't go looking in Bogota for it, I'm more likely to get spiked and robbed—or killed." Braelyn was speaking rapidly now, like she wouldn't get a chance to finish.

"Buy what, Brae? The flowers?" Russell was astounded she was still pursuing this. "I am gratified to hear you at least know to stay away from drug traffickers in Bogota!"

"I'm not stupid, Russell, just because you got the lion's share of the brains. I was sprinkled with a few drops of gray matter before that shaman dusted us. And you *know* what. Yes, the flowers of the *borrachero* tree. Or some other *Brugmansia* plant!

The stuff that—that—did this to me. Did this to us! It messed me up completely, but it sure seems to have helped you. Maybe it can help *me* this time too."

"Brae, you're obsessed."

"I know I am, Russell, but I can't control it. I have to figure this out. It took my life from me!"

"You don't know that. Neither of us know what our lives would have been like if we'd never gone there. There are lots of people with manic depression who drink and don't take their meds and end up in similar predicaments to yours. I think it would be more productive to work on getting yourself together rather than blame it on some crazy substance that we *may* have been exposed to forty years ago. We can't go back in time."

Braelyn quieted, and Russell instantly regretted his tirade. His sister was mentally ill, that wasn't something she had control over. If she would just take her meds…. She looked at him with that vulnerable face that used to get to him when they were kids, and sat back down on the sofa like a dog who'd just been scolded.

"I started talking to a new psychiatrist about it, someone who specializes in the effects of hallucinogens," Braelyn said quietly.

"And…? What did she say?" Russell asked. This could be promising, he thought to himself.

"*He* knew about it. He said it was something that has been experimented with in the past, mostly by the military."

"He knew about the *borrachero* plant?"

"Yes. He said it was unethical to use on human subjects, but since I had *already* been exposed as a child, he wanted to study my brain chemistry. He suggested the effects might be reversible using the same technique, or at least my reaction could possibly be mollified, but the stuff is illegal in this country, so he couldn't get any. I mean, it's not like he said he would give it to me if he had it or that I should go buy some, or anything. That was my idea. And he also didn't know exactly how it was used the first time or what other herbs it was mixed with, just that in the mountains, it was usually used as part of a cocktail. Daddy didn't tell me what was in the stuff, if he even knew; only that they used it on me when they were trying to make me 'behave.' I have some memories, but not enough, and it was all done in Spanish anyway."

Russell sat back. Apparently he and his sister had had very different experiences during their time in the mountains, at least according to their father. The only similarity seemed to be the ancient guru and the Spanish.

"They were trying to make you 'behave'?" Russell asked. He had worshipped his sister back then; he never dreamed she had done anything to be admonished for, certainly not at the age of seven. All that had come later.

For a split second, Russell remembered the damp, muddy earth, the mist in the jungle that smelled of mold, mosses, and dew, the still silence, and the feeling of a thousand hidden eyes watching him and murmuring in a language he didn't understand, and a fleeting terror that he might never see sunshine again. Everything brown and gray. But Braelyn, his big sister, was always there, telling him not to give in to fear, that they were going home soon, that he would be all right. She was his anchor, his strength. He remembered hugging her fiercely, but quietly. Russell had always been a quiet kid. His brain ran at the speed of light but he never voiced his ideas. Back then, his thoughts came so fast, there was no time to put them in words. He'd had to teach himself to stop and organize his thinking; it made him appear less sociable to others. Or, did that start *after* his meeting with the shaman…?

"That's what Daddy told me, that day I spoke to him. He said I was sick from the altitude and I wouldn't eat or drink, and I was yelling at people to go away. They told him they were going to give me something to take away the altitude sickness, and that it would also help me behave. And I guess it did, for a while. I *told* you all this."

Russell rubbed his chin. He needed a shave. Most men would not have cared at this stage of hair growth, but Russell was more obsessive compulsive than most. "Our father didn't tell me anything like that. Just that I ended up—inhaling the stuff, and that the shaman made suggestions to me in that hypnotic state. He said I was in the wrong place at the wrong time. I vaguely remember something… in this little hut… it smelled strongly of something unique and weird… and I remember an ancient man with paper-thin skin and a long white beard, and I remember his eyes. But he wasn't really scary, just… peculiar." Russell looked up nervously, as if for a single instant, he were a little kid again. "I dream about it sometimes, but I never think of it as having been real."

"Daddy said after they 'treated' me, you went into the hut, and Daddy wasn't allowed to follow you. Why did you go in there?"

"I don't know," Russell said. "I do remember the hut; that's where I saw the… I used to think of him as the Hollow Man. And I remember being curious. I've always been insanely curious, about everything, you know that. I must have just wanted to see what was in there."

"That was really brave, especially for a three-year-old," Braelyn said.

Russell broke out laughing. "No, dear sister, not brave. Maybe stupid. Three-year-olds aren't experienced enough to be brave; they have no idea they *should* be scared of anything. Especially if they have a big strong sister around to protect them. By the time children become seven, they understand there are dangers out there to avoid. But not at three!"

Braelyn laughed with him, and the laughter bonded them for an instant, as if the last fourteen horrendous years of heartache and argument hadn't happened. Russell glanced at his watch and reality returned.

"Look, Brae, we have to figure out what to do. You were arrested with two kilos of coke in your suitcase. That's a big deal. You're going to have to explain that or serve time. You have to tell me what happened."

"That's the thing," she said. "I have no idea. Yes, I used cocaine years ago, but mostly I've been on and off the booze now, not the hard stuff. And I've never, ever dealt it."

"Do you know anyone who would have used you to get it back here? Or anyone who wants to hurt you?"

Braelyn shook her head. "I did have a few moments in the airport when I felt kind of sick, but then it passed."

"Did you leave your bags and go to the restroom?"

"No, Russell, I told you I'm not stupid. I know people worry about bombs and shit like that. I wouldn't do that."

"Did you bring anything else back with you?"

Braelyn stopped and looked at her brother. "You mean, like flowers from a *borrachero* tree?"

"Or any part of any of its related trees?"

"I did," Braelyn said. The challenging look appeared on her face. "At least I had it in the airport. I even checked my bag to make sure they were there. I opened the wrapping, and that was when I felt sick." Braelyn shrugged her shoulders. "I figured I could just play dumb about them, since they aren't listed specifically as an illegal substance that I know of. I would have just said I liked the flowers. But they're gone now. And I went to a *lot* of trouble to get them."

She pulled the suitcase over from the corner of the room where she had all but discarded it. She flipped it open and started rifling through the mostly dirty clothing and occasional hairbrush or pair of shoes.

"Look at this mess," Braelyn said. "They pulled everything out to search it and then just stuffed it all back—except the flowers. They took those, and then they had the nerve to call it cocaine!"

Russell noticed a faint, vaguely familiar odor that he could not quite place at the very reaches of his awareness, and it made him queerly dizzy. The smell niggled at him, like he should know what it was, but it was so indistinct, he wasn't even sure if it was really there or just the smell of dirty clothes that had been in a suitcase for too many days.

"Did anyone ask about the flowers?" Russell asked.

"No, no one has mentioned them, so either no one cares about them or no one noticed. All anyone is talking about is this supposed cocaine, which I had nothing to do with. For all that, I'd like to see this cocaine that they are accusing me of possessing. Are my fingerprints even on it?"

A reasonable question, Russell thought, but his head was feeling entirely strange, and suddenly, he needed fresh air desperately. "Look, Brae, I've got to go. But Jeremy will be back to see you tomorrow, and you have to tell him *everything*, understand? I don't mean necessarily all the details of life at the age of seven or why our parents split up, but the fact that you brought back the flowers, what they do, and what the psychiatrist told you. All of it. Tell me you understand."

"Yes, little brother, I *understand*. But I don't know everything the flowers do. Do you?"

Russell got up abruptly. "Okay, I'll call you tomorrow."

"Wait! What do they do? Do you know what they do? You know, don't you? Russell!"

He paused at the door. "I have no idea how they used the flowers with us." He walked down the hall and into the elevator where Braelyn, with her ankle bracelet, could not follow.

———

Braelyn watched the elevator close behind her brother. Her frustration was supreme; she felt like a rubber band that would snap with the slightest increase in tension. She was driven to go running after him, shake him, and make him tell her everything he had learned about these plants, but she also knew if she took one more step, the police would come get her and throw her back in that disgusting cell with Tattoo Lady who smelled like the New York City sewers. She teetered, on the razor's edge between a full-blown manic attack and the abyss of depression. Every time she looked into that chasm of despair, she feared she might never be able to climb back out of it.

Braelyn believed herself cursed. She saw life as it essentially was and people for what they truly were, and it was often nearly unbearable. Beyond the illusions of civilization, past the deception of intimacy, Braelyn looked at New York City and saw her fellow humans as empty carcasses of flesh meandering meaninglessly through their lives, desperately trying to gorge themselves on abundance and wealth to distract themselves from the hollowness of their meager existence. Unconsciously trying to deny the ultimate aloneness of each's presence by searching for fashion and lavish belongings, "must-haves," intuitively frantic to keep themselves from staring into this very void that haunted Braelyn. They were successful; not so Braelyn. She used to throw herself into sexual relationships precisely to drown out the knowledge of how isolated she really was. She was locked in a dark labyrinth from which there was no real escape, and from which Braelyn did not have the luxury of looking away. The shaman had made sure of that.

She had medication for her "condition" in her room, but it blunted her brain too much. She couldn't think clearly when she took it, and while she didn't get herself into much trouble nor did she notice the abyss in front of her when she was on it, neither did life hold any appeal for her either. Living was reduced to a net zero. Another kind of nothingness, one that she didn't care about when she took the pills. And Braelyn *needed* to care. She had little else that was "hers" outside of her emotions. The irony of her dive into the world of alcohol and drugs, which produced a kind of nothingness all its own, was not entirely lost on her, but she was a desperate soul.

Braelyn had always known that Russell's experience was very different from her own; he was not plagued by the intimate, existential knowledge of his being. Either that, or he had an entirely different way of understanding it. And now, she suspected that Daddy had given him completely different information about Peru from what he had told her. Did the shaman do something different to her baby brother? Was it only *her* that the shaman had cursed with this "wisdom"?

She was pretty angry at her father, for so many things. Leaving them when they were children, for starts. No explanation, no forwarding address. And then showing up four years ago to drop a bomb on their heads about their history, separating them for the tales, which just magnified the distance between her and her brother, and dying two days later. And not even remembering details. Like, was it Peru, was it Ecuador, was it Colombia? All he knew—or all he *said* he knew—was that it was in the mountains, the altitude was over 11,000 feet, and that had made Braelyn sick. She had tracked it to Peru and the Northern Andes. She wished her mother had been more forthcoming as well, instead of taking most of the story to her grave. Why the hell was there so much secrecy about a family trip to South America? A family trip that, apparently, had gone horribly wrong.

And why wouldn't Russell tell her what happened to her son? Something nagged at her, like maybe there was a connection between her and Josh's "mishaps." Braelyn often felt like she was "psychic," but that just fed the notion to herself and to everyone else that she was certifiably out of her mind.

Braelyn put her head in her hands and cried. She hated

herself for not being able to be a proper mother to Josh, for being so unpredictable, irresponsible, and rootless. For all the strength she'd had for Russell when they were children, she had none for her own son. Her moods were labile and uncontrollable, and she knew—now that she had been speaking to the new shrink—that this was rooted in her uncanny intuition and a mental ability and insight that she did not understand, had no control over, and that frightened her tremendously. She was sure Russell had these flashes too. How did he manage them?

She went to her computer and did another search for the plants called *Brugmansia* and *borrachero*. Russell knows all this, she thought, as she skimmed through the few articles she could find. He had never studied medicine *per se*, but he could gather an understanding of any subject in a matter of hours, and no doubt, he had researched it all. He also had access to journals and essays that she did not, due to his friendships with scientists and physicians. In Braelyn's mind, there was no subject Russell could not master if he put his head to it, and it often infuriated her. Her own above average intelligence was no match for his genius, and she felt like an imbecile next to him.

Feeling determined, Braelyn expanded her inquiry to focus not just on what roles the plants played in the ancient rites of Andean ritual practices, but also on their current uses—and misuses.

What she learned threatened to break the ground beneath her and swallow her up.

CHAPTER 10

Maya was just putting dinner on the table when the phone rang. Her brother always seemed to call at exactly the wrong time, but she felt like she had to take his calls. Both Maya's brother and sister still lived outside of Dallas with their families, near their ailing father who was pushing eighty. Dad required a lot of care, and the family philosophy was to take care of your own. It made Russell that much dearer to her that he felt the same way about Joshie. Since Maya could not be present in Dallas for the day-to-day home care and verbal abuse that came with an elderly parent suffering from dementia, she felt guilty if she didn't do everything she possibly could for them by phone. But sometimes just listening to her brother Martin was enough to drive her batty. She was often grateful they did not do video chats.

"Hi, Marty," Maya answered on the fourth ring.

"I was thinking you weren't going to pick up," Martin snapped. "Nice to have a good excuse to stay out of the loop."

"Oh no, what did he do now?"

"What didn't he do? A new young nurse was in today. He

grabbed her by her scrub pants and insisted she was trying to seduce him, *while* he was sitting on the commode, mind you! And he wouldn't let go. He is so embarrassing. I wanted to crawl under the bed and hide. Then he refused to eat unless she fed him every bite. You don't know how good you've got it, Maya, being far away in that *leeb-er-ay-al* city of yours, where family problems never touch you." Martin's Texas twang turned "liberal" into a four syllable word.

"Now, Martin," Maya started, "I have certainly had my share of family problems all my own." Why did he always try to turn things into a political discussion?

"Nonsense. You don't even have a family, just that half-moron of a kid you've been looking after for Russell's sister."

Maya sat down. There were few things that could hurt her so deeply, and Martin knew it. "What do you need, Martin?" she asked. Her voice was chilly.

"A little assistance, dear sister. We need to be away next month, and I was hoping you could come down for a visit and sit with Dad while we're gone. Make up for lost time. You know."

"When next month? The first is next week. We've got a bit of an issue going on right now, and I don't know if it will be resolved by then. I may not be able to get away...."

"Family first, Maya. Blood family. That's how we were raised. We're leaving in ten days for an Alaskan cruise, and we'll be gone for a week. Your sister Melinda is coming too, with her brood, so it's up to you. You know I've always wanted to see the Northern Lights."

"I don't know, Marty. I—I can't commit right now. Don't they have services for elderly folk down there? Someone who can come check on Dad every day?" Inwardly, Maya seethed. It was just like her siblings to ask for favors at the last minute, expecting her to drop everything and run to help. They were playing on her guilt for being so far away. It broke her heart when she recalled the times the three of them used to go away together, but those days were long gone. That was before the whole country polarized and political differences of opinion became family feuds.

"No, we don't have that kind of round-the-clock care here unless we pay through the nose. We're not socialists like y'all are up north. And neither Melinda nor I have filthy rich spouses to cover everything like you do. You had the right idea, marrying for money."

Maya did not understand how caring for the elderly constituted socialism, but she let that part go. She was not going to let him poke at her marriage. "I did not marry for money, Martin. Russell and I love each other very much. You haven't given me much notice; we might have to hire someone for Dad this time. I'll try my best, but I'm just saying."

"Well you let me know when you're good and ready, then, *sister dear*. But don't wait too long. These tickets are nonrefundable."

Maya hung up the phone. She knew that Texas did not have as extensive social services for the elderly as New York did, but they did have some, and Maya also knew that care for a week could be purchased. Her brother was just playing her, and no matter how often he did it, she always ended up feeling totally inadequate. Oddly, it also strengthened her resolve to stay active in her Undivided group and work to bring equal rights and care to everyone, including the elderly.

It really pissed Russell off when Marty did this, and Russell had said on many occasions she should just bring Dad up to New York. They could hire twenty-four-hour care for him, and she could check in on him as much as she wanted.

Maya wanted to cry. All the stress of the last few days, Joshie covered in blood and with no memory of several days in his life —brutal days, perhaps—and now with Braelyn in jail for drug trafficking. And on top of it all, this reminder of the shredding of her relationships with both her siblings stung like a Portuguese Man o' War.

Even though their views were very different, until a few years ago, she'd been close with both Marty and Melinda. But once the new president had been elected, Maya saw lie after lie adopted by her siblings. She would try to argue that the health of the planet took priority over feeding coal and oil companies, and they would retort that it was only because she had everything she desired that she could ignore the average American who needed these jobs. They barely had any respectful dialogue anymore.

Maya found President Ganaffe so juvenile, so narcissistic, and so power-hungry, that she could not understand how her siblings could possibly support him. He was such a bully! Then he changed his mind several times an hour on the same subject and impulsively spouted rhetoric on social media, igniting the white supremacist movement and inflaming the discord in their society; she found him exhausting. He should have been having thoughtful, rational discussions with the American people he was supposed to be *serving* and engaging in enlightened relationships with the civilized, *democratic* countries of the world.

Marty and Melinda didn't see it that way, though. They believed America should take care of America and never mind the rest of the world, and that no one deserved a handout. They worked hard for everything they had, and they expected others to do the same. But how could they live so close to the Mexican border, have hired Mexican and El Salvadorian nannies for their children growing up, treated them like almost-family, and yet turn a blind eye to the isolated, sick, and starving children at the El Paso border? Marty *used* to say he wasn't against immigration, but it needed to be regulated. And well he should! His own wife's family was from Sweden, although she was born and raised here in the States. Now he justified separating poor, sweet children from their parents, saying America would take care of the kids temporarily but the parents weren't welcome.

At one point, Maya had actually called Marty a deplorable racist, because he didn't stop with immigration. He periodically railed against Blacks and Jews and was violently against gay marriage. What did Marty care if someone wanted to marry someone else of the same sex? But he said it was an abomination against God and started quoting scripture at her. Scripture! As if she hadn't had the same religious education he had. That was when she told him he was a homophobe and a moron. He'd been referring to Joshua as "that half-moron kid" ever since. And now, they couldn't have a civil conversation for even thirty seconds.

Maya was vaguely aware that in older days, they could have had spirited discussions about their opinions without it coming to verbal blows. What had happened to their family? Now it had become a matter of pride, and neither could back down to reconnect with the warm feelings they used to have.

Maya had almost fought with Russell over the subject. He told her she should have expected nothing less from Marty after calling him a "deplorable, racist, homophobic moron." Russell had been cool and rational about it, refusing to take sides, and that was the most infuriating part of all!

Maya never could read Russell on politics. On the one hand, he supported equal rights for everyone—although he would ask her why anyone would care what he thought of gay marriage as long as no one was getting hurt—but then he would not get active in the ACLU. Russell contributed a huge amount of money to programs designed to reduce carbon emissions, develop green energy, and he cared deeply about the planet. He had also opened up a sizable food kitchen in the city to feed homeless people, yet he was lukewarm to her Undivided friends. All the while, he remained an entrepreneur through and through, believed people should be paid more for harder and more successful work, and would never support anyone who wanted to put a cap on his attainable wealth. That notwithstanding, he firmly believed society should take care of the disabled and the elderly, and he *had* made the pledge to give 50 percent of his earnings to charity every year, and he stuck to it.

Russell teased her when she became distraught about his unwillingness to jump on her bandwagons and said that they balanced each other perfectly and presented as a very temperate couple. But Maya had never even been able to determine how he voted on election days, which annoyed her for some reason. Russell always seemed to keep his own counsel, at least from her. His manner of being unceasingly unruffled, calm, and competent was one of the things that had attracted her to him from the beginning, but it also exasperated her to be so left out of his thought processes.

She did wish he would share his secret for managing his stress. Maya knew he felt the same emotions she did, and the rare times he would confide to her his fears or pressures he faced at work made her feel so close to him. Mostly, however, Russell seemed to glide through life as if nothing really touched him. She knew it was not so, but she was the emotional type who wore her heart on her sleeve and could get flustered in a heartbeat. She wished she could master herself the way he did.

CHAPTER 11

Russell was feeling stressed as he made his way back home from the Village. He didn't understand what had happened, and that always made him uncomfortable. He believed Braelyn when she said that she did not knowingly smuggle cocaine into the country, all the more because she so readily admitted to bringing back the flowers of the *borrachero* tree. *That* was the worse contraband, and while he doubted his sister understood that, she surely knew it was not an accepted practice. Her last words, "Were my fingerprints even on it?" gave him pause. Who had found this alleged cocaine, was it a certainty that it was hers, and why no mention of the forbidden flowers? Russell felt like he couldn't get their aroma out of his nostrils, and he still felt the strangeness he had in her apartment; like his brain was too big for his skull. At the very least, the customs agents should have had her present when they examined the contents of her suitcase.

In Russell's typical style of leaving no stone unturned, he called both Jeremy Southpine and Police Commissioner Harrows while waiting for the Uber and asked for each to explore the possibility that the cocaine did not, in fact, belong to Braelyn; he decided not to mention the flowers. He already had to make it a favor for Harrows to "humor" him. Don't all criminals lie?

His mind swam in the back of the car. Traffic was even worse than usual, and his stomach growled. He had an eidetic memory, so he remembered all the details of the one conversation he'd had with his father four years ago. He replayed it in his head.

"Braelyn seemed to benefit from the shaman. She calmed down right away and became so biddable and sweet. And the whole community had adopted you—tiny boy that you were. They watched over you, fed you, and were all very protective of you while we waited for Mama to get better. So, I didn't think about it when you wandered up the hill. No one, not even the natives were allowed to just wander into the Curandero Grande's *hut without permission. When I saw you heading inside, I ran to get you, but the natives pulled me back and wouldn't let me get within fifty feet. Three men held me! And all I could do was wait.*

"When you came out, you were… different. Not like Braelyn, who just looked calmer, you seemed, somehow… older. And more aware, of everything. You looked at me, and it was as if you looked right into my soul. My God, Russell, you were barely three, and you looked ancient somehow!

"Otherwise, I mean, you seemed no worse for wear. Braelyn's 'treatment' wore off in a couple of weeks, and she swiftly became a very difficult child. But you—you had already been speaking in sentences, but after that day… you were slower to answer, but when you did, your sentence structure was way beyond a three-year-old's. At one point, I started to think I had imagined your language skills advancing faster than they ought, but after we'd been home for a few months, I couldn't deny it. You remembered everything you were told, you were doing addition and subtraction, could read at a second-grade level, and

later that year, you started playing the piano. At barely four, mind you!

"I took you to our doctor and told him everything. I was sure they had done something to you and Braelyn, and who knew what else might come to pass in time. And then these people came, from the CIA and the DEA and the NSA... Mama was terrified they were going to take you both away from us. We started to fight all the time. Pretty soon, Mama began to insist you were just naturally a genius and Braelyn a rebel, and I think Mama even started to believe it herself. And then she was afraid—even after several months when the government left us alone—that if anyone found out we'd allowed our kids to be drugged in the Andes, we'd lose you both for sure!

"In the beginning, I thought it was more important to know what happened to you... But your Mama, she just blamed me for everything. She had been sick and holed up on that mountain, and I was supposed to watch out for you. I 'let it happen,' she said, and she was right; it was all my fault. It tore us apart, and eventually, your mother threw me out. I wanted to be in your lives, but she forbade it, and then I started to think she was right. I was a terrible father. And perhaps I was even being selfish to consider taking this gift from you.

"I'm sorry, Russell... I wanted you to know the truth now, just in case... I doubt Mama ever told you anything, but you and your sister deserve to know, and I... I haven't been well these last months."

The Uber stopped abruptly, and the driver honked at the car in front of him, and Russell tried to put the memory out of his head. That had been a traumatic year: finding and losing his father in the space of a couple of days, left with an outrageous story to which he'd have preferred to remain blissfully ignorant. His father had asked him what happened inside The Hut, but Russell had no memory of that; his only memory was *going into The Hut*. At forty years old, it all just seemed like a dream, a dream largely irrelevant to his life. Only his father's story made him wonder....

Russell lost his mother twenty-six years ago. Her autoimmune disease had overcome her. The psoriasis resolved forever after their visit to South America, but the joint pain returned within a year, along with other autoimmune syndromes. She developed lupus and chronic inflammatory demyelinating polyneuropathy, but it wasn't until she contracted giant cell myocarditis that she became dangerously ill. She patently refused to talk about her husband or answer any questions about the time in Peru for her entire life; it was like it had never happened and Father had never existed. She died of heart failure at the age of forty-four. Russell was only eighteen and Braelyn twenty-two when they found themselves completely on their own.

Their father either did not know or didn't care that Mama had died, and he was not heard from until four years ago when he reappeared in time to tell the story their mother had never disclosed before it was lost forever. Russell had never paid too much attention to the fact that their father did not bring Russell and Braelyn together to tell such a tale, but rather visited with them each separately that first and only time. And then Father died of a stroke the very next day. He must have known his time was up.

On reflection, it seemed the two siblings had very different experiences in the smoky hut all those years ago. Different experiences with quite different results, if the *Brugmansia* concoction was truly a factor. Russell had researched it extensively—as he did everything else that captured his curiosity—and it seemed the shamans, or *curanderos,* mixed the drug of the *Brugmansia* with the San Pedro cactus, a plant known to contain the hallucinogen mescaline. It was the combination of the two that allowed the shamans to commune with the Spirit and that influenced the body and mind in order to alter one's reality—or so it was said. Russell learned that some shamans added additional herbs, but what those herbs were was not discoverable knowledge. He had never shared any of that information with Braelyn;

at the time, she was absorbed in her psychopathy and Russell hadn't wanted to fuel any delusions.

All of the *Brugmansia* species, of which *borrachero* was one, contained derivatives of the substance called hyoscine, commonly known as scopolamine, which was used regularly in modern medicine in a hundredth of the dose used by the shamans. Since it had valid medicinal use and was not well known for abuse, it was not part of a routine toxicology screen, and it was too rare to be searched for at the borders.

But in high doses, scopolamine was known as the "zombie drug" as it could produce a wakeful unconsciousness. In the past, the United States military had experimented with it in the interrogation of prisoners and the Nazis had utilized it briefly as a truth serum. Now only known to be used in these doses for criminal purposes, primarily in Colombia, it could bend someone entirely to another's will. A person could be manipulated to perform any act and would appear quite awake and normal while doing so—and have no conscious knowledge or recollection of it afterward.

People dosed with the dust of the flower had been known to "willingly" empty their bank accounts or give over their most valuable possessions while those around them reported they seemed of sound mind so they did not interfere. In the ancient Indian tribes in the Andes, wives of chieftains were given the drug and told to climb pliantly into their husbands' coffins and were buried alive alongside their deceased mates.

To make the matter worse, just a smidgen more of the dangerous stuff was lethal. Even the drug lords in Colombia were terrified of it. It had been referred to by news media and scientists as the "scariest drug in the world," but in its raw, pulverized state, it was simply called Devil's Breath.

Who knew what kind of suggestions were made to Russell's and Braelyn's tiny minds in that vulnerable, hypnotic state, or how the effect would vary on their very young, undeveloped brain tissue? Russell had accepted many years ago that he was… unusual. He had himself tested once, and his IQ was 182. But this was the only reality he knew, and he just accepted it. He did not consciously remember being different before The Hut.

Braelyn had been obsessed the last four years since her conversation with Father. And who could blame her? She'd been in so much trouble all her life, and desperately unhappy. Who wouldn't want to attribute it to something outside her control? And for all he knew, she was right. Their father intimated that she had not been "difficult" until afterward, that she was a very normal little girl before she saw the shaman.

The Uber stopped outside his home and Russell thanked him. As he walked in the door, a thought suddenly hit him like a brick, all the more because he felt in his core that it was a certainty: Joshua had been spiked with scopolamine!

Russell stood in the vestibule of his co-op on East 59th Street in Sutton Place. He owned the penthouse suite, a three bedroom plus loft, three and a half bath, majestic residence that looked out over the spectacular New York City skyline on one side and with a view of the East River on the other. He had taken the elevator up to the thirty-third floor, but before going inside, he stopped and called Jim Werner. He was surprised but gratified when the CEO of New York-Presbyterian picked up on the second ring. Leaving Jim a message would have meant a call-back, and he didn't want Maya to hear that conversation. He wasn't quite ready to share this with her yet.

"Hey, Russell, what's up? How's that patient of ours doing?"

"Thanks for picking up, Jim. I am calling about him. He seems fine, except no recall yet. Any chance you can have his blood tested without alerting the usual crowd to its result right away?"

"Strange request. What did you want to test for?"

Russell took a breath. "Scopolamine."

Silence for a long minute. "You mean scopolamine as the

reason why he can't remember anything? That would have some very serious implications, if it's positive. I mean, I guess it would answer a bunch of questions—and raise a ton more. Where is this coming from? Who would do that to him, and why?"

"It's just a hunch," Russell said. "Probably completely off-base."

"I've learned over the years that your 'hunches' can be quite uncanny, Russell. I'll look into it, my friend. I'm sure we still have the blood; I'm not sure we do that testing on site. You do know a positive result would become a police matter in an instant, maybe even federal."

"Thanks, Jim, I know. I would just ask if you could let me know the results before raising the alarms—if it does happen to be positive."

"I can do that. I'll get back to you."

CHAPTER 12

On Friday, Maya was organizing her Undivided committee materials while Joshie was upstairs taking a shower, his first since the day he'd come home from the hospital. He had told Maya in the morning he wanted to go back to work today; he felt absolutely fine, except when he tried to remember last weekend, the details of which he was most uninterested in knowing anyway, and he was quite bored. They compromised instead, and Maya convinced him to wait until Monday to go back, but he could go to his Cingulate Services group session. That seemed harmless enough. Maya was sure that once he was back in the office, he would be descended upon by the police again, and she didn't think he was ready for that.

Maya was going through her emails and found one that looked to be from the New York City chapter of the Undivided Movement. It congratulated her on being such a vital contributor and praised her dedication to the cause. It asked if she would be interested in taking a more active role for the good of the country, and if so, would she meet with the chapter chair named Harris in New York City next week. They were going to be initiating a new methodology for spreading the truth, and he needed a sub-chairperson to spearhead it.

All Maya's worries were instantly transformed into joy. Imagine! *Her* meeting with the Chapter Chair. She was being selected to head up a new committee—and this had nothing to do with her husband's influence! She could barely contain herself and couldn't wait to tell Russell the good news.

Maya's primary focus was on bringing political reform that would address civil liberties and protections. She believed it was every citizen's duty to safeguard human rights and make the planet a better place for the next generation. So, she and her fellow Undivided cohorts had written postcards and letters to the editor in favor of humanitarian platforms, and to endorse their chosen candidates, and had led several campaigns to petition for the preservation of environmental protections. Her fellow chapter members congratulated their team success, and perhaps she had made a difference in many instances, but the fact that she couldn't even convince her own family to talk to her with open minds made her frequently feel like her work was never going to be enough and she, herself, was largely irrelevant.

It didn't help that she was always comparing her work to Russell's; his success felt like a shadow that lay over her, making her feel inferior. Somehow Russell sensed this and had once chided her about it, saying he was only building physical structures while she was changing the world, but she imagined he was just patronizing her. She dreamed that one day her efforts would have a more far-reaching effect on their cause. Perhaps because she'd had no children of her own, Maya *needed* a legacy.

She was sitting at the solid acacia wood dining table to go through her email, although she did have her own desk in the room Russell used as his home office. Somehow, she always felt she was intruding on his space when she went in there, even though he did most of his work at the Sixth Avenue address.

Maya looked around her beloved home. The ceilings were fourteen feet high, with floor to ceiling glass windows and marble floors. The terrace outside wrapped around to provide a nearly 360-degree view of the city. She had decorated in grays and whites, in a warm but somewhat minimalist fashion, except for the colorful, cozy throw blankets and thick area rugs. The seven room luxury dwelling in midtown Manhattan always made her feel utterly transported from the fast-paced, often grimy streets below. Yet, she frowned thinking of how privileged she was. She wasn't sure what to do about that other than what she was already doing. She didn't want to give up her home, and she knew Russell wouldn't downsize. He believed in spreading the wealth to those less fortunate, not restricting it from himself.

Another unwelcome but familiar thought began to circle through her head, taunting her: how little she herself contributed to their financial circumstance. That in itself was part of what fed her insecurity; it wasn't just leftover emotional baggage from her family as the "bad egg" who moved away. Even though it went against her principles, she still ofttimes measured her worth in terms of dollars and cents. No matter how involved in social action she became, her successes never seemed to be enough by that standard. Therefore, Maya was not enough. Not compared to what her husband did for the world with the money he made.

Maya hesitated; maybe she shouldn't share her news with Russell yet. She could just picture his response. He'd say, "That's terrific, honey," and that would be the end of it. Oh, sure, he would mean it and all, but he wouldn't be excited for her the way she was. He was head of so many committees himself, and involved in so many important business agendas, it wouldn't be spectacular to him. For Maya, this would be her very first opportunity to make a large-scale impact after her hopes for Cingulate Services had dissolved. And she could throw herself into something she would be proud of: the grassroots revolution to bring human rights back to the citizens of America on a city-wide scale. So much more important than money itself, right? Hmm. Maybe she should call one of her girlfriends first instead.

She heard the water from Joshie's shower shut off and decided to wait. This wouldn't be a two minute phone conversation, and Joshie would be downstairs very shortly. She knew he would be excited for her and would hug her with glee, although she wasn't sure he would grasp the tremendous implications.

She answered the email and said she would be incredibly excited to contribute in this way and asked for the details of the meeting, and immediately, she was feeling thrilled all over again. She took a moment to reread it and then toned down her emotions in the email, saying instead that she would consider this a privilege. Living with Russell had taught her to go short and sweet when answering anything official, and that "less is usually more."

Joshie came bounding downstairs, kissed and hugged her in response to her news, and even jumped up and down with happiness for her before he dashed out of the house headed to his group.

CHAPTER 13

Russell had just gotten off the phone with Jim Werner and stood outside, gazing at his closed front door, collecting himself. He loved what he did, so the prospect of it being Friday didn't give him the joy it did for many others, even his own employees, but he had been troubled all week. He couldn't stop ruminating over what Joshua could be entangled in. What if it was found that Joshua had committed a murder and had been totally unaware of it? He suddenly wished they were staying in their house in the Catskills. Maybe this would be a good weekend to go upstate. He took another moment to compose himself, just as the door burst open and Joshua ran out, nearly crashing into him.

"Whoa, there, Josh," Russell laughed. "Where are you off to?" He caught Joshua by the shoulders, but they both nearly fell to the floor.

"Hi, Uncle Russell!" In his excitement, Joshua seemed almost oblivious to the fact that he'd nearly knocked over his uncle. "Aunt Maya said I can go back to Cingulate group tonight." He frowned then. "She wouldn't let me go back to work until Monday, though."

Russell nodded and straightened his shirt. "I think that's wise. Do you have your phone with you? You know… your mother has been trying to call you."

Joshua stopped short, looking like he'd been slapped. "No, Uncle, I don't carry my phone anymore." He looked suddenly frozen; his jaw slackened a bit.

"Why not?"

Joshua answered slowly. "I… I don't know. I just don't. It gets in the way. Too distracting." His posture changed abruptly back to normal, and he reached down to tie a shoelace that had come loose in their collision. "Mom's back? Is she home? How come she didn't call me?"

Russell grinned in spite of himself. "Maybe because you haven't been carrying your phone?"

Joshua laughed. "Good point!" he said and started past Russell down the hall to the elevator.

"Wait, Joshua. I think you should get your phone and take it along. In case anything happens and you need to call us. Or if one of us wants to reach you."

Joshua stiffened and stared at him, stared *through* him. Russell considered that Josh had never gone against a single thing Russell had told him to do in the fourteen years since they'd taken guardianship of him, even on matters of much greater moment than this. Obviously, Joshua did *not* want to do this, something so simple he would normally do every day: carry his phone. What twenty-four-year-old didn't carry his phone? Feeling again the strangeness in his head that he'd felt in Braelyn's apartment, and in that queer way of *knowing* that Russell took for granted, he *saw* Joshua struggling with this as if against a mental concrete block, and Joshua seemed almost paralyzed with the effort. Russell put his arms out again instinctively, as if his nephew were really going to fall this time, but Josh stood rock still. His eyes were glazed and distant.

"Josh?" Russell shook him gently, angling his face to look into his nephew's eyes, *reaching* into Joshua's head. It was something Russell knew he sometimes did reflexively. Now he watched himself do it with intention, as if some part of his consciousness purposefully extended outside of himself and—in this case—into Joshua's mind.

After a minute, Joshua suddenly inhaled deeply and exhaled for longer. He shook his head like a dog shaking off the rain. "I'm sorry, Uncle Russell," he said quietly. "I'll go get my phone if you think it's important." He went back inside.

Russell stared after him. What the hell had just happened?

Shaking his head much like Joshua had just done, Russell walked into the co-op apartment. Maya was sitting at the dining room table with her laptop, and while she looked outwardly completely normal, she had an air of sheer happiness around her. Russell was feeling super sensitive to moods and mental phenomena, something he considered himself to have mastered decades ago. He knew this ability of his was an anomaly, and also that it was one of the things that bound him deeply to Braelyn; he also vaguely acknowledged that it dated back to his earliest childhood, maybe even The Hut experience. But why was it so pronounced now?

In order to survive the onslaught of thoughts, emotions, and intuitive feelings, Russell had learned as a very young child to slow them all down and pick them apart, organizing them before he would speak. It had made him appear to be an abnormally quiet, contemplative kid, and he had not had many friends growing up, but that never bothered him. He was so busy keeping his mind orderly that he paid less attention to his social environment, which always brought a fresh barrage of information that needed to be sorted through. In this way, he kept himself sane. And as he grew up, he seemed to attract friends anyway; people wanted to be around him for his success.

He knew Braelyn was prone to the same kind of information assault, but Russell recognized that she was not able to control her mind like he was. Maybe because hers had started when she was older? Or maybe because they were just different. Russell had no idea how to explain to her what he did in his head that kept his mind performing in a disciplined way.

Right now the process had been on overload since he was in Braelyn's apartment; Russell understood that much. He watched as if from another world as Joshua left the house again, looking much more subdued than he had when he nearly knocked Russell down in the hallway; he felt Maya's happiness as a palpable thing in front of him, and yet, it was like he was behind a window that he could not reach through.

"Russell!" Maya said. "You're home! I'm sorry, I got so distracted, I didn't put dinner on the table for you."

"You don't have to wait on me, Maya. I can find food for myself."

Maya frowned, the happiness diluting in front of Russell's eyes. "That's silly, Russell, of course I do. You work so hard, and provide so much, and what do I contribute? Nothing. I wonder sometimes how you even love me. I must bore you to tears."

Russell pulled himself out of the clarity state he'd been in, realizing how distant he must have seemed.

"Why would you say that, Maya? Of course I love you." He reached into the cupboard to get dishes and started fishing through the refrigerator. He hated when Maya waited on him, as if he were deserving of some sort of reverence instead of just an ordinary guy.

"But I'm so stupid and you're so smart, and you make millions while I mostly spend your money." She started to pout, and this was threatening to become a fight. Russell was not in the mood for another one of her insecurity tantrums. He stopped and wondered if he should just let her get him dinner after all.

"Maya, you're being silly. You are nurturing, loving, generous, and kind, all things that cannot be bought with money or procured through the intellect. You contribute the more important things in life. Things that I never had enough of until I met you." He went to her to give her a hug, which she accepted briefly before turning away. Apparently, she was not to be placated. Something else was going on.

"But how *do* you abide the stupid people in the world?"

"Maya, you are NOT stupid!" Russell never raised his voice, so his response surprised both of them.

"I wasn't talking about me," Maya said quietly as she took his plate and loaded it with salmon and faro and put it in the microwave. "There are so many *idiots* out there, who like to hurt people just because they're different, who carelessly destroy the planet—I *know* you care about that—and who are out for only one purpose, to feed their bank accounts! I know that's not *you*, Russell, but how do you stand to share the world with these people? Carrying guns and bullying others just because they come from a separate culture? Telling women what they can and can't do with their bodies... It's worse now than it ever was! How do you stay so—so—unfazed while it all goes on around you?"

Russell leaned back on the counter. Maya had been to another of her Undivided meetings, no doubt. Undivided was a nationwide movement of thousands of volunteer-led local groups that engaged in progressive advocacy and electoral work at the local, state, and national levels. She often came back fired up, and Russell frequently got the brunt of that.

"I can't change the whole world, Maya. I try to do my part. I donate to The Sierra Club and Environmental Defense Fund, to Doctors Without Borders, Planned Parenthood, St. Jude, Wounded Warriors.... Geez, Maya, you know the list. And together, you and I started two soup kitchens, in Harlem and on the Lower East Side. Six months ago, you said your Undivided group was doing a midnight run to give clothes to the homeless, and I gave $10,000 to the cause, and let you shop for them as you pleased. What else do you want me to do?"

Maya quieted. "Maybe I want to make my *own* contribution too, Russell. Maybe I want to do something as Maya Vaderman that isn't just getting petitions signed, writing letters, or distributing my husband's money. I want to do something more hands on."

"Well, no one is stopping you. *I* certainly have never tried to stop you. Do you have something specific in mind?"

"Well, yes, actually, I do," Maya said. She nodded to the chair at the table and Russell took a seat. "I received an email today inviting me to head up a subcommittee for Undivided NYC. I'm going to do it." She took the grilled salmon and faro from the microwave and placed it in front of him, and then tossed a salad with white balsamic vinegar.

"Great," Russell said, thinking how much more enthusiastic he would have been about this if she hadn't been so argumentative. "What will you be doing?"

Maya handed him the salad bowl and gathered up her laptop. "That hasn't been disclosed yet; I'm having a meeting with the chairman next week, and then I'll be able to plan."

Russell looked up from his plate. "Don't you want... to know what you'll be asked to do before you agree to do it?"

"You really don't understand! What could they possibly want me to do that I wouldn't be willing to do? I want to help this movement, and I'm honored that I've been selected. And it came from the top." She went out to the patio... overlooking the New York City skyline and closed the sliding glass door.

Russell shrugged to himself and turned to his dinner. For all his high intellect, he would never understand women.

CHAPTER 14

Thomas Brunner sat nervously in the side office waiting for the class to come in. He had arranged the snacks on the table. Everyone got a single "sugar" cookie, which was warmed in the microwave as per protocol, assorted donuts if they wanted more munchies, and as much milk, coffee, or soda as they wanted. They made the cookies a game to encourage discipline, so that the clients prided themselves on each taking one and only one.

What a week for Wheeler to sit out, Thomas thought. Or maybe he was just late. Thomas and Mark Wheeler had been doing this group session together for nearly a year. The progress of the students was incredible, better than Thomas had ever imagined it could be. Their ages ranged from eighteen to fifty, but most were on the younger side. If these kids had had this supplemental learning in their teens, they'd all have been rock stars and going on for advanced college degrees.

Thomas only barely understood how it worked. After the clients had their cookies, they did a group review with discussion about their week. Who interviewed for a job or who impressed a friend, who got a raise, or just general horsing around. Then he led them in a relaxation technique that was like a guided meditation. In it, Thomas repeatedly suggested to them how much smarter they were becoming, how easy it was for them to master materials and remember data, and how confident they must feel in their mental abilities; that the world was at their feet and they could pursue any career they wanted. Then they did either math exercises, studies in science and technology, or vocabulary and reading, depending on the week. Sometimes they split into groups, and the older crowd was given tutoring in computer programs and apps; the youngsters rarely needed help with that stuff. The sessions were two hours long, but there was always a little time for a brief current events discussion about the great job Ganaffe would do when he won the presidency and the dangers of ultraliberalism and the Antifa movement. At the end of each session, they had exercises to practice, and they could work together or ask for help with them if needed, and then homework to do for the next week. There were songs and socializing. Everyone loved it, and they really did seem to be getting smarter.

One thing was sure, if Wheeler didn't show, there'd be no breakout groups today. Thomas couldn't ever remember his just not showing up. Wheeler had been with Cingulate Services for years and said he loved watching the little group thrive. Thomas had only been there nine months and knew there were a lot of other arms to the organization, about which he knew next to nothing. Now he realized he didn't want to know any more than he did.

Thomas had been mildly surprised to learn that they cushioned their success on the use of a drug that made the mind more pliant and subject to suggestion. The clients were not to know that was why they had "sugar" cookies every week, but it was unclear to Thomas if knowing would negate the effects. Thomas didn't pursue the matter much; it had seemed like a harmless enough ruse for the incredible strides these people were making, people who had never before dreamed of making more than minimum wage and who transformed into managers and office workers getting twenty-five dollars an hour or more.

Two months ago, Wheeler included Thomas in a conference call. He was told the uses of this drug to influence the mind could have many excellent benefits, and that Thomas was going to have the lucky opportunity to contribute to the well-being of their nation on a larger scale. Thomas soon realized this was primarily for monetary ends, benefiting some group or other, but he didn't object since he was promised a cut of the dividends, which amounted to an extra $2,000 a month. In a million years, he would never have dreamed it would involve murder.

Clients started wandering into the suite, greeting and poking fun at each other, and digging into the cookies and other treats. There were nineteen students total, and they were an amazingly friendly, happy group who gelled easily and enjoyed each other's company. They also genuinely cared about their comrades' progress and encouraged each other along the way. They waved cheerfully to Thomas in the side office where he'd left the door open.

Of course, there would be only eighteen today, Thomas thought. Donny was never coming back. He wondered if he should ask if anyone had seen him or volunteer that Donny had left the group. He decided against volunteering anything; if the police thought he knew Donny had left, they'd want to know his source of information and where he had gone.

Joshua was one of the last to arrive. Usually perky and playful, he looked somewhat dispirited, and Thomas felt his heart rate increase. Joshua kept to himself tonight, even when his friends tried to include him. He sat in his chair and waited for class to start. Thomas wasn't even sure Joshua had taken his cookie.

Thomas swallowed his fear and walked over to Joshua's desk. "Hey there, Josh. You feeling all right? You're not eating."

"Hi, Mr. Brunner. I'm just not hungry tonight. My aunt made a big dinner, and I guess I pigged out a little."

Thomas wasn't sure if this would be a problem. They never forced anyone to eat, but it was clear that those who imbibed received far greater benefits from the program. Any other week, it wouldn't have been so unnerving. Thomas put a hand to his heart, feigning insult.

"But Joshua… I made them from scratch!"

Joshua looked torn, as the boy was foremost a people-pleaser. He said, "All right, Mr. Brunner, I'll take one, just for you." Thomas breathed a sigh of relief, but later noticed that the cookie remained untouched for the entire session.

During ending exercises, one member named Jonathan piped up and asked where Donny was. Thomas's heart skipped a beat and he looked around anxiously.

"Has anyone seen Donny?" Thomas repeated the question to the class. Everyone shook their heads and looked around. Thomas glanced briefly at Joshua who seemed suddenly terror-stricken.

"Hey, Josh," Jonathan asked him. "You and Donny are friends. Don't you guys go for pizza and shit? Have you seen him?"

Joshua sat motionless, a look of horror on his face. Jonathan called to him again.

"Joshua, did you guys get together last week?"

"I… I don't remember. I don't think so." Joshua finally answered. He literally looked like he'd seen a ghost.

Thomas jumped in. "I think that's it for this week. You can all finish your assignments for next time."

But Jonathan wouldn't let it go. "Mr. Brunner, he was in the office with you and Mr. Wheeler last week after class, I remember. Shouldn't you call his house and see where he is?" Jonathan turned to Joshua. "Or can you call, Josh? I'm worried about him. He loves this place, he never misses."

"I'll see to it, Jonathan," Thomas answered, taking the pressure off Joshua, who had turned completely white. Joshua was already collecting his materials and heading for the door; he looked at Thomas for a second as if trying to figure something out, and then raced out.

———

Joshua walked quickly, in a state of near panic. He wasn't even sure why. He wanted to go home. Not to his aunt and uncle. Aunt Maya was whom he sought when he wanted to be enclosed in love, and Uncle Russell was his source when he needed his problems solved. But right then, he needed to figure stuff out, and after the brief encounter with his uncle in the hallway tonight, he was afraid to see him. Something creepy had happened. So he headed for the East Village and his mom's place. He nearly took the subway, but at the top of the stairs, he stopped short and couldn't make himself go down to the station. Weird.

He decided to hail an Uber on his app, hoping his uncle wouldn't mind the charge too terribly much, but then could not bring his phone out of his pocket to use it. It was like his hand was made of lead. He looked at the subway steps and thought about his phone and decided to walk instead. He headed downtown for a few blocks and realized it was going to take a long time to get to the Village and he was suddenly exhausted. He *felt* Uncle Russell in his head telling him to take his phone "in case anything happens." He looked slowly at his pocket and pulled his phone out. Nothing seemed amiss. Finally, he opened the app and then waited impatiently at the corner of Eighth Avenue and 29th Street for the Uber.

He was breathing hard and his head was starting to hurt

again, like it had on *That Day*. Like a knife was boring into him. He knew he should call and tell Aunt Maya where he was going, but he didn't want to use his phone again, and especially not to talk. As much as he recognized how off script that was for him, he couldn't get past it. He had only taken it with him at all because Uncle Russell was insistent. More weirdness, like the subway steps.

When the Uber showed, he got in and sat forward in the seat, tapping his foot the whole way.

CHAPTER 15

Braelyn's second meeting with Jeremy Southpine had not been much more productive than her first. It was her word against the customs agent's that the cocaine was not hers, and although Russell knew her well enough to consider the possibility that she was telling the truth, Jeremy only wanted to talk about a plea bargain. She dutifully told him about the *borrachero* flower, but he didn't seem to know what to make of that either. Even when she told him it was taken from her and she wanted it back.

Why did Russell have to leave so abruptly yesterday? Didn't he know he was the only person in the world she could rely on? She unzipped her suitcase and started picking the clothes out to throw in the laundry. They smelled weakly of *borrachero* flowers and Braelyn felt giddy for a second, but she clamped it down. Maybe because she had been exposed as a child, it had been easy to learn how to block the effects of the plant itself, which she'd had to do the first time she went to Colombia looking for it. Whatever transformation this stuff had caused in her brain years ago was water under the bridge, but the plant couldn't hurt her anymore. Which is why she was so outraged that someone could have made a switch on her at the airport. She did not believe she was deceived with any chemical assistance; she would have known. She did not believe a switch was done at all. They lied to her, plain and simple. Of course, verbalizing that would label her a paranoid schizophrenic. She knew how this world worked.

She started poking through her fridge, wishing she had put more items on the Peapod order or had asked Russell to bring her groceries. She had a pizza delivered and ate two slices, but she really wanted something more substantial and healthier. She'd been eating junk food for the last few days, and she hadn't exactly been watching what she was eating in Colombia before that. Except, of course, to make sure it wasn't tainted. She was bored, and frustrated, and yes, a little scared. She did not understand what had happened to her.

She fingered a bottle of gin in the bottom of her credenza. It wasn't supposed to be there, she was supposed to have gotten all the booze out of the house when she got sober (again) six months ago. She found it sort of an exercise in futility. No one believed her anymore, and no one cared to celebrate with her when she reached sobriety milestones. She guessed she couldn't blame them, but it made it harder to stick with it when no one encouraged her. Her new shrink told her she had to get sober for herself, never mind anyone else. But life right now was so upside down, what could it hurt? And it was the only way she had ever been able to escape the chaos in her mind.

As she reached for the bottle, she heard the key turn in the latch. She jumped, nearly knocking the bottle over and stood straight up in time to see Joshua coming in the door.

She was so glad to see him. It felt like she'd just been given a long drink of spring water after a month in the desert.

"Joshua!" She ran over to give him a great big hug.

He smiled at her mildly. "Is it okay that I'm here?"

Braelyn stopped and took a good look at her son. He looked terrible. Worn and ragged and haggard. Then she realized she was looking *into* Joshua, for his clothes were neat and tidy, his hair was clean and combed, and he had recently shaved. He was standing there peacefully, but she felt a war raging inside him. Her psychiatrist had told her that these insights were what made her feel like she was losing her mind.

"Oh my God, Josh, of course it's okay! You *live* here... at least, whenever you want to. Do you want some pizza? I put it in the fridge, but it's just from tonight." She started over to get it out, hoping he hadn't observed her stooped under the credenza. Joshua knew better than anyone where all her liquor hiding places were. But he hadn't seemed to notice.

"No thanks, Mom. I'm not hungry. I just wanted to crash here tonight. Is that okay?" Joshua fidgeted with the strings on his sweatshirt and didn't meet her eyes.

"Of course! Did something happen with your aunt and uncle?" She guided him into the living room to sit down together.

"Oh, no, nothing. I just wanted... space."

Braelyn nodded and they were both quiet. Maya frequently did not allow for "space." With all good intentions, she could smother someone with love and affection, and be completely oblivious that what they really needed was for her to back off, so this was a most reasonable request. And Braelyn was really tired of being alone, except for the occasional visit from that imbecile lawyer. The moments dragged.

"How was your trip?" Joshua asked. "Did you do any fun stuff? Maybe I could go with you one day, I'd like to go to South America and see the sights. Maybe tomorrow we can go to the park, like we used to...." His voice trailed off.

So, Russell really hadn't told Joshua anything, Braelyn thought. How was she going to explain? Joshua wouldn't believe her either.

"Joshua...," she started. "I can't go anywhere right now. I... I was arrested when I came back to New York."

"Oh." It was just like Joshua not to ask anything further. He unzipped his sweatshirt and started taking off his shoes.

"But I didn't do it! I swear I didn't!"

"Didn't do what?" Joshua had that look on his face that Braelyn had seen for so many years. That heartbreaking look that said: *My mother is a mess, and I can't rely on her. I'm all alone.*

But this time it was different. This time Braelyn had *not* been the disappointment. This time it wasn't on her.

"They said they found cocaine in my suitcase. But I didn't put it there. I swear, Joshua, even though I know you probably won't believe me, but I did *not* pack cocaine in my suitcase."

Braelyn found herself on her knees in front of her son. "Joshua. It wasn't mine. I *need* you to believe me! It wasn't mine. The stupid lawyer even asked me if maybe I forgot. Forgot! I would *know* if I put contraband in my luggage, how could I forget?" She shook her head as she put it in her hands and wept. "Something very, very weird is going on in my life right now, Joshua, and I don't understand it at all." Tears were flowing down her cheeks.

Joshua looked down at her with something that surprisingly looked like he might actually believe her. "For me too, Mom. And I'm really scared."

CHAPTER 16

Thomas Brunner watched the last client leave and then called Mark Wheeler. How could Wheeler leave him alone to deal with the class today of all days, with the Plessman kid now an unknown and having to account for Donny being gone—forever.

There was no answer to his call just as there'd been no answer to the texts or email he'd sent during the class. Thomas began to sweat. His gut was talking to him, and it was saying something very unpleasant had happened to his senior colleague, something directly related to the disaster they had potentially created with Donny and Jackson. He did *not* like that guy Trenaman, did not like him at all. He looked like he had a heart of stone. How was this going to come back on Thomas?

He gathered his materials and collected the food and replaced it all in the shopping bag he'd brought. There was a maid who came in and cleaned everything after the sessions, but he never left food there, especially not the cookies. He looked at Joshua's desk and the uneaten cookie. It had a mouse-sized bite in the side but nothing more. What if Joshua would not eat them anymore? Would it matter in terms of the "command" they had given the kid? Would his memory continue to be a blank? Did he need to keep consuming the stuff at group meetings, or was the initial encounter enough? Should they kick him out if he wouldn't eat?

Thomas's mind was racing so much he barely noticed the man in the black suit and white shirt standing in the doorway. He jumped.

"Mr. Trenaman," he stuttered. "I didn't see you."

"Obviously," Trenaman said.

"Have you… did you… I haven't been able to reach Mark Wheeler. He's usually here tonight. Do you know where he is? I mean, is he okay?"

Trenaman looked at him coolly, and Thomas felt his blood turn to ice. "Mark Wheeler will not be back. His employment with us has been terminated." Then Trenaman smiled. "You, on the other hand, have been promoted to senior administrator for this phase of operations. That comes with a hefty pay raise and only requires a few more hours per week of your time. I think you will be pleased with your new compensation. You will report to the main office uptown, not the timeshare, on Monday morning, where your new duties will be explained carefully."

Thomas trembled. No one was asking him if he was interested in this new "position."

"Will I not be running these Cingulate sessions anymore?"

"Oh, yes, you'll still be here, and we'll get you an assistant. We want the students to have continuity with familiar faces. See you at 9:00 a.m. on Monday."

Trenaman walked out and Thomas again noticed the limp, which was more subtle than the last time they'd met; Thomas collapsed in his chair as he watched him leave, his bowels threatening to turn to water.

This could not be good, Thomas thought. They had been involved in a murder. There was no way Wheeler would have been allowed to just walk away. Not knowing what he knew. And now Thomas was being asked—no, told—to take his place, which meant he was trapped.

Thomas began to panic. He calculated how much cash he'd managed to squirrel away in the last six months, and it was nearly $20,000. He was hoping to move out to the suburbs and buy a little house, so he had banked all those extra incentive checks. He considered giving all the money back but decided quickly they'd probably kill him for even considering it. So, he'd have to get away. Far away.

Where could he go? And how soon would they miss him? He had, of course, given them his bank account numbers for direct deposit; would they be tracking him if he took his money out? Would they suspect he might run?

Thomas had never been known for his bravery. He was never cruel or a bully, and he never sought to hurt anyone, but he didn't stand up for anyone either. He had gotten a degree in business and always planned to go on for an MBA, but didn't want to put all that work in. He was a guy who liked to slide by. He had never found a job that paid him what he thought he was worth, so when Cingulate Services came along, he jumped at it. He hadn't really cared what they were doing, as long as he was getting paid.

Thomas grew up in rural Pennsylvania. His father was a farmer, and his mother taught elementary school, but Thomas mostly just liked to play video games. He spent enough time outside when his father needed help, and he wasn't much of a team player for sports. He knew how to handle a gun and to hunt, but he didn't like killing anything, even though he loved fresh meat for his dinner. When he really thought about it, he was fairly mediocre. Maybe that was why he liked Cingulate Services so much; he was cleverer than the people he was teaching, and it gave him confidence. Except lately, the clients were getting smarter.

He wondered if he could go home for the weekend. He could say he knew he would be putting in more hours and wanted to see his parents before his extra duties began. Could he talk to his father about what to do? He'd get yelled at for sure for getting mixed up in something so criminal—and so stupid. But honestly, how was he supposed to have known? He didn't have a lot of real friends, mostly they were drinking buddies, no one he could trust with this. He knew he had a cousin in Majorca… Could he go there? Would that be far enough away? Did he need a visa to go to Majorca? If he did, that probably wasn't happening over the weekend. Where else could he go?

It was nearly 10:00 p.m. At the very least, he needed to behave normally. He grabbed his briefcase and headed out into the street and down into the subway station, his brain on overload. He discarded the idea of Majorca. He barely spoke any Spanish, and besides, he seemed to remember his cousin's area spoke mostly Catalan. If he wanted to go to Europe, he should probably do it in a more circuitous way, anyway, like maybe go to the Bahamas first. Thomas had a headache.

CHAPTER 17

At 10:30 p.m., Russell turned the desk light off in his study and got up to stretch. He should be working on designs for a new structure in Germany. It was an honor to be asked to bid on the new rail station they were constructing in Berlin, and his submission was due in ten days' time. He wanted it to be uniquely compelling, but he wasn't really concentrating, and he finally gave up completely.

Jim Werner had called from New York-Presbyterian an hour earlier. He sent Joshua's blood in for scopolamine screening with NMS, the National Medical Service labs. The turnaround time was eight days—fifteen if it was positive—since it involved high performance liquid chromatography with tandem mass spectrometry. So, there was nothing for Russell to do now but wait, but he was having a hard time putting it out of his thoughts.

He walked into the living room to find Maya working on a soft, powder blue baby blanket. They had no friends with small children, but Maya loved to knit and donate blankets and sweaters to distribute to low income families in the city. She proudly claimed that each one was made with love as if it were going to her own blood.

Russell sat down next to her on the couch, hoping her pettish mood had passed. "Have you heard from Joshua?" he asked. "Isn't he usually home from group by now?"

"No," Maya said. "Maybe he went out for a bit with that friend of his. What was his name, Donny? I suppose I could call." She picked up her phone and dialed, but after five or six rings, she put it down. "It says his voicemail is full. That's odd. Now I'm worried, Russell."

On a hunch, Russell picked up his own cell. Something was queer about this business of Joshua and his phone, but after their strange encounter in the hall, Russell felt Joshua might respond better to him. He texted Joshua.

Hey, Josh. Let me know where you are.

It didn't take but a minute for Joshua to text back.

I'm staying with Mom in the Village.

Nothing more, like how long he planned to stay there. Well, he was twenty-four years old, and he was with his mother. What could Russell say? Still, it made him uneasy for some reason.

Maya was neither warm nor cool to him, but very involved in her knitting and in the latest news reports about the United States pulling out of the Paris Climate Agreement. Russell announced he was hitting the hay and headed off to bed. Once he tucked himself in, he fell asleep immediately.

The air was thick and heavy, and the ground was a soggy mixture of mud and grass in the forest clearing. The foliage was nearly impenetrable beyond the circle of trees that were so tall, it was like being surrounded by wall-to-wall towers. Everything was larger than life—

or maybe Russell was just very small. He climbed the little hill in the gray mist, putting one foot inexorably in front of the other. Part of him wanted to stop, to go back, but he could not. He was being pulled forward, like a magnet, and it was useless to try to resist.

The Hut loomed up in front of him. The sides consisted of rows of thin tree branches tied together, and thatch covered the roof. A faint smell of sage and something else he couldn't quite identify radiated through the walls. The door was slightly ajar, and he found himself walking through….

Russell jerked awake, his heart pounding. The room was still, and Maya had not yet come to bed. He got up and threw cold water on his face and considered going back out to the living room, but picturing Maya sitting with her knitting convinced him that wasn't where he wanted to be. It was only 11:25 p.m.

He lay back down, but it wasn't until he heard Maya come in quietly and slip under the covers in the dark next to him that he finally closed his eyes.

The funny smell was stronger inside The Hut, and it reminded Russell of the smell of Braelyn's dirty clothes in her suitcase; for a moment, Russell thought he was alone. There was a little table off to the side with a candle burning and it cast shadows about the walls. It seemed to be neither day nor night, but some otherness time, not like or unlike twilight.

There were small pottery dishes on the table and larger ones against the wall, and another in the center of the room, which held the smoldering herbs. The haze and the smell came from there. Then Russell noticed the man. He was sitting on a little bench gazing at Russell, the little boy who had entered his space, but he didn't look disturbed by the intrusion, rather, Russell understood that he had been summoned by the man himself. There was a commotion outside that sounded like Russell's father yelling, but the Man in The Hut passed his hand across the air between them, and the noise muffled and disappeared.

The smoke in The Hut was even thicker than the mist was outside, and little Russell was afraid to breathe because he thought he would cough, and he was sure he was not supposed to cough in front of the man. His head felt funny and he associated it with the dense smoke and he wanted to leave, but he was also intensely curious about the man, and his feet remained planted in the ground. Then the man beckoned him to come forward, and Russell found his feet moving forward again, his eyes locked on the man's, unable to look away.

The man's eyes were peculiar. Opaque white, and yet Russell knew they looked at him, looked into him, looked right through him. He kept walking closer in the smoky little space until he could see nothing but those white, blind-looking eyes and the surrounding mist.

The man passed his hand between their faces again, and then spoke to him. It wasn't really speech, because Russell only heard it inside his head, and he didn't really hear it. He just felt the meaning. Like a series of visions. Some part of him recognized it was not English, but it didn't matter, because he understood exactly, and yet the ideas were very big for his little-boy brain. It felt like images, but not visual images. Symbols that made perfect sense.

"You are gifted, young child. You will be blessed.
Your mind shall have no limit; no door shall remain closed
to you.
You shall be a Curandero Grande, even as I am.
You will see into the hearts of others and you will enter their
souls at will.
The Spirits have foreseen your coming, and today I make it so.
When next the Holy Plants find you, all doors will open...."

Suddenly the world expanded, larger and larger, and Russell was not standing on solid ground anymore but floating in space, the thatch ceiling of The Hut stretched higher and higher until he was ten feet off the floor, but he still could not touch the ceiling. He started to panic and reached out frantically for something to hold onto, and then he was falling—

"Russell! Russell, wake up!" Maya was shaking him. She had turned on her bedside lamp and her tousled hair fell across her face, but Russell could see her eyes, so white—no, wait. That was the dream. Maya looked quite like Maya, albeit desperately worried. And no doubt; Russell could not remember ever waking up screaming from a nightmare before. Not in his adult life, anyway.

"What was it, Russell? Tell me! What happened?"

Russell shook himself and sat up in bed. He swung his legs around the side and stood up, and Maya followed right behind him. He sat down in a chair and motioned her to wait a minute. He couldn't speak yet. His heart was racing, his breathing rapid, and he had to take a minute. He motioned at the main light with his hand, and after a moment Maya understood. She turned it on and squatted down next to him.

Russell let the light wash over him, hoping it would carry the dream away. The images dulled but they remained. Maya was looking at him expectantly. He finally found his voice.

"I'm so sorry, Maya." Russell heard himself speak and thought he didn't even sound like himself. His voice was hoarse, and he wondered how loud he had been screaming, but he was afraid to ask. "I guess I just had a bad dream."

"No kidding, Sherlock," Maya said. "What were you dreaming?"

But Russell found he couldn't put any of it into words and wasn't sure he was even ready to. He needed to be with it for a while first and process it.

"Was it the Man in The Hut?" Maya asked.

Russell's head snapped back to look at her. What did she know about the Man in The Hut?

"Huh? You know about The Hut?"

Maya sat back on her heels, responding to his return to normal speech. "When we first got married, you told me about those dreams you used to have as a child. I just don't remember your having one since we've been together. At least, you never mentioned them, and you *certainly* never woke me up with it."

"And you remembered that all these years?"

Maya sniffed and stood up, heading back over to sit on the bed. "Of course, I remember. It must have been important in your life, or you wouldn't have told me." She paused. "I think we shared more of ourselves with each other back then. Bound to happen as marriages evolve, I guess, and we start to take intimacy for granted."

"I'm sorry. I guess I get very involved in work these days and get caught up in my own head," Russell said, grateful to change the subject. "Maybe we should go upstate this weekend. We haven't been away, just the two of us, in a long time. It's great hiking weather. And looks like Joshua is staying with Braelyn, for better or for worse."

Maya brightened and reached for her robe that was hanging on a chair. "That sounds absolutely lovely! But what about the dream? You see how good you are at deflecting me?" She was laughing in spite of herself as she said it.

Russell laughed too and shook his head. "I have to figure it out myself first. Right now, it feels like a smudge on a lens, nothing is clear. Maybe in the morning I can sort it out."

"If you don't forget it by then," Maya said. "That's what often happens to me with my dreams. Coming back to bed?"

"In a minute. You go ahead, I'll be right in. I'm just getting a drink—no, sit, Maya, my love. I can get it." Russell went into the kitchen, needing a moment alone. The "smudged lens" could just be the hazy, smoky nature of the dream. That was about the only thing that was clear. But one thing was for certain, Russell was not going to be forgetting this dream anytime soon.

Until tonight, the "dream" had always stopped when he arrived inside The Hut and saw the Hollow Man, but he was never able to remember what he said. Suddenly Russell realized: This had *never* been just a dream. It was a memory. And the rest of the memory had been lost until just now.

CHAPTER 18

Braelyn looked at her son as if seeing him for the first time. He looked vulnerable and frightened, something he hadn't shown her in years. He always presented as the picture of happiness, unfazed by the world around him. Since he'd gone to live with his aunt and uncle, that is.

He had never been diagnosed as learning delayed, but by second grade it was obvious he would be no genius. He struggled even in elementary school. Braelyn always blamed herself because those were the years she was heavily into drugs, a rebel in full force, thinking she could run from the monsters in her mind. She had married Keith Plessman on a whim, maybe to prove she was "normal." She thought she had found someone who would make the world a friendlier place; instead he just helped her flee from it. Keith used to deal cocaine and meth—although neither Braelyn nor Keith really used the methamphetamine. In those days, Braelyn had felt like everyone in the world was against her, even Russell, who seemed to be able to gather his wits no matter what was going on around him. The pregnancy was an accident, but they were married, so she figured, why not?

Keith was murdered in a drug deal gone bad just before Joshua was born, and Braelyn was wholly unprepared to be a single mother. She couldn't help but feel that Joshua's lack of mental acuity was because of all the chemicals she had put in her body while he was developing inside her, and later, not spending time teaching or reading to him when he was a toddler did not help his lack of development. He was a constant reminder of how difficult it was for her to keep it together, even when another life depended on her.

Joshua loved her anyway, in that unconditional way that young children love their parents. Always affectionate and forgiving of her absences, until Russell and Maya had taken him to live with them. Josh tried many times to come back home, but once Braelyn saw he would be taken care of in her brother's household, her drug and alcohol use went wild. Why couldn't she be like "normal" people? Why was she, of all the impotent humans of the world, uniquely aware of the existential isolation of every soul? Others glossed it over with store-bought *things* and the fantasy that they were not alone in the cosmos, but for Braelyn, that knowledge could not be buried or outrun. It stared her in the face every moment of every day for almost as long as she could remember.

Joshua would come to her sometimes, wanting to spend time with her, and she would be high as a kite, fleeing her demons in whatever manner she could find. Eventually, reality set in, and he started to get that look in his eyes that told her he had given up expecting anything from her at all. Even the dumber kids finally learn. Ironically, that was when Braelyn started restricting herself to booze, but it didn't assuage her guilt.

Russell truly adopted Joshua as his own. He spent hours with him, tutoring English and algebra so that Josh could graduate high school, and Maya loved Joshua and praised him on his progress every day. Braelyn could never have done all that; she just didn't have the patience.

Now Josh was making great advances with the Cingulate Services group, and Maya had even suggested he could go to college if he wanted, but Joshua wasn't the studying type.

Braelyn sat down on the couch and looked at her son. "What happened to you? Russell said you had a 'mishap,' but he wouldn't tell me anything about it."

Joshua looked at his hands. "I don't know, Mom. I can't remember. And every time I try, I get this terrible headache. But last weekend… I don't know. I don't know anything!" Joshua put his head in his hands and started bawling like a baby.

Braelyn went to him and held her son. She pulled him over onto the couch with her. It felt awkward at first, but after a few minutes they clung to each other as they had not done since Joshua was a very small child. Finally, he sat up and rubbed his eyes with his sleeves.

"What is it like?" Braelyn asked. "When you try to remember?"

Josh puckered his eyebrows, concentrating hard. "It's like this bright light that blocks out everything, and it hurts my eyes and my head. And I must've done something bad because when I woke up, there was blood on my clothes. And dumb things keep happening, like… like my phone…." Joshua pulled his phone out of his pocket as if it were contaminated with something and he didn't really want to touch it. He placed it gingerly on the coffee table in front of the couch with two fingers.

"I didn't get your calls because I wasn't carrying it. I still don't *want* to carry it. And I don't know why!" Joshua's voice started rising, out of control.

Braelyn looked at the phone, then at Joshua. He needed her and she desperately wanted to be the mother she'd never had the capacity to be before. Simple questions seemed the best route to go. "So, how come you brought it tonight?"

Joshua shook uncontrollably for a couple of seconds. "It was Uncle Russell. He told me to take it with me. It was like a... a... compulsion—is that the right word? It was like he *made* me take it. No, that's not right... It was like he made me ignore the part that was making me *not* take it. That's what it was. Oh, none of this makes any sense, Mom. But my head hurts, and I don't remember anything, and I'm not *supposed* to do or say some things or see some people, and I don't understand! It's like my brain is all broken." He started crying again.

Braelyn was speechless. How could Joshua suffer this kind of mental anguish? He almost sounded like he was feeling what she felt, when her mind went wonky—which was practically every day. Her thoughts and emotions would get all balled up inside her and threaten to explode. There was just too much information that came in. And she couldn't find anything stable in her mind to anchor to, so it was all a mishmash. Then her only two options seemed to be to explode with it or shut down completely and dive into the abyss. But Joshua had never been in The Hut, had never met the shaman, never had the sinister liquid stuffed in his nostrils with the resultant assault on his senses that never seemed to stop; no, Joshua was safe from all that. Maybe Braelyn was just plain crazy after all, and maybe it was genetic.

"And, I didn't realize *any* of this until Uncle Russell did... whatever he did tonight! And now I'm scared to see him again," Joshua finished.

Braelyn almost didn't hear his last sentence, as she poised for a nosedive into the chasm of self-contempt and despair.

"Wait," she said, "what? What did Uncle Russell do?"

Joshua sat up and dried his eyes. His confidence in Braelyn took away some of her shame and self-deprecation, but panic loomed just at the periphery of her consciousness, as it always did.

"I don't know, Mom. It was like he reached into my head

somehow and deleted that program. Or like he changed the password, because I can still feel it in there somewhere, but now I can choose not to follow it. But it's *hard*. I know that doesn't make any sense. I feel like a fruitcake. I was hoping to talk to you because, well, because people say you're a fruitcake, and so I thought maybe you wouldn't tell me I made it all up."

Braelyn didn't know whether to laugh or cry at that. In perfect Joshua character, he had no idea he had just insulted her. Well, apparently her mental drama was good for something. She tried to focus on her son's crisis; she was determined to be here for him this time.

"Tell me what he did. Try to remember. It's okay, don't be scared."

Joshua's brows crinkled again. "It was like that time I went fishing with him, and my line got all tangled up. And Uncle Russell pulled the strands apart and untangled it. It was kind of like that. But how could he get inside my *brain?*" Joshua started to shake again.

Braelyn wondered if he hadn't just explained to her how Russell handled his own mental overload; she knew her brother was subject to it just like she was, only Russell had a method. He had a "workaround," and she had begged him countless times to share it with her, but he always denied doing anything special.

"You saw your brain as 'strands?' Like, like… neurons?" Braelyn wasn't sure Joshua knew what a neuron was, but she knew *she* sometimes felt like her neurons were all crossed and tangled.

"Huh? No, it was like my brain was all knotted up and blocked inside. Like a line I couldn't cross, like it was clogged. I can't describe it." Joshua was unconsciously playing with the hoodie strings of his sweatshirt, twisting and untwisting them, as if demonstrating what happened in his head.

"Did it hurt when Uncle Russell did that?" Braelyn glanced

at the strings and wondered if she could try that with her own thoughts sometime.

Joshua thought about that. "No, not really," he said quietly. "But it felt *weird* as all get out. Please don't make me see him again right now. Can't I just stay here for a few days?" Josh pleaded. "I don't want to go back there."

"Of course, Josh. This is your home, and I am your mother. Stay as long as you want."

CHAPTER 19

Monday came around quickly, and so did Maya's first meeting with the chair of the NYC Undivided Movement. Joshie had spent the weekend with his mother, which bothered her, because she knew Braelyn would not care for him nearly as well as she did, but Russell insisted she leave it alone and let him be. Whether he showed up for work today or not would tell the tale.

So, Maya decided to focus on herself. She was incredibly excited about her meeting with the mysterious "Harris" who had emailed her last week. She had been to the salon over the weekend and had the blonde highlights touched up in her otherwise medium brown hair, which was cut to shoulder length and styled. Then she had her nails done in a muted red color that she hoped made the statement that she was both classy and capable. She went through her walk-in closet for the fourth time, trying things on and discarding them, feeling like nothing really looked good enough for what she wanted to convey: professional, enthusiastic, competent. She gave up on perfection and found an outfit that was acceptable, gave her hair another comb through, and went down to meet the Uber.

Maya arrived ten minutes early and waited near the door just inside the restaurant for Mr. Harris to arrive. She shifted her weight nervously, not sure if she should ask to be seated while she waited, but when she said whom she was meeting, the *maître d'* did not give her that option. The restaurant she had been directed to was quite upscale, even for her experience, being married to an inconceivably rich yet completely unpretentious man such as her husband.

While he was certainly not frugal, Russell hated to overspend or be wasteful. This place dripped ostentation, and Maya felt increasingly self-conscious of her black skirt and pumps, and pale camel-colored blouse and black blazer. She had been a firm and desirable 135 pounds in her twenties, but now she struggled to keep the scale below 150. Russell never seemed to care, and always made her feel attractive, but just at this moment, she was wishing for her former figure and accompanying confidence in her appearance.

The tables were set with white linen cloths, crystal wine goblets, and small tulip arrangements, with candles burning in the low light. About half the tables were full, set well apart from each other to allow for private conversation, and all the discussions seemed discreet. It made Maya feel like she wasn't *supposed* to look at anyone. Despite the sun blazing on the street, the tinted windows gave the impression she had walked into another world, and there were hand-painted pictures of Italy hanging on the walls.

The door opened again at exactly 12:30 p.m., and a middle-aged man walked in wearing a tailored, ash gray Armani suit and matching tie with a silver shirt. He wore round wire-rimmed glasses and had a short, neatly trimmed, graying mustache and dark wavy hair that seemed neither long nor short and was the only unkempt thing about him. It looked like his hair was rebelling against the rest of his pristine demeanor. He walked up to her and took her right hand in his, one on top and one on the bottom, and spoke softly.

"Maya Vaderman, I presume? I am Harris. I trust you found the restaurant without any problem?"

"Oh, yes, Mr. Harris," Maya nearly stuttered. She felt completely out of her element! It wasn't just the rich décor; the ambiance and Harris's demeanor were much more formal than she was used to. Russell's meetings, when she was invited, did not stand on so much ceremony. "No problem at all," she said.

The man smiled, still holding her hand between his. "It's 'Harris.' Just Harris. We don't use last names at this level of the organization. For security reasons. You understand, don't you?"

Maya squirmed. She definitely did not understand, but she nodded anyway.

"Come," he said. "Let's take the booth in the back so we can talk. Can I get you a glass of Dom Perignon?"

"Oh, no, no wine for me. I never drink at lunch." Maya wondered if she was being inappropriate.

Harris led her to a private booth at the back and held the chair for her. When she was seated, he took the bench seat so his back was to the wall. The *maître d'* brought them each a menu and Maya glanced through it, but her mind was racing. Is this the way Russell's other meetings go—the ones she did not attend? she wondered. So formal and high profile? The menu dishes were classic Italian, but the prices were three times more than she would have ever dreamed of spending, even at some of the ritzy places she had gone with her husband. Unless it was their anniversary or something. What would she tell Russell if she were expected to pay for this lunch?

Harris made a few suggestions of excellent choices, and she chose the least expensive. A baked pumpkin ravioli with marinara and a side salad and hoped she could eat it without choking. Why was she *so* nervous about this?

They talked of the weather and then more seriously about the climate and the political state of the country, and by the time they were halfway through lunch, Maya began to relax. This was her topic, and she found herself excited again to be talking to a kindred spirit who felt the current state of government was a menace, operating with no regard for the rights of women and minorities and causing America to become increasingly isolated from the rest of the nations of the world. By the time they were finishing the main course, she felt completely at ease, and couldn't imagine what had been in her head to upset her. Just because he obviously had money? *She* wouldn't want to be judged like that.

Harris ordered cappuccinos for both of them, which came with an almond biscotti, and he nodded to the waiter and told him to put lunch "on his tab." Then he leaned back and looked expectantly at Maya. Maya took that as her cue.

"Thank you for this delicious lunch. How can I help the Undivided Movement? Up until now, I have been mostly writing postcards, making phone calls, and inviting candidates to speak at our meetings. It would be a privilege to get more involved."

"I'm so glad you feel that way, Ms. Vaderman—"

"Please, call me Maya. Especially since I am to call you Harris." Maya smiled at him.

"Okay, Maya," Harris said, smiling slowly back. "Do you have time available to you? I understand you have no children."

This set off a silent alarm in the back of her head. Her inability to conceive was always a sore spot, but, really, how did he know that she was childless? Had he checked her background? But then she hushed herself. Of course, he would check her out; he would not want to waste his time and money interviewing seventeen different candidates when he could rule certain things out in advance. She did wonder what else he had looked for about her, and why having children might have been a problem.

"Well, no, I don't have my own children, but I've been raising my sister-in-law's son since he was ten. He's twenty-four now, and quite able to take care of himself." Maya suddenly wondered if that was, in fact, true, since they were still trying to determine what had happened to him a week ago.

"How wonderful of you," Harris said, which definitely stroked Maya's ego. "Tell me about him. Has it been difficult?"

"Oh, no, Joshie is the sweetest boy. Like the child I never got to have. He's fairly self-reliant now."

"Not completely? You said he was twenty-four…."

Maya back-pedaled quickly. "Joshie has been doing great. He did have some learning challenges, but he has worked super hard and made fantastic progress. He has a full-time job, and he has his own friends and spending money. He could afford to live on his own if he wanted to, but he splits his time between our house and his mother's in the Village so he can save." Maya could not quite shake the eerie feeling that Harris already knew all of this. But that would be ridiculous, wouldn't it?

Harris nodded and seemed to consider her. Then he appeared decided and sat up straight. "Actually, Maya, I apologize, but I have not been completely transparent with you, and I must correct that. I am not directly part of the Undivided Movement. Our organization works closely with several societies, including Undivided, societies that share our interests, mainly in keeping our government accountable. As you may have guessed…" He looked around pointedly and grinned at her. "…we have a tad more funding to get work done than Undivided has, which places us at a huge advantage."

Maya was startled. She had felt something wasn't quite right. It must have shown on her face.

Harris continued. "If you do not want to involve yourself with us, then it was my pleasure to take you to lunch and we can part ways. But if you would like to do more than you can accomplish through Undivided, then I invite you to join us."

"Who are you, then, and what exactly do you do?" Maya asked.

Harris sat forward, looking directly at her. "First of all, I would need your word to keep what we do completely confidential, even from your husband. Can you do that?"

Maya frowned. She never kept anything from Russell, not for long, anyway. He was definitely the wiser, more experienced, and had always been a kind of protector—not that she'd ever needed to be protected from anything, but he made her feel safe.

Harris must have seen her hesitation. "This is important, Maya, because some may not understand our intentions. For example, does your husband share your enthusiasm for the Undivided Movement?"

Maya knew Russell was not nearly so enamored with Undivided, but he certainly cared about people and the earth, and he put his money on it. Yet, she found herself unable to say so with real conviction.

"Not *so* much with Undivided, but we share the same dreams for our planet." As Maya said this, she wondered if it were, in fact, true.

Harris looked at her for what seemed like forever. "Will you at least wait to discuss this with your nearest and dearest for the first month, until you completely understand what we are doing and why?"

"I can do *that*," Maya said. It sounded perfectly reasonable. She desperately wanted to be a part of something impactful.

Harris smiled again. He did have the most charming smile. "Good. Because we influence the population on a grand scale." He sat back again, letting that sink in. "The ultraconservatives have been playing dirty by using 'brainwashing' techniques; it's time we started fighting back."

"They can't do that! Isn't that illegal? Why would anyone let them get away with that? And *how* can they do that anyway? People have their own minds; why don't they think for themselves?"

"Why, indeed? How, indeed…?" Harris asked. "Let's end for today. Think it over, and I will be in touch. Only say yes if you can keep it confidential—for now."

He pulled her chair out for her and held her elbow as he walked her to the door; then he went back inside, leaving her to call for an Uber.

"Thank you again for lunch—" Maya called to him, but he had already turned away.

Well, now I've blown it, she thought. He thinks I'm a baby who can't make a decision on my own. She was ashamed of herself for being so juvenile and resolved that when he emailed her again, she would agree to his conditions and come on board to help out. Imagine! Brainwashing people, here in the United States of America. Of course, they had to fight back.

CHAPTER 20

Thomas Brunner ate his chicken calzone in silence. He had considered and discarded all the options he could think of that would get him away from New York City and Trenaman. He didn't want to endanger his family by going there and neither did he want anyone to know he was looking for an escape route by planning a vacation. He had nowhere to go and no one to visit if he left the country. Besides, he wasn't even sure these people limited themselves to the United States. Going to the police did not seem to be sensible, since he could be convicted of accessory to murder. It wasn't like he had tried to back out when he first heard the plans. He decided to toe the line for now but take out $500 every few days and start stashing the cash under his mattress so he could make a run for it.

When he had arrived at the main office for Cingulate Services Monday morning, no one even blinked. They gave him paperwork to fill out and materials with which to familiarize himself in his new role. He had skimmed them without anything really registering at first. It was mostly stuff about how the program worked and the philosophy behind it, all things he already knew. The basic premise was, if the mind could be convinced at an unconscious level that it had the capacity to learn, it would learn. And the drug simply tapped the subconscious learning centers in a region of the brain called the cingulate gyrus.

He started getting interested when he read a study about dementia patients compared with "normals" who were taught a video game and asked to play it for a half hour every day. Each time, the researcher had to reintroduce himself and repeat his request to the dementia patients because they couldn't recognize him from day to day, nor did they remember the game they had played the day before. After a couple of weeks, researchers found that the learning curve for both groups, normal and demented, was the same, even though each day, the dementia patients did not recall having ever seen the game before. They concluded that the part of the brain that learned was not necessarily tied to short-term memory or conscious thought. This opened new avenues for education.

The file suggested that because the cingulate gyrus was a kind of bridge between the emotions and the intellect, and the drug—whatever it was—acted on these centers, it enabled emotional learning as a part of the intellectual process. It did this by associating feelings—in the case of Cingulate Services, the positive feelings the counselors provided—with logical thought. He also discovered why they were instructed to always nuke the cookies to make them warm and aromatic before serving. Apparently, the sense of smell was one of the most basic and primitive functions of the limbic system, which regulated instincts, memories, and anchored emotional experiences in the psyche in the strongest possible way.

Further on, he read the section explaining the chemistry of the drug, most of which Thomas did not understand. They were using hyoscine, a "muscarinic antagonist," that acted in the brain and had the effect of making someone highly sensitive to suggestion. This drug was routinely used, albeit in much, much smaller doses, in everyday scopolamine patches to treat seasickness. So, how bad could it be?

Thomas hardly noticed the passage of time. At noon, he ordered his calzone and continued mulling all this over while he munched, and at 1:00 p.m., Matthew Trenaman walked into the office. He stopped first at the front desk to converse quietly with the secretary, and then came over to Thomas in the cubicle where he had been reading.

"So, Mr. Brunner, what do you think? Are you starting to understand why our program is so important?" Trenaman asked.

Thomas had decided early in the day that the safest thing he could do was say very little, but he was increasingly curious about this chemical and its potential uses. "It is quite... quite fascinating," he finally said.

"Indeed. We've decided, given the little 'misadventure' with Mr. Wheeler, that we should educate you a little more than your predecessor. Then perhaps you will understand the need for care and discretion, not only in your conversations, but also in how you carry out your tasks. You already know more than Mr. Wheeler was told."

Thomas gulped. The last thing he wanted was *more* information. That would just make him more likely to get knocked off if he appeared to act the slightest bit suspicious. He said nothing.

Trenaman continued. "I hope you appreciate what an honor it is that you have been invited to work with us in this position. This work has been sanctioned at the highest level of our government. However, that also means no mistakes will be tolerated. Are you a patriot, Mr. Brunner?"

"Of course," Thomas said, without hesitation. But I was hardly "invited," he thought. More like commanded.

"Good. Then you will understand that what we learn from the studies you are assisting with will help in matters of the highest national security as well as being an exciting new avenue for educating our population. For that reason, you will be beyond discreet. And in turn, we will take excellent care of you." Trenaman smiled.

"Thank you, sir," Thomas managed to croak. "May I ask which branches of government will I be working for?"

Trenaman eyed him closely, and Thomas regretted his question immediately.

"That is on a 'need to know' basis. You do not need to know."

"Of course, sir," Thomas said, his face turning red.

Trenaman limped over and grabbed a chair from the empty adjoining cubicle, brought it back, and turned it to face Thomas. He sat back and crossed his good leg over his lame one and folded his fingers together in his lap, as if he did not have a care in the world. "Tell me about last Friday evening's class. How was the Plessman boy? Any issues?"

Thomas took a breath and accepted he was in this for better or worse, at least for the moment.

"Plessman was quiet, more so than usual. I mean, he's normally quite gregarious, but on Friday, he was just… quieter. But he didn't say anything about what happened last week. Oh, and he wouldn't eat the cookie. First time for that, but he said he'd had a big dinner."

"Anything else?"

"Umm, yeah. One of the other clients, his name is Jonathan Samuels, asked about Donny." Thomas couldn't help but squirm when he mentioned Donny's name. "He asked Joshua—I mean, Plessman—if he'd seen him. He said he knew they were friends; he kind of pressed him even."

"Hmm. What did Plessman say?"

"Nothing. I mean, he said he didn't know, but he looked real uncomfortable, and left the room fairly quickly. It was the end of the session anyway."

Trenaman raised his interlocked fingers so his chin was leaning on them, his elbows on the side rests of his chair.

"Do you think Plessman remembered anything?" Trenaman asked.

"To be completely honest, Mr. Trenaman, I have no idea. Joshua isn't the kind of kid to prevaricate. He's just not sophisticated enough to play dumb, so I'd say no. But he wasn't acting normal either. He was disturbed. I don't know if he understood why."

"So, you just let him leave?"

Thomas trembled. "Well, yes. What else could I do? Everyone can have a bad day, and I thought if I made a big deal about it, that would be worse. I mean, if he remembered, we were screwed anyway, and if he didn't, why pull it out of him? But seriously, I don't think that kid is capable of 'pretending' to not remember. And why would he come back to class if he did?"

Trenaman seemed pleased. "I knew promoting you was a good move. You think on your feet. Yes, Mr. Brunner, I think you handled it appropriately. We shall see next Friday; if he shows up, and, *how* he shows up."

Thomas let his breath out and relaxed a little. Maybe he could do this after all.

Trenaman got up to go but stopped at the door and turned back. "By the way," he said, "you'll find a $5,000 bonus in your account tomorrow. Just a little thank you for coming on board."

Thomas nodded. "Thank you, sir," he said. He hated himself for prolonging this interaction, but he plowed ahead anyway. "Mr. Trenaman? Why are we so interested in Joshua Plessman?"

"Oh, that's simple. His mother is one of only two people we know of who were exposed to this drug in large doses as a child. She has had, shall we say, certain permanent 'side effects.' We are studying the genetics of this substance on mental processing to see what might have been passed on if her egg cells were affected as well at that tender young age."

"Who is the other?"

"The other is none other than her brother, Russell Vaderman. We have been watching him too, for many decades, and he is quite remarkable. Unfortunately, he did not have any children for us to study."

Trenaman left then, leaving Thomas to wonder at his own audacity and with even more questions than he had before.

CHAPTER 21

Joshua went to work Monday morning with trepidation. He had wanted so badly to get back to his normal life, but that was before his uncle had poked around in his head. While he did not need to check in when he was working on a project, it had been over a week since he'd been in the office, and Joshua couldn't avoid coming in to collect his new assignment.

Joshua had started working at Vaderman Ventures a couple of years ago with simple tasks, more akin to being a scut puppy and delivery boy. A combination of familiarization through time and his work at Cingulate Services had allowed him to progress to doing web searches for his uncle on diverse requested topics and chasing down foreign regulatory restrictions. He basked in the trust Russell had placed in him and wanted more than anything to be successful. He wasn't able to predict time expenditures for new ventures or calculate the material costs of various projects, but he knew he was making a contribution to his uncle's business, and he was quite proud of that. Normally. Today his head just hurt. Again.

Joshua had been trying all weekend to piece together what

had happened between him and his uncle last Friday night. It helped that his mother didn't think he was nuts, but then, he wasn't sure her vote on that subject was legit. He still wasn't certain that anything had *happened* at all; maybe he had just imagined the whole thing.

He was standing outside his uncle's door, stone-faced and frozen, exactly like he had felt when Uncle Russell told him to take his phone along, when Rosalee, his Uncle's secretary, walked up.

"Joshua, are you okay? Your uncle isn't with a client now, you can just go in," she said.

"I brought my phone," Joshua said.

Rosalee looked at him sideways. "Okay," she said. "That's good."

At that moment the door opened and Russell stood looking at them both. There was an awkward silence between the three of them for a couple of seconds. Rosalee handed Russell a folder she was carrying.

"Here are the plans for the German Underground structure. They were just printed." She gave them both a questioning look and went back down the hall to her station near the entrance to the office.

"Come in, Joshua," Russell said and he absently dropped the folder on his desk. Joshua took a seat in one of the two plush silver armchairs in front of Russell's desk, but Russell did not go around to his own chair; rather, he half sat on his desk facing Joshua.

"I brought my phone," Joshua said.

"That's good, Josh. You know, you never used to go anywhere without your phone. What made you want to leave it behind?"

Joshua didn't answer. He didn't know what to say. He looked down and saw that he was literally wringing his hands.

Russell reached over and touched him on the shoulder.

"Josh, this has to do with the time you lost, doesn't it? We've got to talk about it."

Joshua felt frozen again. Finally, he looked up at his uncle. His mouth moved, but no words came out. Russell kept his eyes fixed on Joshua, but there were no prying tendrils worming into his brain this time. It was just his uncle. His rock, his security from his earliest memories.

Joshua had never known his father, but Russell had been as near to a father as he could have ever hoped for, and he'd been there all Joshua's life. Finally, he blurted it out.

"I'm scared! I'm scared, Uncle Russell. I'm scared about what you did on Friday!"

Joshua was sure his uncle was going to deny he had done anything, or else was going to tell him he was mad like his mother and they needed to get him help. He was ready to bolt out of the office and run back to his mother's or jump in the river—anything but being told he was crazy like *that*.

"So am I," Russell said quietly, which completely shocked Joshua.

"What...?"

"So am I. I'm scared too. I didn't know I was going to do that until I did it, and I'm not entirely sure of exactly what I did. I am very sorry it frightened you so much. I wished you had come home over the weekend so we could talk about it, but maybe we both needed a little space. Was Mom helpful?"

Russell shifted his weight and plucked a piece of lint off the desk. He seemed to Joshua to be almost as uncomfortable as he was, and Joshua calmed down. So, he wasn't crazy. But if Uncle Russell didn't know what was going on, how could anyone? Uncle Russell knew everything!

"She… she asked me what it felt like. When you did that."

Russell turned back to Joshua, looking quite serious. "Now *that* is an excellent question. What *did* it feel like? To you, I mean."

Joshua got nervous again; he wanted to get this right, to look good in front of his uncle. He always wanted to look good in front of his uncle, who was so smart and capable. Russell read his mood change in an instant.

"Don't be afraid, Josh, it's okay. Whatever it was, is what it was. There is no right or wrong answer here."

Joshua looked up and saw only kindness in his uncle's eyes. He didn't question that Uncle Russell seemed to have no knowledge of what he himself had done. He knew that Uncle Russell loved him, and that was all that was important right then.

"Like I told Mom. It was—do you remember when we went fishing upstate two years ago and my line got all balled up? I caught a big fish too, remember? But I couldn't reel it in because the knot got stuck in the roller part, and so I lost the fish! That was going to be our dinner too. You always say, don't catch and release. Catch if you're going to eat it, and then say a prayer of thanks to the fish for giving up its life for your dinner."

Russell chuckled. "Yes, that was the day you gave up eating fish. It really brings our actions home when we acknowledge their effects on life around us."

Joshua laughed, remembering the day. He had found it hard to eat any meat after that if he'd had a glimpse of what it had looked like before it arrived on his plate. Remembering good times spent with Uncle Russell definitely made this easier.

"Go on, Josh," Russell said softly.

Joshua puckered his brows together. "It was like that in my head. Like my brain was a knotted up ball of fishing line. And everything was all blocked out. And then you..." He glanced up at Russell again, still worried that his uncle might get angry, but he saw only curiosity. "You *reached into my head*, Uncle, and you untangled it." Joshua put his head in his hands, feeling embarrassed. It sounded completely senseless.

Silence filled the room. After a minute, Joshua looked up. His uncle had the strangest look on his face, like he was sorting through something Joshua couldn't see. He looked intent, and perplexed, and even somewhat excited, like he was making a discovery. He seemed to have forgotten Joshua was in the room.

"Uncle...?"

Russell turned back to him. "You're right. I think that's exactly what I did. I have no idea *how* I did that, or how I *knew* to do that, but... but that's what I *always* do in my own head. That's how I manage the... But how did I get in *your* head? I felt it happen, but I don't actually know how I did that. My God, Joshua, I must have terrified you!"

Joshua found tears running down his face. Uncle Russell believed him, even understood why he had gotten so scared. He, Joshua, wasn't nuts after all; he wasn't even in trouble. He jumped up and threw his arms around his uncle and buried his head in his shoulder. It felt weird as soon as he did, since he hadn't hugged his uncle like this since he was much younger, when his face was at Russell's chest level or lower. Now they were virtually the same height, with Russell only about an inch taller. Joshua thought he was much too old to be crying on a man's shoulder, but Uncle Russell held him close and stroked his head. After a moment, Joshua sat back down.

They sat in silence for a few minutes, but this time it was a comfortable silence. Russell took the other plush silver armchair next to Joshua, and they just sat there each, with their own thoughts.

"Josh, do you think you can remember the rest now? Where all the blood came from? What happened to you two weekends ago?"

Instantly the fear returned. The bright light, the headache, the shard of glass through his eyes.

"No, no, I don't think so. I don't want to go there, Uncle, please don't make me go there."

"Easy, Josh. I won't *make* you do anything you don't want to do; I promise. But don't you *want* to know?"

The intercom buzzed and Rosalee's voice came through. "Mr. Vaderman, Detective Rodriguez and Officer Greenstone are here. They want to speak with you and Joshua."

Russell walked over to the intercom, and Joshua started to visibly shake again. He was definitely not ready for this; Aunt Maya had been right after all.

"Can you ask them to please come back later? This isn't a good time," Russell said.

"I tried, Mr. Vaderman, but they were most adamant. Liam is trying to stall them, but he really can't stop them."

"Okay, thanks." Russell turned to Joshua.

"I can't talk to them, Uncle, I'm not ready."

"I know you're not. Come here, I'm going to send you down the back stairs, and I'll talk to them. But we have to get to the bottom of this, Josh. We'll do it together, you and me. Okay?"

"There's a back stair?"

Russell started laughing. "Indeed there is, and now that you know about it, I need you to keep it 'Top Secret,' okay? Where are you going to be tonight, with Mom or with us?"

"I want to go back to Mom's. Please?"

"Okay, sure, but I'm going to come see you there tonight. Hurry now, and be quiet as a mouse. Once you go down a few flights, you can exit the stairwell and take the elevator the rest of the way."

Russell led Joshua to the coat rack in the corner and showed him a small alcove hidden behind it. Sure enough, there was a door at the end with a sign that said "EXIT." Joshua slipped through very quietly just as he heard the knock on Uncle Russell's office door. He closed the door gently and tiptoed down the stairway.

CHAPTER 22

After his conversation with Thomas Brunner, Matthew Trenaman went into his own office at main headquarters. Unlike the little cubicle Brunner had been provided, he had a real desk, shelves, glass windows overlooking the city, and a door that locked. There was a small black leather couch off to the side for those nights he had to work late.

He had reported the incident with Donny and the Plessman kid to his superiors in the NSA. He'd had no choice. It came as no surprise when he was told Wheeler was now collateral damage and had to go. Trenaman understood they could not abide such carelessness in a sensitive project like this one, but he was disheartened, nonetheless. He had liked Wheeler and thought he had potential.

Trenaman was in this project for the good of the country. He ardently believed people just did not know what was good for them, and if you got enough subjects together, they followed each other like sheep anyway. Why not provide them with proper direction? They were going to follow someone, right? He vaguely understood that those defining this direction were the ones in power, and in the back of his mind, he wondered if they were true to themselves or true to their wallets and egos. But Trenaman had been a career Navy man all his life, and he did not question orders.

He had risen to the rank of captain before he'd had to retire due to injury. His left leg was blown off in an explosion aboard his command aircraft carrier as it cruised peacefully offshore of Iran several years ago. He had lost good men that day, and now he himself had a prosthesis from above the knee. After he rehabbed, he signed up with intelligence so he could still do his part for Homeland Security. He hadn't been ready to go sit at home by the fire at the age of fifty-two.

It was a good career move, but he missed the physical operations. Mental maneuverings were probably more important, but Matthew Trenaman used to pride himself on being a man of action. Still, both brain and brawn were necessary in any war, and this battle of ideology was a war as sure as any other.

Trenaman didn't get to the rank of captain for nothing. He was not only a shrewd strategist but he could read people well, and he had recognized immediately that Brunner was terrified and considering flight. Trenaman was also a pragmatist and preferred not to take life unnecessarily. The prudent course would be to win Brunner over rather than kill him off, although it might be necessary. He hoped that between financial incentive and presenting enough information to draw the younger man in based on Brunner's sensibilities would be enough to make him a loyal servant. Playing to his patriotism was planned; Trenaman knew Bruner's father had served in the Marine Corps.

The NSA consented to Trenaman's plan to shift Brunner's role and authorized him for bonuses and a higher level of security clearance based on Trenaman's judgment. But if he strayed at all, Trenaman was to neutralize him. It was the best he could get.

Trenaman himself only received information on an as-needed basis. He looked at the cryptogram on his desk, realizing he himself was now deemed as needing to know the next layer. He went to his laptop and decrypted the program that would read the new file for him. He was not terribly surprised to see that it was referencing Plessman's mother, Braelyn. It took him ten minutes to satisfy all the security steps, and then he was in.

> *The subject was stopped at reentry point JFK.* Borrachero *plant specimen found in suitcase and appropriated. Replaced with cocaine. Subject was arrested. She is now on bail at home with an audio transmitter in her ankle bracelet.*
> *Historically, this subject has been completely refractory to suggestion, as has been her brother who was comparably dosed; subject's offspring appears quite susceptible but with side effects. Please monitor for insight. Is this a genetic modification?*
> *Addition: Why did subject bring* borrachero *plant to the US? Follow encrypted link below to download recordings every twelve hours, and report. Link will expire after each use and a new one will be provided.*

That's quite suspicious, Trenaman thought. Why indeed would an innocent citizen want to bring Devil's Breath home with her, if not to use in some sinister way? He was quite aware of who the "subject" was, and who her "offspring" was as well. Trenaman knew the NSA wanted to know as much as possible about the long-term consequences of scopolamine dosing, including its effects on future generations.

In the case of Braelyn Plessman, who had been on the Watch List for as long as Trenaman had known there *was* a Watch List for this, she was noted to be obstinate and unpliable, even when dosed. In fact, dosing her seemed to intensify this oppositional effect, and while it had been tried surreptitiously on a multitude of occasions, she proved completely refractory to suggestion every time. It seemed to have the opposite effect and made her excessively contrary.

It was quite unusual to find anyone who did not immediately succumb to the effects of scopolamine, and the Braelyn Plessman anomaly had been attributed to her being induced at a very young age. It was unclear if she were an exception or if youth played a role in susceptibility. Her brother was a much more complicated subject to follow. Partly because Russell Vaderman was a prominent public figure, in whom an induced change of trajectory would be more noticeable, and partly because his responses were harder to gauge; he seemed to be thoughtful and maddeningly unflappable on every front. His mind was deemed unique; unfortunately, he did not have any biological children to study.

At a certain point, the NSA had recruited several women to tempt and seduce Vaderman, as his children would bear watching, intending to keep any pregnancies a secret, but he did not take any of the bait—strange in itself. It was not hard to get volunteers; he was a wealthy, handsome man, in good shape, and gentlemanly with women. He was only in his forties, so the effort was still ongoing, but for now, it was Braelyn Plessman's son who was being watched to see if any effects were transmitted genetically. Trenaman knew just enough about scientific research to know that an n of one was never going to make a case for anything, so he assumed that there were others out there who had been deliberately dosed in childhood and who were now growing up under the government's watchful eye.

Trenaman opened the link to decrypt the first recording. Damn, was he supposed to listen to all twelve hours, twice a day? That would take his entire life from him. He looked over the code and noticed that he could zero in on where there was actual conversation—or at least patterned noise.

He settled in and listened to a conversation between the Plessman woman and her lawyer. She denied the cocaine, and

Trenaman had a fleeting moment of sympathy for her; no one would ever believe her. But he soon buried it under his understanding of the need for the greater good.

The next conversation sounded like it was with Russell Vaderman. He paused and hobbled over to the Keurig he kept on his shelf and poured himself a cup of coffee. He eyed his couch for a moment; this was going to be a long night.

CHAPTER 23

Russell headed to the East Village after work. He preferred to walk when the sky was this blue and there was just a slight breeze, and he would have if he were going back to Sutton Place, but it was too far to his sister's apartment. It seemed he did some of his most troubling thinking in the back of Ubers these days.

After Joshua ducked out the back door, Russell fended off the NYPD detectives with the honest answer that Joshua had been there but had left, and Russell was not exactly sure of his destination when he did so. It was not that Russell did not respect the police force, he most assuredly did. His relationship with Commissioner Harrows was based on genuine high regard and friendship, although their connection had its roots in Russell having been threatened a few years ago and needing support. But Russell was very protective of his nephew, and was sure Joshua was not ready for an interrogation. Russell also believed he was the best hope of getting to what was in Joshua's head; he fully planned to share that information with the police as soon as it became available.

Russell had already checked a reverse phone lookup for the number that had called Joshua's cell that Monday night. It was registered to a Peter Jackson. When he had asked Joshua who that was, Joshua had drawn a genuine blank; Josh had no idea. Russell searched the name without finding anyone local and then looked in missing persons reports. No one by that name was found on the long roster of the New York City missing, so maybe it was just a wrong number. Forty-three seconds was not an unreasonable amount of time for a caller to confirm whether he had misdialed, and Joshua did not remember any details about the night at all.

When the NYPD officers finally left, convinced Russell was not withholding anything, Russell called the commissioner. He told him outright that he planned to do his best to uncover whatever was buried in Joshua's head, and promised to report back immediately. He also asked about the fingerprints on his sister's alleged cocaine package and was disturbed to learn that not only were her fingerprints not on it, but the bag had been completely wiped clean; that would hardly exonerate her.

Harrows then revealed that construction workers had discovered quite a lot of blood on the ground in the subway station at 57th Street and Sixth Avenue. The blood type matched the blood found on Joshua, but other than that, no one knew whose blood it was, and there had been no bodies discovered. There was a string of missing persons, to be sure, but that was not unusual in New York City, where runaways and ne'er-do-wells abounded.

Russell felt that the victim would soon come to light, however, and he had a pressing need to get Joshua to open up to him before then. He rolled his brain over the memory of what he had done with Josh in the hallway last Friday night, and he realized as he was doing it that it felt like he was running his mental fingers over it. This was such a familiar process to him, he never considered it to be unusual, but he was starting to wonder if many of the mental practices he took for granted were actually his unique way of using his mind. Was this a product of that smoky mist he had inhaled that made his mind expand and feel clear and muddied at the same time? Was it all because of that episode in The Hut?

For years, Braelyn used to hound him, demanding to know what he did to keep the "demons" at bay. He had never recognized them as demons. It was just his reality. Information always flew at him from a hundred different places at once, and he always paused to unpack it—and yes—*disentangle* it. He just always thought that was normal.

Could he teach that to Braelyn? Would it help her find peace? Perhaps she would no longer be at the mercy of her "mental sensations." And was that even her problem?

The immediate question was, could he help Joshua peer through the smaze in his mind into whatever happened to him? The blockage might be just traumatic shock to his senses, because Harrows intimated there was enough blood to imagine someone had bled out and died. Or, was there something happening in Joshua's head that was similar to Russell's and Braelyn's?

The scopolamine test results were still at least four days out, and that was if they were negative. If not, that would precipitate another testing procedure to rule out any false positives. It could be up to another ten days before they'd know for sure. While that would, at least, prove Joshua innocent of any conscious criminal act, Russell felt an urgency to solve this before that time.

The Uber stopped in front of Braelyn's apartment and Russell headed upstairs. He found them chatting away at the kitchen table over paninis. There were unpacked grocery bags on the counter, and the front door had been left ajar again.

Joshua jumped up when Russell walked in. "Hi, Uncle! I went shopping for Mom and picked up sandwiches from La

Bottega on the way home. You said you were coming, so I got you your favorite grilled vegetables and balsamic with goat cheese and avocado. I figured you'd be hungry."

"Thanks, Joshua," Russell said as he realized his stomach was rumbling in response to the food. He walked over and kissed his sister on the cheek and touched Josh on the shoulder. He peered in the grocery bags as he passed. "Do you think we should put this stuff in the fridge first, so it will stay fresh?"

"Don't worry, I'll do it later," Braelyn said.

They ate in silence for a few minutes, and Russell felt like he had interrupted one of the few healthy interactions between mother and son that he'd seen in ages. After they finished their paninis, Joshua reluctantly spoke up.

"What did you tell the police?"

"I didn't tell them anything, Josh, there's nothing to tell—not yet. They found blood in one of the subway stations that's under construction that matches the blood that was on your clothes. Do you remember being underground at 57th and Sixth?"

Joshua stiffened immediately, but Braelyn broke in.

"Remember, we talked about this, Josh. We know it's scary, but we're here with you. Don't be afraid." She looked to Russell for confirmation, and he nodded to Joshua.

"Okay…," Joshua said. "But I don't think I can get there myself." He gulped and looked at Russell. "Uncle Russell, can you do that thing you did before and help me remember?"

Russell felt flustered, a very unusual emotion for him. *Could he?* "I don't know. I don't really know how I did that before. I guess I can try."

Joshua turned to face him and visibly forced himself to relax. The blind trust he was placing in Russell was almost more terrifying than what he was supposed to know how to do. And he had no idea how to do it.

Russell sat up straight in the kitchen chair and faced Joshua. He relaxed his mind in the way he naturally did when the outside world hammered at him. He was vaguely aware of Braelyn watching him, almost hungrily, as if she would be able to see what he did in his head.

Russell ran his mental fingers over the memory of what he had done a few days ago, when he searched for why Joshua wouldn't carry his phone. He had tilted his own head to catch Joshua's eyes so he could look into them, into Joshua… Russell found himself speaking in a whisper. "You can remember, Josh…." And then he *reached*….

He felt it immediately and backed off. The blazing light Joshua could not see past, and then the pain, searing into him, and Joshua cried out.

"Stop, Uncle, it hurts!"

Russell pulled back into himself. Both he and Joshua were shaking.

"I'm sorry, Uncle Russell. I didn't mean to—"

"No, Josh, it's okay."

Braelyn was watching and not *seeing* anything. "What happened? What did you do?" she demanded.

Joshua was whimpering and Russell put his hand out onto his nephew's shoulder. "Are you okay?"

"Yeah, I'm okay. I think you just startled me. And it was like it was *That Day* all over again, all sharp and painful." Joshua looked up innocently. "Uncle, I don't think we can do this."

Russell collected himself and pulled apart in his head all the steps of what had happened. He was starting to recognize his thought processes, which used to be automatic and unconscious.

"Maybe I was too rough; I was trying very hard," Russell said. "On Friday, I didn't *try* to do anything, it just sort of happened."

"I think you should both take a rest from this, that's what I think," Braelyn said. "This is painful for me to even watch, and I have no idea what you're doing. Russell, do you even *know* what you're doing?"

"Not really," Russell confessed. "But let's try again, Josh, if you can. Come over to the living room and relax."

"Okay...."

Russell and Joshua settled on the couch, facing each other at angles. Braelyn sat on the chair. Joshua licked his lips and looked from Russell to his mother nervously.

Russell let his mind go blank and tried to recreate the emotion of curiosity, of the sort he'd had when he was so puzzled by Joshua's not wanting to carry his phone. He looked into Joshua's eyes like he had that evening, and very gently extended his mind while softly stating *you have nothing to fear, you can remember, you do remember.*

The light burst open again, but this time Russell held his ground, softly prodding with a mental "finger" as if through a curtain of shimmering light or a waterfall.

No pain this time. Just "otherness." Russell felt a massive tangle of something bright and ominous, but he was prepared for it this time, and he started to pull it apart, just as he would do with any other unwelcome, disorganized morass of information. There were multiple layers, and though they were weightless, as only light or thought could be, they felt dense and heavy at the same time. Strand by strand, he unraveled each one tenderly, and with each milli piece he moved, the ball became less bright, less painful to Joshua, and more transparent. In his own mind, Russell had never let his thoughts get this jumbled, probably because he knew instinctively how hard it would be to clear them. Some distant part of himself wondered if this was what his sister went through and how overwhelming it must be. He felt like it took forever, but at last, it was done. Joshua's mind was free, and Russell nearly collapsed against the chair. Twenty-five minutes had gone by.

Braelyn was staring at him, her jaw slightly slack. Joshua had his eyes squeezed tight, and Russell was sweating in the cool apartment. He got up to retrieve his seltzer still on the kitchen table and drank thirstily.

"Josh?" Russell finally called.

Joshua was sitting rigidly on the sofa. He opened his eyes cautiously, and Russell saw recognition in them, but his eyes were filled with terror. He looked like he was in shock all over again.

"I'm not supposed to tell *you*, Uncle Russell. Especially not *you*."

"Not supposed to tell him what?" Braelyn asked.

Joshua looked back and forth between his mother and his uncle and started rocking on the sofa. Finally, he focused on his mother.

"Not supposed to tell what happened. In the subway station." Joshua's eyes were wild. "It was horrible, Mom, horrible! When I got there, this guy, he was dead!"

"What guy?" Braelyn asked. Russell just watched them both, almost afraid to move.

"Some guy. I don't know who he was. Donny knew who he was—Donny called me and asked me to come—I think… but I'm not… I'm not to have anything to do with Donny anymore. Donny is gone. No more Donny." Tears started streaming down Joshua's face. "But I *liked* Donny…," he whispered. "He was my friend."

He started crying uncontrollably then and Braelyn moved to the couch to hold him. Russell sat on the chair she vacated because he was too drained to stand. He was afraid to make a sound and focused on trying to piece together what he had done; and more importantly, *why* he had needed to do it.

Joshua quieted finally and turned to Russell. "I know what you did," he said softly. "I saw it in my head. Instead of letting everything come at me in a rush, you pulled it back, and only let one thought piece through at a time. I might… maybe I could do that myself some time. I don't know. I'm thirsty."

Joshua sat on the sofa sipping the cool spring water and gingerly exploring his memory. Flashes of recall came at him now. It was like Uncle Russell had separated everything so it was recognizable but nothing was in the right order. He was very confused and incredibly frightened. Frightened of what had happened and frightened that he might lose this clarity and revert back to the chaos and darkness from before. Funny, but the sensation had been blinding light and yet it had felt like darkness because he couldn't see in it.

His mother wanted him to sleep on it, but Joshua knew he had to spill everything right then, in case it all went away again. He started blabbing it all in no particular order, words just pouring out of his mouth.

He remembered that he fell, and there was a dead man with a lot of blood. There were cinder blocks and an old camp trunk. Some powdery stuff blew in his face. There were two men in the empty subway station, and there was a fog over their faces, but something was familiar.... Donny called him, hysterical, and begged him to come to the subway station (or did that happen before?). There was a voice telling him not to use his phone. Never tell his uncle, never, never, never tell his uncle. It was just their little secret. He must hide underground until morning. Donny was there but then he wasn't there, and Joshua was never to look for Donny again. Donny is gone. Joshua started crying again at that.

He remembered sleeping fitfully on the cold floor of the station and waking at some point, stiff and afraid of rats, but he couldn't make himself leave; he wasn't supposed to leave yet. Something very bad would happen if he did. Something very bad *had* happened, but nothing bad had happened. It made no sense. But it would all be all right if he just waited there until morning and went home. It would all just go away, if he never,

never told his uncle, never used his phone, and never remembered Donny.

By the time Joshua was done, his mother was in tears over what her son had been through, and his uncle looked astonished for the first time—ever. Joshua just felt cold, like he was still lying on the pavement and he couldn't get warm. He grabbed the throw blanket on the couch behind him and wrapped himself tightly in it, but he couldn't stop shivering.

And then, gradually, a new recognition filtered in and Joshua sat straight up, holding the blanket so tightly, it nearly tore apart. His eyes were wide and his pupils dilated.

"The men… Uncle Russell, I know them!"

CHAPTER 24

Matthew Trenaman settled down with his coffee to listen to the audio file. He put his right foot up on his desk, and his left prosthesis rested on a little ottoman that he kept nearby for that purpose. The white noise generator hummed at the side of the locked office door.

Most of the file was footsteps and shuffling of materials, the nature of which Trenaman had no idea. At one point, The Alan Parsons Project was playing, and there was nothing to hear but the music and occasionally Braelyn Plessman's voice singing slightly off-key. That was annoying, because it was hard to distinguish the waveform of music from the waveform of conversation, and Trenaman was forced to let it run through. Then silence. When he looked at the logged time, it was 1:00 a.m. when the music had shut off.

He fast-forwarded it to the next cluster of waves that looked like conversation, and heard Braelyn leave several messages on her son's voicemail. He concluded that at least part of the "conditioning" had taken root if Joshua Plessman wasn't answering his phone. But that was sorely suspicious. He cursed Wheeler under his breath.

There was silence for a couple of hours that he could skip over, and then a man's voice opened conversation. After listening for a few sentences, Trenaman concluded it was her brother, Russell Vaderman, and he sat up hoping to get some useful intel from this. His watch said 5:45 p.m., and he was getting antsy.

He listened in amazement to the two siblings talk. How could it be that they weren't sure which country they'd been in? Or what exactly had happened to them? Had no one taught these two their own history? Trenaman started to think he knew more about their childhood than they did. Vaderman did not immediately assume Plessman was lying about the cocaine; he seemed to suspend judgment on that and was not really surprised that she had packed a *borrachero* flower. That was also concerning. No one was supposed to know about that, and it had been expected that no one would believe Braelyn Plessman's story.

Plessman mentioned a new shrink, someone the NSA should have had on their radar, but although he listened to the complete exchange twice, he didn't get a name. How could surveillance have missed that?

He smiled at the irony of hearing Braelyn say she had been dosed for the purpose of making her a more biddable child, as it obviously had the entirely opposite effect. Or maybe she had just always had an inverse reaction to this drug. There had to be some people who were innately resistant. Maybe she was one of them, because the woman had been nothing but trouble since her tweens.

The fact that neither sibling seemed to have clear memories was not a surprise, given their ages at the time and the amnestic properties of the drug, but he would have thought the parents, at least, would have explained what had happened to them. The reason these kids were even *on* the radar was because the father had looked so hard for answers to the effects of the drug and the changes he was seeing in his children, that he had alerted intelligence. And then his wife kicked him out, and he dropped out of their lives, seemingly forever.

How fragile families were, Trenaman thought. He had been estranged from his own wife for a decade now, but they hadn't split up. Too much habit of tradition. They lived separate lives in the same house. Their one son, Andrew, was grown and living across the country in Arizona with his family. Trenaman had hoped Andrew would follow in his military footsteps, but after a brief stint in the Air Force, he had settled down in civilian life. Trenaman hadn't heard from him in months.

He stopped for a minute and listened to parts of the tape again. He hadn't had a full briefing but was pretty sure no one knew the father had reappeared fleetingly before he died to tell his children about South America. There had been a watch on him, but for so many years, he never made any gestures indicating he wanted anything to do with his former family. Last Trenaman knew, Vaderman senior had a domestic partner of sorts, not official, and had made a new life for himself in Europe.

Trenaman took a break. He wrote some cryptic notes on a pad, got up to stretch, and walked outside to the main reception area. Everyone had gone home. He glanced at the little cubicle where Thomas Brunner had been studying for his new role and checked his phone app to see where the tracker was. He knew Brunner might want to flee, so the last time he used the restroom, he'd had a trace placed in Brunner's phone to keep tabs on him. He looked at it now, hovering over the Upper East Side where his apartment was.

Not today, he thought; Brunner's not leaving today. We'll see if we can recruit him for real. Trenaman sighed with relief. Brunner had potential, and he was a good kid. He'd have to eliminate him if he panicked and fled, and it would take another small piece of humanity from Trenaman's soul to do so.

Trenaman was vaguely aware that he presented as tough, demanding, and uncompromising on every level. Even his family saw him that way, and that was probably why he had limited attachment to them. Most people did not understand the sacrifices that he made for the security of their country, and he couldn't exactly explain it to them without compromising that same security. So, he accepted that he must remain aloof, even from those nearest and dearest to him.

Trenaman went back to his office and turned the audio file back on, catching it just before the time expired and he'd have had to sign in all over again. He heard Vaderman admonish his sister to be straight with the lawyer and then said goodbye; it was obvious the brother understood more about the plant than the whacko sister did. Plessman was heard crying, and after that ceased, there was just quiet for the next several hours, so Trenaman called it a day. Geez, this was going to take forever. He hoped he'd glean some information that would make it all worthwhile.

CHAPTER 25

Joshua was beside himself after he remembered the dead man and Donny, and realized the other men in the subway station were none other than his counselors at Cingulate. While Braelyn finally put the groceries away, Russell weighed the risks of whether either Joshua or Braelyn could be considered safe in her apartment. While there was a police officer downstairs to make sure Braelyn didn't leave, if Joshua had been followed to his mother's apartment, there was no one there to prevent anyone suspicious from entering. No one was looking for that.

He questioned Joshua at length about his group three days ago, even to the point where Joshua was starting to squirm in fear. It didn't sound as if anyone knew they would be identified, but there was no question that Joshua could not return there, and as soon as he stopped going, that would tip them off. If it were known Joshua was visiting his mother, Braelyn could be a target as well.

Russell tried unsuccessfully to get Commissioner Harrows on the phone. Should he call Greenstone and Rodriguez? They had been less than understanding of a kid with psychological shock and memory loss, but perhaps they were just doing their job.

Russell sank into himself for a minute and let their essences swim before his mind. Rodriguez was a hard ass for sure, but underneath, a good guy. Russell felt it. He had struggled to climb the ladder to detective, fending off discrimination at every turn, and he'd been lied to so many times by suspects as well as his superiors that he expected nothing better, but there was a heart under there that cared about people and about justice. And Greenstone… Russell ran his mental fingers over his picture of Greenstone, something he had just recently realized was how he "figured things out." A big part of Greenstone's image was blotted out, and Russell couldn't see him. He was popular, a player with the ladies, capable in action, and never afraid to chase down and tackle a criminal, but there was something… Russell shook his head.

"You're doing it, aren't you?" Braelyn asked. "That thing you do, when you're stumped by something and then it all becomes clear."

"I guess so, Brae. Until you and Joshua pointed it out, I had no idea; it was just automatic behavior."

"You need to teach me to do that! Please, Russ!" Braelyn pleaded.

Russell looked right at her, took her hands, and said, "I promise I'll try. But not right now. Right now, we have to make sure you and Josh are safe."

"Can you stay here tonight, Uncle Russell?" Joshua asked. "I feel much safer with you here, and I don't want to leave my mother."

That would mean leaving Maya at home alone. Taking Josh home would mean leaving Braelyn. He should call Rodriguez about Josh, but he would want to ask for protection for his sister, and that would mean explaining to Rodriguez that Braelyn had been arrested with two kilos of coke, which would not do wonders for the credibility of any of them—although the NYPD probably knew about that already. It all ran through Russell's brain in a split second.

Finally, Russell did try to call Detective Rodriguez to tell him Joshua had remembered what happened and needed police protection, but he was off duty. Russell decided it could wait until morning, as if Josh had not remembered anything yet, but he decided it was safest to take Joshua home to Sutton Place. Russell sternly admonished his sister to keep her doors locked and not to let anyone in, and this time she seemed quite convinced. Then he stopped to chat with the police officer outside Braelyn's apartment and asked him to keep a sharp eye out for anyone requesting access outside of immediate family.

———

Maya, Joshua, and Russell sat at the breakfast table eating quietly. Maya kept looking at them both, sensing they had a secret she was not part of, and torn between being insulted and irresistibly curious. She questioned Joshua about his nice slacks and button down shirt, which was better than how he usually dressed for work, but he merely grunted at her, his mouth full of yogurt and granola. It was an unusually subdued meal without Joshua excitedly talking about his day.

No one asked Maya about her meeting, and on the one hand, she was glad she didn't have to evade, but on the other, she was hoping she could get some nonspecific affirmation from Russell that she was engaging in a worthy project.

But no one really spoke to each other that morning at all, except for Russell stating briefly that they were going to the police precinct before work, and then they were gone. Maya sat frustrated. She had anticipated sharing her meeting excitedly with her Undivided group, but if these people were not actually from Undivided, and she wasn't supposed to talk to Russell about them, she most certainly shouldn't be sharing with her girlfriends. It was a most unnatural state to find herself in; Maya was a fiercely social person.

She cleared away the breakfast dishes, feeling disconnected and alone. She frequently helped out in Russell's office, and she supposed there were things she could do there to busy herself but she was reluctant to go in today for some reason. She had an unprecedented desire to withdraw from her life.

The phone rang, and even before she got to it, she knew it would be her brother, Martin. She hadn't gotten back to him about going to stay with Dad while they were away. She lamented again over their broken relationship, with Martin so enamored with President Ganaffe and his whole cabinet; it was almost as if he had been… brainwashed? Could it be?

She went to her phone. "Hello, Marty," she said.

"That's it? That's all I get? No, 'Sorry I didn't call you back. I know you need help right now,' just 'Hello, Marty?'"

Maya groaned to herself and sat back down at the now clean kitchen table.

"I'm sorry," Maya said. "There are just a lot of complicated things going on right now, and I've been distracted." Maya paused for a few seconds, and silence ensued. "Look, I really am sorry. I can't come down right now. I've just become involved in a new project, and…"

"And nothing, Maya. What you're saying is you won't be here for your family when we need you," Martin said. "What if someone were seriously ill? Would you still stay up there in your commie state with your socialist friends, ignoring your own blood?"

Maya was exasperated. "Now, stop that, Martin. No one is sick or dying; you just want to go on vacation, and if you had needed my help, you should have consulted me before you made plans." As she said it, she realized no one could have predicted Joshua's misadventure, and she would not have wanted to put Harris off, but if she had made a commitment, she would have stuck to it.

"I didn't realize you needed to clear seeing your family with that rich husband of yours. Does *he* need you to stay up there and help him in his business? Can't he hire a secretary? Or are you afraid he might get it on with her if he did? I thought you liberals have different ways. Is 'swinging' not part of your scene?"

"Why do you make every conversation political, Marty? We never used to fight so much, I hate this," Maya said, longing for the brother she loved in childhood.

"You've changed, sister. You used to know to back each other up, as family should. Before you got all involved with those 'Undying,' or whatever you call that socialist group—"

"Undivided, Marty. For God's sake!"

"Undivided, Undying, it's all the same. You used to tell me to stay away from Tea Party meetings, and now look at *you*."

"And did you? Stay away from the Tea Party meetings?" Maya asked.

"'Course not! Them's our people, right there. I don't know where you got to. It all started when you moved to that Yankee city of yers for college, and it's gone from bad to worse. Why didn't you just stay home? I miss my sister too."

In the midst of her frustration, a lightbulb went off in Maya's head.

"Marty, do they serve food at those meetings?"

"Of course, they do, what d'ya think? Ya think only *your* folk got etiquette?"

"What... what do they serve?" Maya asked.

"What do you care? They take care of us, right enough. Better than you do. I see we will have to hire a stranger to look in on Papa. And don't you go thinking you can buy your way out of this by footing the bill."

"I was going to say, I can contribute…." Maya's voice trailed off. Although she knew Russell wouldn't mind, she shouldn't feel obligated to pay for an expense that was part of her siblings' vacation.

"Never you mind, Maya *sister*. We'll make do without your help. Just think twice if you ever need yer family for anything." The phone went dead.

Maya was suddenly tired. Martin was wrong; she hadn't "changed" when she came to New York. She'd known since she was a little girl that she didn't belong in her family's ultra conservative environment, so she left it to find a place she could be more comfortable.

Maya's father was a fiercely independent man who had grown up on a ranch. As an adult, he made his living working for oil refineries and had done well enough. He carried his shotgun in his pick-up truck as a matter of course, as was legal in Texas, even when he was drinking, and when Maya's father drank, he became mean. Maya was frankly afraid of him, which made her the brunt of jokes from Martin and Melinda, who thought it was way cool that their father was a "badass." Maya followed them everywhere back then, the baby sister looking to be protected from Papa.

Maya was always quite bright, even if timid as a child, and when she was a senior in high school, she applied to New York University and was accepted with a scholarship. She excitedly came to live in the city she had romanticized most of her life as a pinnacle of diversity, hoping to find a new perspective on life.

In college she began by studying liberal arts where she was introduced to novel ideas. She was drawn into the atmosphere of tolerance that resonated in the intellectual facets of the city and she realized very quickly she would never return to the backward neighborhood she was raised in. Maybe if she'd grown up in a progressive city like Austin or Houston, but Maya had lived in the boondocks in an area where attitudes were mostly old school, and people built up their egos by putting others down. She couldn't seem to find her niche anywhere within her family. For one thing, Maya loved animals—all animals—yet her family prided themselves on hunting for dinner or for sport. By her last year in high school, Maya had become a vegetarian and even stopped eating meals with them.

Ultimately, Maya majored in business, seeing how expensive it was to live in New York City and being determined to make it on her own there. She had expected to go on for her MBA in the Stern School of Business, but she started dating Russell that year and decided instead to work for him when he suggested it. She figured they would have lots of children, and she would be a business partner of sorts in Vaderman Ventures, so she let her previous aspirations take a back seat. But then, children were not to be, and although Russell did pay her well for her time, so she always had some personal money of her own, his earnings took care of every possible thing she could ever want or need, and she ended up feeling largely superfluous. Maya never did broach the subject of becoming a partner once she saw that Russell's business was built on his personal brilliance and the uniqueness of his talent, something she couldn't hold a candle to. He just didn't need her in the business sphere at all.

She sat at the clean table sorting through her email and hoping for a second email from Harris. She wished she hadn't been such a baby with him; she had so many questions to ask. Like how long this brainwashing has been going on, and how could they possibly stop it. She wondered if Tea Party meetings were just the sort of places he had been talking about, and if perhaps her brother had been "influenced" to believe horrible things about his own family. Could this conditioning overcome families' love for each other? Was it that strong?

Maya had a memory of having climbed a tree as a child of six or seven and not being able to get down. She must have been up there for an hour when she'd started to cry, afraid she would never get out of the tree. But shortly after her tears started, her strong, confident brother Marty came along to extract her. He teased her relentlessly for weeks, of course, but he was so gentle gathering her from the tree and setting her safely on her feet, and she always believed he would protect her from anything.

Was it some darkly conceived political influence that had changed Marty and Melinda from the loving siblings they'd been? Sure, they had always had their differences, but lately it was magnified to the point they could barely talk to each other anymore.

Maya wondered if it would be poor form to email Harris today and tell him she had considered his offer to work with his organization and wanted to proceed. She vaguely wondered again about the secrecy he seemed shrouded in, but she guessed once she was involved and he could see that she was trustworthy, he'd share more with her. After all, he had to be careful to protect his strategic response to such underhanded tactics by conservatives.

CHAPTER 26

Joshua was shaking on Tuesday morning as Uncle Russell led him into the police precinct. His mouth was dry, and he couldn't stop licking his lips. The station was abuzz with activity. Once they were brought back into the main area, he noted multiple desks scattered in the large arena, several with animated conversations going on, and all was happening at once. Instinctively, he took his uncle's forearm and gripped it harder than he intended.

Russell turned to him. "It's all right, Josh, you didn't do anything wrong, and the police exist to protect you. I'll be right by your side."

Detective Rodriguez caught Russell's eye and motioned them to come into a smaller office off the main area. The detective's name was on a small plaque next to the door, and there were a couple of chairs on the other side of his desk that he and his uncle sat down in.

The desk was massively cluttered with papers, folders, and desk trinkets. There was a five by seven picture of the detective with his arm around a woman and three children in the foreground, all looking to be in their teens. Rodriguez closed the door and sat down across from them, and swept the area immediately in front of him clean with his hands. He pulled out a fresh pad.

"So, Mr. Plessman, you remember everything now?" he asked.

Joshua swallowed hard. The detective seemed angry and disinclined to believe anything Joshua could have to say, and Joshua was incredibly nervous. He glanced at his uncle, who was sitting like a rock next to him, and took a breath.

"Yes, sir. My memory has come back. Well, not as well as I'd like, but I remember snatches of things. Really scary things…." Joshua's voice trailed off. This guy was never going to believe him, he thought. It was too crazy a story.

Rodriguez said nothing; he just stared at him and waited.

Russell reached over and squeezed his hand and nodded to him.

Slowly, Joshua started to describe the snatches of memory he had regained, trying to put them in the right order, but not sure he was doing it properly. He ended by nearly whispering that he recognized the two men.

"Why didn't you come straight to the police to report this when it happened?" Detective Rodriguez asked. His voice was cold and menacing.

"I… I couldn't," Joshua said.

"Why not?"

"I don't know, I just couldn't. Like I couldn't remember it, and then they told me I *had* to stay there until morning."

At that moment, there was a knock on the door, and Officer Greenstone walked in without waiting for an answer. He had a permanent playboy grin on his face, which seemed to turn into a sneer when he saw Joshua and his uncle sitting there.

"About time you guys decided to show up," Greenstone said. "Now that the leads on murdered persons have gone cold and you've had time to figure out what story you're going with."

Uncle Russell broke in. "Look, Joshua is here voluntarily. He was unable to remember anything until last night. Now that his memory is coming back, it's no wonder. He sustained quite a shock. The neurologist predicted it would take a few days, and that has turned out to be accurate."

"So," Rodriguez said to Joshua, "you have no idea who the dead man was, but you know for sure your friend Donny was there, and you think the men from your tutoring group were also there? How do we find Donny, and can he confirm this? What is Donny's full name?"

Joshua shifted uncomfortably in his seat. "I'm not sure about his last name. I know him mostly as just Donny. Maybe Anderson? But I haven't seen Donny since."

"What did I miss?" Greenstone asked Rodriguez.

Rodriguez turned to Greenstone. "See if there's been a missing person report filed on a 'Donny' or 'Donald' Anderson, or anyone else with that first name." Greenstone took out his little notebook and jotted down the name. "And apparently, there was some kind of powder that was blown in this young man's face, right, Mr. Plessman? And this made it hard to remember until now. It turned you into some sort of obedient slave who couldn't do what you were supposed to do, which was run and get help." Rodriguez made more of a comment than a question.

Joshua was nodding but Greenstone snorted. "No such thing as a powder like that," Greenstone said. "And why would anyone care to do that to you, anyway? Sounds like they would have just killed you if you were a victim. C'mon, now. Come clean with us."

Russell stood up. "Okay, that's enough. I get that this sounds bizarre, but I believe Joshua is telling the truth." Russell turned to Greenstone, his gaze intense, steady, and bordering now on malice. "I guess you're not up to date on your drug pharmacology, *Officer*. Drugs like that do indeed exist, and they are very dangerous. When a drug is used in a criminal manner, I would have thought it is the role of our police department to investigate it."

Greenstone smirked at Russell at first, but found he couldn't keep eye contact, and soon had to look away. Joshua had never seen this side of his uncle before, and felt a swell of pride, while praying he never needed to have a confrontation with him.

Russell continued. "Why Joshua was subjected to such a drug is the real question. If I were you, I'd look to the counselors at the Cingulate Services group, Matthew Wheeler and Thomas Brunner, and I would find out from them where to find Donny Anderson. Furthermore, Joshua is going to need round-the-clock protection. I think it's a given that they did not expect him to remember anything, and once you start asking questions, it will become necessary that he be watched over."

His uncle didn't say more, and Joshua knew in some new way of *knowing* stuff, that it was because Russell didn't want to scare him by finishing that thought.

Rodriguez frowned. Joshua wondered if the man ever smiled; even in the photo on his desk, he seemed content but was not smiling. "I thought his toxicology screen was negative. Wasn't he tested at the hospital?"

Uncle Russell nodded. "You are correct, Detective. But that screen has limitations, and it only looks for certain substances. Some that can do this are not on that panel."

Greenstone piped up again. "Rohypnol is absolutely tested for. I can't think of anything else that has such an effect on memory."

Russell completely ignored Greenstone and continued to stare at Detective Rodriguez, who was tapping his fingers on his desk and staring right back at Russell. Finally, Rodriguez shrugged. He glanced at his partner for a moment, appearing slightly annoyed with him.

"Rohypnol is in that toxicology screen, but that drug has a very short half-life and would have been metabolized in the first few hours. If Mr. Plessman's story is correct, it would not have been traceable by the time he emerged from the subway station. I have also never heard of it being aerosolized."

Rodriguez stood up and turned to Greenstone. "Let's take another look at the subway station at Sixth and 57th and then pay a visit to Cingulate Services as well. And if anyone named Donny was listed as missing, I want to know that too." He turned back to Joshua and his uncle.

"You two, stay available for further inquiries. No more jilting us if we come by with more questions."

Uncle Russell did not move. "And police protection?"

Rodriguez was quiet and Greenstone was smirking again, but his uncle made no move to leave.

Finally, Rodriguez nodded. "We'll send a couple of uniforms to watch your office and home. And there's no need to bother the commissioner about this, Mr. Vaderman. I understand the ramifications."

Uncle Russell just smiled his closed-mouth smile, which Joshua had learned wasn't *really* a smile, and they walked out together.

Joshua jumped along like a puppy next to his uncle on their way to the office. When he started to speak, his uncle just put a finger over his lips, so Joshua held his tongue, but he was bursting with questions. He could never have gotten through that interview by himself, not without being reduced to tears and embarrassing himself.

He followed his uncle into the elevator at Vaderman Ventures, and as they passed Rosalee's desk she smiled at Joshua and spoke to Russell. "Commissioner Harrows left a message for you, sir. He apologized and said he can't be here this afternoon as he'd planned. He'll be in touch later or tomorrow."

"Thanks, Rosalee. Hold my calls for now, would you?"

Joshua felt strangely important. He never had Uncle Russell's undivided attention like this when they were at work!

Uncle Russell closed the office door and told Joshua to have a seat. He went to his mini fridge and offered Joshua a vitamin water, which he took, and sat down on the edge of his desk to drink his own as well.

"I'm proud of you, Joshua. That was a tough interview. The police are rough on murder witnesses in your situation."

"But I didn't see anyone get *killed*, I just saw the—the dead body." Joshua shivered.

"I know," Russell said. "I did have an additional test run on your blood from the hospital. The results aren't back yet, which means there is a high likelihood they will be positive. Negatives are reported early; positives are confirmed with additional testing."

Joshua felt scared again. "What is the drug, Uncle? Is it that powdery stuff they blew at me? I never heard of anything like that either."

"It might be, Joshua. The drug we're testing for is called scopolamine, and one source is a plant also known as Devil's Breath that can be turned into a powder, like the one you described."

Joshua sat very still. He was quite pleased that Uncle Russell said he was proud of him, but this drug sounded evil. Yet, Uncle Russell seemed calm, and Joshua took his strength from there.

Russell looked at Joshua for a couple of minutes. "Cingulate Services seems to have helped you a lot, I think—"

"Uncle Russell, I don't ever want to go back there!" Joshua said, bursting into a frenzy.

"No, no, Josh, you misunderstand. I'm sorry, I'm musing a

little out loud. Let me start again. No, I agree. You're never going back there."

Joshua relaxed.

"But," Russell said, "they *have* helped you a lot. You seem to have made incredible strides in your ability to not only retain information but also to process it. In short, I think you have become *smarter*. Do you feel that too?"

"Um, yeah, I kind of do," Joshua answered, playing with a button on his shirt and feeling somewhat embarrassed. He knew his intellect would never come anywhere near his uncle's, so it seemed insignificant to him.

"Both your mother and I have had… experiences with that substance. Or something similar. Has she ever told you about our time in South America when we were children?"

Joshua squished his eyebrows together, a sure sign he was struggling to remember something. "Maybe," he said. "Mom's talked about these flowers from Colombia and Peru, but I thought she was having one of her… well, one of her rants. Sometimes she doesn't sound quite right. I know I shouldn't say that about my own mother, and I'm probably wrong about her. I mean, what do I know?"

Russell chuckled. "No, Josh, your mother definitely 'rants' sometimes. And the flower stories sound crazy even if a more rational person talks about it. I avoid the subject entirely myself, just for that reason. But there is a tree that grows wild in parts of South America and was used in ancient rituals by some of the local tribes. Rituals for healing, mostly, but also for divining of a sort. It seems a shaman used this, probably in combination with another plant or plants, on both your mother and me. We were very small, and I remember almost nothing about it. Mom was seven, and she remembers more."

"Was it dangerous, Uncle?"

Russell shrugged. "I seem to have turned out all right—some say, better than all right, though apparently my intellectual journey has been unique. But your mom thinks her psychiatric problems stem from then. Look, Joshua, I have a hunch about what may have happened to you to make you feel compelled to follow your counselors' instructions, and why your memory was a blank. But I don't understand *why* it happened, or why it happened to *you*."

Joshua didn't know what to say. He had the feeling there was more that he hadn't remembered yet, and he still had an aversion to looking deeper. It made him feel like his blood was icy cold, just considering it.

His uncle was determined, however. "I'm going to want to go over everything that you can recall about the last several weeks. That's why the commissioner was supposed to be here as well. We were going to all walk through it together, but we can start ourselves for now."

Joshua stood up and started pacing. "Weeks? I don't know, Uncle Russell, you know my memory isn't as good as other people's. And why the commissioner? Is it because you guys are friends? So, why did we go to the police station anyway? What if I can't remember anymore? I'm scared, Uncle Russell. There's still that voice in my head that says something really bad will happen if I talk about it. And those police officers don't like me, they think I'm doing all this on purpose. What if they lock me up?"

Joshua's thoughts were spilling out as if he couldn't think linearly, kind of like when Uncle Russell was in his head and his brain felt all knotted up. He didn't want his uncle to do that to him again, even if it could help him remember.

"Whoa, slow down, Josh. No one is going to lock you up. I know this is scary, and I'm sorry it's happened to you, but we *have* to find out what transpired. Someone died. That person was someone's father, brother… uncle? And what if Donny is in trouble? He's your friend. We need to at least find out if he's okay, don't you think?"

Joshua walked over to the window and rested his forehead on it. It felt cool and sweet on his hot face. He vaguely remembered the counselors talking to Donny privately and giving Donny separate instructions. And then Donny left, carrying something, it looked like. But Joshua wasn't supposed to pay attention to any of that.

"No more Donny… not friends anymore…," he whispered, but even as he did, he knew it wasn't his own thought. He could almost see the mental strand in his head that came from somewhere *else*. It was a different color. Dark, devious, and blood red, where the rest of his thoughts were bright green and blue and violet. How could that be? Had his thoughts always been in color? What had happened to him? And how could he have a thought in his own head that wasn't his own thought at all? Joshua shook his head vehemently, but he didn't know exactly what he was trying to negate. His mind felt heavy and like it belonged to someone else.

Joshua looked over his shoulder at his uncle, who was staring at him intensely, as if he could look into Joshua's mind again. Joshua searched wildly for a way to block him out. Surely Uncle Russell would see the truth, that Joshua was insane. Like his mother.

———

"Uncle, don't. Stay OUT of my head!"

Russell felt Joshua's mental barriers slam shut on him. It was like literally having a door hurtled in his face, and he reeled with the vibration of it. He hadn't even known he was trying to gain access, he had not done so consciously. What the hell was happening to him? He was doubly shocked because Joshua had never before challenged him, on anything.

"I'm sorry," Russell said, shaking his head. "I didn't mean to do anything."

They just looked at each other. Joshua was still standing at the window and Russell stayed perched on the edge of his desk but had twisted around to face him. Joshua seemed different ever since Russell had deliberately gone into his mind to unravel it. He seemed stronger somehow, and older.

"Let's start with more recent events," Russell said. "What happened at your last Cingulate group meeting? Were your counselors there as usual?"

Joshua walked over to his uncle and plopped back down in the plush chair in front of the desk. "Mr. Brunner was. He's always there, but Mr. Wheeler didn't come. Mr. Brunner seemed a little distracted. Oh, and he got kind of upset when I wouldn't eat my cookie this week, even though I told him I had a big dinner."

"What cookie?"

Joshua told Russell about the game they played, how everyone eats one and only one cookie every meeting. They were maple flavored and were heated up to smell delicious, but they were limited to one and never allowed to bring a cookie home. "It's just a stupid cookie," Joshua said. "I don't know why he got so uptight about it."

Joshua also told Russell about the exercises they did, which were second nature for him now but used to be really hard, and that he didn't really enjoy the session last Friday as much as he usually did. Joshua had initially attributed that to their encounter in front of the co-op just prior to class, in which Russell had basically commanded Joshua to take his phone along, but Donny was not present in class last Friday, and Joshua felt uncomfortable when Jonathan kept asking about him.

The cookie was new information, and Russell tucked it away for future thought. Given how uncomfortable Joshua was, he decided to just let it go and wait for whatever the police would turn up.

The next few days passed outwardly uneventfully, but inwardly, Russell was trying to make sense of what had happened to his family.

Certainly Joshua's brain chemistry had been affected, and although it never occurred to Russell that Joshua had gone insane, he recognized the terror it provoked. Russell attributed it to the effects of the drug and his own eerie tampering in Joshua's mind.

Two days later, the blood test did indeed come back faintly positive for scopolamine. It had been drawn many hours after the incident, and the fact that it was still detectable at all meant that Joshua must have received a massive dose.

Jim Werner notified Russell first, as he had promised, and then reported the findings to Detective Rodriguez. He reinforced that Joshua should see a neurologist for follow up but changed his referral recommendation to a neuropsychiatrist that Werner knew personally.

CHAPTER 27

On Wednesday, Maya decided to go into Vaderman Ventures and do some cleanup bookkeeping and check their investments. She was still waiting to hear back from Harris and wanted to be professionally attired and ready at a moments' notice anyway, and going to work would revitalize her feeling of being part of the business world and distract her at the same time. She mentally kicked herself nearly every hour that went by that she did not receive a follow-up email.

Russell was involved in his new Berlin project and had been spending some extra time with his sister, which made sense, given she had been arrested and the bail money had come from Russell, not to mention the mess Joshie found himself in. Maya managed to ascertain that Russell and Joshua had uncovered some of the mystery surrounding Joshua showing up doused in blood. Maya had not asked much about it, though. It seemed to be an incomplete memory anyway, and to be honest, the whole thing unnerved her enough to not really want to know all the details. As long as her loved ones were okay.

Somehow, she never had gotten to talk to Russell about her first meeting with Harris, which Maya supposed was fine, since she wasn't supposed to reveal anything anyway, but she wished she had someone to talk to. She was used to sharing everything with her best friend, Katrina, but they both worked with Undivided, so Maya thought she probably shouldn't mention it. Damn, it was difficult going it alone.

Maya did not believe in keeping her own counsel, although she was great at advising other people what to do in sticky situations. She could be unbiased and dispassionate for her friends, and she knew she gave good guidance. But when it came to counseling herself, she never could see what the right thing was to do; she just couldn't be objective. She was much too emotional.

She was busy in her office at VV, which was how they all referred to Vaderman Ventures, when she saw an email from Harris come in, asking if she had made a decision. He suggested that if she wanted to proceed, she should meet him for lunch again at the same restaurant. Russell was tied up in meetings of his own, so Maya packed up and left without leaving word where she was going. Russell could get quite wrapped up in his own work, and when he was in that mode, he didn't register the extraneous things going on around him anyway. She checked her tailored suit and makeup in the ladies' room and headed out.

———

The waiter brought the bruschetta on freshly baked, toasted bread in the now familiar booth at the back of the ritzy Italian restaurant. Harris motioned to Maya to take one and she did, savoring each bite. It was a few moments before he spoke.

"So, you have considered what we spoke about, and you

want to be involved? Have you discussed our meeting with anyone?"

"Well, my husband knows that we met, but I didn't tell him anything about it, and he didn't ask."

He smiled and reached for his Pellegrino. "Very good. Are you prepared to keep these conversations private?"

"Yes, yes. At least for a month, like you said, and probably longer. I mean if you show me why that's important, I will give it a month at least to understand." Maya was getting more and more anxious. What if he turned her down?

Harris looked at her over his glass for a long, silent minute. Then he leaned across the table and spoke to her intently.

"Maya, what if I told you that people follow President Ganaffe because they don't think for themselves?"

"Oh," Maya said, slightly disappointed. She had been expecting something far more momentous. "I know they don't think for themselves. It's a 'mob mentality.' That's the whole problem."

Harris continued. "No, what if I told you they do not have the *option* to think for themselves. They are no longer capable; that choice has been taken from them, and they do not know it."

Maya felt confused and it must have shown on her face.

"Maya, there has been a movement afoot, a very successful movement, of real-life brainwashing on a grand scale. It is being accomplished through the use of drugs hidden in drinks and food served at the Ganaffe rallies, Tea Parties, and many other assemblies of conservatives. The effects are then reactivated by certain slogans circulating on Twitter, Facebook, and Instagram, and on television network news. It is alike to a subliminal suggestion that social media cues tie into. And this movement has gathered momentum and is now sweeping the country, multiplying, and bringing in thousands of new victims daily."

Maya did not know what to think about that; it sounded outrageous. "Wouldn't that be illegal? How could anyone get away with that? Obviously, it's known; you're telling me about it. So, why hasn't anyone put a stop to it?"

Harris chuckled and sat back. "What do you think drives the world, Maya dear? Is it fairness? Truth? Justice?"

Maya had a flashback to something Russell had once said to her. It was a jolt, as he had used so similar a phrase. *No matter how well-intentioned in the beginning, the driving force in this world is always money. The ones with money are the ones with power. If you want to figure out why something is the way it is, just follow the money. Maya, my love, never let me fall prey to that thinking. Never let that be my motivation. I want the purpose of our money to be for making a better life. Never let me make our life be for the purpose of making money.*

"Money," Maya whispered as she remembered. "Follow the money."

Harris raised his eyebrows. "Very good, Maya dear. *Very* good. And I thought I would need to make you see that."

"Russell—my husband—says that. But what has that got to do with this… drug?"

"Money and power. The drug bestows power, power yields money, and money, in turn, buys more power. The people who want to stay in power use this drug. People follow them mindlessly, and it makes them rich. Which in its turn, gives them even more power."

Maya was still confused about what she could do about this, and for a fleeting second, she had a gut feeling that she shouldn't be there, that she was way out of her league. She deeply regretted her promise not to discuss anything with Russell.

She fiddled with her napkin and took a deep breath. "How can *I* help with this? I doubt my husband would put up any capital to fight these drugs without knowing all about it anyway. I mean, I don't know, but you don't want me to talk to him about it, and I can't take a large amount of money from our account without explaining what I need it for."

Harris broke out laughing. "No, no, dear Maya. I am not asking you for money. I am just giving you background about the problem we face."

Maya relaxed a little but was more perplexed than before. "So…." She trailed off.

"What we need to do is to fight fire with fire. We have been waging a losing battle against the extremists because they have been, frankly, playing dirty. We are going to come back at them and give them the same as they are giving us."

Maya looked at him, silent alarms going off in her head. "You want to drug people too?"

Harris leaned forward across the table and looked right into her eyes. "We *have* to, Maya, or we will surely lose. This war of the minds has been going on for a very long time, and we need to even the playing field."

"What do you want me to do?"

Lunch arrived at that moment, and Harris motioned her to start. He also dug into his meal so hungrily that Maya wondered why he hadn't touched any of the savory bruschetta. It was so tasty, she had had two pieces. After a few minutes, he continued.

"It is really quite simple. I am going to ask you to throw some parties. You will have a budget, and there will be no out-of-pocket expenses for you, just time. You will run a pre-arranged curriculum of sorts designed to persuade the attendees of our philosophies, which are mostly philanthropic, and refreshments will be served. Some of those refreshments will contain this substance. There will be no harm coming to anyone, and your guests will not even know they are ingesting anything unusual. You will be completely confident there will be no harm done because you will be right there with them and you will see, their behavior will not change a whit. It will all be quite safe. You will be doing a great service to our cause. If you feel there are any visible ill effects, well, I want you to let me know imme-diately, and we will discontinue everything."

Maya distantly noted a change in his tone; for a moment, he sounded almost like he was ticking off points in a lecture. But it all sounded perfectly reasonable to Maya, especially if she were free to cancel at any time. She felt almost compelled to agree.

"This *is* something you would be comfortable helping us with, isn't it?" Harris asked.

Maya found herself nodding her head even before she was done hearing his question. "Oh, yes, Harris, that would be easy for me to do; I love to throw parties, and I would be grateful for the opportunity to participate in something so important and so useful."

Harris sat back in his chair, a warm smile on his face. "Won-derful," he said. "We will make all the arrangements."

Maya wondered why she had entertained any doubts at all.

————

Harris took the call in the back of the restaurant after watching Maya get into the Uber. She had been humming happily as he walked her out.

"Yes, it is all in place," Harris said into the phone. "She is quite sensitive; I think we may be able to start Phase II sooner than planned."

Harris hung up and opened his laptop. He started ordering supplies and set up a guest list for Maya's first "party."

CHAPTER 28

Braelyn stared at the closed door after the damn lawyer left. She wanted to throw something after him. Something heavy. Jeremy kept insisting she needed a stronger defense to explain how cocaine could have gotten in her suitcase if she wanted to plead innocent, and she kept arguing that it wasn't hers, and in this country, she was supposed to be innocent until proven guilty. The fact that it was found in her suitcase was happenstance; she couldn't explain it. That was the problem, so, they were at a stalemate.

She repeated to him that she had brought back the flowers of the *borrachero* plant and that these had been confiscated and no one had mentioned them. They must have confused the two. Not surprisingly, Jeremy had never heard of a *borrachero* plant and dismissed the notion of shamans in South America as having any validity in the civilized world at all. Begrudgingly but as promised, she scribbled the name of the shrink she'd been seeing on a scrap of paper and gave it to Jeremy, but she specifically did *not* give permission for them to discuss her situation.

That was personal. Jeremy had left looking completely unraveled. Good, Braelyn thought. She hated lawyers.

Sitting on her couch, Braelyn realized she should call her shrink anyway. She hadn't spoken to him since she returned to New York, mostly out of embarrassment. She wasn't sure he would believe her either, and she knew he certainly hadn't meant for her to go bring the flowers back, and he might feel responsible. Here she was now, with no flowers and under arrest to boot. The tension in her body made her feel she would burst, and she couldn't even go for a run or to the gym to drain some of it off. "Damn that Jeremy," she screamed at the wall. "Damn them all!"

There was an old exercise bike in the extra bedroom, which had been a gift from Russell years ago. That room was crammed full of "stuff" that Braelyn couldn't seem to part with, and getting to and then clearing off the bike to use it was a monumental task. But she had nothing else to do, so she started after it. In her current mood, instead of putting things away or sorting out what should go in the trash, she just threw everything around the room, making bigger piles everywhere else.

She finally cleared off the bike seat and a space around the petals and got on, prepared to spin off all her pent-up frustrations, when the gears slipped and she couldn't pedal. Too late, she remembered it was broken and that was why she had stopped using it. She screamed again, grabbing at her head as she did so. Then she hushed and waited for a neighbor to complain.

As if her thinking of him had attracted him to her, her phone rang, and she saw it was Dr. Mitchell Gray. He was probably the only person in the world who didn't keep telling her she was crazy. Since he was her new psychiatrist, that tickled her somehow.

"Braelyn? It's Dr. Gray. I'm just calling to check on you. I

haven't heard from you for nearly a month. You had an appointment today that you missed. Did you forget?"

Damn, Braelyn thought. She really had forgotten. No wonder
he was on her mind, though.

"I'm sorry, Dr. Gray. I'm in such a mess!" Braelyn broke
down sobbing and told him everything.

She could almost see his astonishment right through the
phone. "You actually brought the *borrachero* plant back with
you? I don't think that's legal. Did you declare it at customs?"

"I didn't have a chance to declare anything! They came for
me and my bag before I got to the front of the line. They took my
bag away from me and stuffed me in an office, and then they
came back and told me I was under arrest for carrying cocaine!
They never mentioned the flowers, they never showed me this
supposed cocaine, and when they returned my suitcase, the
flowers were gone! I went to a *lot* of trouble to get those! It was
the whole purpose of my trip."

He was quiet for a moment. "Did you ask anyone where they
went?"

"No," Braelyn muttered softly. "I was afraid to."

"The whole thing is very strange, Braelyn. Customs should
have had you present when they searched your bag. Do you
think they knew you were carrying the flowers? My God, what
possessed you to bring something like that home? Where did
you even get it?"

"I wanted to give it to *you*, Doctor. I thought maybe you
could figure out how to use them to make me 'normal' again.
Oh, I don't know!" Braelyn flopped down on her couch, her
manic phase turning swiftly to depression. She hated the way
her moods flipped so easily. She dug her hands behind the cush-
ions and found a pen, no doubt having come from one of
Joshua's pockets.

"Dr. Gray... My son Josh *also* had something really weird
happen to him, and he's supposed to see a neuropsychiatrist.

That's you, right? I mean, they gave him a referral, but I'd rather he see you." As Braelyn gave him the details, she realized how much it sounded like her son had been dosed with the same flowers she had brought home.

Dr. Gray listened carefully until she finished. "Yes, I can see your son, if he wishes. But why in the world would anyone want to do that to him or his friend? Braelyn, this is starting to sound like you and your son may be at some risk. I told you the government experimented with this many years ago, remember? I don't want you to be alarmed, but perhaps we should talk somewhere more private; can you come to my office?"

Braelyn laughed. "I'm stuck here, Dr. Gray. They've got an ankle bracelet on me. And even if I was allowed to leave with it, they'd know where I was in an instant. If they wanted to bug my apartment or follow me, there's not a damn thing I could do about it. Why do they care about me anyway? I'm just a mental nutcase who can't hold a job or keep it together for more than five minutes."

"I don't know…" Dr. Gray sighed heavily. "I don't normally do house calls, but I could make an exception one time, I suppose. If you want, that is."

Braelyn felt the first ray of light she'd known in a week. "Would you? Oh, please, Doctor!"

———

Mitchell Gray hung up the phone. Why had he offered to do that? He knew Braelyn was unstable. How smart was it to go to her apartment? He doubted she would do anything that could compromise him professionally, and he *did* see her in his office alone, but he still felt uneasy for some reason.

Braelyn Plessman was not only an interesting challenge for him, but she had also reawakened his questions from nearly twenty years ago. He had been a young whippersnapper neuropsychiatrist back then and had been incensed by the stories coming out of Guantanamo Bay regarding the methods used to question suspected Taliban prisoners. Not that he didn't agree they needed to keep America safe from terrorists. Mitchell's own sister, Andrea, had worked in the North Tower and had been a victim of 9/11. So, he had mixed feelings, but he'd heard rumors… rumors that scopolamine was being used in massive doses both to question and control suspects. As much as he wanted justice for his sister, taking over a person's mind felt so ethically wrong to Mitchell. He had been all twisted up inside at the thought.

So, Braelyn's story felt close to him. He recognized the fact that her auburn hair and slight build, so similar to his sister's, played into that for sure. Braelyn was also no prisoner or Taliban suspect. Just a woman, who as a very little girl had been subjected to something she could never understand, her mind going in directions just to survive that made her think she was near lunacy. Was she? Had the drug done that to her? Or was her behavior just a "normal" reaction to her circumstance of exposure? And was there even a difference at this point?

Since hearing Braelyn's story, Mitchell had done his own research into the practices of the shamans in Northern Peru. There were not many of them, and it was not easy to dig up information, but for some reason he had felt driven. Maybe because he had always had an interest in the paranormal, a little fact he shared with few because it tended to get him labeled in ways he preferred not to be known.

He discovered the *Brugmansia* plants (of which the *borrachero* was one) were not used alone in ancient tribes but were usually mixed with the San Pedro Cactus and other hallucinogens. Under the command of a *curandero*, that mixture was said to be harnessed for healing purposes of both the body and the mind, and this same mixture was said to serve as a conduit for a shaman to speak with spirits.

The most revered of these shamans, *El Curandero Grande*, was said to have developed his mental abilities far beyond those of typical humans and that this *curandero* had developed his extrasensory abilities past even the instinctual senses of primitive times, when those abilities were sometimes all that kept humans from being discovered and devoured by other animals.

Some reports also said this shaman displayed telepathic and telekinetic power under the influence of these drugs, and that in the last few decades, he had spent all of his time in a chronic state of intoxication. From another source, Mitchell found that the present *Curandero Grande* was in Piura, coinciding eerily with where Braelyn Plessman indicated her family had gone when seeking healing for her debilitated mother, and that he was almost two hundred years old. Some even thought he was from another planet entirely.

It was impossible to know how much of these stories were real and how much was inflated; the human mind was capable of so much more than what mere humans typically accessed. Instances of superhuman abilities were well known when under supreme stress—people lifting cars off loved ones, communicating over distances, and even controlling fire and light with the mind.

Probably most of what Mitchell had "uncovered" was fantasy, but he was wise enough to know that all myths had *some* basis in fact. Peeling away that truth was the tricky part.

Since he met Braelyn two years ago and heard her story, Mitchell had wondered increasingly why the US government hadn't pursued what happened to her and her brother. Braelyn's brief report that her parents split because her father looked for help from the medical community and her mother wanted to hush it up once the DEA and CIA became involved, convinced Mitchell that the government *had* to have known *something* about it. So, he'd decided that perhaps the Feds didn't think it was important.

But now he wondered… What if they were still following her? Why else would customs arrest Braelyn and confiscate the flowers without even mentioning them? Somehow the Feds must have known she was carrying them. Which meant someone had to have been watching her. Which meant they'd been watching her for a very long time.

CHAPTER 29

By 7:15 a.m., Trenaman was in his office and making himself a cup of coffee. He thought wearily of the task before him but hoped to get some real mileage out of the day so he could quit listening to taped conversations by 2:00 p.m. and still have time to address other matters in his life.

He waded through the morass of security protocols needed to listen to the next section of the recording from Braelyn Plessman's ankle bracelet. He found it at least possible to skip the down time and recognize when the sound wave pattern reflected voices, and he fast-forwarded to the next conversation.

The young man's voice was apparently the son, Joshua, and Trenaman's ears perked up in sheer curiosity to see what had come of the impromptu experiment with true Devil's Breath powder. Up until then, Trenaman had only utilized scopolamine ingested in food or drink, since the dusting seemed to be too difficult to precisely direct.

Listening to Joshua describe what it felt like to be dosed and not "allowed" to remember was remarkable, and Trenaman didn't know if they had ever had an opportunity to study the effects in this way. The kid had come up for air covered in blood, so obviously *something* had happened to him, and Trenaman cursed Wheeler again for allowing that to occur. If Plessman had just returned to life as usual, wearing unstained clothes and without much loss of time, it could be hoped the kid would remember nothing about the incident and have had no need for soul-searching. He frowned. This was a completely botched use of the drug.

It was fascinating to hear someone describe what it felt like when confronting a command given to the mind under the influence, and Trenaman felt pity for the poor kid, who sounded quite young on the tape. He even cried. But Trenaman's ears perked up in alarm to hear that the uncle, who would be none other than Russell Vaderman, had managed to override the command. How was that possible?

So now the kid was carrying his phone again, which in theory, he should never have been told not to—too conspicuous, but he had dissonance with that. The sheer naiveté of this kid was also a problem. A more sophisticated person might have been too self-conscious to tell anyone about the discordance between his feelings and his behavior. This kid was blowing the lid right off the whole process.

Trenaman listened three times to the part where Joshua explained how his uncle got into his brain. He concluded that the kid, at least, believed this, that it was not a dramatic interlude, and there could be something to it. They knew Vaderman was an anomaly, having been heavily dosed as a toddler, but no one knew exactly what brain deviations had occurred. While they had certainly tried over the years to test him subtly, he seemed impervious to influence, until ultimately, they'd given up. No one had used the drug on him since he was a teenager, when they met with an unprecedented result: Vaderman had stopped in his tracks, put his hands to his head, then looked at the "researcher" and accused him of trying to poison him. Then he had simply walked away.

Damn. On the one hand, the man was getting horribly in the way, and on the other—they needed to study Russell Vaderman! Trenaman turned the system off and sat back at his desk. He was completely floored. What might they learn from this guy?

CHAPTER 30

Russell was greeted at home by the smell of sautéed garlic coming from the kitchen. A quick peek confirmed his favorite grey sole *au gratin* had just come out of the pan and was ready with pasta and broccoli on the side. His mouth watered.

"Hi, Russ," Maya said cheerfully, and leaned over to give him a kiss. "Perfect timing, dinner is just about ready. I'm just finishing the string beans."

"Excellent, I'm starved," Russell said, dropping his keys on the counter. "You're in a happy mood."

"Yes! I just received my first project, and I'm very excited about it. Russ, this is *really important* work!"

Russell smiled. "I'm very happy for you. What will you be doing?"

"Actually," Maya began, "I would love it if you would join in. I'm throwing my first big event this weekend, but I hosted a small group of ten over lunch today, kind of to get my feet wet. We met at the Olive Garden, and oh, everyone was so favorable! We discussed police brutality and the cruel abuse of force on

Black folks. It's so important to spread the word right now; I feel like this was such an opportune time to get involved! There's so much that needs to be done."

Russell nodded. "It's horrible, I agree. I don't understand why people can't see beneath the color of one's skin."

"And the police!" Maya jumped in. "They're barbaric! They enjoy hurting people just because someone doesn't look like them."

Russell was setting the table and stopped suddenly, thinking that not *all* the police were barbaric. "There needs to be better accountability from our police officers," Russell said, choosing his words carefully. "We need to get rid of the ones who went into the force as an opportunity to bully and hurt others, and we need to train the good officers on how to protect themselves wisely and how to cope better with suspects who have mental illness. So many good cops are terrified of going to work right now."

"We need to get rid of the police altogether!" Maya shouted.

Russell cocked his head and gave Maya a half-smile. "Now, what would we do if we didn't have any police? We'd be at the mercy of any hooligan who wanted to cause trouble. Maya, darling, that's not what they mean by 'defund the police.'"

"Look at this, Russell!" She grabbed her tablet and pulled up a picture. It showed a group of five police officers on the right, protected by hard face shields and fully armed, and the one in the forefront had a pistol of some sort and it was aimed at head level. In front of the cop was an African American man with a very little girl on his shoulders. At first glance, it looked like the cop was pointing at the man's face.

As Russell studied the picture, something didn't feel right about it. Suddenly, he was standing over the scene, and in that weird way his mind always turned, the photo seemed to float for a moment in 3D space. He shook his head.

"Look, Maya dear. The officer is not pointing his gun at the man with the child. This picture is taken with a telephoto lens. It makes it look like they are right next to each other."

He wasn't prepared for her reaction.

"Russell! How can you say that! Just look at it, the gun is leveled at this poor man's face while his child is looking on."

Russell moved alongside his wife and put one arm around her shoulder while pointing at the tablet with the other. "Maya, sweetheart, look at the size of the man's face. Now look at the size of the police officer's face. They're not equivalent. They are at very different distances from the camera. Also, look at the officer's expression. He looks frightened, vigilant, not mean or cruel. There's plenty of real horror going on, there's no need to hyperbolize it like this. It's unnecessarily inflammatory."

Maya looked at the image again, and Russell *saw* her see it, and then it was like a brick hit her in the face, and she shook her head vehemently. "No, Russell, you don't know what you're talking about. It's right here in black and white. We're going to be talking about this at my event, and then we will be joining the protests in the city. Really, Russell, how can you be so callous! You're actually making excuses for these barbarians."

Russell stared at her. He knew she had seen what he saw, in that uncanny way he had of knowing—which, for some reason, was getting increasingly more prevalent since he'd had a whiff of Braelyn's clothes that smelled of the *borrachero* plant. But he also saw her shut it down. It was not like her to do that. It almost reminded him of what had happened to Joshua—but that was ridiculous. He changed the subject.

"Tell me about your event," he suggested quietly.

Maya nodded, put her tablet down, then started bringing the food to the table. "I'm so excited to be a part of this! On Saturday, there will be fifty of us meeting in a very fancy Italian restaurant, where we'll have the back room to ourselves so we can project photos and outlines on a screen. Afterward, we'll jump on with the protesters. Oh, and don't worry, it won't cost us a dime. It's all covered by the organization."

"Undivided has money for that?" Russell asked.

"Um, no. Harris is covering it—he's with an ancillary agency that is attached to Undivided."

They sat down to eat, but Maya suddenly looked uncomfortable.

"As long as you're happy, darling. Just be very careful in the protests. Most of it is peaceful, but I don't want you to get caught up in the small faction that has become violent. Keep your eyes and ears open."

"Nonsense," Maya said, passing him the platter of fish. "They wouldn't send me into anything dangerous."

"No one can predict what happens in these things, they have a life of their own. I'm not saying don't go, just be careful."

"Fine," Maya said. She sounded anything but fine.

Both were quiet as they started to eat. Presently, Maya asked about Joshua.

"Is he still at his mother's? I wish you would tell him to come home, Russ. You know she can't take care of him."

Russell sighed to himself. As happy as Maya seemed when he walked in, she had made a complete transition to one of her contrary moods. "He's twenty-four, Maya, he's not supposed to need taking care of by now. We should leave him be."

"Does he remember what happened to him?"

"Actually, he does. Much of it, anyway. I think he needs some space to process it, but at least we know Joshua didn't hurt anyone, and the police are keeping him under surveillance to make sure he's safe."

"Of course he didn't hurt anyone! But you are ready to trust the police with Joshie? Brutes are what the police are! How will they keep Joshie safe? He should be here; at least you own a gun." Maya pushed her plate aside, unfinished.

"Maya, I thought you hated that I own a gun." Russell couldn't help but chuckle as he finished his last bite of grey sole.

"I did, but now that we have to police ourselves, it's different. I trust you much more than I trust the police these days."

Russell just sighed. He didn't have the energy just then to try to push past her sudden resistance. He had wanted to talk about his day, but just then, he decided not to share the report from Detective Rodriguez that confirmed Donny Anderson was missing. His mother had filed a police report almost two weeks ago, but so far, no one had found him. The precinct originally chalked it up to a kid wanting out of his parents' house, since he was twenty-two years old, but after hearing Joshua's story, they started searching for him in earnest. No luck as of yet.

Josh had checked in with Russell a couple of hours ago, per Russell's request. He was trying to practice doing in his own head what Russell had done to him, and he said he was making progress. The whole incident still didn't sit right with Russell. He had always known he was different, but not *this* different. How had he gotten inside Joshua's head? But then, if he had shown Joshua something he could use for himself, what a boon that was, and once they got to the bottom of it, maybe Braelyn could use his "technique" when she suffered from her own information overload. How strange it felt to Russell to think about his mental processes as a "technique."

"Where did you go?" Maya asked him. Her lower lip jutted out, and she looked sulky.

"I'm sorry, I was just musing," Russell said.

"Obviously? I wish you didn't shut me out like that. Hey, I want to give you something special for dessert. It's leftover snacks from the luncheon today."

"I'm really not hungry now," Russell said. "That was an outstanding dinner. You outdid yourself."

Maya looked insulted; she was already getting up to get whatever it was she wanted him to taste, and Russell did not want to get into an argument with her. He could see this would not end well unless he tried the treat she wanted to give him.

She handed him a biscuit and looked at him expectantly. It looked like a fairly ordinary biscuit with rivers of cinnamon running through it. He couldn't read her mood at all, which he found strange.

"Here, I'll make you some tea to dunk it in, unless you want coffee?"

"No coffee, it's late. This is fine." He took a bite to appease her as she went about fixing some tea anyway."

The biscuit tasted quite ordinary, but he nibbled at it anyway to appease his wife. He watched her getting the hot water from the cooler and add the tea bag to the mug. He saw the hot water evaporating slightly into the air, even though it shouldn't have been hot enough to be steaming so visibly. She placed the tea in front of him, and as Russell watched, the tea bag expanded and the flavor sifted through the tea bag membrane and spread in swirls into the hot water. The texture of the water changed as the flavor infused, and Russell felt the tea rising up to touch his face.

"You really need to rethink your faith in the police, Russell. They are brutes, through and through. We need to send them all packing. Why don't you come with me this weekend, and we can march together after the luncheon? I'm sure you'll enjoy the food, and that way you can watch out for me, make sure I don't get arrested or anything. People listen to you, Russell. If you tell Commissioner Harrows to disband the police, he'll do it! Besides, we never do anything really important together. Come with me."

Russell almost found himself promising to go, promising *himself* he would go, and thinking to *himself* how much sense Maya was making. How could he have seen it differently?

Some reflex in his head slammed the brakes down hard on this path of thought. Something felt desperately wrong. Russell had been completely enraptured in the teacup for some reason, and as he looked up, the table stretched out in front of him as if it were twelve feet long and growing. He blinked, and it was normal sized again.

He put his hands on his temples and sank into his head; slowly and deliberately, he unpacked what he was feeling and thinking, automatically, as he had done since he was... was three? No, *he* didn't believe all the police were brutes. Some, yes, not all. *He* didn't want to tell off his friend, Commissioner Harrows. What *he*, Russell, would do was talk to Harrows and ask what was being done and if there were something he could do to help diffuse the situation and change protocols for police behavior so these injustices would never happen again. He heard Maya calling him, but he shut her out as he used to do when he was a kid, feeling pummeled by the questions of adults.

Finally, his head felt ordered again, and he let go of his temples. He sat back in his chair and breathed in deeply. He saw the lines of thought untangle in his head, and he kept the ones that were his own, discarding the foreign strands that had come from... where? He looked at Maya.

His mind felt normal again, but his body was exhausted. Clearly he could have just bounded off and done whatever he was told to do—he almost had!

Russell continued to look at Maya, and she looked back with something that resembled smugness before it changed to concern. "So, you're coming, right?" she asked. She smiled with some uncertainty.

Russell stood up, suddenly needing to move. "No," he said, and went into his study. Maya seemed shocked, too shocked to follow him.

He closed and locked his office door behind him, still somewhat dazed. He leaned against the door and replayed this last encounter and could almost see Maya's thoughts, laced with excitement, a measure of guilt, and then shock when he shook it off and walked away.

But at least he was in control of his brain again. Having recognized that he almost wasn't was quite disturbing. Was this his "technique" then? He searched the lingering sensation in his mind. Oddly, he felt like he'd been here before somehow, or somewhere similar.

Russell delved into his memories, and abruptly the Hollow Man was in front of him, speaking directly into Russell's mind, exactly as he had in the dream. But this was no vision, he seemed quite real, as if Russell could reach out and touch him....

"When next the Holy Plants find you, all doors will open...."

Russell started to panic. One thing to dream this, but he was wide awake.

He squeezed his eyes closed so tightly they hurt. His breath came in short bursts, as he felt the mist and smelled the musty incense. Yes, it was the same smell that was in Braelyn's apartment. No, that wasn't right, he was just remembering the suitcase smell. He opened his eyes and found himself in near darkness, staring at the ancient man with paper thin skin, a long white beard, and white eyes. Those eyes that could not see looked deep into Russell's soul and Russell heard the whisper that was not a whisper, in another language that might have been some dialect of Latin or Spanish. Except he wasn't hearing the words, he was just receiving them.

"You are gifted, young child. You will be blessed.
Your mind shall have no limit; no door shall remain closed
to you.
You shall be a Curandero Grande, *even as I am.*
You will see into the hearts of others, and you will enter their
souls at will.
The Spirits have foreseen your coming, and today I make it so.
When next the Holy Plants find you, all doors will open...."

The vision, or whatever it was, faded. Russell stood in his office staring at the lamplight reflecting off the glass pencil holder on his desk, like a faint flame dancing up to the ceiling; he clearly recognized the effect of a hallucinogen. He turned abruptly and burst out of the door and back into the kitchen.

"What did you give me?" Russell demanded of his wife, his glare scorching her for the first time in nearly twenty years of marriage. At first she just stared at him, as if he were from some other planet, but as his gaze bored into her, she began to cower.

"It was just a tea cookie. Everyone ate them at lunch, including me. They were a big hit. No one else had any reaction to them." Her voice was squeaking slightly.

"You drugged me!"

Maya shook her head, backing away from him. "No, no I didn't. I wouldn't. Russell, I love you, I would never hurt you...." Her voice trailed off and Russell could see her thoughts, wild and twisted, as she sunk into a chair. She trembled and put her hands to her throat, as if she couldn't take a breath. Her mouth froze and her lips started to turn blue. She seemed to be willing herself to die by refusing to breathe.

Russell strode over to her in two steps, and placed his hands on her head, not kindly. He *reached* into her on instinct and commanded:

"STOP!"

CHAPTER 31

Thomas Brunner looked at the boxes in the back of the truck. Simple stuff, mostly water bottles and the same cookies they served in the Cingulate group. Over the last several days, he had been given a rented truck and told to deliver to multiple parties all over the city for meetings of the Kiwanis and Rotary clubs, and next week he'd be going to meetings of the Elks Club, Knights of Columbus, and VFW.

Even though Thomas did not have a problem serving the students at Cingulate those same cookies (and maybe it was in the milk and soda too, for all he knew), that was to help them develop their cognitive abilities so they could make a better life for themselves. Yeah, they had some learning exercises that, now that he thought about it, were fairly political in nature due to the examples they utilized which always praised President Ganaffe as a hero, but it seemed a small price to pay for making them better wage earners, more equipped to succeed in society.

Now that Thomas knew what Cingulate Services was *really* about, he felt slightly scummy delivering "food and beverages" to any place with a political agenda. The $2000 bonus he was told he would receive for each day he made deliveries did make it somewhat more palatable, and he told himself sternly that if he didn't do this job, someone else assuredly would. So, why shouldn't he get the money for it?

His third delivery stop was in Central Park where they were holding an outdoor rally of sorts. President Ganaffe himself would not be attending, but many of his party's representatives were there. Thomas was told he needed to stay for the event and encourage anyone taking the free water bottles or wrapped cookies to stop and listen for a while, and he was to use a "trigger" phrase after they started to drink or eat: "vote Ganaffe Again for a Great America." He was also handing out red, white, and blue hats with GAGA printed on them.

Trenaman stressed the importance of this verbalization, saying it would ensure and reinforce the correct political message. When Thomas started to object, he was admonished that they did not want people drugged and turned loose to be vulnerable to anyone's whim. That would be irresponsible. And indeed, Thomas heard the same phrase used multiple times by the leaders of the rally, and he realized he'd also heard it used in primetime TV and radio ads. In fact, it showed up frequently on his Facebook and Twitter feeds, even though he did not follow anything like that, and Instagram promoted hats with the same logo.

Thomas felt like he needed a shower, but he didn't know if it was from the summer heat or the knowledge of what he was doing. The sun was hot, and he almost cracked open a bottle of the cold water from the cooler before he stopped himself. No way he was going to let his mind get manipulated by these people. Trenaman intimated that Wheeler had been under the influence and less able to think for himself, which may have led to the botched mission a few weeks ago. He said he *wanted* Thomas to have his wits about him, and to that end had gotten him a higher level of clearance. But it was even more than that for Thomas. Thomas wanted to have the ability to decide to run if that became the appropriate thing to do—not that there was likely to be any safe place to go.

So, he sat in his lawn chair and handed out cookies and water bottles from the cooler, all of them with a sticker that said "Ganaffe Again for a Great America" on one side and "Re-elect President Ganaffe" on the other with the "GAGA" logo underneath, and invited pedestrians to stay for a few minutes to hear some of the speakers. Two thousand dollars for three deliveries and a couple of hours sitting in the sun doing this could feel like Thomas was the one taking advantage of Trenaman.

The speaker was good. He knew just how to animate a crowd, calling for cleaning up crime in the city and making it a great place to live again. At first, Thomas didn't catch the very subtle reference to racial division as a fulcrum for accomplishing this. The speaker was saying that Ganaffe was the least racist person in the country, yet he also seemed to be encouraging mistrust between Blacks and Whites. Thomas also noted that Ganaffe did not censure the neo-Nazis who rallied and supported him even as they harassed his opposition. No one seemed to catch the contradiction.

Thomas was not generally a particularly political person. As long as he could find work and no one bothered him, he didn't get much involved in what the rest of the world did. He knew that recently, there'd been more and more outrage over police violence toward the Black population—at least that's what made the news—but for Thomas, getting stopped for a driving viola-tion would make his own skin turn cold, so he tried to imagine how his darker-skinned brothers must feel.

And what most people didn't know was, Thomas wasn't entirely white. His mother's grandfather had been Black, but the genes had diluted enough so that Thomas just looked like he had Mediterranean skin or something like that. He hadn't thought anything about it as a kid, until a classmate once made him feel mildly like an abomination, so he never spoke of it again with anyone, but it made no sense to him. They had learned about adaptation in science class, and that darker skin was more protective against the sun's rays. Thomas thought it was cool that he didn't get a sunburn as quickly as most. And besides, evolution suggested that all humans had descended from *homo sapiens,* who originated in Africa, so, what was the big deal, anyway?

But the speaker went on, berating the protesters who had been out *en force* for a couple of weeks now, calling them all looters and rioters and encouraging the crowd to oppose them. Many people listened for a moment and left, or just walked on by with their heads down. Amazingly, not a single person left who had drunk the water Thomas served; they all seemed riveted to the speaker. A chill went up Thomas's spine, even in the warm summer air.

New York City was a pretty liberal and tolerant metropolis, as cities go, and the speaker was only partly successful in converting residents to follow his example. But for those whose attention he had, they were shouting and raising their fists in the air. There was a police presence protecting the speakers, and Thomas noted that some of the officers were Black or Hispanic, and many of the cops, regardless of color, looked uncomfortable with what was being said, even though it was supposedly in defense of the police force.

Thomas thought back to his last conversation with his father a couple of days ago. He couldn't escape by running back to his childhood home, that felt too dangerous, but he had called Mom and Dad out of a need to feel sheltered by his parents. Of course, he didn't reveal his troubles, but it was comforting just hearing his parents' voices. His father then admonished him to be careful with the protests and the riots and to stay in at night, but Thomas knew it was generic concern. What would his father say if he knew what a mess Thomas was really in?

The rally was breaking up, and Thomas could overhear some of the chit chat as people walked by, mostly agreeing with the sentiment to "take back the city" from minorities. Thomas was appalled. Had he been party to that? He looked around and consoled himself that he was in a city of over eight million people; even if he had been, this was such a tiny percentage of the population, it couldn't possibly make any significant difference in the long run.

CHAPTER 32

Joshua went back to his mother's after work on Thursday. He didn't quite want to be alone with his uncle right now. Even while he fully recognized Uncle Russell loved him and meant him no harm, neither one of them seemed to understand what was happening between them, and that just made him uncomfortable.

Braelyn had been cooking. It was such an unusual sight that for a minute Josh thought he had entered the wrong apartment. It smelled good.

"Hi, Mom," he said as he came in the door.

"I knew you would come home tonight. I made dinner. I hope you like it."

"Smells great. How did you know?" Joshua put his things down on the couch and came into the kitchen.

Braelyn shrugged. "I have no idea. Sometimes I just seem to know stuff."

"Like Uncle Russell," Joshua said. "He does weird shit like that, too, sometimes."

"I'm glad you're here," Braelyn said. She finished setting the table and sat down. "It's lonely and frustrating being cooped up in this place by myself. The worst is that I have no idea how long it's even going to be. And then I'm afraid that once they arraign me, or whatever it's called… what if they say I'm guilty and send me to jail?"

His mother looked like she might break down at that, and Joshua stiffened. He really wanted to be with someone in his family who was acting normal. Well, anxiety *was* normal for his mother, but this was deserved anxiety, not her usual craziness.

"Let's put some music on, Mom, that always cheers me up. You like The Beatles, right? That's from 'your time.'" Joshua pulled up his Apple music, and his Bluetooth connected automatically to the speaker set. He'd used it tons of times before when his mother was away.

They sat down to eat, and even though the music was pretty loud, his mother let him keep it turned up. It definitely dispelled some of the awkwardness they sometimes felt between each other.

Dinner was sweet and sour chicken and rice with the steam-in-the-bag Brussels sprouts Joshua had stocked the freezer with a month ago. He thought it was just as good a dinner as his Aunt Maya could make, and he was proud of his mom. He got about halfway through with dinner before he felt brave enough to ask questions.

"Mom, Uncle Russell doesn't even know what happens when he gets in my head, and he never did that before. Why is it happening now?" Joshua was afraid to look up. He took some more rice and spooned the sweet and sour sauce on it, deliberately spreading sauce over every grain.

"I don't know, Josh. Why would you think I could know? I watched the two of you, but I have no idea even what you were experiencing, much less how he was doing it." Braelyn was eying Joshua's swirls of red sauce on the white rice.

"But, Mom, he said you both had something happen to you

in South America when you were little. So, if it happened to you too, how come you don't know what he's doing?"

His mother put down her fork and knife and turned her full attention on her son.

"Uncle Russell talked to you about South America?"

"Not much. Only that a shaman—I don't know if I said that right—used some plant on you and him. Something for rituals and healing. And, and divining? What's that mean? And what is a 'shaman?' If it was supposed to heal you, how come you're so messed up?"

His mother burst into hysterical laughter, but Joshua did not see anything funny. He was getting increasingly frightened of his world, and none of the adults in his life were in any way helping him cope.

"Did your uncle say anything else?"

"Nope. We were going to talk more later, but I chickened out. I didn't want to have that conversation, so I didn't go home."

"Blackbird" was blasting from the speakers, but neither moved to turn it down. For Joshua, the music gave his mind a familiar thread to follow so he didn't have to think too much. They were sitting catty-corner at the table, and suddenly his mother took his hands and pulled him close so he could not move away. She looked into his eyes very seriously.

"Joshua, would you do something for me?"

Joshua squirmed. This can't be good, he thought. Mom often had crazy ideas and requests, and he had finally learned not to promise anything until he found out what she wanted. He looked at her, now wishing he had gone back to his aunt and uncle's place after all.

"Josh, this is very important to me."

He had a terrible sinking feeling, but he said nothing. Just waited.

"Josh, would you ask Uncle Russell to come to my psychiatry appointment tomorrow at 3:00? Maybe my new shrink can figure out what's been happening."

Joshua relaxed. Somehow he'd been sure his mother would want him to explore what went on in his and his uncle's head by walking back through it, right then, with her, and not only did he not think he could, he didn't even want to go there.

"Oh," he started.

"I would ask him myself, Josh, but I don't think he'll come if I ask. He doesn't take me seriously."

Joshua had an idea. "Can I come too?"

CHAPTER 33

Trenaman shut off the recording and scratched his chin thoughtfully. He had just spent the better part of a day listening to mostly music and white noise with a few conversations thrown in. But this last… he had just listened as a man deprogrammed a subject who had been dosed with Devil's Breath, without using any chemical intervention. Both memory and mental control had been restored to the kid, yet Trenaman had learned nothing about how this had been accomplished. The implications of this for military use were stunning! The United States was certainly not the only government availing itself of the use of scopolamine in clandestine operations, but being able to "turn off" the effects and restore memory and cognition was a function they needed to acquire.

Physostigmine was a drug long used in medicine that could routinely reverse the effects of standard or slightly increased doses of scopolamine. However, in the doses the military employed, such a large amount of physostigmine was required that it was frequently fatal in and of itself, or it was known to produce its own delirium, depression, and cognitive disruption.

In short, it required a careful titration by IM or IV injection to nullify such high doses of scopolamine, and a captured espionage operative treated so was ultimately rendered incapable of giving the government any useful information. Vaderman's ability to remove the drug's effects while preserving the mind and the memory of the subject was beyond remarkable.

Trenaman took a mental step back. The immediate threat, his task at hand, was catastrophic: Plessman knew who had drugged him and must therefore know who murdered the subject, Jackson. It was only a matter of time before Donny Anderson turned up dead, and there was no mistaking what would happen from there. Wheeler and Brunner were compromised. Well, Wheeler was dead and gone, but Brunner… Trenaman hated to waste the kid.

Trenaman considered carefully. He did have connections in the NYPD, just as he had connections in US customs. They didn't know *why* they were connections, of course; they'd been specifically selected for their usefulness and kept motivated at various influential gatherings to offer unconditional loyalty. If Trenaman could make the murders "go away," then Brunner could be spared. If not, he'd have to take the hit; Brunner would have to be dead when they found Anderson so he couldn't spill his association with Trenaman in the murder.

Trenaman called the National Security Agency on an encrypted line and was put through to President Ganaffe's secretary. He secured permission to negotiate with Russell Vaderman regarding acquiring his skills, but the word was final: Brunner had to go. There were too many loose ends to cover if he survived. It needed to be visible, and it needed to be an accident.

Trenaman understood. He spared thirty seconds to feel sorry for the kid, and then turned cold and mission-oriented.

CHAPTER 34

Maya was in a panic. She knew she shouldn't have given Russell the biscuit. But Harris had been so reassuring about them. When she'd picked up the materials for both the small luncheon yesterday and the larger gathering tomorrow, Harris gave her the standard biscuits and then a small bag of "special" ones. For those who were not catching on as quickly, he said, she should use the cinnamon biscuits. He assured her everyone would love them and would love her, and he had been spot-on.

Last night, Russell had been so *difficult*! He wasn't seeing things properly at all. So, she had tried one of the special biscuits on him; was that so horrible? But she knew it was, and she was still shaking from it.

Maya had always known her husband was a formidable personality and that people instinctively did not cross him, but he had never been so with her. He could be stern on matters that were important to him, but he was generally so easygoing that while she often said she pitied the poor soul who ran up against him, she had received nothing but love and support from him for the last eighteen years. Russell had never, *never* unleashed that anger at *her*. He had barely ever raised his voice.

Now Maya was terrified. Terrified of her own husband. He had met her with such wrath, with such force—she still felt him in her head: *"STOP!"* What had he done to her?

She remembered how confused she had been, knowing with surety that he must comply and agree to accompany her to her event. Finding that he wasn't going to do so had made her dizzy, short of breath, and her heart had pounded. In that moment, she was sure she would stop breathing! And then… then Russell cut through it all and touched her head. No, he must have struck her, and very hard, because her head felt like it had been smacked with a brick. But for all that, she couldn't find any marks on her. And then she had started breathing normally again.

Her emotions were in turmoil. She barely slept, and stayed out on the couch all night, and at 5:00 a.m., she dressed, gathered all her supplies for the meeting, and headed out. She didn't know exactly where she was going, but she didn't want to think about coming home for a while. She didn't know if she could face him.

She sent Harris a desperate email and realized for the first time that she had no way of reaching him quickly in an emergency. She still felt her breath catching in her throat, but the sensation that she would simply stop breathing was gone. As if Russell's command had banished it.

Maya went to the ritzy Italian restaurant uptown. She didn't know what else to do, and every time she had met with Harris, it was there. Of course, the restaurant wasn't open at such an early hour, so she reluctantly sat in a Starbucks across the street, sipping tea. Mindlessly, she munched on one of the cinnamon biscuits. After a few minutes, she found herself angry at Russell for making such a commotion over something so harmless, tasty, and delicious. She certainly felt no ill effects from it. How was it that she had never known how violent he could be? To strike her, for God's sake. Perhaps she should see a divorce lawyer.

Thinking along this line brought her to wonder what her brother and sister, with their perfect families, would say. How mean they would be to her. Well, it was no matter. She wasn't going back to Texas anyway. They probably thought the police were justified in butchering minorities, especially Blacks. They affirmed anything and everything President Ganaffe did or said.

She was sure she would be entitled to half of Russell's money, and she would insist on taking Joshie with her. She was still his best protector, and she ardently believed he still needed a mothering spirit, even if he was already twenty-four.

When 10:00 a.m. finally rolled around, about four biscuits and much tea later, Maya walked back across the street to the restaurant. She felt a little unsteady on her feet, and she attributed it to getting virtually no sleep and being in an agitated state.

The restaurant still didn't look open, but she could see shadows of people milling around inside. She knocked on the door and waited. After a few minutes, she knocked again, louder this time. She *needed* to speak to Harris, and the way he was treated here, especially since he put everything on his tab, made her sure they would know how to contact him.

She cupped her hands around her face and pressed up against the window to peer inside. She jumped when she found a face staring right back at her. Maybe she should leave. But where would she go?

As Maya stood uncertainly near the door, it opened, and the *maître d'* she had seen on the last few occasions looked out at her.

"How may I help you, *madame*?"

Maya stuttered, feeling suddenly foolish.

"Harris. I need to speak to Harris. I don't know how to reach him, but it's an emergency, and I thought—I hoped—you would know how to find him. Please help me!" Maya realized she was speaking frantically, and it made her feel even more distressed.

The *maître d'* looked her up and down for a moment as if she were a puzzle. Maya blanched, sure she would be turned away.

"Come in, *madame*," he said instead, and Maya gratefully went inside.

She stood in the vestibule of the restaurant with her purse slung over her right shoulder and her bag of supplies for tomorrow's webinar hooked over her left arm. She fidgeted continuously, turning her wedding band around and around on her finger. What if Harris decided she wasn't up to this project and let her go? Maya was literally wringing her hands as the minutes ticked by.

Finally, the *maître d'* motioned her over to a table on the other side of the restaurant from where they usually sat. He held a chair for her and presently brought her some tea and bruschetta. Maya stirred the tea absently. She'd already had so much tea, she felt like she would float away, and the biscuits sat like a rock in her belly. She couldn't put a thing in her mouth.

After what seemed like forever, but was really only fifteen minutes, Harris came out from the back of the restaurant and walked toward her. Maya was shocked. Had he been there the whole time? No, there must be a back door. She was sure she heard the *maître d'* refer to him as Horatius.

"Maya, love." Harris took her hand and lifted it to his lips. "What has you so troubled, my dear?"

Maya was still trying to get her bearings. "You were here? Do… do you *live* here?"

Harris laughed and sat down. "No, of course not. But this is my family's restaurant. My family is from *Italia*. Now, tell me, what has you so upset?"

Maya wanted desperately to present herself as cool and rational, but she couldn't help it. She broke down. She told Harris everything that happened last night, and he listened with fascination. He didn't interrupt nor appear to judge, although Maya was sure she sounded hysterical.

She finally finished. "I should never have given him the biscuit. But he was being so cross and adversarial! Like he couldn't see our point at all! You've been right about everyone else, Harris—no one has been anything but agreeable and enthusiastic! What happened? And then when he came back out of the office, he hit me! And, and… well, it was strange. I actually felt better after he did. I could breathe again. Before that, I thought I was going to die! But then, I ran away. I've never seen my husband so angry at me, and he has never attacked me before. What do I do, Harris? I hope it's okay that I came here, I didn't know where else to go."

Harris stayed silent as Maya hiccupped and pushed her plate away. "Thank you for sending food, but I'm afraid I've been sitting in Starbucks and I was eating biscuits—the ones with the cinnamon. I had four of them, I think. I hope you don't mind—how could Russell have possibly found fault with them? They were delicious. And he only had one bite! And then he *accused* me… It was horrible, Harris, just horrible…." Maya hung her head in her hands, ashamed of her outburst, and sure Harris would be completely disgusted with her and send her packing. She was afraid to look at him.

When she finally looked up, she was surprised to see Harris looking amused. As if this were funny!

"You ate four biscuits this morning, did you?" Harris asked.

Maya thought she would explode. With everything she had just told him, *that* was what he chose to focus on!

"I'll pay you back for them…."

Harris waved his hand as if it were of no importance. "No, my dear, no need for that. But I would say you should probably not do that again. There may be some unhappy consequences. Beyond a stomach upset, that is." He continued to smirk slightly. Or was Maya imagining that?

"Tell me a bit more about your husband and his history. Do you think... perhaps he has been previously brainwashed by President Ganaffe and his cronies? You know, when one person receives suggestion from two opposing sources, it can be quite complicated. We are working on making our efforts stronger by using a slightly different concoction than the conservatives are doing."

"I don't think so. The most maddening thing about Russell is that he rarely gets fired up about *anything*."

Except for last night, of course, she thought. But Maya stopped for a second, realizing how true this was and that she had never realized it before. It was exactly what frustrated her about him. He would mostly agree with her on matters of humanity, he just wouldn't put much gusto into them. And yet, he'd give money, he'd make presentations at times that swayed people of influence, and he would work for change. He'd set up the soup kitchens from nothing. But he was never *emotional*. Maya was so emotional that Russell often infuriated her.

"So, he's never been subjected to any brainwashing techniques before?" Harris pressed her.

"Not that I know of. I don't think Russell *can* be brainwashed. We call him 'unflappable' because nothing phases him. He once told me it was because since he was a little boy, he made sure he took his sweet time deciding how he wanted to react to something. It made his life tough as a kid, but now, some say it's his greatest asset."

Harris was listening with extreme interest. "Has your husband told you anything about his experience with hallucinogens in South America?"

Maya's ears perked up. "Hallucinogens... I don't think so. Just the dream... wait, how do you know about South America? No one knows about that I don't know the whole story. I'm not sure Russell even knows; he rarely ever mentions it."

"Many powerful people know that your husband was

compromised in Peru as a very young child. President Ganaffe and his men have been watching him for years, but so far, they haven't found him to exhibit any special qualities that bear closer inspection. If he can identify and throw off these effects so readily, and if the government were to get wind of it, he could be in very grave danger." Harris sat back and crossed his hands in front of him and waited for Maya to speak.

She didn't know what to say. Her anger at Russell was dissolving, even against her will. Was he in danger? Her beloved husband? She started to collect her belongings. "I must go warn him," she said.

Harris put his hand over her wrist. "Easy there. Think. What will you say? Perhaps you should bring him here, to me, and let me speak with him. Better still, just ask him to meet you, and I will meet him instead. You should probably not be here when I meet him. He may still be very angry with you."

Something sounded off about that. Russell in danger, but Maya was not to tell him? Russell to meet Harris instead of her even though she would say she would be there? Russell wasn't even supposed to know about Harris or his organization, was he? But Maya's head felt lulled and finally calm after the drama of last night and all the dizzying biscuits, and the fear she had been feeling all night and this morning. She just wanted someone to tell her what to do. Harris's voice was so reassuring, and she trusted him completely by now.

"Okay, that sounds good," she said. "I'll set it up."

CHAPTER 35

Russell woke up and looked around warily. It was mid-morning and the sun was shining through the bedroom window. Maya was nowhere in sight, but the clock said 9:40 a.m. He had obviously overslept, which was uncommon in itself, and she had probably left early without waking him because she didn't want to face him after last night.

He swung his legs over the side and stood up slowly, testing his body. He felt normal, the effects of last night's drug and the vision were gone. He pictured the biscuit and wished he had kept it to have it tested. Perhaps there were more still in the house.

A careful search of the kitchen did not reveal any, and the bag Maya had carried them in was missing. He opened the trash. No, it had not been emptied. Taking out the garbage was usually Russell's chore, and today he was grateful for it. He fished around and found the remainder of last night's biscuit. He slipped it into a baggie and washed his hands, but as he touched it for that brief second, the memory flooded back in a rush. He sealed the bag, and the feeling was gone.

Russell showered quickly and dressed. He was too late to do his usual workout in the gym downstairs, so he headed straight out to New York-Presbyterian, biscuit in hand, to see his friend Jim Werner. While on his way, Joshua called and asked him to come to his mother's psychiatry appointment. Under other circumstances, he would definitely have declined, but after last night, he found himself almost eager.

Werner took the biscuit doubtfully but promised to have it analyzed.

"I'd much rather test you, Russell, and check you out thoroughly. Are you sure you're feeling okay?" Werner asked.

"I feel fine now, really," Russell replied. In truth, he knew that something about him was different, but he doubted it would reveal itself in standard laboratory testing, and discussing it with his friend Jim was not likely to be at all helpful. He might even get labeled a kook.

He chose to walk the twenty blocks to his office, trying to substitute it for his missed workout. The cool air on his face foretold that summer would soon be over, and he drank it in as he puzzled over the memories last night had brought back. As a small child, he almost never responded immediately to anything anyone asked or told him. If it weren't for the fact that when he did respond, he was so obviously bright, he would have been placed in remedial classes and passed over.

Russell's acumen in math, reading, and vocabulary as a little boy kept him from being labeled mentally challenged, but he had few friends because he often just nodded and took what most labeled an inordinately long time to answer anything. He was sifting through information, always. He remembered it well. If he had been born ten years later, they would have said he was "on the spectrum," but it just wasn't a popular diagnosis when he was a kid. As he got older, he became more efficient at this task and could process what was happening in his surroundings more quickly, and then have ordinary conversations and behave more socially "normal." He started to fit in more, and he stopped noticing himself as being so different.

Last night when the drug hit him, he automatically reverted to his childhood survival skills. It had been instinctive. And Russell was starting to feel certain that he had been drugged with a *Brugmansia* derivative. Scopolamine.

He went through his day on autopilot until 2:30, when he called an Uber to take him to the Village and Braelyn's apartment.

Russell walked in to find Joshua shifting nervously on the couch and Braelyn pacing with her standard frown. Joshua jumped up to say hello as Russell came in.

Braelyn studied Russell intensely for a long minute.

"You look like hell," she said. "What's wrong with you?"

Russell started. Did he really look that bad? Then he realized, Braelyn had many of the same skills he did, but in an undisciplined form; she could see right into people. It was a big part of what made her seem so contrary and antagonizing. Russell smiled thinly, the smile that Joshua would say was not *really* a smile.

"So, I get to meet your new shrink," Russell said, ignoring the question.

At that moment, a man knocked lightly on the door and walked in. He was small, about five feet six, clean-shaven, in a light brown tweed jacket. His shorter height belied a strong presence, and he looked around quietly, sizing up the group.

"Dr. Gray!" Braelyn said. Russell couldn't remember seeing her this happy to see anyone in a long time.

"Hello, Braelyn," Dr. Gray said. "I see you brought guests."

"Whoa," Russell stepped up. "I thought this was all planned." He turned to Gray and extended his hand. "I'm Russell Vaderman, Braelyn's brother. If I'm intruding, I apologize. I can leave." Russell turned to the door, feeling quite annoyed. It was just like his sister to ask him to show up uninvited.

"No! Don't go!" Braelyn nearly shouted just as Dr. Gray waved his hands in front of him.

"Please, Mr. Vaderman," Gray said, "I'm quite pleased to meet you. It's just unexpected, is all." He turned to Joshua. "And you must be Josh."

Joshua looked shy. "Mom just asked me to invite my uncle and I asked if I could stay too. I hope it's okay."

"Of course," Gray said. "It sounds like there's a lot going on, and I've wanted to meet Braelyn's family for a long time. I'm sorry it has to be under such..." He looked at Braelyn's ankle bracelet, "...circumstances."

Braelyn brought iced coffee, and they all sat down in the living room. Russell felt awkward, but Gray grabbed the reins and began with his voice very low.

"First off, Braelyn, as I said on the phone, it may be that you are being listened in on. Perhaps we could put on some music?"

"Cool!" Joshua jumped up. "Music always calms me down." Joshua went for the sound system.

Russell started to speak, but Dr. Gray put a finger to his lips until The Beatles were playing "She Loves You" loudly in the small apartment. Joshua joined in with own version of the chorus, singing, *"yup, yup, yup..."* as he bobbed his head and tapped his fingers on the coffee table like a drummer.

"What's with The Beatles, all of a sudden?" Braelyn asked her son.

Joshua shrugged. "I don't know. You and Uncle Russell like them; they're from your younger days."

Braelyn snorted. "You keep saying that. The Beatles were definitely before my time, Josh, but they are classic. You have good taste." Joshua blushed with pride, reminding Russell of how desperately Joshua needed his family's approval.

Joshua sat back down, and Dr. Gray didn't miss a beat now

that they were four instead of two. He began with an outline of why he thought they should take precautions to avoid being overheard.

Twenty years ago, the Department of Homeland Security had used all manner of untraditional methods to gather information from terrorists and suspected terrorists after 9/11. Some of that had taken the form of scopolamine as not only a truth serum of sorts, but, when used in larger doses, individuals were manipulated into going to their former contacts and doing anything from extracting further details about future attacks to murdering the cell's leaders. Frequently, these patsy zombie-suspects met with retribution from their own, but not until precious information had been extracted by means of wiretaps and surgical strikes against Taliban leaders were accomplished.

Gray further explained that the NSA had been overly interested in the specific formula used by Peruvian shamans, as it appeared more potent than straight scopolamine or pure Devil's Breath. When Braelyn told Gray that she had been given this drug when the family visited the *Curandero Grande* in the Northern Peruvian Andes to search for a cure for her mother's autoimmune illnesses, Gray's curiosity had been piqued. The story that Braelyn and Russell's father had tried to get information from local doctors upon their return, triggering interest from the DEA and NSA, had given Gray to wonder if the family was still on government radar *somewhere*, even though the event had taken place forty years ago.

"I wonder if our father *was* being watched, if that was the *real* reason he disappeared," Russell said. "I searched for him about fifteen years ago. I even hired a private investigator, but she couldn't find any trace of him, so I figured he'd started a new life and didn't want any reminders of us at all. But I remember the PI was totally puzzled. She said everyone leaves *some* trace of their previous lives, somewhere."

Braelyn stared at her brother. "I had no idea you did that. Why didn't you tell me?"

"You weren't well, Brae. It was the height of your…" Russell shrugged. "You were a big reason I tried to find him. I thought it would help you sort things out. When I came up empty, I didn't see the point of telling you."

Braelyn stared at him like she'd never seen him before.

Joshua kept looking from his mother to his uncle and back again. "That was when I first came to live with you, Uncle Russell, wasn't it? I remember you being really secretive. I thought it was because I was in the way and you didn't want to tell me."

"God, no, Josh, not at all!" Russell put his hand over his forehead. "Yes, that was around when I started to look, but I never meant for you to feel that way. I didn't want you to know because I didn't want to give your mom false hope, and I thought you might mention it if you knew. I didn't want to ask you to keep secrets."

Russell got up and walked over to Joshua and took him by the shoulders. "Joshua, please believe me. You have been such an incredible gift to me. You are the son I never had. You're my family, my blood. I love you."

"Yeah, but I wasn't part of 'the plan.' You only took me in because Mom…" Joshua threw a cautious glance at his mother, "…because Mom couldn't take care of me."

Dr. Gray stepped in. "Joshua, it seems to me that you have reason to feel very much loved. Your mother may not have been able to care for you well, but she loved you enough to let you live with your uncle and aunt who could, which allowed her to still be in your life. And from all that I have heard, your uncle and aunt loved you and raised you as their own."

Joshua dropped his head and nodded. "I don't mean to complain, Uncle Russell."

Russell sat back down. "It's okay, Josh. It's probably a

normal reaction, given the circumstance, right, Dr. Gray? You know, Maya and I—that's my wife—we talked about having Joshua go into therapy, but he seemed so well adjusted…"

"And I didn't want to!" Joshua said. "I didn't want to bother anyone any more than I already was."

Dr. Gray was surveying all of them. "You know, I think it would be a good idea to pursue this topic at a future date, but we really need to focus right now on Braelyn." He turned to her. "I now think it's quite likely that our federal government has been following both of you, and you, Braelyn, have been set up with the cocaine so they could steal the *borrachero* flowers. The question is why, and how can we help you?"

Braelyn started to cry. "Thank you, Dr. Gray, thank you for believing me. No one ever believes me. Russell, you didn't believe me!"

"Actually, I did believe you," Russell said. "That's why I posted bail. That's why I have Jeremy Southpine working on your case."

"Jeremy!" Braelyn said. "He's not even a friend of yours. He knows nothing about us!"

Russell chuckled. "I don't share our history with any of the people I know, Brae. It's private. Jeremy is a great lawyer. He looks under every rock and crevasse. He's chased down the cocaine they claim is yours and put an isotope tracer on it to see if it really originated in Southern Columbia. It's a stretch, I grant that, since most of the cocaine we confiscate comes from that region and that's where you were, but if it originated in, say, Bolivia, for example… Well, it doesn't prove it wasn't yours, but it makes it less likely that you obtained it near Bogota. It was Jeremy's idea to trace it."

Braelyn looked stunned.

Russell looked at Gray. "I don't know if it's connected, but Joshua was involved in an incident that resulted in the likely murder of one person, whose name we do not know, and there's still another boy missing." Gray nodded, as if this was not news to him, so Russell continued. "Josh had no memory of anything, so I asked to have his blood tested for scopolamine. It was positive. That means the Feds will almost surely need to be notified."

Braelyn looked even more astonished. "Why haven't you told me any of this?"

"These are all recent developments. I had planned to tell you today when I saw you. Also...." Russell trailed off and didn't finish his thought. He felt like he needed to get this out but couldn't seem to form the words.

They were all looking at him, and Russell felt tongue-tied and self-conscious. How could he even say this?

"Why *did* you agree to come today, Russ?" Braelyn asked after a minute. "I didn't expect you to say yes, that's why I wanted Josh to ask you. Something happened. Spit it out."

Russell took a deep breath and licked his lips. They had a long history of his sister seeing into his head the way Russell could sometimes see into others', especially when they'd been young children, but he wasn't used to feeling so uncomfortable. He tended to retreat inside himself and figure everything out before responding to anything, and he didn't see how he was going to be able to do that right now.

"My wife... Maya drugged me last night."

He couldn't say anything more. He saw the shock on both Joshua and Maya's faces. Perhaps he shouldn't have said it in front of Josh, but the kid was twenty-four, and whatever was going on, Joshua was up to his neck in it. He deserved to know whom he could and could not trust. They were all staring at him, waiting for him to continue, Braelyn with her mouth open.

"It was a cookie or a biscuit, or something like that," Russell said. "She wasn't going to let it go until I ate it. But after one bite...."

"What was in the cookie?" Dr. Gray asked.

"A hallucinogen. Something very similar to what we were given in Peru, I think. It felt very similar, anyway. I sent it for analysis this morning." Russell glanced at his sister. He wanted to continue, but found himself clamming up. Russell suddenly couldn't bring himself to talk about the dream that was not a dream, even though that was the primary reason he thought speaking to the shrink would be a good idea. It was as if he had just exposed a terrible weakness in himself, and he felt extremely vulnerable. The silence dragged on.

"Like the cookies at Cingulate Services," Joshua broke in with excitement. "They always want us to eat their stupid cookies."

Russell looked up sharply, remembering Joshua's story when he had described the events preceding his memory loss.

"None of this makes any sense," Russell said, giving up on expounding further. "All three of us have had encounters with some form of high dose scopolamine in the last few weeks. Do you have any ideas, Dr. Gray?"

Gray was gazing intently at Russell while stroking his chin, and Russell felt even more exposed. He *knew* Gray could tell he was holding back information, but the psychiatrist said nothing about it.

Russell's phone beeped and he looked at it almost gratefully. It was a text from Jeremy. He read it and brightened up.

"Good news, Brae." Russell read. "Jeremy got the court to lift the restriction on your movements. You can move about in Manhattan only. The bracelet has to stay on so you will be tracked, but at least you can get out and about. It's possible the investigation into the cocaine's origins have them realizing we're going to fight it, and this won't be quite the slam dunk they were expecting."

Gray's eyes went immediately to the bracelet. "Let me see your ankle, Braelyn." As she put her foot up on his lap, he put a finger to his lips again, and Braelyn and Joshua stifled giggles.

His finger moved along the bracelet. He released her leg and said softly, "you have a transmitter in the bracelet. I'm afraid none of your conversations have been private."

Russell went to the kitchen counter and took a newspaper flyer that was lying there, and some scotch tape from the drawer. He pulled apart the pages and crumpled and twisted them into a linear shape. Then he walked over to Braelyn and knelt down at her ankle, wrapping several layers of paper around the ankle bracelet and taping them loosely in place. "There," he said. "That should cause enough static to interfere with voice, as long as you move your leg periodically and speak softly."

Braelyn looked at him with tears in her eyes and suddenly flung her arms around her brother. "Thank you," she whispered. "Thank you for taking care of me after all I've put you through."

Russell softened. "Brae, you took care of me all those years. It was just the two of us, like forever. Remember?" She nodded, unable to speak.

Gray was nodding. "Okay, let's evaluate what we know. First of all, Joshua and Russell, I want you both to know, Braelyn is not crazy. Her mind has had to function with way more information than any of us normally do, and it's caused her tremendous difficulty." He turned to Russell. "Except I understand you had the same experience but learned to deal with it quite effectively."

"And he's taught me some of it!" Joshua broke in. "I want to learn more, except… well, except that it scares me."

"No doubt," Gray said. "It's pretty scary stuff."

All eyes were on Russell. He felt caught in a snare. He stepped back into himself, into his automatic behavior of silence. He couldn't have spoken if he'd wanted to. He had *not* dealt with last night. The room fell out of focus, and he sensed his own all-encompassing fear and confusion.

Slowly, quietly, Russell began to unpack the morass in his

mind. He picked at it gently with his mental fingers, careful not to "break" anything, just ordering his mind. He was familiar with fear *per se*, but he recognized *these* fears as being colossal. He stepped back and carefully separated them out, strand by strand, and tucked them away in a safe corner, isolating his emotions away from his intellect, and he felt his thoughts become crisper. He rolled his mental fingers over the hallucination of last night, aware abruptly that his panicked attempt to flee from it was exactly what was causing him to feel so muddled. He started to untangle the vision he'd had, and the clarity with which he knew that there was something real about it (that was the terrifying part). He saw again the face and heard the voice and he cringed, but then he straightened up and faced it slowly, as if turning very slightly toward a light that hurt his eyes.

Somewhere in the backdrop of his mind, he heard Braelyn calling his name, but just like when he was a very small child, he ignored it. Or, in truth, he was unable to acknowledge it while he was so busy mentally. He felt the shaman in front of him, knew he was in fact far away, and that somehow he could reach Russell over the distance. Something known in the paranormal world as an uncanny and farfetched possibility, and the sheer unlikelihood that the shaman would reach for him, *Russell*, so outlandish....

And then he remembered the words, propelled as images into his mind in some other language.

"You shall be a Curandero Grande..."

What had the shaman done to him? What had the ancient man pronounced upon him? Did Russell have control over the command, or did the command control him?

He saw it then. The blessing/curse that Russell was marked with that day in The Hut. His three-year-old brain... altered somehow under the spell of a ritualistic medicine man prophesied to have superhuman abilities. Abilities he seemed to bestow upon Russell to be awakened *when next the Holy Plants find you.* Well, they'd found him, all right. First through the odor of the *borrachero* plant in Braelyn's suitcase, and again through that tea biscuit. Russell was sure of it.

He had a fleeting memory of a similar feeling after someone gave him a soft drink as a teenager. The feeling had been so confusing, and Russell had accused the boy of trying to poison him. Those days, he would still get bullied from time to time. Funny, he had not recalled that until just now, but he'd felt weird for a few days afterward—like he was somehow bigger than himself. It was after that incident that he began to process his thoughts at lightning speed, and then he started to find himself surrounded by people who wanted to be friends with the "genius."

Russell opened his eyes. He had not realized they were even closed, and he had no idea how much time had passed. Braelyn, Joshua, and Dr. Gray were all staring at him. Only Braelyn was not worried. She was nodding slightly. She knew. She'd seen him do this before, when he was a little boy. How many times had she defended him against the bullies who accused him of being daft or mentally ill when he would retreat to his private place for sanity?

"You went *there*, didn't you?" she asked. "I haven't seen you do that in decades."

"Yes."

"Why? What sent you this time?"

"The dream... the dream that was not a dream. The vision. From last night...."

So, Russell told them about the hallucination that was more like a visitation. He told them about the dream he'd had a couple of weeks ago, which he now realized happened after catching the scent of the plant from Braelyn's suitcase. He told them about the prophecy, and about finding himself in Joshua's head when Joshua was blinded by the Devil's Breath. He told them that when Maya was holding her throat dangerously, seemingly unable to breathe, he had reached into her head and commanded her to stop. He stated his experiences in matter-of-fact terms; he did not ask them to believe him. He didn't know if he believed it himself.

No one said a word.

"I think I'm starting to understand what I do, in my head. To stay 'sane,'" Russell said finally. "Joshua helped me see it." Russell smiled at Joshua, who looked very serious, and like he knew he was being treated as one of the adults and wasn't sure if he wanted to run back to the safety of childhood instead. Russell turned to his sister. "I think I might be able to help you now, Brae. I never understood that part before. But…."

Russell sent a pleading look to Dr. Gray. No one spoke. The album changes and "Imagine" started playing. Russell's head felt like it was twisting sideways.

"Is this even possible?" Russell asked Gray. "What did this guy do to me? Can what I'm feeling—seeing—knowing in my head—can this be real? Have I lost my mind?"

Dr. Gray half shrugged. "I'm not in your head, Russell. I don't know. Do you feel like you've lost your mind?"

Russell put his hands on each side of his head. "I don't know!" He shouted. "I don't know what 'crazy' feels like."

Gray smiled and reached out to touch Russell's hand. "You seem quite sane to me, if that helps. As for whether it's possible… *something* has happened, so that question is moot. *How* it happened is another issue. The reaches and the abilities of the human mind are so minimally understood, but lack of understanding is hardly a reason to deny reality."

Russell relaxed a bit. So, he wasn't insane. But that meant… had he communicated with the man from The Hut? Was it a memory or a visitation?

Dr. Gray stood up. "We're going to have to stop here, but a lot has come out of this meeting. If the government gets wind of who and what you are, you could be in serious danger, Russell. And with that transmitter," Gray nodded at Braelyn's ankle, "figure you may have been compromised already. So all of you should stay wary and look around you at all times.

"Russell, I think it would be extremely helpful if you could share your understanding of your thought process with Braelyn, and perhaps a little more with Joshua as well, to protect them. All three of you have to ask yourselves why you've been targeted just now. Why did your wife try to drug you, Russell? What is her involvement in this? Why was cocaine planted on Braelyn? Why was Joshua dosed?"

As Gray turned to the door he said, "Russell, I feel you are a kingpin. You are immune to this drug. In fact, exposure seems to have made you stronger. I doubt anyone counted on that. Braelyn, you are probably also immune, but the scattered nature of your thought patterns has made you vulnerable in other ways, so try to learn and emulate what your brother does to order his mind. A vital question here is: has scopolamine been targeted at you as a family, or is it just that given your peculiar circumstance, you understand what's happening to you where others would not? In other words, is this an individual or a pervasive occurrence? Above all, be very careful who you trust."

Joshua looked very serious. "We should stay together, us three. Until we find out what's wrong with Aunt Maya. She was so happy last week, too! Getting promoted in her Undivided group and all. You know, Uncle Russell. What even happened to her?"

CHAPTER 36

Thomas sat in puzzlement at the bar. Trenaman had invited him out for drinks and made it sound quite sociable, but Thomas was sure it was not an invitation he could refuse. The last thing he wanted was to get friendly with the guy, or to learn any additional secrets to make it harder to leave on friendly terms once his job was done. If that were even possible at this point.

Right on time, Trenaman limped into the pub. He smiled an unreadable smile at Thomas and took a seat on the barstool; the height of the seat exaggerated his disability. Thomas tried to look away from his frailty and smile back at the same time. He was so confused and, frankly, so terrified, he thought it must have looked more like he was grimacing. He felt himself starting to shake.

Trenaman ignored Thomas's discomfort completely. He ordered a couple of gin and tonics and made small talk about the week. Thomas found himself unable to focus.

"Do me a favor, Thomas. Would you mind picking up one of

those menus by the door? This leg of mine is aching—I expect it's going to rain soon," Trenaman said.

Completely baffled but intimidated into complying, Thomas went to fetch a menu from the waitress at the entrance to the pub. This is crazy, he thought. Why not ask the bartender for one? Admitting such a weakness seemed out of character entirely, and since when had Trenaman ever called him by his first name? Red lights were going off in his head, and he told himself to stay vigilant.

Thomas came back and handed the menu to Trenaman who began to peruse it slowly. "Are you hungry?" he asked Thomas.

"No, not at all," Thomas answered, belatedly thinking he might be giving Trenaman attitude. Thomas picked up his drink and downed half the glass in three sips. His nervousness was looking for some outlet, and drinking seemed to satisfy two requirements. It gave his hands something to do and the liquor promised to calm his nerves.

Trenaman remained quiet, just browsing through the menu. He seemed to take forever, and time felt like it was stretching out. Thomas just wanted to go home. He finished his drink and after another few minutes, he spoke up.

"If it's all right with you, Mr. Trenaman, it's been a long day. I'd really like to be going home. Thank you for the drink," Thomas said, and worried he might be slurring his words. Could he be drunk on one glass of gin?

"No worries," Trenaman said. "It was very nice having a drink with you. You should definitely go. As you cross Eighth Avenue, you will wait for the perfect moment and throw your-self in front of the first large truck you see that is exceeding the speed limit, one going at least thirty miles per hour or faster."

"Okay," Thomas said. Something felt off, but he was so relieved to be getting away, he would have agreed to do anything the man asked of him, as long as he could leave. He got up and walked toward the door. It was like he was seeing the world through cellophane, and he felt an urgency to step out of the bar and walk to Eighth Avenue. Behind him, he heard Trenaman's lackadaisical goodbye.

"It's been a pleasure," Trenaman said.

Thomas nearly stumbled onto the street and didn't get his footing until he was outside in the open air. The breeze felt good, and the sun was just starting to set. He took a deep breath. The colors were so pretty. So out of sync with the smells and sounds of the city.

Thomas walked down 54th Street to Eighth Avenue and turned right. Traffic was coming toward him, and he could see the whole street. Cars and trucks honked their horns occasionally, and the air smelled like hot dogs and burned pretzels. He walked over a steaming subway grid, which was always an assault to his olfactory senses. He looked up over the tall buildings, catching another glimpse of the sunset, knowing the deep pink and orange actually bespoke air pollution, but it was gorgeous and the sky seemed pretty clear tonight. Thomas wished he were walking all the way to Battery Park to sit by the bay. Maybe he would. He could catch the ferry and ride it roundtrip to Staten Island, just to gaze at Lady Liberty. He used to do that sometimes when he first moved to the city.

He found himself thinking of his old girlfriend for the first time in a year. She used to love sunsets. Especially over the water.

Thomas continued downtown along the street, watching the traffic coming at him as he went. He weaved through the mass of pedestrians, most walking at a rapid clip, some smoking cigarettes as they went. Few people made eye contact, and everyone seemed to know exactly where they were going. Suddenly tired, Thomas stopped at the curb, halfway between 52nd and 51st. There was a newsstand to his left and someone selling gyros to his right. Across the street next to the CVS was a fruit market, and he thought about the fresh melon he had picked up yesterday on a whim. He was anxious to get home to it.

After a few minutes, he saw the ReadyRefresh by Nestle's water truck coming toward him in the left lane. It made him thirsty, and he wondered why his drink at the pub had been so unsatisfying. Thomas stood on the edge of the sidewalk as if he wanted to cross. Jaywalking was illegal in New York City, but people still did it, of course—just usually not on such busy roads. The driver looked right at him, and Thomas met his eyes and nodded. *Yup, I see you.* The driver gave a nearly imperceptible nod back and accelerated. Just as the truck was about to come parallel to him, Thomas took a flying leap in front of it.

CHAPTER 37

Maya headed back to the co-op in Sutton Place. As she got closer, she began to slow her pace until she was walking so slowly, people were looking at her funny. What would she say to Russell? Would he still be angry? Maybe he had forgotten. Maya had been surprised that many of her party attendees did not clearly remember the luncheon, even though they remained enthusiastically on board with the philosophy discussed. Russell had, after all, been drugged too. Maybe he wouldn't remember much.

Harris hadn't seemed terribly concerned about Russell's reaction, only that he might be in peril. So, either Russell wouldn't remember or he would, but he would be fine. Either way, he shouldn't be mad at her. She hoped.

She rode the elevator up to the thirty-third floor and hesitated before she turned the doorknob. This is *my* home, she told herself. I am entitled to be here. In the back of her mind was the tape that always played about Russell providing everything in their life, but she ignored it. They were married and that gave her half ownership. She walked in.

Russell was sitting at their baby grand piano by the window, playing *"Für Elise"* softly. Simple as it was, it was one of his Beethoven favorites, and he was rendering a slower, more melancholy version than his usual. Maya put her things down near the door and waited for him to finish before she spoke.

"Hello, Russell," she said. "Dear."

Russell turned and gazed out the window that looked onto Central Park without acknowledging her presence. Maya's heart sank.

Normally, Maya loved to listen to him play, but this was ominous. Panic was rising in her throat, like pure acid, and she was afraid she would vomit.

"Did you have a good day?" Maya tried again. Her voice was definitely squeaking now. "I—I'm sorry I left without saying goodbye this morning. I couldn't sleep, and I didn't want to wake you."

Russell turned to her finally. She tried to avoid meeting his eyes. Those deep blue eyes that held the mysteries of an ocean, eyes that could see right into her, into her heart and into her dreams, eyes that had charmed her from the day she met him. She strained not to look, but in the silence, she finally caved. And when her brown eyes met his blue ones, she felt like he locked onto her, and she was incapable of looking away. He held her like that for several minutes, without speaking.

Maya felt him tear into her then, and yet, Russell didn't move, didn't twitch, absolutely nothing. But Maya felt the layers of her soul open up and expose her for who she was and what she had done, knowingly giving him a tainted biscuit, all because she wanted him to agree with her. She watched helplessly as all her insecurities were laid bare, her fear that he wouldn't love her, that she did not contribute enough to their life and was a parasite, that she couldn't give him children… her lesser intellect, her need for acceptance that he never seemed to share. And the empty space in her heart that she yearned to fill but could not. All her secrets were somehow revealed in those few minutes, and Maya was left naked, frightened, and alone. And yet, neither of them had moved at all. Finally, Russell released her and looked away again.

"You're drugged," he said.

That was it. No mention of the evil Maya knew he had seen inside her, and no sympathy for her suffering. Just those two words.

Maya suddenly felt the strength leave her knees, and she stumbled to the recliner and sat. She literally couldn't hold herself up any longer.

"What?" Maya asked.

Russell did not look back at her. "You're drugged," he repeated. Then slowly, he shook his head and turned to her.

"You do know that, don't you? You were trying to drug me too, last night. *That* you were clearly aware of. What I don't understand is why? Tell me why." Russell turned his gaze on her full force again, but this time, she did not have that feeling of being reduced to a lump of emotion and failure. He was simply demanding an answer.

"I don't really know, I guess...," Maya said. "I'd been feeding the biscuits to the people at the party, and I have more for tomorrow's event... it seems to calm them down and I'm able to explain our political situation to them, so that... so that..."

"So that they'll agree with whatever you tell them, right?" Russell finished her sentence.

"Yes," Maya whispered. Then louder, "But Russell, you don't understand. The conservatives are playing dirty, using this substance to brainwash people. We have to even the playing field! We can't let them win."

"So, you play the same dirty game as they do?" There was ice in Russell's voice, and Maya cringed.

"No, Russell, it's not the same. This is for their own good. For our country's good."

"What happened to the woman who believed so fervently that every human being deserves to have their own voice? The woman who stands up for the rights of every individual? You're claiming to be doing what's best for *them*, but really, you are doing what *you* believe is best, and you are silencing the very people you have always wanted to set free."

Maya sat on the chair, her mind so confused, she felt again like she could not breathe. She felt frozen, locked in her head. Russell's words tugged at something deep within her that felt right somehow, but she couldn't reach it. She was lost, and suddenly she was spiraling, her mind spinning off like a tetherball whose rope had been cut.

Dimly, she became aware that Russell was next to her. His hands were on her temples, and the vertigo stopped. He seemed to hold her mind between his fingers, and he rubbed away the fog that had settled there as smoothly as Maya would wipe the bathroom mirror down with Windex cleaner. She hadn't even known she was behind a haze until it was gone.

When he was done, Russell got up and went to the fridge. He brought two sealed bottles of Dasani water and handed her one. She drank thirstily.

"What did you do to me?" Maya asked. She noted that her voice was lower pitched, normal even, without the note of hysteria that had been present before.

"I can't explain it. Not yet, anyway. I… I removed the drug effect. You were under its influence, I don't know for how long."

Maya *did* feel clearer in her head. She looked down at the water bottle. "I don't remember buying this," she said.

"You didn't. I'm not eating or drinking anything in this house that I didn't personally bring in and have the ability to track," Russell said. "Now, tell me what the hell you've been up to the last couple of weeks and how you got yourself into this mess."

Maya didn't know where to start. She still felt a little woozy, and she looked at him helplessly.

"Start with the biscuit. Where did it come from, and who told you to give it to me," Russell said. He was still not being kind, but that awful iciness was no longer in his voice, and Maya took heart.

She wanted to tell him about the organization that was affiliated with Undivided, but wasn't *actually* Undivided, and realized she didn't know what it was called. To her it was just Harris, and Harris was so charming, it didn't matter what he called his organization as long as she could be part of it. Yet she wasn't supposed to discuss it with Russell, she'd promised. Maya felt a tug-of-war going on in her head, and she felt she might freeze up again.

Again, Russell's hand touched her temple, and the panic receded. She felt the fear separate from the compulsion and then from the facts in her mind, and she remembered Harris saying he wanted Russell to come alone to meet him, so obviously it was okay if Russell knew about him. As Russell continued to hold her face in his hand, Maya *saw* the coercion that had been placed on her. It made her angry and she struggled against it, but Russell seemed to smooth out her rage and set it aside, as if to be dealt with later. He continued to detach the warring impulses in her brain, and when he was finished, she could see her own thoughts and ideas as distinct from Harris and the pressure to make people agree with their agenda. In a moment, the miasma cleared, and Maya saw what she had done. To her friends, her fellow citizens, and oh God, what had she done to her husband?

Maya turned to Russell, feeling a horror in her gut that she had never imagined. It all flooded into her; how she had been willing to sacrifice her husband and all of her values... it had been so easy to get sucked in, and she was filled with self-loathing. "Oh my God, Russell! What have I done? I could have… I could have hurt you… I could have turned you into one of Harris's *drones*…."

Russell gave her a peculiar half smile. "Welcome back," he said.

———

Russell was weary beyond measure. Whatever he was doing with his mind—now more and more casually, it seemed—was taking a toll. He was mentally exhausted. Part of him remained confused by the whole notion that it should be happening at all, but the process was becoming clearer, and the method by which he was touching other minds was crystalizing, even if he couldn't explain it with words.

Maya was fidgeting tearfully on the edge of the recliner, but she was once again in control of her thoughts and actions. A part of him felt he should get up and comfort his wife, and in the past, Russell wouldn't have thought twice about doing that. Rationally, he knew her choice to feed him the biscuit was largely a result of her having been deeply under the influence, for days, maybe weeks, but she had also admitted that she had not been specifically directed to give the tainted biscuits to him, only to her event attendees.

Russell stayed seated on the couch while Maya sat with her own thoughts, sniffling periodically, and he examined his own feelings. He knew Maya's penchant for emotionality, her passionate involvement in causes she believed in, and her propensity to be effusively loving, expressing all those warm, fuzzy emotions that did not come easily for Russell, and that was exactly what attracted him to her. He had always sympathized with the turmoil she went through, which he felt stemmed from her longing to erase the isolation that made her feel so insecure, one that every human soul struggled with. Yet she had always seemed to be a sheltered haven in his storm of mental managing. Now something was eroding. His trust, maybe? She no longer felt safe to him. He still loved her, of course, but something in their relationship had just died in him, and he wondered if he would ever get it back.

After twenty minutes of silence between them, Maya got up and announced she was going to make dinner.

"What would you like, Russell? Pasta okay?"

"No thank you, I'm not hungry," Russell said.

"But it's late. Did you eat at the office? You never do that."

Russell gave her a crooked smile. "Not quite ready to eat anything here, Maya. I'm sorry."

Maya started to cry. That had not been Russell's intention, but he was never one to pretend a truth. He thought of himself as actually very simple. Take the world as it is, a piece at a time, until he had a grip on what was real and what was illusion and had put all the parts together. He had adhered to that ever since he could remember. He recognized that many people were happy to fool themselves because it was an easier path, but it was never a simpler one. He supposed he could have said nothing, but eventually Maya would figure out that he had no intention of eating anything she prepared for him. At least not yet.

Maya came to the couch and sat next to him. "Russell, I'm so sorry! I will never do anything like that again, I promise. I didn't know what I was doing. I didn't understand what was happening to me. Russell, please! Please forgive me."

"I do forgive you," Russell said, knowing that it was true. Forgiveness and trust were two very different things. "Maya, you must learn how to prevent yourself from succumbing again. I think I might be able to teach you. But you will need to be exceptionally honest with yourself. When you think a thought, you must have the patience and integrity to look at it dispassionately, to determine if it is truly your own or was planted in your mind."

"You mean, with *every* thought? How…?"

"In the beginning, yes," Russell said. "After a time, you will begin to recognize the differences more easily. In particular, beware of snap judgments or phrases you hear others say. Your own mind will produce ideas that are of a different weight and texture, that will have been derived from your own considered beliefs and values. And before you adopt those views, ask yourself if you have all the facts you need to make a judgment. Too often people don't look further than the headline of an article or take the time to discover why some don't agree with their philosophy. Get the *whole* picture before you create an opinion."

Maya looked confused, and no wonder. Russell had developed this method over a lifetime. Maya was impulsive and emotional, and this was totally strange to her.

"I don't know if I can, Russ, but I will try."

Russell smiled, patted her shoulder, and got up to go to the bedroom, having no appetite for dinner. Maya jumped up and blocked his way.

"Russell, wait! I have to warn you. Harris says… he *says* you are in jeopardy. He says the government knows about you and your ability to resist this—this drug. Whatever else he is, Harris is right about that. He wants to meet with you, to help you. Russell, please meet with him. I can't bear it if anything happens to you. He can help you."

Russell looked at her with incredulity. "You really think I would meet this guy who brainwashes people, including my own wife?"

"But Russell, he can't do that with you, and he knows that. He has good, *liberal* intentions. He wants to spare our culture from the influence of the conservatives and President Ganaffe! Russell, you don't favor Ganaffe, do you? Ganaffe is racist, anti-science, and—and a menace! He accepts support from conspiracy groups, like QAnon, that spread lies and call us cannibals and pedophiles, just because that feeds his feeling of power. All he cares about is money and profit. Don't you see? The conservatives are trying to make us all hate each other!" Maya suddenly stopped and put a hand over her mouth. She calmed herself visibly, took a breath, and spoke quietly. "That *is* my own thought, I know it is. Russell, do you really support Ganaffe?"

"Of course I don't support Ganaffe," Russell said, looking exasperated. "You know where my heart is, Maya. But I am not going to stoop to the same malice of playing with people's minds and eliminating their freedom to make their own choices. Why would you ever think that I would?"

"But Harris is on *our* side! He is helping our cause!"

Russell touched her chin, gently this time. "Maya, darling. This is exactly the problem. Can you put your principles *before* your party? Don't 'pick a side' and follow it blindly. Instead, weigh your own values—with all their nuances. It's the only way to stop polarization. Almost nothing is black or white the way they want you to believe. If our society can't learn to do that…." Russell lifted his hands in the air. "Hate comes from both directions. Do you understand?"

Maya burst into tears. No doubt, a consequence of severe stress over her own mental faculties, which Russell had tampered with, and now Russell was suggesting she completely reorder the way she thought about life and politics, plus there were the aftereffects of being drugged. Russell wished that over the years, he could have found some way to help her feel more confident so she didn't have to seek out ways to prove herself. He also wondered if this struggle was not at the root of the human condition, including the political battle for supremacy on each side. Maya was not all that different from the average American, after all.

"Please, Russell," she said. "Just say you'll meet him and hear him out."

Russell didn't answer. Had he really expected her to think differently after one conversation? He turned and walked to the bedroom, his own exhaustion overwhelming him.

CHAPTER 38

A crowd was gathered at Pier 35 on the East River, a usually idyllic little esplanade with a view of lower Manhattan and the bay. It had been renovated and given the name Mussel Beach, and residents and tourists loved to come and sit on the benches to watch the water move in and out with the changing tide. Some took to rollerblading along the boardwalk as barges navigated the inlet. In truth, the East River was more of a tidal estuary than a true river, since the water did not flow consistently in a manner that would easily carry anything out to the ocean, even as it bordered the entire east side of Manhattan Island. It did make for a peaceful respite from the bustle of the city proper.

Today, the tide had gone out, leaving a figure washed up on the rocks. Police were called and began clearing pedestrians out of the way, and presently, a crane lifted and then deposited the body onto the boardwalk with a gentle thud.

The coroner gloved up and knelt to examine it, estimating it had been in the water for at least a week or two. Definitely a male, in his early twenties. They'd have to hope for matching DNA, dental records, or fingerprints on file somewhere to be able to make a positive ID; the face had swollen and was no longer recognizable and discovering the manner of death would likely be difficult, as evidence would be distorted by the water. Of note were faint cord marks or abrasions on the wrists where they appeared to have been strapped down or tied to something heavy. Given the location of its emergence, the body could have made its way into the river from anywhere along Manhattan, the Bronx, or theoretically, even on a circuitous journey from the Long Island Sound.

The body would be cross-checked with the long list of missing persons in hopes they could narrow down its identity.

When Officer Greenstone heard about a body uncovered from the East River and looked at his list of missings, Donald Anderson was first on his suspect list. Vaderman and his nephew had made quite an impression on him, with their white privilege and apparent assumption of special treatment. Greenstone was pretty sure the "dumb" act was just for show, and he was itching to put that Joshua kid behind bars. Maybe now that they had a body, since the kid was the last person to see him alive, they could nail him.

As instructed, Greenstone had tracked down the so-called counselors of the Cingulate Services group, and both had turned up dead. Wheeler died in an accident at Coney Island, falling out of the Ferris wheel. Apparently, he'd been so drunk, he had thought it cool to find a way to release himself from the safety bar. He should never have been allowed to ride it in the first place, and the whole thing looked suspicious to Greenstone. Men that age don't amuse themselves at Coney Island, not without a child—or at least a woman—along for entertainment. The other guy, Brunner, conveniently threw himself in front of a truck a couple of days ago. These were not normal New York

City deaths. Back to square one, and the only lead was the kid, Joshua Plessman.

He discussed all of this with his partner Rodriguez, who was less enthusiastic about the Plessman kid being responsible but had not offered a better explanation.

CHAPTER 39

Russell was walking to the office in the morning when a man fell in step beside him. The man was about Russell's height and walked with a subtle limp, but stayed abreast of him and kept the same pace. Russell sped up a little, and the man sped up as well, although he looked like the increased pace was uncomfortable for him. Russell slowed down, and so did his new companion.

Russell stopped short and turned abruptly to face the man.

"Who are you and what do you want?" Russell demanded.

The man stopped two feet away and seemed unfazed. They eyed each other for a moment, and then the man glanced past Russell to the doorway behind him.

"My name is Trenaman, and I would like a word. May I buy you a cup of coffee?" Trenaman looked pointedly at the door to Starbucks behind Russell, and then shifted back to focus on Russell's face.

"No, thank you," Russell said crisply, his new heightened awareness revealing the other man's discomfort standing on the street. "Whatever you have to say to me, it can be done without refreshments."

Trenaman looked amused." Okay, how about we sit inside, and I get a coffee, and you keep me company for a few minutes?"

"And why would I want to do that?"

"Because I work for the NSA, and your country has need of you right now, Mr. Vaderman."

They stared at each other. Russell was annoyed but not surprised that the man knew his name. He *felt* this Trenaman was telling the truth about the NSA, but he remained wary.

"If you prefer," Trenaman said as he flashed his badge, "I can make an appointment to see you in your office down the block, but I thought this would be more… discreet."

Russell glanced in the window of the busy Starbucks. There were a couple of empty seats near the back, but there was so much traffic in and out, it hardly seemed like much of a risk. Nevertheless, Russell found himself mentally rehearsing his black belt training in Tae Kwon Do. He hadn't been to a dojo in over a year, which he regretted at the present moment, yet this guy was obviously already handicapped. He gave a slight nod and they walked into the coffeehouse.

A table at the window vacated as soon as they entered, and Russell walked to it directly. He wanted to be as visible as possible. Trenaman joined him and did not bother with ordering coffee. Russell felt the other man's relief as he sat down. The shape of the leg under the trousers gave Russell the impression of a prosthesis.

Trenaman put his elbows on the table and crossed his fingers under his chin. "I'll cut right to the chase. I know a lot about you, Mr. Vaderman. In particular, I know where you spent your family vacation when you were three, I know about your peculiar talent and your apparent immunity to chemical influences, and I know you can teach others to resist drug-induced effects. I also know about your sister and her troubles. You have something your country needs; I have something to give you."

Russell kept his gaze steadily on Trenaman. He was getting a barrage of information in his usual fashion, but he was so much more aware of it now, and he struggled to unpack it without flinching. This would have been second nature a couple of weeks ago, so what was the matter with him? There was a lot to this man's story, and in his usual style, Russell wasn't saying a word until everything was laid out on the table.

Trenaman kept his gaze with a mixture of curiosity and amusement. When Russell didn't speak after a full two minutes, he continued.

"I have to say, it is a privilege to actually meet you, Mr. Vaderman. You've been on our radar for years."

The silence continued. "I'm waiting to hear what it is you want from me," Russell finally said.

"Something very simple—for you—and imperative for us. You know how to deprogram someone who's been dosed with scopolamine."

Russell considered he might have wanted that coffee after all. He broke the gaze and looked at Trenaman's hands, measuring how they moved and if they appeared to indicate he was being anything less than honest. He looked back up at Trenaman's face.

"What if I did? Who would I be 'deprogramming?'"

"Ah," Trenaman seemed to relax. "You would be teaching us how to do that, so that we could emancipate miscreants and spies from their compulsion to do harm to the United States. You would not be dealing with these malefactors yourself, but rather would be educating us so that we could do it without you. There is no need to involve you in sensitive information that would complicate your life. In return, you will know you have served your country, and you will be well paid and protected."

Russell smiled his closed-mouthed smile. "I'm sure you know, I don't need money. Financial considerations are not a temptation for me."

Trenaman bit his lip slightly and nodded knowingly. "But you are a man of known integrity who I should think would *like* to serve his country. And, of course, there must be something you *do* want."

"How long have you been watching me and my family, and why?"

Trenaman waved his hand in front of his face. "Details are not important. We have largely left you alone all these years. Do you yourself understand how you removed the block in your nephew's mind, and can you teach someone else to do that? That is all that is important to us. Teach us and we will continue to leave you in peace."

Russell's thoughts were on overdrive. What had this guy *not* said? He said they'd left him "largely" alone. Trenaman apparently knew what he had done with Joshua and that was in Braelyn's apartment, before they met with Gray and learned they were being listened in on, before they turned up the music and covered the ankle bracelet with crinkly newspaper.

It was suspicious that Trenaman hadn't asked what happened to Joshua causing him to have such a "block" in his mind in the first place, so he must have already known. Therefore, Trenaman had not left them completely alone. He had been spying on them, at least in part, with the transmitter in the ankle bracelet, but undoubtedly before that. The bracelet itself was from Braelyn's arrest at customs—for something she said was planted on her. Trenaman had to know about that as well.

"What do you know about my sister's troubles?" Russell asked. "And what is your involvement in them and with my nephew?"

Trenaman cocked his head to the side briefly. He seemed to

be trying to decide how much he should keep private and how much Russell would figure out anyway.

"I know she was found at JFK to be carrying cocaine—"

"No, you don't," Russell said. "If you know anything, you know that cocaine was planted on her. And something else was taken. I'd like to know why."

Trenaman smiled slowly. "We wanted the flowers."

His blunt admission took Russell by surprise. He placed his palms flat on the table. "For what? And why arrest her, why not just confiscate the *borrachero* flowers? Why plant the cocaine? If you really are with the NSA, you can have her cleared."

"We did it for leverage. And I *can* have her cleared," Trenaman said. "Is that your price for helping us?"

"I don't know," Russell nearly whispered. "Clearing my sister would be helpful, but since you are responsible for her arrest in the first place, it hardly seems much on which to establish trust or goodwill."

"Ah, but I do not need to establish anything of the sort, Mr. Vaderman. Consider that it is advisable for *you* to remain valuable to *me*. It could make the difference between life and death." Trenaman turned his gaze out the window and allowed that to sink in. "At the moment, we feel there is much to learn from both you and Braelyn Plessman. And perhaps your nephew as well." He turned back and faced Russell. "Let's pray that continues."

A chill ran up Russell's spine, and he sat back in his chair. He found himself *reaching* toward Trenaman in that weird mental way that seemed to be happening so frequently, searching for distortion of truth. He spared a moment to wonder if he had always done this but had only just become aware of it. He decided Trenaman was being honest but incomplete.

"You're not giving me the full story, and you're creating a precedent for future blackmail," Russell said. "Why did you need to steal the flowers if you were just looking to learn how to dispel them? And you haven't explained why you had my sister arrested on a bogus charge."

The two men stared at each other for over a minute. Russell knew Trenaman was sizing him up, deciding what he could lie about and what he should reveal. But Russell was evaluating Trenaman as well, on a much deeper level. Where were his strengths, his weaknesses, how committed he was to his cause? And Russell knew that Trenaman felt his probing. It was making Trenaman sweat.

Trenaman reached a decision. "The substance of the flower in both its natural and synthetic states is being used to guide the population on a rational course. Left to their own devices, human beings are restless, unruly, and prone to violence. My job is to assist in smoothing out the currents of society to bring about the greater good."

"Who decides what that greater good is?" Russell asked. Trenaman showed a flicker of surprise that his statement produced no astonishment on Russell's part, but he covered it quickly; he was a man used to playing with a poker face. For Russell, the idea of brainwashing on a mass scale synced so neatly with his discussion with Maya last night that he barely raised an eyebrow. "And how do you justify removing people's free will to determine their own life course?"

"People don't think for themselves anyway, and as such, they don't exercise their free will," Trenaman said. "I know you know this. They are like sheep. People will follow whoever has the loudest, most charismatic voice. They read only the head-lines, they don't bother to read the story. They are even less likely to evaluate the merits of those stories. They have already abdicated their right to freedom."

"In many cases, you are right," Russell said.

"In nearly *ALL* cases, I am right!" Trenaman said. "And you *know* this to be true. People are not inclined to put in the effort. They merely go along with what their friends say they believe.

They are damned from the start. They need a strong leader to guide them forward."

"But they have the right to choose that leader in a democratic process—"

"There *is* *no* democratic process, Vaderman! Your average schmo goes along with whatever his friends think, or his parents think, or—however *we* steer them to think. And then, they can steer others. That's how it's done. That's how it's been done for centuries. Occasionally, someone throws a monkey wrench into the machine, and it always results in unnecessary bloodshed. We've merely taken the reins in a process that has nothing to do with free will anyway. It is for the Greater Good. Trust me."

Trenaman finished his tirade, and Russell sat quietly unpacking it, as he always did. He had no doubt that Trenaman sincerely believed he was doing a good thing. Russell could even see the logic in it.

"Who chooses the future?" Russell asked.

"Our government. We are the paragon of freedom and justice. We lead the world in righteousness."

Trenaman sounded like such a believer that Russell would have expected to find traces of scopolamine on him, but when he had pressed his mind, Russell had found none.

"That sounds like the road to dictatorship," Russell said. "Do you trust that the people running our government will always make just decisions? It seems that of late, we have not been such a light unto the world. Children separated from their families at our borders, insufficient food, shelter, and healthcare for American citizens, prejudice against people for the color of their skin or the religion they practice, and the abandonment of our planet's needs in favor of profit for large corporations. We are hardly an example of righteousness. I have also heard President Ganaffe has stated he will not leave office even if he is voted out. That, in particular, is not the sound of a 'great democracy.'"

Trenaman fired back. "Would you have us leave our borders

wide open to any terrorist or criminal who wants to cross? Do you know how disproportionate our contribution to the Paris Accord has been? Do you understand how many people still could not afford healthcare under the Affordable Care Act?" Russell could see Trenaman was enjoying this discussion.

"Vetting who comes into our country is obviously important. But taking little children from their parents… you may as well breed a generation of people who hate us and are destined to form the next revolution—there are ways to manage our borders that are humanitarian. Relegating the fate of the Earth to corporate moguls is a suicide mission for the entire planet, and not providing for our elderly and our sick is unconscionable in a country as wealthy as this one. Under the current government, this 'great' country is behaving like a petulant, self-interested adolescent, more concerned with the accumulation of wealth and power than the practice of kindness. We have become a country without a heart, with a leader who blatantly and unapologetically distorts facts and lies to the public. So," Russell continued, "you haven't answered my question: Do you truly believe in the worthiness of the people running our country?"

Russell saw Trenaman hesitate. He'd hit a nerve.

"I've been a Navy man all my life. I believe that order comes from discipline. If officers question what our superiors do, we flounder. I've devoted my life to serving my country. So to answer your question, it doesn't matter what I think about our leaders. They are our leaders."

"Kind of like the Germans who were 'just following the orders of the Third Reich…,'" Russell mumbled quietly, but Trenaman heard him and grew angry.

"Tell me I'm wrong! Tell me people actually think when they take a stand! Liberal protesters get riled up over a few unfortunate incidents and respond with bullets aimed at masses of innocent people."

Russell raised an eyebrow. "And you tell me why we have a

president who encourages civil conflict and white supremacy. Tell me how you can support leadership that gives false information to the public in order to be elected."

Trenaman's demeanor changed, and he lowered his voice ominously. "You cannot tell me that people weigh the pros and cons of a bill that is brought to Congress, or that your average person bothers to think through why a tax is proposed on *any* given article rather than simply reacting when someone suggests they shouldn't be paying it. The masses simply jump to conclusions, usually based on whichever slant the media applies in their favorite rag."

Trenaman rubbed his hands together. "You're a smart man, Vaderman. Have you ever noticed how people want full services but do not want to pay any taxes? Americans believe they are innately privileged, entitled not just to 'Life, Liberty, and the Pursuit of Happiness,' but to comfort, convenience, and a clear conscience at no personal cost." He leaned forward across the table. "We are merely harnessing the emotions of the people who *do not think for themselves anyway.*"

Russell frowned. "You're right," he said. "About most of that, you are right. There is no longer any obligation for news media to report on both sides of an issue, and both sides take advantage of that. But you're taking the easy way out. The people need to be educated. They need encouragement to spend the effort understanding what's at stake in any given matter before they make up their minds. It's not about 'your' way or 'their' way. The population must learn to evaluate the issues in totality, and find their own minds. And then the liberals and the conservatives might discover they're not so far apart after all."

"You're dreaming," Trenaman said. "It will never happen. Your average human being has relinquished their free will because it's not worth their time to seek the truth. They are already damned."

"Perhaps," Russell said. "But by using a drug to enforce the mob mentality of President Ganaffe's choosing, you have removed from the population even the *possibility* of redemption."

Trenaman stood up abruptly. "It's too late for redemption, Mr. Vaderman. The liberals are doing the same thing we are. If we stop now, we lose. Think about helping us. Think about serving your country. You will soon find that the obstacles in your life may be too great to surmount without my help. I will be in touch." Trenaman limped out the door.

CHAPTER 40

Officer Greenstone sauntered into Detective Rodriguez's office with his usual smirk amplified and sank into a chair.

"We have confirmation on the body found at Mussel Beach," he said. "It's Donny Anderson, all right. The kid needed a wisdom tooth extraction a few months ago, and weird as it is, he kept the tooth. Parents found it in his bedroom drawer, and we compared it to DNA from the body. It's the kid's, all right. I'm going to go find that Plessman kid and link him up."

Rodriguez looked up from the notebook he was reviewing. "Why?"

Greenstone was incredulous. "Why? Because the Anderson kid is dead, and Plessman is the last person to see him alive, that's why."

Rodriguez frowned. "Did you find any of Plessman's DNA on the kid? Or in the subway? He already gave us a statement and told us he saw Anderson. Do you have anything to connect him to the East River?"

"No," Greenstone said. "But he already admitted he saw

Anderson covered in blood, and instead of trying to help, he hid underground all night. Also, there was a call made to Plessman's cell phone on Monday night from a phone registered to Peter Jackson. No one has seen Jackson for weeks. Why hasn't Plessman mentioned this? There's more to this story than what he told us, I know it. He's holding out on us."

Rodriguez shrugged. "Okay, bring him in for questioning. Maybe his memory has been jarred since we last spoke."

"And maybe if he can't hide behind that uncle of his, he'll start spilling his guts," Greenstone said and spat into the garbage can.

———

Joshua was on Sixth Avenue, just heading back into Vaderman Ventures, when a police officer stepped off the curb and collared him, and then yanked Joshua's arms behind his back. Joshua felt hard metal on his wrists.

"Going somewhere, Plessman?" Greenstone appeared behind them and patted down Joshua's pockets and shirt. He took Joshua's phone. The other officer wrenched Joshua's arms back harder. The cuffs were tight.

Joshua started to panic, and the more he struggled, the more his wrists and shoulders hurt. He asked to call his uncle, but the officer pushed him into the back of the police car and said he could call from the station.

The ride was terrifying. Joshua was sure he had done something horrible, but he had no idea what it was. If only Uncle Russell was there, he always made everything okay. When they got to the precinct, Greenstone hauled him roughly out of the car and into the building, and then threw him in a room with a table and two chairs and chained him to the steel table that was bolted to the floor. There was a large mirror against the wall that reminded Joshua of the one-way windows he had seen on *Law &* *Order*.

Was he under arrest? No one had read him his rights, so he couldn't be under arrest. He tried to remember an episode on television where someone was in a room like this and was not under arrest.

Greenstone put his face close to Joshua's. "Where is Peter Jackson?"

"Who?" Joshua asked.

"Why did you kill Donny Anderson?"

Joshua just stared at him. It was like years ago, when he would get so frightened that he couldn't think straight, and everyone called him stupid. That was before Cingulate Services. Before Donny. Before he got "smart." But, was Donny dead?

Joshua tried to ask about Donny. He tried to ask for his uncle. He knew he had never heard of any Peter Jackson. He tried to be really grown up and ask if they had arrested him. But nothing came out of his mouth. His voice cracked and he started to shake, and then he started to cry. Eventually, Greenstone left, looking quite satisfied with himself.

Joshua sat in the room alone for at least a half an hour, and finally Detective Rodriguez came in and sat down across from him. Joshua thought he was mean the last time they'd met, but Rodriguez looked softer today than Joshua remembered. At least compared to Greenstone.

"Hello, Mr. Plessman."

"Can I speak to my uncle? Is Donny really dead? Why did you bring me here? Why did you handcuff me? I know I'm not under arrest because no one read me my rights. You're supposed to read the rights if you arrest someone, right? What did I do?" Joshua had found his voice, and the questions spilled out of his mouth.

"Should you be under arrest?"

"Well, I'm in handcuffs." Joshua's voice was shrill.

"Officer Greenstone didn't read you your rights because you haven't been charged with anything, Mr. Plessman. We just want to talk to you," Rodriguez said.

"Then why did he handcuff me? He could have just said he wanted to talk to me instead of putting handcuffs on me." Joshua pulled at the cuff on his right wrist that was chained to the table, and it clanged loudly. "I'm supposed to get a phone call too. I want to call my uncle. Please let me call my uncle!" The more Joshua said, the more hysterical he sounded.

The detective looked at the chains and frowned, making Joshua even more frightened. Then he got up and walked out. Through the open door, Joshua could see Rodriguez give Greenstone a glaring look, then shake his head before he came back with Joshua's cell phone and some keys. He unlocked the handcuff and Joshua was free, but the table and the detective were between him and the door.

"I'm sorry if Officer Greenstone was rough with you, I'll speak to him about it. We really do just want to talk to you."

"I want to call my uncle!"

Rodriguez handed over the cell phone and Joshua called Russell, his hands shaking. It rang five times, but there was no answer.

"Look, Mr. Plessman… It's Joshua, right?"

Joshua nodded. He was trembling and sweating and gripping his phone like a life raft.

"Look, Joshua. We just wanted to get some additional information from you, now that we found Donny Anderson's body."

"Body…?" Joshua's voice was barely a whisper. "Donny really is…?"

"Yes, I'm afraid so. Your friend Donny is dead. I need you to tell me again what happened the last time you saw him."

Joshua licked his lips. He tried to speak, but he couldn't think straight. Donny was dead! He started pulling on his hands and found the phone in them, so he looked down at it and dialed his uncle again. Another five rings, and no answer. It went to voicemail, but he did not leave a message. Tears came to his eyes. Where was Uncle Russell?

"I told you everything already."

Officer Greenstone barged back into the room. He picked up a chair and threw it against the wall. Rodriguez was not especially kind, but at least he hadn't been mean. Greenstone seemed so angry, and Joshua had no idea why. Joshua was terrified of him.

"Spill!" Greenstone said and glared at him.

Joshua squeezed his eyes tight. He tried to remember what Uncle Russell had done with him in his mother's apartment. Joshua could sort of see the bright ball of confusion that had blocked him before, how it had been smoothed out, and now it was balling up again. Only this time it was different. This time Joshua was doing it himself, he knew he was. It wasn't from a drug. The more Greenstone glared at him, the more pressured Joshua felt to answer, which made him panic, and the more he panicked, the more tangled the ball became.

Joshua tried hard to remember what else had happened while Mr. Brunner was speaking to him. He remembered seeing Mr. Wheeler talking to Donny, but he hadn't heard what they were saying. He'd been too shocked to find the body, the blood, and then to see his counselors.

Greenstone spat on the floor and grabbed Joshua by the shoulders. "C'mon, you little prick, you told us nothing. Anderson's mother says her son went out on Monday night and never came back. But *you* saw him that night; you told us that. So, what happened to him?"

———

Maya sat alone in her living room, thinking they should have gotten a dog or cat when Joshua had begged them to years ago.

The weekend had passed without much further exchange between her and Russell, and Joshua was spending an inordinate amount of time with his mother these days.

The event Maya had hosted for Harris had gone well. Everyone loved the refreshments and the video, and there was a lively discussion about voting rights and how the protesters were entitled to damage some property because lives were worth so much more than material things. One person had complained that his friend's business was destroyed and now had no way to support his family, but he was practically booed out of the room. Several people signed up to help register voters who might otherwise not take the trouble. They were never going to get Ganaffe out of office if they didn't get their constituents to the polls. Maya *should* have felt accomplished.

She reported back to Harris that all had gone well and tried extra hard to appear dignified to make her breakdown from a few days ago a thing of the past. She was embarrassed by her behavior. She also felt not quite the same in her head since Russell had slapped her two nights ago and then she had eaten all those biscuits the next day. She *guessed* Russell was trying to help her, since he seemed to understand later, but she couldn't overcome the shock. And the question loomed ever-present in her mind… *had* he slapped her? How could she be so unsure about something like that?

It was all still so muddled in her memory. Russell was never violent—he was barely emotional at all. Why did she keep thinking he hit her? And then the next day, he hadn't *really* gotten inside her head, he had just explained things, right? For the tenth time, she examined her face in the mirror, looking for bruises and finding none.

Ultimately, she broke down and called her best friend, Katrina and told her that she and Russell had a terrible argument. She didn't go into a lot of detail—also not normal for her, because she usually gave the long version of any events that upset her. But Katrina had family visiting and wasn't able to talk for long, and Maya felt so guilty about sharing anything since she had promised Harris not to speak of their organization, and she and Russell *had* sort of made up, that she did not press it. Katrina apologized and assured Maya they would catch up in a couple of days, so Maya sat in the house wishing she had a closer relationship with her siblings.

Maya bemoaned again that she had not been able to have her own children and the big family she always dreamed of. She wished she had pursued a separate career from her husband so they would have something fresh to discuss over the dinner table. She wished she had gone for her MBA, so she could feel more equal to him. Although, how could she ever be equal to Russell Vaderman? He was superior to her in every way, especially mentally. Maya piled it all onto herself, one personal failure after another, until she thought she might be better off dead.

She went to the minibar and poured herself some apricot brandy. Russell kept the brandy for entertaining guests, along with a supply of gin, scotch, vodka, and a variety of mixers. Strange, actually, since Russell almost never drank. Russell was always completely in control of himself, and Maya was often such a mess. And she knew he saw that, especially "that" night —he had seen it so clearly. He had seen right into her. And he wasn't even surprised. Like he had always known. She felt humiliated all over again every time she thought about it.

The phone rang; it was Commissioner Harrows looking for Joshua. Joshua was not there, of course. Just Maya in one of her moods. She suggested he try Russell or Joshua's mother.

The commissioner wouldn't tell Maya what the call was about, and Maya was puzzled that he had called their home. Why not call Russell? Or work? The strangeness of the call took her mind off her personal troubles, and she dialed Joshua's cell, but after a few rings it went to voicemail.

CHAPTER 41

Russell stepped out of the elevator at Vaderman Ventures, still shaking slightly from his encounter with Trenaman. He'd been threatened before, with court actions, or by street kids near the soup kitchen, and by extremists on both sides who objected either to his wealth or to his support of the indigent. He had never been threatened by the US government.

As he walked by Rosalee, she gave him an exceptionally friendly smile.

"Good morning, Mr. Vaderman! That friend of your wife's is here. I let him wait in your office."

Russell stopped short. "What friend of my wife's?"

"Why, Harris, of course," Rosalee said. "Here, have a chocolate truffle. He brought us a whole box. I know you don't usually eat chocolate before lunch, but these are *so* good. They're hand-made!"

Russell looked at the box of chocolate and at Rosalee, then at the door to his office. He grabbed the box and, pivoting on his heel, stormed into his office.

A man was lounging in one of the oversized chairs, gazing out the high-rise window as if he hadn't a care in the world.

Russell closed the door and walked to his desk. He tossed the box of chocolate into the trash and looked around. He took in his immaculate desk and the mild-mannered, forty-something-year-old man with the round glasses and disheveled hair all at once. Nothing looked out of place, but his desk *felt* wrong. He found himself sweeping the contents of the drawers with his mind, without even opening them, and noted the lower right drawer had something in it that didn't belong. He said nothing to the man in the chair, who had started smirking quietly when Russell tossed the chocolates, but went right to the drawer, opened it, and removed a small roll of Scotch tape that did not belong to him. He threw it on top of the desk.

Suddenly a wave of vertigo came over him as he realized what had just happened. How had he done that? What was *happening* to him? He put his hand to his forehead and felt a buzzing in his head.

Harris looked alarmed for a moment and shifted uncomfortably. "That was very impressive," Harris said. "I didn't see any cameras in here."

"Oh, there are cameras, be certain of that," Russell said, relieved to be able to brush it off as if it had a logical explanation. There were, of course, cameras that surveyed the entire room, but they were discretely hidden in crevices that blended perfectly into the walls. Russell wasn't an architect for nothing. Fortunately, this man would have no way of knowing that Russell had not actually accessed those cameras just now.

The buzzing started again, and he turned to his pocket. His phone showed a call from Joshua. He silenced it and turned back to Harris, who was pristinely dressed in a dark gray designer suit with matching tie and ash gray shoes. "What are you doing in my office uninvited?"

"Oh, but I assure you, I was invited. Your charming secretary showed me in and said I could wait for you inside." Harris rose and extended his hand. "My name is—"

"Harris. Your name is Harris. And Rosalee wouldn't let the FBI wait unattended in my office for me unless *I* gave her explicit instructions to do so. So cut the bull," Russell said. He ignored the outstretched hand and kept his voice quiet and even, but he was filled with fury.

"Perhaps I can be more… persuasive… than the FBI." Harris smiled again and dropped his hand.

Russell picked up the Scotch tape and examined it. He ran his fingers over it for a moment until he realized it contained a tiny transmitter in the center. He pulled the minute disk out of the tape cartridge and squeezed it hard, wishing he had a hammer close by so he could smash it. The uncharacteristic intensity of his emotions was unnerving him, and a faint visage of *El Curandero Grande* swam before his eyes.

When next the Holy Plants find you ….

Russell rubbed his temples and shook his head to clear it, and his phone started vibrating again. At least he knew it was the phone this time and not the "Man in The Hut" buzzing in his brain. He saw Joshua's caller ID and silenced it again.

"What do you want?" Russell demanded. He perched on the edge of his desk directly in front of Harris and folded his hands in front of him.

Harris turned serious. "I am here because your life is in danger, my friend. I am here to help you."

"You are not my friend, and you are not my wife's friend."

"Ah, but I am, Mr. Vaderman, if you only knew. Strange things are afoot in your life. The NSA is on your heels, and they can be even more 'persuasive' than I can."

"So, what? You're going to drug me and everyone in my life into a stupor so I won't be bothered with any of it?" Russell swept his arm toward the door and Rosalee's desk beyond.

"Nothing of the sort, Mr. Vaderman. May I call you Russell?"

Russell did not answer.

"Very well, then. Mr. Vaderman. We are building an army. An army to defend the American people against the dark influences of the conservatives and our government. Against those whose primary concern is the wielding of power and the attainment of wealth. It has become clear that this movement has targeted you for your… uh… abilities, so it was necessary to get close to you. We do not want you to fall defenselessly into their hands."

Russell was starting to feel the vertigo again. He was getting the usual influx of information from Harris: words said and unsaid, body language, hidden meanings versus the stated agenda, and their implications for Russell's life and current reality. He couldn't quite separate the emotions from it, which was a cornerstone of how he evaluated his life, but despite that, he seemed to be processing it all at lightning speed. He knew Harris was showing a completely different side of his character to Russell than he had to Maya, almost as if Harris were two separate people.

The image of an ancient man with paper-thin skin, opaque eyes, and white hair and beard that practically glowed in a misty light hung before his face just out of reach. Russell was so nauseated, he thought he might start retching at any moment.

Russell walked stiffly to his chair and sat down behind his desk, trying to hide the weakness he was feeling in his knees. "How do you think you can help me, and why do you think I would want you to? What's in this for you? After you drug my wife and my secretary and place a bug in my office, you expect me to trust you?"

"Your dear Maya was a bit overly enthusiastic, that dose was never intended for her. It became necessary for me to come in to see you myself." Harris chuckled. "It's good she did not eat too many more… Please understand that those tea biscuits were never intended for you either, for that matter. She indulged in them quite on her own and offered them to you without my knowledge."

"But you have been intentionally dosing her," Russell said flatly. Harris gave a half shrug and said nothing.

"The drug you are using is scopolamine, which is lethal at high doses. The biscuit is being analyzed as we speak, so there's no point in lying or trying to hide it."

"I do not lie, Mr. Vaderman, you will learn this about me. Sometimes I have need to stretch the truth for a short period, but I always come clean." Harris stretched out his legs and crossed them. "Yes, it is synthetic scopolamine. Our rivals are using the same and also experimenting with several species of the natural flowers themselves and searching additionally for the other 'ingredients' that were mixed with them in more ancient times. There is evidence that a particular recipe could confer upon a human quite unusual, paranormal abilities."

Russell kept his face impassive, but his mind was running a mile a minute. He had long ago learned that in a face-off, the first one to blink, loses.

Harris shrugged. "You may have some knowledge of what I am referring to."

Russell's vertigo was starting to subside. "Why are you here, Harris? Just to bug my office?"

"I am here because I am sure that the NSA will be contacting you. I think we both know they have been watching you. Once they discover you are immune to the effects of standard scopolamine, to them, you will become either an asset or a threat. Assets they acquire; threats they eliminate. I would like to help you appear to be an asset, which could save your life. But I also want to convince you to resist them. Their priorities are not aligned with the integrity and compassion for which you are known."

"So, you want me as *your* asset," Russell said.

"Of course," Harris said. "I told you I will not lie to you.

More to the point, I would like the opportunity to present our goals and let you pass your own judgment. I hope that you find them more favorable to society than those of President Ganaffe's."

"Who are you? Who funds you? And what are your objectives?"

Harris straightened up in his chair. "I would like your word that this conversation will remain confidential. Whether you decide to sign on with us or not."

"I'm not making any promises," Russell said.

Neither spoke for half a minute. Finally, Harris shrugged. He sat up straight in his chair and interlaced his fingers in front of him. "No matter. We are the 'opposing party' to those currently in power. We oppose actions that compromise the planet and its inhabitants, especially the human race. Anything that infringes on the rights of individuals, based on gender, skin color, religion, or social status, or that contributes to global warming by raping the planet of its resources in order to put money in the pockets of big corporations, is a threat to life on Earth. We oppose that. To that end, we are fighting back at administrations that encourage conflict between peoples and extortion of planetary resources. Our aim is to work in harmony with our planet and our neighbors." When he finished speaking, Harris brought his index fingers up to his chin and waited.

Russell huffed. "That is quite an eloquent speech. It seems you should hardly need my help in inducing anyone to follow you. In fact, why do you need to use drugs to convince anyone of your rectitude? It all seems pretty self-affirming."

"Perhaps, Mr. Vaderman, to you and to me. And to many others. But to those who think only in the short term, the prospect of making money is too seducing, or the effort of changing their livelihood from the only lifestyle they've known is too frightening or cumbersome, and it creates a blind eye. The coal miner does not want to learn how to manufacture solar panels. Add to that the conservative's use of pharmacological persuasion, and you have the mess we find ourselves in. We have no recourse but to fight fire with fire."

"So, you feel justified in using the same pharmacological persuasion as those you criticize?" Russell asked.

"Unfortunately, we have been forced into it. We begin with the dry run on our own like-minded people, and then place them strategically to battle those who do not care to see beyond the next quarter's earnings."

Rosalee's voice came over the intercom. "Mr. Vaderman, Commissioner Harrows is here. He asked if you would meet with him. I told him he must try the chocolate truffles!"

Russell frowned. "Ask him to please give me five minutes, Rosalee, and I'll be right with him."

Russell turned back to Harris. "This makes no sense. How can so many people stay in a drugged state for that long? If you keep dosing them, aren't they more likely to follow whatever suggestion next comes their way?"

"Excellent question," Harris said. "The government uses key words, phrases, and events as triggers to reignite the basic command. So that if someone has been 'programmed' to support racial discord, it is amplified every time they encounter the trigger, and reinforced when they encounter the drug. Even if there is no representative present, after a short time, the movement becomes self-propelling."

"Sounds disturbing, if it's true. What do you want from me?" Russell asked.

"For the moment, I want only to help you. Consider me a resource. It is unclear what tactic the NSA will take but be sure they will pressure you. I work with very powerful people with influence in many places."

Russell stood up with an air of dismissal. "Stop drugging my family, employees, and associates. Otherwise, we will have nothing to talk about. Now, this has all been very interesting, but you've taken enough of my time; I must get to work," Russell said.

Harris stood up. "Very good, I will let myself out." Harris placed a card on Russell's desk. "You can reach me here," he said. "And Mr. Vaderman. Take care with whom you discuss these things. You should know that the conservatives have infiltrated… pretty much everywhere." Harris' eyes flashed to the door and the waiting commissioner.

Harris walked out of the office as Russell's cell buzzed again with yet another call from Joshua.

Russell picked up on the fourth ring.

"Thank God, Uncle!" Joshua sounded beside himself. "I've been arrested, Uncle Russell. Please come down to the precinct and help me. They handcuffed me and everything, but then they uncuffed me and said I wasn't arrested—"

"Wait. What? Slow down, Joshua. Where are you? Why did they bring you in?"

"I'm not sure. But they found Donny, and he's dead! They think I know how he died, but I don't. I swear I don't. All I remember is Mr. Wheeler talked to Donny while Mr. Brunner talked to me. Then Donny left, I think, and I stayed because he told me to. But I don't know where Donny went or why. I'm scared, Uncle Russell!"

"Hang tight, Josh. I'll be there shortly. Same precinct we were at last week? And this is important: Don't say anything to anyone, Joshua. Don't talk about Donny, don't answer their questions about *anything* at all, do you understand? Just say you're waiting for me and for your lawyer, and I told you not to say a word until we get there."

Russell hung up and asked Rosalee to let the commissioner in.

———

Walter Harrows walked in the office and looked around. "Wow, Russell. I haven't been in here since you redecorated. Very nicely done."

"Thank you," Russell replied, as they shook hands. Russell indicated for Walter to take a seat. "Can I offer you some coffee or a vitamin water?" Russell noted that his hand tingled slightly at the handshake.

"Oh no, thank you. I did hear something about some exceptional handmade chocolates, though." Harrows grinned.

Russell frowned. "Trust me, you don't want any of those."

Harrows mocked a pout. "Too bad. I love chocolate. Well, this is just a courtesy visit. I want to talk to you about the scopolamine found in your nephew's blood test. We did notify the FBI, especially since Joshua's circumstances put him in the middle of a potential murder scene, but the thinking is, there was not enough scopolamine in his blood to account for his memory loss. That level could be accounted for by a simple seasickness patch, so we brought him in for questioning. He has not yet been formally charged, but he's being interrogated as we speak."

Russell blinked. He was about to answer and stopped himself. He had always considered Walter Harrows to be somewhat of a friend and certainly a reasonable human being. Something wasn't right. The drug would have been mostly cleared by Joshua's liver by the time Joshua showed up covered in blood the next day. Russell had been about to explain this, when he realized that Harrows already knew it. So, what was he about?

"That blood value represents a level found at least twelve hours post exposure," Russell said, feeling the need to spell it out anyway. "You know the half-life of scopolamine. If you did not before, I'm sure you checked. Furthermore, the blood found on Joshua did not belong to Donny Anderson, but allegedly to a man who was in the subway before Joshua got there who has yet to be identified, and who, for all we know, may be alive."

Harrows nodded. "Yes, we know. We've decided to hold Joshua on charges of depraved indifference in Donald Anderson's death. There's also the matter of the missing Peter Jackson, who called Joshua and then was never heard from again."

Russell stared at Harrows. A forty-three second phone call from Peter Jackson, missing or not, was irrelevant. It was probably a wrong number, and there was nothing else to connect Joshua to Jackson and no clear evidence that he was even "missing," which was why Russell had never brought him up. And Jackson could have just left town. Did he really have to explain this to Harrows?

Harrows went on to justify his action, saying that Joshua clearly saw his friend Donny was in trouble, acknowledged the blood and the presence of what was described as a corpse, and still Joshua spent the night alone in the subway without alerting the police or trying to reach Donny after that. Weeks later, Donny shows up dead with an estimated time of death about two to three weeks prior, or just about the time Joshua last saw him, and the last activity from Jackson's cell phone, a known drug dealer, was a short conversation with Joshua.

Russell listened in amazement. If Harrows had notified the FBI about the scopolamine, then he undoubtedly understood its effects and its known propensity to render a victim in a zombie-like hypnotic state. Harrows should know Joshua would have been unable to assert his own will over that which had been commanded of him, and the amnestic effects that followed. It was only because of Russell's weird mental prying that Joshua had remembered anything at all.

Something was terribly wrong here. Russell *reached* gingerly toward Harrows, not knowing if he could voluntarily use his newfound ability. So far, his talent seemed to emerge quite on its own. He found himself reluctant to be invasive, but immediately Russell sensed a block in Harrows' mind, and as he gently probed further, now committed to exploring it, he recognized it as having the same flavor as the block that had been in Joshua's mind, and Maya's as well. Had Harrows been drugged too? He remembered Harris' statement that the "conservatives have infiltrated pretty much everywhere."

"Thank you for the *courtesy* notification," Russell said, trying to keep the sarcasm out of his voice. "I was just on my way down to the precinct. I need to make a call first to a lawyer to have him meet me there. I trust you will not question him further without an attorney present."

CHAPTER 42

Braelyn was thrilled with her newfound freedom. She could now go shopping for herself, walk in the park, and make her next appointment with Dr. Gray in his office. Even when a court officer had stopped her on the street and made her remove the paper around her ankle bracelet, saying it interfered with transmission of her whereabouts, she remained cheerful. It had been pretty crinkly sounding when she walked, but she couldn't help wondering that if it interfered so much, how was he able to find her on the street so easily?

When she got to Dr. Gray's office, she told him what happened, and they resorted to writing notes back and forth to each other, which was awkward and time consuming, and Braelyn had to concentrate to keep her handwriting from coming out as a scrawl, but it gave her secret pleasure to know they were foiling the authorities. After their appointment, Dr. Gray put all of their notes into his shredder.

Braelyn told Dr. Gray she had finally pinned Russell down and that her brother spent a half hour explaining to her what he did when he "unpacked" his thoughts and emotions, categorized them, analyzed them, and fitted them back together.

She finally understood why her brother was always so "unflappable;" his emotions never got inputted back into his mindset. Braelyn saw this as a weakness. She believed the emotions were the seat of "knowing" and could not be discarded. Not that they'd ever done her a whole lot of good. Mostly she'd ended up either in some dramatic, manic, mischief-precipitating state, or she was pulled into the rabbit hole of depression and despair, and a few times, she had nearly taken her own life in the process. After her talk with Russell, though, she became convinced there had to be a way to make her emotions work for her instead of against. They were just too powerful to discard like he did.

The talk with Russell made her feel better on many levels. She felt cared for by her brother, and grateful that she was important enough to him for him to have taken the time. He had tried to "show" her what he was doing with his head, and she sensed his own terror at the new ability he had developed. This made him more human to Braelyn, who always assumed her brother was fearless, needed nothing from anyone, and was completely at home in the world. Seeing his vulnerability made her feel better about having her own weaknesses. She was able to recognize that she had some of these same mental capacities too, which was part of what made it easy for her to follow what he was doing, and that her unconscious application of this ability had contributed hugely to her belief that the world was right when they told her she was insane.

Braelyn and Dr. Gray "discussed" it all via pen and paper. It was cumbersome and took forever, but Dr. Gray was very pleased and told her so with real words. In truth, he had always had faith in her, and Braelyn had held fast to that the last couple of years, like an exhausted swimmer holds onto a buoy in the middle of the bay.

Dr. Gray explained some of the research in paranormal phenomena, and the idea that all humans are capable of exhibiting it, especially under times of extreme stress, but very few are able to bend it to do their will on demand. In modern day, it was believed that there had to be a precipitating event, but it was also theorized that the way *homo sapiens* had survived before technology, when they clearly were not the strongest nor the most agile nor did they have the keenest hearing, sight, or sense of smell, was through the use of an extrasensory perception that warned them when danger was near, or what plants were safe to eat.

In 2020, this ability remained as the prickling of the hairs on the neck when someone was being watched, or the "knowing" that a food has gone rancid and shouldn't be eaten; a mother's instinct that something happened to her child, or even the intuition that everything is really fine even if the lab result says otherwise. In this age of science that they lived in, Dr. Gray said, there is a tendency to explain everything away with subliminal markers, but there is no explaining a dream that comes to pass or a father who singlehandedly lifts a car off his trapped daughter.

Dr. Gray went so far as to say that much of what is called mental illness, especially anxiety, may merely be a person connected to intuitive powers that are not recognized by the society at large. When that individual is instructed to dismiss what they believe in their heart that they *know*, the discordance can be crippling.

Walking back from the appointment, Braelyn felt the first real sense of calm that she had felt since… since… maybe since she was seven years old.

CHAPTER 43

Russell declined a ride with Commissioner Harrows and took his own Uber to the precinct. He needed some time alone, just to breathe and process the bizarre morning he'd had so far. He called Jeremy and asked him to represent Joshua. Even if they had not formally charged his nephew, he could be held for forty-eight hours as a "person of interest," and he would need counsel. Russell arranged for Jeremy to meet them at the precinct and advised him it might or might not be connected to Braelyn's case. Russell wasn't sure of anything anymore.

Despite having told Braelyn that he did not share his childhood with people like Jeremy—or anyone else—he did consider Jeremy to be a friend and a confidant. They had known each other some twenty years and had been known to have a drink together on many occasions. Taking stock of their relationship, Russell realized he didn't have many "close" friends, largely because he shared so little of his soul with anyone. Not even Maya. He knew that drove his wife crazy, but it was who he was, and he had never changed. She, of course, had made a mission to try to change him, and had been unsuccessful.

Suddenly, a visage appeared in the seat next to him. The Man in The Hut, *El Curandero Grande,* sat calmly next to him, stroking his long white beard. Russell blinked, glanced at the driver who noticed nothing amiss, and turned back to the mirage.

Surely there was no one there. Russell's mouth was dry; he wanted to speak but knew he'd sound like an idiot to the Uber driver. He opened his mouth and closed it. *El Curandero Grande* gave him a slight, knowing smile.

Russell felt a rush of wind and, abruptly, he was no longer in the car. He was on a mountaintop, and the trees were a lush green and smelled of forest and a far-off bonfire. He found himself walking alongside the ancient man. The air was thin, and his breathing felt labored.

The Ancient One stopped and motioned for Russell to sit. Russell did and *El Curandero* gracefully lowered himself onto the ground where he sat with legs crossed as easily as if he were a man in his thirties. He looked at Russell kindly and nodded, and then he "spoke" directly into Russell's mind.

"Ask me."

Russell had so many questions, but he could hardly articulate them; he wasn't even sure any of this was real. He felt like the three-year-old child of his memory and an adult all at once. He had been afraid to vocalize anything in the Uber, but… was he even in the Uber anymore?

"How… where are we? How are we talking? Are you real? How did we get here?" The questions tumbled out.

The Ancient One reached over and patted Russell's hand. *"It depends how you define 'real,' my son. Reality has many more dimensions than you acknowledge. Yes, I am real. We can be anywhere. You can be anywhere. You are chosen, Russell. I told you this many, many years ago. I know you remember."*

"I always thought it was just a dream."

The Ancient One shook his head and waited.

"What... what am I chosen for?" Russell asked, but was afraid of the answer. "Why me? Why is all this happening now?"

"You are chosen to lead the people of Good Heart. Now, because the world has need of you now. You were one preordained from long ago. There are a few in every era. The evil that is ravaging your world has activated your ability. Your re-exposure to the essence of the holy plants was the catalyst, and together they have set these predetermined neurophysiological processes into play, but you were initiated as a little tiny boy. It was inevitable. We expected to have need of you."

The technical words sounded odd coming from a shamanistic visage. This isn't helpful, Russell thought. It was confusing him more, but he didn't know where to start to ask for clarification.

"What am I to do? Who is this 'we?'"

"The world as you know it is about to change. There will be a Great Transformation."

"Who are the people of 'good heart?'"

The Ancient One smiled. *"You will know them."*

That made no sense at all to Russell. "My sister also—"

"Your sister needs your guidance. She has been given ability, but she is very angry. She will not be able to fully use her talent until she can put aside her rage."

Russell did not understand what the shaman was saying, and it made him supremely uncomfortable.

"What has happened to my mind? Why can I do these— these things?"

"There are many more things you can do that you do not yet know about. They will come to you as you have need of them. Do not fear them. Use your mind for Good. We are watching over you. We will be with you."

"Who's we?" Russell's voice choked as he asked a second

time. The image of the Ancient One started to fade before his eyes. "Wait! Don't go! I don't understand!"

An instant later, Russell found himself back in the Uber. His heart was pounding, and he was sweating, and still breathing heavily from… from the altitude? He was at sea level here in Manhattan. The Uber driver was calling to him.

"Hey, man, are you getting out, or what?"

Russell shook himself, set his facial expression to neutral by sheer force of will, and got out of the car. His phone buzzed at him, and he left a large tip on the app for the driver. He took an uncertain step toward the entrance to the precinct just as the commissioner came walking up the street. As Russell walked in the door, Jeremy fell into step beside him. He gave Russell an odd look and patted his shoulder.

"Don't worry, Russ," Jeremy said. "We'll get this all straightened out. They've got nothing on him."

Russell felt a rush of gratitude mixed with total confusion.

CHAPTER 44

Joshua sighed with tremendous relief when he saw his uncle walking into the precinct. But Uncle Russell looked upset, and Joshua was sure he'd let his uncle down somehow. There were two men with him. One looked vaguely familiar and carried himself like he was in charge, and the other was more aloof to the police staff and stuck to Uncle Russell's arm like a well-trained dog. Presently, this man came over to Joshua.

"Hello, Josh. My name is Jeremy Southpine. I'm a friend of your uncle's, and I'm a lawyer. I'm going to be with you every step of the way. From this moment on, I don't want you to say *anything at all* to the police until we have discussed it first. Do you understand?" Joshua nodded. "I also want you to understand that all of our conversations will be private." Jeremy looked pointedly at the officer watching Joshua. Jeremy's manner was comforting to Joshua, and he trusted the lawyer immediately.

The officer scowled and left the interrogation room, just as Uncle Russell joined them and closed the door. Russell hugged him and echoed that Joshua was to tell Jeremy everything he could remember, but when it came to what he would say to the police, he should defer to Jeremy.

Jeremy asked a bunch of questions about the Monday night Josh spent in the subway, and Joshua told him everything he could recall. It was surprisingly clearer than Joshua expected, but he wasn't panicked talking to Jeremy like he had been with the police officers earlier, and besides, Uncle Russell had already helped him sift through the hard stuff. The parts he didn't know then, he still didn't know—like what was said to Donny before he disappeared or what had happened to the dead body, but Jeremy didn't yell at him for that. He just nodded and said it was okay if he didn't remember.

"Are you sure the other man was dead? Did you know his name?" Jeremy asked him.

"I—I think he was." Joshua scratched his head. "Donny thought he was. Donny said he—he might have killed him, but he didn't remember. Donny said he found a knife, and there was blood all over him, but—that's crazy, right? I guess I assumed the guy was dead. I mean, I didn't get close to him or anything to check. I didn't know who he was. I know there was blood everywhere...." Joshua started whimpering.

Jeremy squeezed Joshua's hand. "When the police talk to you, only tell them what you know *for sure*. That there was a body there with blood on him, and that Donny told you he found himself in the station and didn't know he got there. Okay?"

Joshua nodded. Uncle Russell sat quietly across the table and listened. It helped Joshua just to know he was there, but he looked so tense, and Joshua wasn't used to seeing his uncle rattled by anything.

When Joshua was done recounting his tale, Jeremy sat back. "Tell me what it felt like when the powder hit you in the face. Do you remember that?" Jeremy asked.

Joshua started to tremble slightly, but he concentrated as hard as he could. "It was bad. First, I couldn't see, because there was dust in my eyes. Then it was like the station got very small, and I could only see right in front of me. Part of me was scared—no, wait." Joshua scrunched up his eyes. "It was like part of me *wanted* to be scared, but I wasn't really. It was like I had a mission, like in the movies, and I knew if I just did my job, everything would be okay." He stopped talking and looked at his uncle. "But it wasn't true, was it? It wasn't okay! Why did I feel like it would all be okay?" His voice squeaked and tears welled up in his eyes.

"You were drugged, Joshua," Jeremy said softly. "It wasn't your fault. Now tell me, why didn't you look for your friend Donny?"

Joshua grabbed his own hands and twisted them over and over until Jeremy reached over and put his hand over Joshua's.

"I don't know," Joshua said. "I really don't know! I wasn't *supposed* to, that's all I know."

Jeremy and Uncle Russell both got up. They each patted Joshua on the shoulder and stepped out for a few minutes, leaving Joshua alone. Time dragged. Joshua thought he'd never been so scared and miserable in his life, except maybe when he was a little boy and his mother hadn't come home until after midnight. It was thundering and lightning outside and he had been terrified. When she finally arrived, she just plopped down on the couch and fell asleep. She hadn't even seemed to notice him hunched over and crying in the hallway. It was shortly after that that his aunt and uncle had taken him in.

Jeremy finally came back in with a woman in a navy suit with her blonde hair tied back. He introduced her as Dr. Jameson and said she was a psychiatrist who worked for the police. He was to answer her questions just like he had answered Jeremy's, but Jeremy was going to sit in on the interview.

Dr. Jameson asked a lot of the same questions, particularly about the way Joshua felt when the dust was blown in his face. She also asked about the day Russell helped him remember. Joshua looked at Jeremy, who nodded, and so Joshua licked his lips and tried to describe how his uncle had helped him. When he was done, she asked him if he were hungry, and someone brought him a hamburger and French fries.

———

Russell sat at Detective Rodriguez's desk with Jeremy, watching the psychiatrist talking to Rodriguez and Greenstone down the hall. Rodriguez was nodding slightly with his chronically sour expression, but Greenstone looked ready to pop out of his skin. Russell could only hear snatches, but he got the gist that Greenstone had been reamed out for not reading Joshua his rights if he was going to cuff him, and instead of taking responsibility, Greenstone was directing his own anger at the psychiatrist. Russell guessed he hadn't received the report he wanted from her.

Nevertheless, Russell watched while lunch was delivered and Harrows and Greenstone helped themselves to pizza and soft drinks. Dr. Jameson had apparently concluded her assessment and left. Rodriguez waved off the offer of pizza. Russell's stomach growled.

Rodriguez came back over to his office scowling with the commissioner beside him and sat down across from Russell. "It seems Dr. Jameson believes Joshua is telling the truth and is describing an incident of being drugged by what she concurs could be 'Devil's Breath.' It's not something I'd ever heard of before, and my partner is inclined to disbelieve, but that will be a matter for the courts to decide. We are likely going to have to arrest your nephew anyway. My question is, if this drug is so powerful, how did you snap him out of it?"

Russell was so tired, but he couldn't let his guard down now. He searched Rodriguez's eyes for a hidden agenda and found none. He gave up. If Trenaman and Harris knew about his "ability," it wasn't worth prevaricating about, was it? But while he found he intrinsically did trust this cantankerous Rodriguez fellow, a glance over at the smirking Greenstone down the hall made his decision.

"Quite honestly, Detective, I really don't know. Maybe because I didn't barrage him with a million questions. I helped him relax, and then I helped him… untangle it."

Rodriguez frowned. It was obvious he wanted to challenge Russell. He clearly understood Russell was holding out on him, but Russell knew Rodriguez had noticed the meaningful glance Russell had flashed at his partner before evading the question, and he stopped himself. It might not be the first time someone hesitated to talk to him because of Greenstone.

"Very well," Harrows said. "But Joshua will be staying here tonight."

"On what charge?" Russell asked.

Rodriguez sighed. "Depraved indifference and negligent homicide. He's being read his rights now, with his attorney in the room."

Russell nodded. He clasped his hands together to keep him from rubbing his temples and showing fatigue. "And of course, we can expect Mr. Southpine to file a motion to suppress anything he may have said to you before now."

"That will be for the DA to deal with," Rodriguez said. He stood up and looked at Harrows. "He will be arraigned tomorrow—as a courtesy. The normal wait time is a few weeks."

"I thank you for that," Russell said. Harrows nodded and turned to leave.

Russell reassured Joshua that he would be at his hearing tomorrow and would post bail, and to just hang tight for one night. He made him promise to say nothing further to anyone and not to worry, and that Russell would let Braelyn know.

Commissioner Harrows walked out into the sunshine with Russell. It was odd that Harrows had come down for this, and Russell had an intuition that it was important to *someone* that Russell understand the commissioner was on board with this arraignment. Russell was *supposed* to be feeling squeezed right now.

Before Harrows turned to walk uptown, he reached over to touch Russell on the arm. "Look, man, I know you love the kid, but it's a pretty bizarre story, and the fact that Joshua did nothing after seeing his friend like that... who then turns up dead three weeks later? He's got to at least give us some information about what happened."

Russell stepped back involuntarily so that Harrows' hand slipped off his arm. "He doesn't *know* more than what he's told us, Walter. That's the nature of this drug. It causes amnesia."

"Yeah, well, he sure seemed to remember enough after you spoke to him, didn't he?" Harrows turned on his heel and walked off into the New York City foot traffic.

CHAPTER 45

aya read over the material for her next meeting. Things were coming to a head. A video of a police officer holding a Black man in a choke hold until he died had gone viral. The officer claimed he was detaining the suspect, but it was clear that undue force had been used, and many were crying out to convict the police officer of murder.

Maya packed her biscuits and a lemonade drink that Harris's distributor had provided her and headed out to the meeting place. This one was being held at a local community center that Maya was not familiar with, and the event had been advertised as a free lunch. She didn't believe anyone would need to be chemically convinced that an atrocity had transpired in the death of the Black man, but she was told people come to events expecting to be fed and, sometimes, expressly for the sake of being fed. Free food always attracted people. Harris arranged for a full lunch of wraps and paninis, so she was merely bringing the dessert and beverages.

Harris had warned her that the city was polarizing and demanding fair treatment for all people of color. Anger over bigotry and discrimination and the war between the White Supremacists and the liberal factions were boiling over. It was all being kindled by President Ganaffe, who then turned around and claimed that he, himself, was not a racist. As if saying so would make it true. Harris urged her to keep herself out of harm's way.

Maya never worried about such things. She trusted that if she just did what was right, the Lord would protect her, and so far, He had never let her down. And she prided herself on always acting from the purest place in her heart and always with compassion. At least she had until the night she fed Russell the biscuit. A dark cloud of guilt hovered over her from that.

As Maya sat in the Uber, she mused over what had become of her relationship with her husband. Over the last few days, he seemed to have put aside her having given him the "tainted" biscuit, as he called it. But they hadn't made love in over two weeks, and that was unlike him. He seemed to have no interest in her sexually. If it weren't for the fact that she felt he was still angry at her on some level, she might have suspected it was because he had found someone else. But it didn't mean he *hadn't* found someone else either, given how angry he'd been at her.

She and Russell did not speak further of her meetings, and truthfully, Maya didn't know if she was "allowed" to talk to him about them anyway.

Russell mentioned once that he had met Harris and had been underwhelmed. He wouldn't say anything further about it, and Harris hadn't mentioned it at all, so she considered Harris had had a change of heart regarding engaging Russell. Maybe he no longer felt her husband was in any danger.

It wasn't like Russell had ever had much interest in her Undivided meetings before, so it could mean nothing that he didn't ask about these, but Maya was so acutely aware that *now* she was doing work of such greater importance than anything she had ever done before, and she longed to discuss it with the man she loved most in the world and to whom she had always trusted to give her the soundest advice and keep her safe.

When Maya got to the community center, the huge space was packed. Maya was getting used to speaking in front of large groups, but there must have been at least two hundred people present today, and her mouth felt dry. She reached for one of the lemonade drinks, stopped herself, and then decided it was the biscuits that were laced with the drug so she should be pretty safe with the drink. She gulped it thirstily. There was a TV on in an adjacent room with the news blasting, and Maya spared a moment to consider the terrible virus that was burgeoning in the West Coast and was rumored to be heading to New York, but she dismissed it quickly as the door swung shut and blocked out the reporter.

Maya showed her video as instructed, having first read the opening remarks personally prepared by Harris and then a brief conversation starter after the video. She felt her gorge rising as she watched and listened to her own words and had a tremendous urge to go confront the entire police force and President Ganaffe right then and there. She had been indignant before and eager to protest, but now she felt enraged to such an intense degree, it made her uncomfortable. There was something distantly familiar about the feeling she was having, but she couldn't pin it down and had to let it go as she became wrapped up in moderating the emotional discussion that followed her presentation.

———

Across town in the Kings of Columbus, another meeting was taking place. It was a weekly gathering, and members were encouraged to bring a guest. They were served pizza and mixed drinks, or soft drinks for those on their work lunch, all catered from the Italian restaurant next door. Today's topic was sexual abomination, in the form of homosexuality and same-sex marriage. After a savory lunch, they read from the Good Book and discussed people they knew who hid their evil ways as well as those who flagrantly displayed their sins for all to see.

In recent times, they were having to fight hard to keep "common sense" values in the public eye. People were becoming complacent, saying things like "live and let live," and "as long as they aren't hurting anyone, it didn't matter." The speaker impressed on his audience that God's word *does* matter, and they must speak up and enforce it.

They all rallied with the speaker for the better part of an hour, and then set their next week's agenda with the topic of Right to Life. Members vowed to bring their family baby pictures to salute the beautiful lives God had granted and to berate the wicked lawmakers that threatened to snuff out potential blessings on this earth. They made plans to follow lunch with a march up the avenue and a protest outside an abortion clinic, so all were encouraged to bring signs.

Trenaman walked in briefly and glanced around. Everything seemed to be in order. He did spot-checks on random sites to make sure his mules were doing their jobs. The man running this meeting was named Randolph, and he was utterly reliable. Since he was completely conservative before he'd been "influenced," having Randolph as an organizer was a breeze, but Trenaman evaluated everyone's performance periodically regardless. It was one of his jobs.

Since Braelyn Plessman had figured out the transmitter in her ankle bracelet and had taken regular steps to avoid being spied on, Trenaman's time was freed up again, as there was not much to listen to. He couldn't say he was sorry, it had been a tedious job. But Trenaman always followed orders, and if that was how they had wanted to use him for now, he would have continued to comply. Having Braelyn under surveillance was now much less useful, although being able to track her whereabouts could still be expedient if her brother became hard to find. It had been many years since she had yielded any particularly interesting insights into the effects of childhood exposure to Devil's Breath, so Trenaman wondered if they would decide to terminate her as well. She definitely knew too much, so after they used her as a bargaining chip in getting Vaderman to help them, it could conceivably go that way. Trenaman did not like being dishonest, but it was not his determination to make.

CHAPTER 46

Russell got home exhausted and hungry and belatedly realized he was not comfortable eating anything in the house. It occurred to him that he shouldn't eat anything delivered to them either. Although he seemed to have some intrinsic immunity to scopolamine, the effect it had had on him was so gut-wrenching, he didn't want to repeat the experience. He went rifling through the cabinets for prepackaged food that had been purchased six months ago or more. He found some pasta and marinara sauce that looked innocent enough and set about preparing himself a simple dinner.

Maya walked in and looked at him expectantly. Russell could practically smell the residue of scopolamine on her, and he felt an overwhelming fatigue fall over him. Could he possibly keep her mind clear of it? Was it everywhere? He vacillated between pointing it out to her and letting it go. He could tell she was already torn between feeling elated that he was home and being terrified that he would reject her. How was he *seeing* this so clearly?

"Russell, my love! How are you? We haven't even seen each other in what feels like ages!"

Russell thought about the revelation he'd had that he shared so little of himself with anyone, including Maya, and how frustrating that must be for someone as effusive as she was. It occurred to him again that he had chosen to marry someone who could express exactly those things he could not, as if to fill a deficiency he had always known he harbored. He forced himself to walk over to her and give her a hug. It was not a particularly passionate hug, but it had the desired effect of allaying her fears that he wanted to be rid of her now.

Maya started to cry. "I'm so, so sorry, Russell. I didn't know what I was doing. It was the drug! I don't even know how I was drugged! I mean, the next day, I ate the biscuits too, but before then, I had never had them." She had already apologized, and it wasn't like Russell to hold a grudge, but it obviously still weighed heavily on her heart.

Russell took her face gently between his hands. "This is bigger than either of us, Maya. When you originally met with Harris, did he feed you?"

Maya's face took an expression of shock and horror. "Why, yes, always at the same restaurant. His family's restaurant. Do you think it was from there?"

"I wasn't there. What do *you* think?"

Maya sat down at the kitchen table. She looked over at the pasta, and Russell took it off the stovetop. Russell proceeded to mix it with marinara sauce and looked for fresh basil and grated parmigiana cheese in the fridge, but then thought better of it, and kept it simple. He served two platefuls and brought them to the table.

Russell dug in hungrily, but Maya played with it with her fork. "Russell, it isn't wrong to want to make a difference in our world. We have to fight what Ganaffe is doing. *I* have to fight it.

I *need* to be doing something for our planet and our country. I thought you agreed with that. Don't you agree?"

Russell reached over and stroked her hair. "Maya, honey, of course I do, but it really doesn't matter what *I* believe. It only matters what *you* believe, in your own heart. When all the facts are at hand."

"Well, I believe that this president has got to go. Remember, he threatened to withhold aid to California when they had the fires last year because the governor isn't a republican? How can he do that? He's supposed to be responsible for the well-being of *all* Americans. And he'd rather we ally with dictators, like in Russia and North Korea! I want him out. And I want equality for all people. Is that wrong?"

"Maya, darling, why are you inviting me to pass judgment on things that are at the core of your belief system? Would it change anything if I either agreed or disagreed?" He took another forkful.

Maya looked horrified and put down her own fork and knife. "You don't feel the same way?"

Russell gave up. He rubbed his head where it was starting to throb. "I *do* feel the same way. But my affirmation or denial should not change your heart, not if you've truly thought it out. Collect as much fact as you can, from both sides, and then form your opinion. Do not adopt a policy merely because I do. That's all I'm saying."

"Okay," Maya said. She still looked confused, but she started eating again.

Russell changed the subject; he couldn't avoid it any longer. He told her Joshua was under arrest and awaiting arraignment in the morning. As expected, the news provoked an outpouring of concern, even after Russell assured her that Joshua was okay and they'd bail him out in the morning, and as always, Maya named Joshua's mother as a bad influence. "See what comes of his spending so much time with his mother?"

"This has nothing to do with Braelyn," Russell said and turned back to his dinner.

They did the dishes together in silence and Russell went to the couch and turned on the news, not a common practice since he usually cruised the web for information, but he was in the mood to give his eyes a rest. In fact, his whole soul seemed to need a rest, and he wanted to take a less active role in acquiring information at the moment. Maya joined him.

A SARS-like virus outbreak appeared to have originated in Asia and was quickly extending to other parts of the world, including Europe. In Italy, the hospitals were so overwhelmed that people over age sixty were being told to stay home to die, as they would not be admitted to the hospital. It sounded completely out of sync with twenty-first-century medicine, like they were living in a Michael Crichton book. Already in the United States, Seattle seemed to have a disturbing number of cases, with a staggering number of deaths for such a small period of time. It was spreading rapidly and appeared to be quite aggressive, with those it was infecting getting seriously ill and many dying. President Ganaffe was announcing that he was no longer allowing planes from anywhere in Asia to land in the United States.

"Look at that," Maya said. He's calling it the 'Asia virus,' as if those poor people deliberately created it. You see what I mean? He reviles anyone who looks different from him. Do you really think any nation would develop a virus and set it loose on its own population?"

Russell grunted, not in the mood for a political debate, even if he agreed with her. In his usual fashion, he was reserving judgment on where and how this virus had originated since he did not have adequate information, but he wasn't up to telling her that. The last month had taken something out of him. The Man in The Hut seemed to be present in his mind at some level nearly all the time now, even when the visage did not clearly manifest, and his head felt strange, as if it were being repro-grammed by something he had no control over. He was perfectly content to let Maya ramble on and grateful that they were back on easy terms again.

But at the edge of his awareness, the news about this new virus seemed particularly relevant to him, Russell, for some reason, and he was too tired to try to puzzle it out. He fell asleep on the couch, dreaming of his "visit" with the Ancient One in the back of the Uber, trying to demystify what had been meant regarding a "Great Transformation" and what that had to do with Russell's destiny, while another part of him scoffed entirely at taking any of it in the least seriously.

CHAPTER 47

Braelyn headed over to the courthouse in the morning. Her brother's cryptic message on her voicemail was not a surprise. She had known from the beginning that Joshua had something to do with the serious injury of another person, even if he had no idea who that person was. So, it had finally caught up with him.

She was astounded by the mental clarity she felt since the evening Russell had spent with her in the park. He had put his hand on the side of her head and spoken softly to her, but it was almost as though he could have done it without words. He explained how he never took information at face value, but always evaluated the baggage it came with—who stood to gain and who would lose with this revealed. Even knowing how advanced her brother's mind had always seemed to her, it was astonishing to Braelyn that he would look at the source of everything he learned, its accompanying emotion, and its perspective: its essential core.

Every thought, every event had an essence, Russell had said. It seemed to Braelyn he was actually thinking with the deepest part of his heart, not just with his head. That was the only way Braelyn could understand it. Russell had learned over the years to do these things nearly instantaneously, but she remembered what a long and painful learning process it had been for him. By the time they were done, Braelyn could almost *see* his mind working as he spoke to her.

In the beginning, she was frustrated. It took a *lot* longer to process anything this way, and Braelyn remembered how children and adults both used to snicker at the little kid who would listen and nod, and then come out with a response sometimes five minutes later. It wasn't until Russell was in his mid-teens that he started to "think on his feet." He was a tremendously lonely child as a result, and Braelyn was one of the few people who took the time to listen to him. He used to pad around after Braelyn like a lost puppy until he was eleven or twelve, and it used to annoy her no end. But she seemed to be at odds with nearly everything and everyone else in her own life and being there for her baby brother was one of the few things she could do that made her feel like a decent human being. Mother wasn't there for either of them ever since Daddy went away. She used to say it was all because of what that nasty medicine man had done to them when they were young, but Braelyn was never able to get any details out of her mother other than that.

Now, Braelyn felt like she was learning to think all over again. Like riding a bicycle when she had read the manual but never actually gone anywhere, down streets for which she knew the map like the back of her hand but had never actually been to. Yet, the more she practiced, the less complicated it was.

She walked into the courtroom and saw Jeremy Southpine up front in the defendant's position, whispering to Russell who sat in the first pew behind him. Maya was sitting next to Russell, of course, and as Braelyn made her way up front to join them, Joshua was brought in by the side door and directed to sit next to Jeremy.

Braelyn *felt* her son's fear and anguish all the way across the room, as if he were broadcasting it. His eyes were wild, and they scanned the room quickly and settled on Braelyn's own. He locked onto her with gratitude, longing, and fear. Braelyn felt tears well up in her own eyes.

In the past, having this experience would have terrified her and served as confirmation that she was nuts. After her conversation—or whatever they'd had—with Russell, and then with Dr. Gray, she began instead to unpack it and note how she had accessed that information.

Everyone rose as the judge came into the room and then were seated, but the prosecution and the defense stayed standing, along with Joshua, who was wearing a dark blue suit and tie. Russell must have brought it for him, but he looked about fourteen standing there facing the judge and trembling.

They started the proceeding as Braelyn's head swam. This should *not* be happening to her little boy! She slipped into a seat behind Russell and Maya. Joshua was being charged with depraved indifference and criminally negligent homicide in the death of Donald Anderson. The prosecution stated that Joshua knew his friend was in dire peril as they were both covered in blood, and yet he did nothing to help him but spent the night on the subway platform while his friend was killed. Jeremy spoke about Joshua's having been a victim himself, that he had been drugged, and cited a blood test and the police department's own psychiatrist who had determined this to be true.

After arguing for ten minutes over whether Joshua was a flight risk, bail was set at $250,000, and Joshua was returned to his cell. Russell took Braelyn's arm as he walked out the door and assured her Joshua would be home by the afternoon.

No one spoke as Braelyn, Russell, Maya, and Jeremy walked toward the courthouse lobby, from which a smattering of hallways branched off. Maya kept dabbing her eyes and whimpering, and Braelyn had to bite her tongue to keep from calling her out on her dramatics. She had never had patience for Maya and her overly emotional displays. Russell told them all to go on ahead and he would catch up with them after posting bail.

Suddenly, several uniformed police officers ran past them back toward the holding area. Russell stopped and asked a clerk walking by what happened. The clerk seemed to recognize Russell—of course, the whole world knew her brother.

"Don't know exactly, Mr. Vaderman. Looks like there was an altercation between two prisoners who crossed paths. Someone managed to get hold of a pen or something and did some damage as a kid was being brought back. Question of bad timing, if you ask me, or else they were sharing a cell. Maybe they knew each other; it's hard to say."

Braelyn caught her breath and expected Russell to go running back in, but instead he was staring at a man leaning on the doorway of the building. The man was looking straight at Russell with a knowing half smile, and as he turned to walk away, Braelyn noticed he had a pronounced limp.

CHAPTER 48

Russell started after Trenaman as the NSA agent walked out of the building, but stopped, torn between running after him and finding out if Joshua was okay and getting him out of this dump. He was sure Trenaman played a major role in both his sister's and nephew's fabricated legal problems, and Russell had no way of tracking the man down.

He grabbed Jeremy and quickly asked him to see to Joshua's bail and to let him know immediately if Joshua had been the one injured before running off after Trenaman, leaving his family gaping after him. He ran down the steps and onto Centre Street and looked around. The guy couldn't be moving that fast, unless he'd gotten into a car.

Russell stopped and focused on quieting his mind. An image came to him of an office in midtown. He could clearly see Trenaman sitting at a desk, with a coffee cup next to him, working with a desktop computer. Russell blinked and it was gone.

He turned uptown and started dodging pedestrians as he ran up the street.

Something made Russell stop halfway up the block. He pivoted around and looked into a coffee shop and saw Trenaman at the counter. His back was to Russell, but he was unmistakable. Russell entered the coffee shop and stood behind Trenaman, waiting for him to finish paying the cashier.

"I expected you'd find me," Trenaman said without turning around. "I told you we would meet again."

Trenaman turned to Russell with a compelling stare. "Coffee?" he asked Russell before moving to a nearby table and calmly taking a seat.

Russell did not answer but stood behind the chair across the table from Trenaman. He noticed the deliberation Trenaman needed to navigate seating himself while holding his coffee cup, how hard he tried to make it a smooth motion as if he had no physical limitations, and Russell felt the other man's discomfort with his condition. Russell also intuited something else. This man was somewhat afraid of him and was desperate to keep that a secret. Well, Russell thought, he was a little afraid of himself these days, but perhaps he could use Trenaman's fear to his advantage.

"Call it off," Russell said.

Trenaman smiled blandly. "Call what off?"

"The charges against my nephew. And my sister. All of it. They're fabrications. We both know that. You are using them to threaten me, and blackmail is a piss-poor way to elicit my help in a function that you claim is so noble."

"I could do that. I could make it all go away." Trenaman sipped at his coffee.

Russell's phone beeped at him. He broke the gaze with Trenaman to glance at the text message from Jeremy.

Joshua is okay. Few scratches only. Another kid got it worse.
Bail posted; he's going home with Braelyn, his choice.

Russell exhaled a bit more fervidly than he had intended in front of Trenaman. He knew Trenaman saw him relax.

"Your nephew is fine. Although, he might just as easily have been otherwise," Trenaman said. "Sit." He nodded at the chair.

Russell sat.

"Will you share your mind with your government?"

Russell tried to penetrate Trenaman's strictly disciplined thoughts but came upon resistance instead. Unlike Maya and Joshua, Trenaman could shut him out. He supposed that a career in the high ranks of the military demanded the development of scrupulous thought patterns. If Trenaman had been a captain of a naval ship, he must have trained to shield himself from anyone trying to break him for information were he to be captured. What Russell did not sense was the scent of scopolamine. Trenaman was a free spirit in that regard. His mind was squeaky clean.

And yet... Russell felt if he pushed Trenaman, he might be able to influence him with his own mental force. Russell recoiled reflexively at that idea. How could he possibly justify manipulating someone else's volition?

"What exactly do you want me to share?" Russell asked.

Trenaman calmly stirred his coffee. "How do you do it? How do you stand apart from the effects of the drug, and how do you detach another person's mind from the influence of scopolamine?"

Russell shrugged and sat back, trying to make it look like he was at ease. "The first part is easy. You can probably do that yourself. Your own mind is rigorously controlled. Do you not understand how well-disciplined you are mentally?"

Trenaman rubbed his left index finger over the lip of his coffee cup. "I have never tested it. You think I would be immune as you are?" Trenaman was letting his guard down, and Russell noted he did not seem particularly surprised that Russell could discern this about him.

"No idea. But it would take a lot more for you to buy a package of hoodoo, I'm sure of that," Russell said. "I suspect you would know you'd been drugged and would fight it. For some reason, you've bought into this government package of 'the greater good through chemistry' all on your own accord. I don't quite understand why. I'd have thought you were smarter than that." Russell raised an eyebrow questioningly.

"Because in your opinion, you disagree with it? People want to be guided. They do not read facts, they respond to emotions. The last thing they want is the responsibility of thinking for themselves. That's hard work. Besides, how do you know for sure this is my own choice? You discovered this about me from just a couple of interactions?"

Russell hesitated. He did not want to show any part of his hand, but he'd have to give the guy something to get him to nullify the sham charges on his family. "I can *feel* the drug when it's there—If I 'look.'" Trenaman perked up curiously and Russell continued. "I can't tell you how. It's as if it leaves a residue, and you don't have it. I don't fully understand it myself."

Trenaman considered that for several minutes. The silence was awkward, but Russell had grown up in awkward silences, so he waited. Finally, Trenaman nodded slowly, as he measured Russell and decided he was being straight with him.

"Okay, Mr. Vaderman. I will make the charges disappear. You realize, of course, that it is a simple thing for me to have circumstances bring new accusations and arrests, perhaps against your lovely wife, or even yourself. You, in turn, will work with me to discover and disclose exactly how you know someone is under the influence and then, how you remove that influence. I believe that you do not fully understand it yourself, so I suspect that there may be much in this process you could learn that might help you personally. I have the entire resources of the NSA and the Department of Defense at my disposal to help you master this... this gift you have. You might be surprised to learn how much your government already knows about psychic ability. Your contribution would be welcome. What do you say?"

"You go first."

CHAPTER 49

Russell walked out onto the sun-drenched pavement. He called Braelyn and confirmed that Joshua was okay. He barely heard her as she related in great detail some other prisoner's brandishing of a stolen staple remover to slash at anyone who crossed his path. Joshua needed a few stitches to his right forearm but was otherwise fine.

He hung up with his sister, his head still wrapped around his conversation with Trenaman. In truth, Russell had no real understanding of what was happening to him, and it terrified him. Was there a way to work with this guy and possibly learn how to control his mental activity without giving away secrets or being controlled by Trenaman and his cronies? Who could he even talk to about such things who wouldn't label him a nutcase straight out of the box?

Russell walked steadily uptown, as if he could leave his whole confusing predicament behind him by doing so. He cut east at Grand and headed up Chrystie Street so he could walk up through the Sara D. Roosevelt Park. He desperately needed the tree refuge.

He found a bench in the park and sat. His feet still felt like they were moving; he wasn't wearing the best walking shoes. He looked up the number for Dr. Mitchell Gray and asked if he could come by and see him.

In Dr. Gray's office, Russell spilled his guts as he never had in his life. The bafflement of information from his earliest memories to the adaptive process he had learned to survive, and how it all seemed to be standing on its head now. Or on *his* head.

"I don't understand what is happening to me, Dr. Gray, or why. Or why *now*. I feel like I've lost it. I had another… visitation, from the vision in my dream, and I wasn't under the influence of any drug—that I know of, anyway. Is this real or hallucination? Am I having a psychotic break? I think this is the first time I have really understood what fear is. Maybe I never had time to be afraid before. This can't be normal."

Dr. Gray nodded compassionately. "This must be tremendously frightening and confusing to you, Russell. No, I do not believe you are psychotic. You have too much insight, too much grounding in reality, and your thoughts are too well-ordered."

Gray got up and brought Russell a cup of passionfruit and ginger tea. The tea was warm in the cool office and Russell was grateful for it.

"I can't explain what is happening to you. I can explain some things that are known in the field of parapsychology, and perhaps that will help you. It has long been known that psychic phenomena exist but studying it has remained elusive. Perhaps that is due to the methodology that's been used. You see, the scientific method relies on unbiased, reproducible evidence, which means it seeks to be coolly analytical in its processes. If it were otherwise, we could not hope to have a world with shared experiences. We need to know that a medication that works for one will also work for most and—to put in architectural terms— that the equations used to calculate the forces acting on a structural beam can be applied to other buildings to make them sound as well. Science stands on its own merit and must be reproducible. The apple *always* falls with the acceleration of gravity. Until the Theory of Relativity came along, at least, and quantum mechanics."

Gray steeped his teabag in his cup, and Russell waited for him to continue. "Much investigation has gone into determining if psi power is real. Whether a person can consistently pick out an image that is hidden from them, or move an object with only their mind, and all of it falls within the context of gathering data to further scientific knowledge. Have you ever heard of the Heisenberg Uncertainty Principle?"

"Yes," Russell said. "Basically, that the act of measuring a thing alters the thing itself, so that the information you gain is about how the thing exists now that it's been examined but does not necessarily reflect what you were initially looking at."

"Just so. Which brings into question whether we can ever know what our current reality is. I can tell you that in studying our world, science takes the emotional content out of the equation, because emotions are not quantifiable.

"It is possible that these conditions of emotionless discovery eliminate the energy that the performance of psychic acts requires for implementation. By which I mean, that the desire to score well in a test of psychic ability may not generate enough emotional energy to achieve that act. Psychic events must have a source of power for their mental function, just as going for a run requires food and oxygen to sustain muscle activity.

"A real-life crisis or state of vital need may create access to a part of the brain that is otherwise unavailable to the logical mind. In short, despite the attempts to quantify psychic ability, it may just not be obtainable in a laboratory environment. To put it another way, perhaps we are trying to understand the limbic system through the eyes of the cerebral cortex. Like trying to smell a flower with our eyes. It may not be possible." Gray sipped at his tea, peered at Russell over the top of his mug, and waited.

Russell had been warming his fingers on his tea. He chortled. "Perhaps Braelyn is right, then. She insists that it is vitally important *not* to remove emotion while unscrambling information. I have no idea how to do that. Taking out the emotion is exactly how I make sense of things."

"She may be right, Russell. Situations of superhuman ability, including what we call 'hysterical strength'—like when someone does something in the crisis of the moment that they 'shouldn't' be able to do—are emotionally charged events thought to hinge on the activation in the brain of the hypothalamus which, acting upon the adrenal medulla, creates an immense surge in the secretion of both adrenaline and cortisol."

Gray rose and retrieved an atlas of human anatomy from his bookshelf. He showed Russell where the limbic system fit below the cerebrum, and then the special relationship between that area in the brain he called the hypothalamus and the organ resting behind the kidneys.

"Once released, these two substances regulate the body's response to danger by activating the fight or flight response. That response delivers exponentially higher levels of oxygen and glucose to the muscles and other tissue, giving them accelerated abilities. Those same increased nutrients are delivered to the brain as well, and that may power the paranormal response that is so elusive in the laboratory setting. You do understand this is complete conjecture, Russell, right?"

"But I am not particularly emotional," Russell said, "so where does my 'power' come from?"

"Aren't you? From what you've told me, I think you feel emotion so intensely that you learned to separate it out for clarity. Perhaps you store it somewhere so that it does not interfere with your thought process. It may be that you convert the energy of those emotions and stockpile it, like charging a 'psychic battery,' if that makes any sense."

"Sure, maybe… but, if that's so… why can I access this when others can't?"

Gray smoothed his hair on each side of his head. "Hard to know, Russ. It is generally believed that all humans have this capacity without knowing how to utilize it. Is it your highly disciplined mind that makes you unique? And there is another factor that likely keeps many from having this ability. Disbelief. You know that it is very difficult to achieve something that you subconsciously believe you cannot accomplish. Our culture does not believe in these abilities. And why not? Because we fear them, at a very base level. This could be our minds' ways of protecting us."

"And this is happening to me now, because…?"

"I can't say for sure, of course. But from what you've told me, Russell, as an infant, you were treated with a powerful combination of drugs that act on the limbic system of your brain. The limbic system is the very seat of emotions, so it is unclear what kind of changes were enacted in your brain chemistry. Your neurophysiology may have been changed in ways we do not yet understand. In addition to that, your 'dream' indicates that a hypnotic suggestion was placed in your subconscious at that time. So at that deep level, perhaps *you* do believe in psychic ability in ways that others cannot. Once your brain was exposed to the same or similar drug again—the scent of the natural flowers in your sister's suitcase and the scopolamine in the cookies your wife gave you, well… limbic memory is primordial and iconic. Consider how the scent of something from childhood can elicit memories and feelings decades forgotten."

"And the vision's reference to my being 'chosen?' Is that based in any sort of 'reality?' Is there a scientific explanation for *that?*"

CHAPTER 50

Russell left Dr. Gray's office feeling adrift in the universe. As a child he had felt his "differentness," but he'd had his sister to buffer the effects of the world around him, and he could retreat into himself and pretend it didn't matter. He doubted going to Braelyn now would help. Too much had changed within and between them, but a part of him longed to run into his big sister's arms. Funny, he never remembered his mother being as much of a comfort. Perhaps it was because his mother felt guilty about what her children had been subjected to, or perhaps it was just that Braelyn empathized on the deepest level, having experienced something similar.

He wandered down the avenue, not much interested in going home. He was sure there had been a huge argument over where Joshua was going after bail had been posted, and he also knew that when Braelyn had won out, it had left Maya incensed and angry, activating all her insecurities. Russell had no desire to step into that setting and get the brunt of his wife's tirade regarding the shortfalls of Joshua's mother, all designed, however subconsciously, to hide Maya's own feelings of inadequacy.

Neither did Russell want to go to the Village and hear his sister's line-by-line depiction of today's adventure. Joshua was all right, and that was enough to set Russell's mind at rest. Braelyn was growing in some way that Russell could feel, developing, strengthening, ever since they had spent the time in the park and he had explained to her, almost mind to mind, what it was that he did to keep himself sane. He felt mildly guilty for not having done that years ago. He had just never recognized that he even had a "method."

He thought about getting a Zip car and driving upstate to his country house in the Catskill Mountains. He could picture it vividly in his mind, sitting on some eighty-seven acres of land, populated with trees, a windmill for clean energy to supplement the solar panels, and a small stream running through it that he and Joshua had fished from. The stream had origins in a small waterfall about twelve feet high to the north of the homestead where he had considered installing a hydraulic head for electricity production, but so far, it was not needed. There was a delightful well that still functioned not far from his back door. He paid a service to go in weekly and keep the place clean and visit-ready.

He could just take a few days off and disappear from everyone and everything for a while, and lose himself in the beautiful sights, sounds, and smells of the mountain forest. Pretend he had never been visited by *El Curandero Grande*, that he had never heard of the Northern Peruvian Andes, that his father had never come to see him before he died four years ago, and that he was just a normal person with a normal childhood.

Russell stopped into a bar on Madison Avenue instead. He ordered a scotch and soda and sat sipping it, pretending to watch the ball game on the flat screen TV. It was interrupted by a news blast stating that the SARS-like virus had spread from the West Coast and was now starting to affect the New York metro area as well, likely fueled by travel to the United States from Europe. President Ganaffe released a statement saying he took no responsibility for its management, and that each state could regulate its own standards. He also stated the virus would "go away" on its own, something Russell felt in his bones was not going to happen.

His head felt foggy, and he wondered if it was because he didn't generally drink or if it was swimming from all the new information he was still digesting about who and what he was. It vaguely occurred to him that he might have been followed and the drink might be spiked, but he found he didn't even care. He was quite sure that if it were spiked with Devil's Breath extract or scopolamine or anything else, it would only heighten his uncanny senses faster, a process that seemed to be inevitably developing no matter if he wanted it to or not.

Russell pondered whether the charges against both his sister and his nephew would be dropped. He felt sure Jeremy could successfully defend Joshua; Braelyn was another matter. That was her word against a US customs agent. If they were dropped, then what? Should he avail himself of the resources of the Department of Defense and the NSA to understand his own mind? Did he even have a choice? He took Harris's card out of his pocket, and stared at it, wondering what Harris could possibly offer as "protection."

As he turned the card over in his hand, a familiar presence parked itself at the next barstool. Russell knew before he looked up that Harris had sat down. Did Russell's thinking about him draw him there, or was it Harris's approaching arrival that had made Russell think of him?

Harris nodded at Russell and ordered a drink. Russell stared back. Never in his life had he felt so out of control. He had spent most of his childhood learning to be quite sure of every next step. But perhaps the sense of control was always an illusion.

"I will assume the NSA has reached out to you, my friend. Any thoughts?" Harris spoke as if to his drink, but it was clearly meant for Russell.

"Exactly what are you offering me?" Russell asked. "You were not particularly forthcoming about those details."

Harris turned to face Russell straight on. "I can't reveal what I have only for you to go running into the hands of the government and then wait for you to betray me. We haven't successfully mounted the Resistance for this long by being stupid." Harris's voice was icy and sharp.

Curiously, that made Russell trust him a bit more. "Okay, I give you my word I will not discuss our conversation with anyone I know to be representing the NSA."

"Or the Department of Defense. Or anyone in the government or sympathetic to President Ganaffe. In fact, I need to know you will keep all of this close to your chest. You do have a reputation for being able to do just that, and I expect that consideration."

Russell nodded. "Fair enough. As long as doing so does not compromise me or my family in any way."

Harris turned on his barstool to face Russell. He glanced around the room, making sure nobody was close enough to overhear them, but they were pretty isolated at the end of the bar.

"I'm guessing they want to get in your head. They'll offer you something quite tempting. If you do not accept, they will either force it on you or kill you. Once you know that they are out there manipulating the population, they need you to be bonded to them. If they get any inkling that you might defect, they'll eliminate you. Do you understand?"

There was a knot in Russell's stomach, and it clenched tighter. He *knew* Harris was telling him the truth. Not the message for the masses, but the harsh, cold reality. He nodded.

Harris's shoulders relaxed almost imperceptibly, but Russell noticed. "All right, then," Harris said. "Let's find a more private place to talk."

They left the bar and walked uptown a bit until a car drove up next to them, and Harris opened the door. He motioned to Russell to get in. They were dropped uptown at an upscale Italian restaurant and ushered inside to a table at the back. There seemed to be few patrons, but it was an off hour, a little before 4:00 p.m. A plate of bruschetta appeared on the pearl-white tablecloths, and a man served them coffee.

Russell stared at the appetizer. Something was off about it. Harris noticed him staring and chuckled. He picked up a piece of the toasted bread and bit into it himself, smiling at Russell's trepidation. Gingerly, Russell picked up a piece and placed it on his bread dish. He put his napkin in his lap, searching for other ways to stall.

"Tell me what you meant by offering me protection," Russell asked. "What kind of protection are you referring to, and what do you want in return?"

Harris finished chewing his bruschetta, running his tongue over his teeth to get the last crumbs. He wiped his hands and mouth on his napkin and took a sip of coffee. Russell sat rock still, the untouched bruschetta waiting on his plate.

"The most fundamental protection, Mr. Vaderman, of course. You have run in with violent people. You need to find a place you can go to for safety, and you will need arms to defend yourself."

Russell was shocked. If he had been eating, he would have stopped mid-chew. "I keep a handgun in my home."

"Mr. Vaderman, you will be dealing with the United States Armed Forces; do you really think your little handgun will be of any use if you fall into disfavor?"

Russell had never thought about the subject in that way at all. "What are you suggesting I do?"

Harris put his elbows on the table and laced his hands

together, intertwining his fingers. He looked right at Russell. "I suggest you give them *something*. Something small. Something to make them believe you are cooperating. And I suggest you *learn*. Learn what they know about the mind, then learn what they are about, what their plans are, what their timeline is. You see, Mr. Vaderman, I know people pretty well. And I do not believe their agenda will sit right with you. I'm counting on that, in fact. I'm counting on your willingness to stand up for what you believe is right. And I am also counting on you being, in fact, able to resist their chemical attacks on your mind. To that end, I am willing to supply you with arms and munitions to protect yourself and your family. And perhaps... your encampment."

At that moment, the waiter brought two steaming plates of pasta to the table and filled the water glasses. Russell felt his stomach growl; he hadn't eaten all day.

"I don't think you really know me, Harris. I don't get involved like that in political issues. I do my best to be supportive—"

"From afar, yes, I know, Mr. Vaderman, and with financial contributions. But this has chosen you. You have no option but to be involved, so now you need to decide what the nature of your *non-financial* participation will be."

Russell took a bite of the pasta without thinking. It was in a savory marinara sauce with some unknown ingredient that made him want to roll it on his tongue. Perhaps it was lemon? Suddenly he felt a rush in his head.

Russell knew immediately what it was but was strangely unconcerned. It was as if on some level, he knew it would come to this. He allowed the hallucinogen to enter his body and watched himself as if from a distance. The Man in The Hut appeared faintly behind Harris and nodded to Russell and stroked his long, white beard.

Russell laid down his fork and took a deep breath. A vision

came to him of his home in the mountains. New structures were built on it, housing for a large community, and he was aware of underground bunkers. His perspective panned back, and he saw his country, the United States, barraged by fires and explosions, men in tactical gear brandishing submachine guns, the Capitol building with its windows smashed and mobs of people shooting at each other, grenades blasting and buildings set aflame. Civil war, beyond which was pure anarchy, while hurricanes, forest fires, and earthquakes pummeled the earth. And then Russell's bird's-eye view of his little community in the mountains was back again. It seemed much larger than his eighty-seven acres. There were apple trees and farmland and people gathering in a community hall discussing the Community Creed. An exclusive society dedicated to people who would uphold new laws of integrity, compassion, tolerance, and mutual support. He blinked and the vision was gone.

"Do you think it would come to that?" Russell asked in a whisper.

Harris cocked his head sideways, and Russell realized Harris knew something had happened but had no idea what. Harris had obviously expected Russell to be either unaware of or angry at the use of the chemical; instead, Harris clearly saw that Russell was affected and unperturbed. The drug did not bend his will nor provoke the defensive reaction it had when Maya had given it to him. Russell could *see* that Harris had needed to do this to know for himself what the drug's effect on him was, and whether Russell would be pliant to anyone's desires if he were dosed.

Russell was seeing the world from multiple angles all at the same time. He felt like he was too large for his body, and the sensation of hovering near the ceiling that he'd had in The Hut dream returned. His stomach lurched ominously. Looking "down," Russell could see the physical aspect of Harris sitting in his chair and that he was fidgeting nervously under the table with the edge of the tablecloth, and he could feel the palpable anxiety in Harris's head and his apprehension about what he had just done by giving Russell the drug. He distinctly saw Harris's conflicting motivations: part indeed noble, to keep the conservatives from planting inclinations in the hearts of their followers, part Harris's own ego, contriving to be the one in power himself, and there was something else Russell could not quite identify.

Russell also saw in Harris's mind a stockpile of firearms, grenades, and defense supplies that could be used to secure a sizable stronghold.

As Russell sat quietly, Harris's demeanor turned slowly to apprehension; a change that he tried to hide and believed to be successfully accomplishing, while Russell felt strangely calm. His initiation into his personal transformation felt complete. While he was still growing and learning to understand this gift that he had, he was no longer fighting it. If he could just figure out how to turn the volume down when he wanted to….

"I am grateful to know that there will be adequate defense equipment if we need it, and I thank you for offering it," Russell said quietly. "Although I'm sure it can also be purchased if I decide it is necessary. I had already intended to work with the NSA in a limited capacity. My question remains: What do you want in return?"

Harris shifted in his chair. "Inclusion. Bring some of our people with you. We can teach you how to manufacture and operate a defense system, one such as would be difficult to buy without raising significant eyebrows. In return, you can deprogram anyone who makes their way inside and tries to sabotage us. We need a new, more secure safe zone. Even if Ganaffe loses reelection, he will hold reins of power for years to come. It is unlikely he will relinquish his office willingly, and he will create as much chaos as he can in his exit. We believe he intends to form a new party from which to pillage the country as dictator;

he, in fact, fancies himself a demigod. There is a grave risk of severe civil unrest lasting into the foreseeable future."

"We?" Russell almost missed the reference.

Harris kept his face neutral and did not answer; although it seemed obvious he could not be operating alone, the specific allusion to others was clearly a slip.

"So, you need to wait out the storm somewhere, and I'm your first choice," Russell said.

"Indeed," Harris stated, and was silent.

Abruptly, Russell stood up to leave. "Well, I'm sure Maya will be pleased that we spoke." Harris jumped up as well, his napkin falling to the floor.

Harris appeared perplexed. "So, you'll join us? I will make arrangements for the defense supplies."

"I will do what needs to be done," Russell answered. "Let's hold off on any weapons' purchases for now." He left the restaurant.

CHAPTER 51

Joshua paced the kitchen in the Sutton Place co-op as his mother and his aunt spoke in the living room. He was still shaking a little from his experience in the precinct and in jail, and then he had to go to an urgent care to have his arm stitched up. When he discovered that Uncle Russell had plunked down a quarter of a million dollars for his bail, he was shocked beyond words. He knew his uncle loved him, and he knew he was well-off, but that amount of money and the trust implied was staggering.

Then there were his mother and aunt talking dynamically in the other room. It made him nervous. While he had known both all his life and associated each with the unconditional love of family, *they* had never seen eye to eye, and always seemed to end up in an argument eventually. Joshua had said he wanted to go home with his mother, but Aunt Maya had insisted they all come first to Sutton Place for dinner and to wait for his uncle. But then his uncle didn't show. Where was he?

Finally, at 5:30 p.m. the door opened, and Uncle Russell came in. Joshua rushed over to hug him and to thank him over and over again for paying all that money for his bail. Uncle Russell hugged him back and smiled at him, putting his hand along Joshua's face. Like the father Joshua never had.

But his uncle did not look well for all that. Joshua noticed strain in his face, and he felt his fatigue, which creeped him out a little bit. He shouldn't have been able to do *that*. And come to think of it, Uncle Russell looked decidedly different. Bigger, or… something. His aunt and his mother seemed to notice it too.

"Russell! Thank God you're home, we were so worried about you!" Aunt Maya said. "Where did you go? Is everything okay?"

Joshua's mother was looking at his uncle with her head cocked sideways, as if she was in on a secret, but she wasn't exactly sure what the secret was.

Uncle Russell put his hand up and said he was way too tired to talk about anything; suffice it to say, everything was going to be fine, and he just wanted to go to sleep for now. He told Joshua he'd see him at work tomorrow and then disappeared into his bedroom down the hall. After a moment, Joshua heard the shower running in the master bath.

So, Joshua and his mother packed up and headed back to the Village, leaving Aunt Maya in a state of disarray.

Joshua and Braelyn took the subway and then walked the rest of the way, as his mother didn't have the resources to spend on Ubers all the time and it was still light out. Joshua might have offered to put it on his credit card that his uncle gave him to use, but after posting $250,000 bail, he didn't want to cost him anything more.

"Mom, what was wrong with Uncle Russell? He didn't look right," Joshua asked.

His mother looked surprised by the question. "That's a noteworthy insight, Josh." She peered at him. "I think that Cingulate

Services group actually did a lot for you." But she didn't answer him, and Joshua found himself feeling frightened again. Now that he thought about it, his mother seemed different to him too, but the change was less striking. She just seemed calmer, where his uncle seemed… bigger.

CHAPTER 52

Two weeks later, Jeremy called Russell to tell him he'd gotten the charges dismissed against Joshua. He had explained to the judge that the prosecution could show no clear connection between Donny Anderson's death and the Monday evening Joshua saw him in the subway station.

According to Joshua, Donny Anderson left the station of his own accord, which presented no picture of clear and present danger that Joshua would be responsible for, and ultimately, Anderson had to have traveled on his own power to the East River, maybe that day or maybe another. It was not even clear if his death was a murder or a suicide. The marks on his wrists might have been from bonds, but there was no way to know for sure. In fact, not much had been determined about Anderson's death at all, not even the time it happened, and while it was important for his family to pursue the matter for closure, Joshua did not much fit into that scenario.

Likewise, while Peter Jackson was "missing," there was no definitive indication that he had come to any harm. A forty-three second call from his cell phone that Joshua, under the influence of scopolamine, could not remember, was hardly incriminating. Jackson's DNA was nowhere on file, and his girlfriend proved singularly uncooperative in the investigation. It appeared she had been abused and viewed Jackson's disappearance as a rather fortunate development. She had, in fact, become a "person of interest."

Russell listened to this news and did not believe this had anything to do with help from Trenaman or the NSA but was simply the work of a good lawyer who was able to keep the case from going to court, a case that would have found Joshua innocent anyway. It wasn't worth "paying" Trenaman for. He thanked Jeremy heartily for his acumen and his persistence to work quickly on the case.

Braelyn's matter was another issue. Jeremy had had the cocaine tested, and the results showed that it had originated in the Apurimac Valley in Central Peru, not a usual source of cocaine purchased in Colombia, since Colombia had its own cocaine for sale in much closer reach. Jeremy sent his brief challenging the origin of this cocaine allegedly being found in Braelyn Pressman's suitcase. He intended to call witnesses to the seizure of the goods to demand to know every detail about what they found and why they thought it necessary to search her suitcase without her present. To that end, the names of the customs agents needed to be disclosed so he could call them to the stand.

At the present time, no one was stepping up to testify as the agent responsible for the search. If no one did, it would be hard to pin the possession charge on her. Jeremy just submitted the paperwork and told Russell it could be several weeks or more before they knew if anyone from customs was going to appear. If there was no one, he would petition for Braelyn's case to be dismissed as well. No promises, he had told Russell, but these guys are like traffic cops who have no time to attend court for contested tickets. It was highly unusual for a search and seizure to be challenged, and they frequently didn't show for the trial.

It was easy to imagine Trenaman pulling the strings in Braelyn's case and making the customs officer disappear. But, seriously, did anyone really want to commit perjury claiming they clearly remembered this contraband coming from that suitcase, nearly two months ago? Sure, it should have all been labeled, but to have to be cross-examined on a lie by Jeremy Southpine, who had a reputation as something of a hard-ass in the courtroom, well, that was asking a lot.

It didn't matter in the end. It was possible that Trenaman was superfluous in getting everything dismissed, but Russell began to find appealing the idea of having at least quasi professionals teach him about paranormal phenomena and how he might come to control what was happening in his mind. He still felt at odds with this new talent he had. It seemed to behave erratically, sometimes foisting itself upon him with unwanted information and sometimes eluding him completely when he tried to call it. It was no secret that the US government had had an abiding interest in the subject for years, so working with Trenaman could be to his advantage, and he felt sure that he could keep Trenaman from knowing more than Russell wanted him to.

He called Trenaman and set a date to start and found himself looking forward to it.

The image of the stockpiled defense supplies that he'd seen in Harris's restaurant swam before Russell's eyes. *That* was significant, and Russell wished he knew why. Yes, he owned a gun, but he was a wealthy man in New York City, and he kept it for defense against petty thieves. He had never used it, never even brandished it, and had never really imagined he ever would. And yet, a vast weapons supply had just been offered to him. Was he going to need it?

Russell closed his eyes in frustration. Instantly, the image of the Ancient One floated in front of him.

There is a Great Transformation coming....

Gingerly, Russell tried to *reach* out with his senses, out into—anywhere. Just "out there." He expected nothing, but slowly, as if being filled in layer upon layer, he saw the planet in a state of flux. Choppy molten lava, like a tempestuous sea, bubbled beneath a world growing ever hotter, permafrost melted away, releasing thousands of microbes that had lain dormant for centuries, storms surged in the oceans and the skies, bringing violent winds and rapidly shifting tides, and animals scurried to find new feeding grounds. The warming oceans sent fishes of all kinds to deeper depths in search of food, leaving birds and dolphins starving nearer the surface.

The focus changed and he saw the United States as a nation literally on fire. The entire West Coast burned, with toxic ash falling over the midwestern states, and Mt. St. Helen's erupted amid the apocalyptic scene. People ran for their lives, fired semi-automatic machine guns, looted homes and businesses, and the government was dissolved. In its place, Russell saw a golden statue of President Ganaffe; his believers lined up for miles to walk by and bow, offer gifts, and kiss the statue's feet. They walked like zombies, cultists, or a new religious faction. Families hid desperately in makeshift shelters and scavenged for food while an armed, grassroots militia with QAnon, Three Percenters, and neo-Nazi insignia marched between burned-down buildings. It was a nightmare, like something from *Fahrenheit 451* or *Soylent Green*. Russell pressed his hands to the sides of his face and shut his eyes tighter. No, no, no....

You will lead the people of Good Heart....

Russell was shaking. He opened his eyes and found himself sitting in his office on Sixth Avenue. His intercom was buzzing, and Rosalee was asking him if he was all right. She must have been trying to get him for several minutes because the buzzing stopped, and there was a knock on his door instead.

"Come," Russell said.

Rosalee walked in timidly. "Is everything okay, Mr. Vaderman? I don't want to intrude. There are protesters downstairs, and it seems the front windows have been shattered."

Russell was oddly unsurprised. "Are Frank and Liam downstairs? Do they need to call for help?"

"Yes, they are there. No one is actually attempting to come in. I'm guessing because none of us in this building have any physical goods anyone can take, like retail stores do."

With Russell's heightened senses, he could sense her surprise at his calm reaction, her loss of emotional equilibrium, and her near panic. Vaderman Ventures had the entire fortieth floor, and were one of several companies with space in the building, but they were all strictly administrative offices. Russell stood up and walked over to her. He touched her gently on her shoulder.

"It's okay, Rosalee," he said. "It's just glass. As long as no one was hurt. Let's close and lock the steel doors on this floor, and then please call a glass company and see if we can get someone to come over and fix it as soon as this is over. Offer them a 25 percent gratuity for making it one of their first jobs. We don't have physical items, but there are a lot of important documents that need protecting. We will stay here until the fireworks are over. Are the police on the scene at all?"

Rosalee took strength from Russell's cool-headed composure and visibly relaxed. "Yes, they are on the avenue. The looting seems to have moved down the street some."

Russell looked out his high-rise window and saw a mob moving steadily downtown. He swallowed hard. He turned on the news expecting it to be covering the protest, but instead it was laying out the projected impact of the new SARS virus that was just hitting the New York City metro region, with Queens being the worst affected. It suggested the numbers would soon hold a comparison to the damage in Italy, whose healthcare system had been completely overrun. The numbers in New York City were rising at an exponential rate and could mirror that need to do the equivalent of war-zone triage in the very near future.

Despite his outward calm, Russell was shocked. Could it be *that* bad? How much of this was real and how much some drug-induced hallucination in his head? Was the world falling apart, *right now*? The reporter cut away abruptly to a breaking story coming out of midtown Manhattan, where rioters were taking the streets, and the police were struggling to bring order.

The center of his soul became suddenly very still, as Russell assessed what he had to do.

First order of business was to secure the safe egress of his employees to their homes, then to assure that whatever Russell could not carry would be secured here in his office, and then get himself home to assemble his vital belongings. He needed to convince Maya, Braelyn, and Joshua to prepare to move upstate. If he were to take his "vision" as genuine, he would need to contract builders, farmers, and manufacturers of various kinds. Would he need Harris's arms after all? And then how would he decide who the people of Good Heart were? If he really could secure safe space amid tragedy, how could he take some and leave others behind? On what basis should he select them? It startled him to realize how seriously he was actually taking this.

He nearly panicked then, until he recognized that the future was not unfolding quite so rapidly as all that. Whatever the course of evolving events, people on the whole were slow to acknowledge, even slower to accept radical changes. He figured he had at least six months, maybe longer, before order fell apart on a grand scale—If that was even going to come to pass. If Ganaffe lost the election and abdicated gracefully, it was possible that it would all be unnecessary anyway. But he couldn't shake the image of the golden statue and its allusion to the "golden calf" of the Book of Exodus. It was just too egregious to be discarded completely.

After the mob had passed, Liam and Frank had boarded up

the windows, and a glass company was arranged for the next morning, Rosalee and his other employees were safely on their way to their homes. Russell stepped outside.

A couple was staring at the damage to the window and shaking their heads. The man looked at Russell's shattered front windows with surprise. "What in the world did they hope to get from your building? Doesn't look like you had any goods or food in there."

"No," Russell answered. "Just letting off steam and frustration, I guess." Russell looked more closely at the couple. There was something about them that he liked. "Are you two just roaming the streets in all this?"

"No," the woman said. "We were just returning from the New York City Department of Health, and had to, uh, take the long way home. The riots are all over the city, protesting another brutal death of a Black American."

"They're mounting up by the dozens," the man said. "I don't understand what the hell is wrong with people who condone police brutality. But rioting does not bring back the dead; it only fuels the flames."

"Do you live in the city? Why were you going to the Department of Health?" Russell asked.

"No," the woman said. "Long Island. I'm a physician; we wanted to get a better handle on what can be done about this new SARS virus. We think it's going to get pretty dicey here in the city very soon. We're trying to decide where to hide out that we can still do some good." She looked at the man with her who put his arm around her protectively.

Russell put his hand out. "I'm Russell Vaderman."

"Troy DeJacob."

"Tobi Lister."

As he shook each of their hands, Russell got a flash of insight. This couple had been through an immense trauma, and they had a fierce and complicated bond to each other that

Russell felt instantly envious of. Had he ever felt that close to anyone?

Troy laughed. "Tobi thinks we should be building an 'ark' and saving what's best of life on this planet before it's too late." Tobi gave him a questioning look, and Russell knew she was wondering why he was talking about that to a stranger.

Troy shrugged. "I can't argue it. She's always been a bit psychic, and the whole damn world is on fire these days—and I don't just mean California."

"It's a good question. We should prepare; we may need a safe place to weather the storm if it comes to that," Russell said.

The three looked at each other for a full minute. Russell felt the ground move slightly, like this meeting was of an importance that he would understand later. He felt *El Curandero Grande* somewhere nearby.

"Hey," Russell said, fishing in his pocket. "Here's my card. Do you have a contact number? I mean, I'm working on developing a sanctuary of sorts. Very early stages. But we might need each other."

Tobi's eyes narrowed slightly. "How do you know you want to include us? We don't know each other at all."

A million answers flashed into Russell's mind, none that were appropriate to tell strangers. "Call it a hunch," he said. Tobi looked at Troy, and Troy shrugged; he scribbled a phone number, and they parted ways on Sixth Avenue.

As Russell headed home to Sutton Place, he got a call from Harris.

"The city is in chaos. I hope you are considering my offer of defensive arms," he said.

"I am considering. No decision yet," Russell said.

Harris paused for a second on the phone. "I hope you do, and that you will be willing to give to the movement in exchange."

"*If* I take you up on it, I will provide safe haven for those who deserve it." The line was quiet. "And I will attempt the removal of corrupt influences from susceptible minds," Russell continued and then waited. He could almost see Harris's brows furrowing through the phone. It wasn't much as payment. "Or, I can purchase my own armaments, *if* I decide it's needed," Russell finished. "Your choice."

"I'm sure we will work something out," Harris said.

After hanging up, Russell called Jeremy and asked him to see what he could do to get Braelyn's bracelet removed. He explained that the crowds of New York City were no place to be if this turned out to be a pandemic, and invited Jeremy and his family to join them upstate if they'd like. Russell felt that if Trenaman had indeed pulled some strings somewhere, releasing his sister should be a simple bureaucratic procedure. There was still half a mil posted in bond money, after all. And it would also be a good test to see if the NSA man would be true to his word.

He texted Braelyn and suggested she and Joshua meet him at home with Maya, and to bring clothing and personal items to prepare for an extended stay in the Catskills. For the time being, he told her it was to wait out the virus. They were walking in the door when Russell arrived.

Once they were all together, Russell assembled them in the living room and outlined in broad brushstrokes his fears about the pandemic and the looming potential breakdown of civilized society, depending on the outcome of the election. He deliberately left out his visions of planetary upheavals, as he thought they would think he was crazy. While Maya looked smugly affirmed of her extreme leftist beliefs, he expected a lot of pushback from Braelyn. To his surprise, they all just listened and nodded. Until then, he had never realized how much his intellect and intuition were respected by his family. But then, they'd all been through the mill between the courts and scopolamine drugs, and the news of the virus, which was becoming pretty terrifying. One look out the window made it obvious that all hell was breaking loose outside as well.

"So, you don't think this will all just blow over." Braelyn made it a statement, not a question.

"Sure it will," Russell said. "This time. And the next. And probably the next."

"I've been saying this for months! This is all because of police brutality," Maya said.

Russell looked at his wife. "In part, yes. But most of the people down there on the street right now who are wreaking havoc are neither 'peaceful' protesters nor police. Do you feel safe?"

Maya opened her mouth to argue, but Braelyn gave her a look that silenced her in her tracks.

"You can take your chances down there if you want, Maya," Braelyn said, "but I don't want to get trampled in those demonstrations. And then, there is the virus… I think it will be bad."

Russell noted how they had all grown in the last couple of weeks, with Braelyn seeming to have changed the most. She seemed much calmer and self-assured, as she allowed herself to believe the information she was processing about her surroundings, even while accepting others might not understand how she gleaned her knowledge. It was as if she finally got it, that *she* wasn't the problem.

Maya nodded in agreement with Braelyn's assessment, remarking how many people seemed to be coughing as they walked the streets. Joshua, too, had noticed this, once his mother had mentioned it. He seemed relieved to hear they would be moving up to their home in the Catskills for a while, but that could also have been his desire to get as far away from the New York City Police Department as possible.

In the morning, Russell looked out the window, and everything was peaceful. He turned on the news, and the talk was of sports, Ganaffe's last rally, and an electrical fire in Brooklyn. No hint of the ominous visions of last night. The world had returned to normal. Again, Russell imagined he was losing his mind or, at the very least, making mountains out of molehills.

Maya picked up the mail and handed Russell a letter from the Bail Department in County Court. Russell expected Joshua's $250,000 bail to have been significantly dipped into, with some nefarious reason cited. He was in complete shock when he opened it to read that a credit for $1.25 million was being deposited in his account. After calling and arguing for forty-five minutes with the bondsman, who swore there had been no mistake, the shimmering shape of an ancient old man with opaque, white eyes appeared at the edge of his peripheral vision. Russell let the matter drop. He felt like he had just been transported into some alternate universe. Which was the "real" world? He had no clue anymore. Is this what the quantum physicists meant when they said anything within the path of a probability curve could be real at any given time—and even—at the same time?

In the weeks that followed, Russell sent carpenters and farmers up to their summer home. They were to build houses, above and below ground, plant grain, fruit, and vegetables, and build a solid bulkhead around the perimeter. He also contracted to have a high tech surveillance system installed.

CHAPTER 53

For a change, Officer Greenstone was not wearing his usual smirk. He stood at Detective Rodriguez's desk impatiently, while Rodriguez read the missive for the second time. Finally, Rodriguez looked up.

"When did you receive this?"

"Just now," Greenstone said. "From Commissioner Harrows. I brought it right to you. This Horatius Marsden guy has just been located and contacted. He admits to the purchase, but he claims he is not in possession of the arms shipment. He does not appear to be much interested in cooperating, so we're sending officers out to apprehend him."

Rodriguez glanced down the hall and saw the commissioner munching pizza with several officers. Greenstone himself smelled like an Italian restaurant, and Rodriguez shook his head. The daily office pizza had become a thing a couple of months ago, but how often could a person eat pizza? Rodriguez started reading the document out loud as Greenstone shifted from foot to foot.

"This memo says this guy Marsden 'contracted for a caravan

of weapons grade machine guns, explosives, and missiles to be bought in Bogota and delivered to Russell Vaderman at his home in the Catskills. One individual, unidentified as yet, was killed during the transaction.' What is their connection, and why in the hell would Vaderman want anything like this, anyway?" Rodriguez asked.

"Beats the hell out of me, but it might be connected to that nephew of his being doped up so he won't remember a murder happening in front of his face. Do you think that sister of his was dealing arms in Colombia in addition to buying cocaine? I knew this family was bad news. They just smell bad all around. They *reek* of privilege." Greenstone sniffed exaggeratedly. "I'm glad our commissioner has finally come around to that understanding."

Rodriguez nodded guardedly. Commissioner Harrows had recently done an about-face on a variety of issues, and while it could be accepted as necessary in defense of the liberals' attacks on the NYPD, the commissioner seemed to be veering toward an almost evangelical intolerance to anything that wasn't White ultraconservative. Rodriguez distrusted Harrows now even more than he had before. Maybe that was why Harrows had started feeding them every day.

The plight of Black people was seminal; well-known, hugely fought for even by many Whites—they even had their own movement. Hispanics like himself were quite another thing. Not Black or White. Not really fitting into a society that more and more did not tolerate difference, and with no compelling voice to protest with.

James Rodriguez's father was from El Salvador, had come to the United States as a teenager looking for work, and had been lucky enough to get a green card and then marry a citizen. But he'd lived under the constant fear, real or imagined, that he might be sent back in a heartbeat. James was born in New York City, but he carried with him his father's legacy of fear and uncertainty. It made him feel all the prouder of his accomplishment in the ranks of the NYPD, but he distrusted anyone who might challenge his legitimacy.

Rodriguez tried to find a connection between Vaderman, his drugged nephew waking up in what was most likely a murder scene but with an unfound victim, and the large-scale weapons shipment. He came up with nothing. Adding in the cocaine in his sister's suitcase, which had somehow recently become questionable, and he got less. Vaderman was annoying, but he had no motive to set up a well-defended fortress in the Catskills. He was an extremely wealthy and successfully established man in New York City, by all accounts happy in his marriage, and middle of the road philosophically. What were the motivators of violence in the upper and middle class populations? Money, power, sex, and political ideology. Vaderman had none of those conflicts.

Rodriguez always tried to imagine what would make *him* commit a given crime or, in this case, what would he want with all those munitions. This thinking often gave him insights into his suspect and made him a formidable detective. But when he imagined himself in Vaderman's place, all he could think was he was being set up. He did acknowledge that could be because he was thinking like a Hispanic living in a world of inequality.

"We need to bring Vaderman in," he said to Greenstone. "Check his office, his home, or trace his cell phone if you have to, even if it's all the way to the Catskills. Find out where he is, and let's get him in for questioning. I want him in here today."

CHAPTER 54

Russell's "lessons" with Trenaman had been ongoing for several weeks. He was tutored in some of the known "Laws of Paranormal Activity," along lines that stated energy is neither created nor destroyed, that matter cannot be created out of a vacuum, *ex nihilo*, and that every action must have an equal and opposite reaction. Basic Newtonian physics that Russell already knew, and he marveled at their conscientious application to behavioral anomalies. He was prompted to attempt "psychic" tasks repetitively, like controlling the roll of dice or reading hidden cards. It seemed fairly useless to Russell, but he figured they were trying to get a sense of what he was capable of.

The lessons also brushed against quantum theory whose relationship to the psyche was ill-understood, but which clearly demonstrated that energy and matter *are* interchangeable. To Russell, this meant it could certainly *appear* as if matter was being created or energy was being destroyed.

To Russell, quantum theory was where the real understanding lay: the concept that reality existed in "superposition," and that an electron (or maybe a thought particle?) *de facto* existed in more than one place at a time as it orbited nuclei because it had an *equal likelihood* of being found anywhere along its orbit. Quantum mechanics said it could not ascertain what is present in a place, only the *probability* of it being so. And within that probability were other possible realities. As crazy as it sounded, the work of Einstein, Bohr, Planck, Heisenberg, and all the frontier quantum physicists had corroborated it, while acknowledging the supreme conundrum it created for the scientific understanding of the world in which they lived. But what if this were true beyond the realm of subatomic particles?

Quantum theory's proposition implied that reality was a continuum of probabilities, which did not collapse into a single reality until it was observed. And if an electron could be in any number of places at any given instant of time, it could also *behave* as if it were in any one of these places, *all at the same time.* This meant that—theoretically—there could be any number of valid alternate realities existing simultaneously, until one was actually experienced.

Physicists called this yet-undeclared existence the "multiverse."

Russell asked himself if this occurred at the molecular level, why not at the macroscopic level, just as the shaman had said? Of course, by the laws of quantum mechanics, the electron could never be somewhere that did not fall within its probability curve; it could not be found outside its own orbit. So, there were limits on what forms reality might take.

But Russell thought to take it further, without having studied the advanced mathematics to prove it, of course. Using the template of light as having both the properties of energy (waveforms) and matter (photons), it seemed to Russell to beg the relationship of thoughts and emotions to particles of energy that existed in that multiverse, or, range of possible universes. How else could *El Curandero Grande* appear in his Uber and then whisk him away to the Northern Andes and back again? The information he was gathering from Trenaman's tutelage was helping him immensely to believe that perhaps he was not losing his mind after all—an idea he had left in suspension since his conversation with Dr. Gray until now. If he had become a lunatic, he was indeed lost.

He did not share these thoughts with Trenaman or his crew. Indeed, the quantum theory module was presented by an expert from the Department of Defense, and Russell doubted Trenaman himself clearly understood the science.

Trenaman's team continued to test Russell with tasks like asking him to move small objects with his mind. He tried and, at one point, he almost felt that he could, but then the impulse dissolved, as if a tire had suddenly gone flat. They asked him to read an image from someone's thoughts and later to extinguish a candle flame or make it flare. He failed miserably at all of them. On another occasion, they gave him latitude and longitude coordinates and asked him to describe what was located there. He did get a very hazy outline of bunkers and a nuclear plant, but when he realized they were asking him to spy on sites in Ukraine, he was purposely vaguer than he might have been able to be. He did not want to be useful to them in that way.

When he was asked to explain how he had unclouded Joshua's mind, Russell genuinely had no answer beyond what he already told them. He "saw" the strands of confusion and disentangled them with his mental fingers. He knew it made no sense to them; it didn't really make sense to himself. He suggested that perhaps it was his emotional connection to Joshua that allowed it to happen.

In other sessions, they took a subject and dosed her with scopolamine and asked Russell to reverse the effect. He truly wasn't able to detect much of a problem, other than the fact that she had been dosed, and he told them so. He conjectured that it was because there was nothing ego-dystonic in the process. She willingly took the drug, and she was not being asked to do anything that, at a deeper level, she would have resisted. He *was* able to accurately identify out of a lineup of ten people, which three had received the drug and who had not.

So after several weeks, Russell thought the training sessions were basically a wrap. It seemed clear to all that in the laboratory setting, with their prescribed tasks, he wasn't of much use. Trenaman asked him in for one final meeting.

In truth, the sessions that had him focusing on the abilities of his mind had taught him to recognize much of what was his uncanny ability versus what was merely in his imagination, and the quantum physics they had introduced him to helped him to believe in himself, so he was a little sorry to see it come to an end. Nevertheless, he felt he had learned all they could teach him, and further study into advanced quantum mechanics was something he could do on his own.

As soon as Russell walked into the room, he knew something was off, although on the surface, nothing looked out of the ordinary. The hairs on his neck rose, and his heart and respiratory rates kicked up a notch.

Trenaman sat at his usual desk, and his female assistant sat on the chair in the corner where she'd been each time before. Russell noticed immediately that she had been dosed, but he said nothing. It was almost like he could smell it now.

Trenaman offered Russell a seat, and he took it. "Today I want to test the effect of the drug on you. I'd like you to drink this milkshake. It is laced with scopolamine."

Trenaman already knew Russell was immune to manipulation, so this made no sense. He looked at the glass. He touched the sides, which were sweating from its half-frozen contents. Russell extended his awareness into the shake. There was no scopolamine in this drink. Something darker and eviler lay within, a poison of some sort. Russell's heart beat even faster and he chided himself to keep a completely even expression.

"Sure," Russell said and scooped the glass up, "accidentally" sweeping it off the desk and onto the floor. The glass broke and its contents spilled, slowly seeping into the carpet.

"I'm so sorry!" Russell said immediately. "My clumsiness." He grabbed a napkin from the desk and bent down.

"No matter," Trenaman said. "Eva, would you mind cleaning that up for Mr. Vaderman?" They exchanged a look and a subtle nod.

"Why, of course," Eva said and walked toward Russell. *Something* alerted Russell and sent him into high gear. Perspiration broke out on his forehead and time seemed to slow down. He whipped around to face Eva just as she pulled a long dagger out from behind her. He grabbed her hand with a strength he hadn't known he possessed, spun her around, and in an instant, he held the dagger against her own throat. She was pinned and struggling madly. Russell carefully backed up against a wall and held her there.

As he touched Eva, Russell could feel the effect of the scopolamine as a gnarled shroud of darkness within her. She was no killer; this was imposed on her. Reflexively, Russell *reached* into her head as he had done with Joshua, but less gently, and saw within the ball of darkness a maelstrom of chaotic colors that were pummeling her brain. Covering it within a mental fist, he squeezed hard. It exploded and Eva dropped to the floor, her breath coming rough and raspy. She lay on the floor in utter bewilderment, while Russell's breath came almost as ragged as Eva's.

Trenaman laughed. "It would appear that there are times when your abilities do come to the fore."

Russell glared back. "Apparently, when there is an emotional trigger, like a threat to my life," he said. Russell stood in a slight crouch, his muscles taut, his eyes darting around the room when they weren't fixated on Trenaman with an intensity that was almost palpable.

Trenaman gave him a menacing stare, and Russell, looking to stall, looked for any keen, new insights that could help keep him alive until he had a plan. He was obviously not supposed to walk out of there today.

"You were once a different man," Russell said. "You were once a man of compassion and integrity. You believed in the human spirit, in human beings. What happened to you?"

Trenaman looked startled for a moment, then sneered. "You see that in my mind, do you?"

"I see that in your heart. A heart that has gone cold. Sealed itself over, letting nothing in."

Trenaman's lip curled. "If you had truly seen what I've seen, the violence that comes of disorder... the meaningless carnage and suffering instigated for the sake of someone's idea of a deity...." Trenaman nearly spit his words. "They blew my leg off in the name of their god. They killed my closest friends. They are nothing but radicals. Fanatics. The way they treat their people... their women and children live in squalor. No, Vaderman, I no longer leave my heart open. I follow the orders of my nation. We stand for righteousness, and I believe we can continue to do so if our people are united in a common cause."

"And," Trenaman continued more calmly, "you have some abilities you have not shared with me. How did you know the shake was not safe to drink? In the weeks we've been working together, I thought I had gained your trust. Can you read my mind?"

"Why would I tell you anything, now that I see you want me dead? This is what you call 'trust?'"

"I needed to test you at the last. If you are not willing to work with me, as it seems you are not, then you are of no use to me. In fact, you are a liability. Surely you understand, I cannot let you live knowing what you now know. But I would like to know how you did *that*." Trenaman nodded at his assistant.

The woman was struggling to get to her feet, confused and

holding her belly as if she'd been punched in the solar plexus. In a way, she had been. Russell reached down and helped her to her feet. She looked at Russell as if she knew she had missed something important. "What happened? How did I end up on the floor? Why do I feel so... awful?"

Russell looked at her with sympathy. "Because your boss here drugged you and told you to kill me." Her eyes dilated in fear.

Trenaman was smiling from behind his desk.

"Our 'training' is over," Russell said.

"Apparently. But do tell me: How did you know the shake was poisoned?"

"I sensed it," Russell said, only bothering to answer in order to stall for time. "There was something not right about it. It wasn't scopolamine, because I've become sensitive to that, but it didn't feel right. But that's... that's something I've been able to do for ages. Maybe not so specifically, and to my knowledge, no one has ever tried to kill me before with poisoned food. But just having the feeling that something is good to eat or not... that feels almost primal."

Russell truly believed what he had just said, while also realizing the contradiction of having eaten Maya's biscuit. For years, Russell was unable to eat mushrooms without getting gruesomely sick—he'd been told he lacked the digestive enzyme for it. Being able to sense whether a food contained mushrooms was something he'd been doing forever. He did have to focus on it, which he had not bothered to do with the biscuit, and he realized not everyone could do this, but it hardly seemed paranormal to him.

"I would like you to teach me to do that," Trenaman said.

At that moment, Russell had no inclination to teach Trenaman anything, especially if it would further his meddling in people's minds. Unless... Would it keep him alive longer to give Trenaman a lesson in how to sense his surroundings?

Surely he already knew this on some level, as a Navy captain. He probably called it "instinct."

"I 'extend' my consciousness into whatever I am looking at. I don't think I can be more specific than that, but I'm sure you've performed similarly when you were in battle."

Trenaman was silent, exuding anger for being reminded that he was now confined to desk work. Russell vied for time, weighing his options. He was on high alert, noticeably in the grip of a fight or flight reaction.

Trenaman nodded with an air of finality and opened the top drawer of his desk. His eyes were riveted on Russell.

Russell was sure there was a gun in the desk. It made sense for there to be one there. As Trenaman reached inside, Russell looked desperately for an immediate way out. He knew he could outrun Trenaman, but he'd have to get through the door first, which was still a couple of feet away from him, and he couldn't outrun a bullet.

The door suddenly burst open and Officers Greenstone and Rodriguez appeared with their pistols drawn.

Russell, Trenaman, and Eva froze.

"NYPD. Hands up, all of you," Greenstone said. To Trenaman he said, "Take your hand out of that desk, very slowly."

Trenaman slowly removed his hand from the drawer. "I'm NSA, Officers. I'm going to reach into my pocket and take out a badge," he said.

Trenaman moved his hand to his pocket while Greenstone's gun stayed leveled at his chest. Rodriguez covered Russell and Eva with his revolver.

Greenstone grabbed the badge from Trenaman and brought it over to Rodriguez to glance at. Then he slowly lowered his pistol.

"Nevertheless," Rodriguez said, with a voice of authority, "Vaderman is coming with us. We have some questions for him.

Unless you can tell us why you are dealing with a man who has contracted on a weapons deal. Is he working with the government? If so, your Horatius Marsden runs a pretty sloppy operation for government work."

Russell felt his stomach drop through to the floor. What was he *talking* about? Who was Horatius Marsden? Yet, Rodriguez's arrival felt like some kind of divine intervention. Trenaman had been about to kill him. The room started swirling in his head.

"You look surprised," Rodriguez said to Russell.

Russell threw discretion out the window. "I don't know a Horatius Marsden. But I *am* glad to see you." Russell nodded his head toward Trenaman. "I think you'll find a pistol in his drawer. You guys just saved my life."

"This is a government operation," Trenaman said to the officers. "Top secret, and you both need to leave. Now. I have this all under control."

Rodriguez shook his head. "Sorry, sir. Vaderman is coming with us." He nodded to Greenstone who grabbed Russell's hands, not gently, and pulled them behind his back and cuffed him. Russell felt incredibly vulnerable. He did not trust the police to necessarily keep him alive, but he hoped they could get him out of there. He turned to Trenaman with a parting argument.

"You know your problem, don't you? You don't work *with* anyone. You act *upon* them. As if people were commodities to be exploited. You are controlling people's minds, leading people around like sheep. You are no better than the fanatics who blew off your leg."

Trenaman looked enraged and stood up, too, moving around his desk as if he would physically hold Russell in the office with him. "People should be led around by the nose," Trenaman said. "It makes *their* lives easier, simpler. They want to be given a purpose to fight for. They are all damned for not using their own God-given brains!"

"That may be true," Russell replied. "But your 'solution' removes all individual autonomy."

Trenaman reached for Russell's arm, but Greenstone pulled him backward toward the door so that Russell almost fell over. "I told you," Rodriguez said quietly. "He's coming with us."

"Munitions are a national security issue. That puts it in federal jurisdiction," Trenaman said. He spoke like a man accustomed to being obeyed. "And this man is a national security risk." He pointed at Russell.

"That's as may be, but right now, he's also wanted in connection with a possible New York City murder. He's ours for now," Rodriguez said. "Take it up with the commissioner."

Rodriguez and Greenstone roughly escorted Russell out of the office and to their waiting car. Russell was more confused than ever. *He, Russell, was wanted for murder?*

A barely present vision of an old man with opaque eyes and a long white beard seemed to nod and wafted out the door with them.

CHAPTER 55

ussell sat in the interrogation room feeling weary in every bone. An eerie feeling of *déjà vu* came over him, and he had to fight to remind himself he had been here recently but it was with Joshua. Being taken into custody, while it likely had quite literally saved his life, was a concept that did not jibe with his sense of who he was. But then, his self-identity was in a frenzied state of flux.

Greenstone read him his rights, and Russell nodded his understanding. If Trenaman hadn't tried to kill him, he would have assumed this was a new "circumstance" that Trenaman had threatened him with. But it hardly seemed worth the effort if he was slated to die anyway. So, Russell found himself intensely curious.

Greenstone sat on the table in front of Russell and leaned over to put his face in Russell's face. A barely shrouded scare tactic, designed to intimidate, and probably would have worked on most people. Russell recognized it as simply Greenstone's adaptive behavior for feeling potentially ineffectual. Russell also detected the residue of scopolamine, something he had become hypersensitive to in his training with Trenaman.

"Why are you buying munitions, Vaderman? Expecting to start a war, are you?" Greenstone nearly spat in his face when he spoke.

"I have no idea what you're talking about."

"Horatius Marsden was delivering the shipment to you at your mountain home upstate. Of course, you know what I'm talking about."

Russell shook his head. "Not only do I not know a Horatius Marsden, I have no knowledge of any shipment, and the workers on my property have not been instructed to accept anything like that. Where did you get this information? I would like some details about what you are accusing me of. If you can't provide any, then I need to call my lawyer."

Greenstone threw the other chair across the room. It landed with a bang against the far wall. But the more violent and angry he became, the calmer Russell felt. He didn't want to ask for Jeremy until he got some information first to figure all this out.

Rodriguez walked into the room quietly. He nodded to Greenstone to leave and picked up the chair from the floor, calmly set it down across the table, and took a seat. Russell sensed Rodriguez's confusion, curiosity, and emotional stability. Rodriguez was in his element: the sleuth. What Russell did *not* sense was any form of a drug-induced state of mind.

"What were you talking about in there with the NSA agent? 'Mind control?' 'Brainwashing?' What was that all about?"

Russell was quiet, knowing how bizarre it all seemed. He wanted to take the moment to organize his thoughts and decipher the information coming at him from his environment. He felt sluggish, like when he was a kid, and his thoughts were so numerous and so jumbled, he couldn't straighten them out right away. As if he had never learned to master himself.

Rodriguez took his silence for lack of cooperation. He raised his voice.

"There is a lot you have not shared with us, Mr. Vaderman. A lot of strange things have been going on, beginning with your nephew's incident a couple of months ago. You see, I can't figure out how all this runs together. And in my experience, when someone ends up even peripherally involved in multiple criminal acts, there is usually a thread of connection between them all. I can't find your thread. But I know it's in there, somewhere. So… enlighten me."

Rodriguez put his elbows on the table and laced his fingers together, rested his chin in his hands and waited. His posture was relaxed, but his eyes blazed into Russell's.

"First, tell me what murder you are accusing me of," Russell said.

Rodriguez frowned. "The transfer of arms was nearly apprehended by customs, and one individual was killed. The package got through, though. We have not yet identified the dead man, but the weapons were purchased on your behalf."

Russell raised his eyebrows in surprise and brushed his hair back with his one free hand. He shook his head. "Honestly, I have no knowledge of this or of anyone by the name of Marsden. What evidence do you have that I made this requisition?"

Rodriguez clenched his fists on the table. "I want answers from you, Vaderman, not more questions. This whole thing is a mess, and you are going to explain it to me. Now."

Russell considered asking for legal counsel, but so far, he couldn't see that they had anything substantial to charge him with. He was really still only a person of interest, they couldn't place him at the crime scene. And in his gut, he trusted Rodriguez. He seemed sincere.

"Okay. I believe I may be a fulcrum in a string of events because of my exposure to a drug from the flower called Devil's Breath when I was a toddler in Peru. I seem to have some sort of immunity that certain government groups are interested in, like the NSA. My sister had a similar experience."

Rodriguez sat back in his chair. This was obviously not an answer he expected, but he kept quiet and waited for Russell to continue.

Russell decided not to hold back. He explained what he knew: that it sounded to him like Joshua had been dosed with this powder, that his sister had foolishly brought one of the *borrachero* plants back with her and it had been confiscated and "replaced" with cocaine, and that Trenaman had sought him out to have Russell explain how he had uncoiled Joshua's mind so they could use this skill for military and political benefit. He told them the NSA was using a similar cocktail to manipulate the population, and that Trenaman admitted to orchestrating the legal obstacles in Joshua's and Braelyn's life.

He did not say anything about the Man in The Hut or his apparent "visit" to Peru from the back of an Uber.

"*If* you can really do all this, why would the agency want you dead?"

Russell gave him his closed-mouthed smile. "Because now I know their manipulation scheme, and I would not help them in their mission. I can't teach them—I have no idea myself how I do it—and the truth is, I don't *want* to teach them. So, I've become a liability. By the way, do you know that your partner has been drugged?"

Rodriguez raised an eyebrow and glanced at the door. He started to say something and stopped.

At that moment, the door opened, and Harris strolled calmly in. He presented a badge for Rodriguez to scrutinize, but it was hidden from Russell's view. Rodriguez straightened up immediately and nearly knocked over his chair as he abruptly stood up.

"Sir. How can I help you?"

"Yes," Harris drawled. "The arms shipment came from me and is slated to be delivered in the Catskills later this week.

Regrettably, I had not filled Mr. Vaderman in on those details as of yet; we are still operating on a 'need-to-know' basis. He had no prior knowledge. He is to be released. Furthermore, you will keep this information to yourself."

Rodriguez swallowed and nodded. "Yes, sir. But there is also the matter of the man who was murdered at customs."

"An unfortunate casualty, we would have preferred to question him. He was an al-Qaida operative attempting to intercept the shipment. We had to arrange his elimination. So," Harris continued, "I will be taking Mr. Vaderman from here."

Rodriguez's shoulders slumped slightly in resignation. He walked stiffly over to Russell to uncuff him. "Mr. Marsden, you should know, the NSA had Mr. Vaderman in custody. We just pulled him away from them, and I'm sure they want him back. I believe Agent Trenaman will be coming to look for him shortly."

"As you know, Detective, we outrank the NSA. You can direct this Trenaman fellow to us." He motioned for Russell to come with him.

Russell stood slowly and looked around as he followed Harris out of the interrogation room. His face must have been one big question mark because Harris just shook his head subtly and led the way out. Standing on the street outside the precinct, Russell turned to Harris.

"What is going on? Who *are* you?"

"As I told you, Mr. Vaderman, I am your friend. I work for a powerful planet-wide organization. We have members from the highest echelons of fifty-four countries, in addition to the Vatican, the Bet Din Hagadol of Israel, and the Sharia of Islam, to name just a few. Virtually every religion is represented, as is every major power in the world." Harris paused and gave him a knowing half smile. "We even connect with certain ancient tribes in the Andes. Our task is nothing less than to save humanity from itself."

"So, you are Horatius Marsden?"

"Indeed. Although you and your lovely wife knew me only as Harris."

"And the NSA will just leave me…?"

"The NSA will do what has been suggested to them to do. They cannot do otherwise. The power they command is formidable, but they have limits, just as we do. They cannot control *all* the fine details. You, for example, have just become a 'fine detail.'" Harris turned to walk down the block, and Russell fell into step beside him.

"Wait," Russell said. "If you are some higher organization, how do you condone the extremism you encourage from the liberals?"

Harris stopped and cocked his head in a half shrug. "Extremism was never the intention, but people will always embellish the truth. It is the nature of the human beast. The best we can hope to do is set a balance of power."

"So, you just let it happen? People are killing each other!" Russell was incredulous.

"If you want a world that is not a constant struggle between polar opposites or, some might say, between good and evil, I'm afraid you will have to build *that* world for yourself."

Harris started walking again. "Now, shall we start to make plans for your mountain oasis? The city is becoming a hotbed of infection, and while your mind may be extraordinary, your physiology is still quite human."

EPILOGUE

Harris was spot-on in his prediction. Within a couple of days, the infection rate in the city was rising exponentially. The word went out to stay home if you were sick but not seriously, as the hospital ICUs quickly filled to capacity and beyond. The morgues overflowed, and refrigerated eighteen-wheelers soon parked outside some Queens hospitals to accommodate the increasing number of dead.

The public received two sets of information. Health personnel stated it was a deadly virus and everyone needed to cover their faces, wash their hands frequently, and stand at least six feet apart, while Ganaffe's people said it was just like a flu, there was no need to worry, and masks were unnecessary.

Each side seemed anchored to their own truth. One side was based on medical science, the other on political shenanigans. The public was likely being manipulated by both sides at the same time, and meanwhile, citizens attacked each other in stores over mask wearing, many claiming the virus was a hoax and that being forced to wear a mask was an affront to their personal freedom.

Russell, Maya, Braelyn, and Joshua moved up to the mountains just as the weather started to turn cold. The outrageous statements coming out of the White House were being accepted and amplified in ways that Russell believed could only be explained by people not having access to their own minds. President Ganaffe himself became infected by the virus as the election loomed. While the media presented him as not being severely ill, it later became known he had a near brush with death. Yet Ganaffe had continued throughout to encourage his supporters to ignore virus precautions, and held rallies where masks were not required.

It was clear to Russell that even once Ganaffe was out of office and the pandemic had passed, the vast number of people believing flaming lies would persist, even when information was disseminated that directly contradicted facts, as long as they were reinforced by media and upstart fanatical organizations. And, of course, scopolamine. It was starkly terrifying. What had happened to America?

The season wore on and ultimately Ganaffe lost. He nevertheless proceeded to wreak as much havoc as possible in his remaining days by claiming the election was stolen, refusing to concede, and encouraging a violent insurrection from his base supporters. It was as if he were starting a coup.

When the Conservative Political Action Conference met in February to discuss the future of the party, a golden statue of Ganaffe was displayed. The picture sent an icy shiver down Russell's spine and reminded him glaringly of his apocalyptic vision. Harris's—or Horatius's—words whispered back to Russell, that Ganaffe fancied himself a "demigod" and would pillage the country as a dictator.

Russell resigned himself to hiding out in the mountains while the plague was overrunning much of the country. It seemed anyone who could manage to do so had fled New York City, and the "city that never sleeps" began to look like a ghost town. Discord raged in the streets and at government buildings around the country as extremist organizations became more vocal, all inspired and fueled by Ganaffe's followers.

By the time the virus passed, the world was going to be a very different place, even if it appeared that democracy had been restored. If Ganaffe's party did not succeed, it would still be a stain on the United States for decades. And if it did, maintaining a safe haven was going to be increasingly difficult.

If Russell was indeed meant for "something greater," he needed to figure out what that was. He decided to follow the Ancient One's suggestion and bring together a community of skilled people in the interim, people who were defined by integrity, compassion, and the desire to build better—to *be* better. But he had, as of yet, no idea from where he would draw these individuals.

In the interim, Russell buried himself in his office in his Catskills home when he was not hiking outside or supervising construction. "Harris" seemed to have disappeared as quixotically as he had materialized, leaving Russell alone to examine his "visions" of the future, which descended upon him erratically. He started to doubt himself and could not quite discern how much was pure imagination and how much really could come to pass. He had never been one to fantasize before, and he had no idea what to do with the phantasmagorias of the future that hounded him.

So, Russell took refuge within the serenity and safety of the clean mountain air, the gurgling stream, and the local wildlife, removed from the screaming suffering of his beloved city, which remained ravaged by plague and violence. The more he explored his mind, the more he found conflicting images of the future present themselves to him on various days. Disturbed in the root of his soul, Russell searched his heart tirelessly to uncover a clear path to a peaceful life ahead. He also continued his study of quantum physics, and he came finally to conclude that any or all of these would-be prophecies might, or might not, come to pass at all.

Or maybe, they might come to pass, *and* they also might not, at the same time.

"Those who are not shocked when they first come across quantum theory cannot possibly have understood it."

—Neils Bohr

In conversation with Heisenberg and Pauli, in Copenhagen, 1952

BEYOND THE PILLARS OF SALT

chapter 1

Devon slid down behind the large oak tree in the thick, darkening forest, trying to make himself as small as possible. His breath came in huge gulps that he was sure could be heard for miles, and he struggled to calm himself while his oxygen-starved lungs gasped loudly. He glanced at the makeshift cart he was using to drag his unconscious mother into the mountains. It reminded him of an oversized wagon he'd had as a child. She made no sound, but the soft rise and fall of her chest reassured him she was still alive. Barely. She had lost a lot of blood.

Another shot rang out from behind them and Devon jumped, even though this time it was fainter. He could more sense than hear the raucous laughter of the Marauders, drunk on their own chaos, and he said another prayer that they would give up pursuit. The smell of the forest was soothing; the buzz of insects and the thick canopy of trees that surrounded them offered the impression of coverage and safety. He'd had to ditch the SUV to get this far, hoping they would not follow him off-road. It was getting harder to navigate the narrow terrain. When all was said and done, the Marauders were inherently lazy folks and not interested in hacking their way uphill through tangled under-growth. That was his hope, anyway.

Not twenty-four hours ago, Devon and his parents happened on an abandoned farmhouse and had planned to hole up there, at least for the night. They soon discovered why it was empty—the previous owners had been slain and left to rot behind the house, a treat left for vultures that scattered as Devon wandered out back. Within an hour of their arrival, the Marauders returned, and Devon had to watch while six men murdered his father. They beat him to a pulp, kicking him in the head and chest, pounding his legs with shovels, and shouting "nigger" and "slave," and then they shot him five times for good measure. There was nothing Devon could do to help, just hunker down and stay hidden behind the old barn where he'd gone to check on any remaining livestock. His mother's condition, weakened by a previous bullet in her shoulder, made it impossible for Devon to leave her. He had been closest to her when the Marauders showed up and had pulled her quietly out of sight. He was about to run to his father's aid, but she had grabbed his arm with her good hand and begged him not to go to Dad. She said he'd be throwing his life away.

As soon as the coast was clear, Devon had run back. Dad opened his eyes for a moment, barely able to speak. "Take care of your mother," he whispered. "Find the Safe Place. Keep heading northwest...into the mountains... Find it, they'll have a doctor. Take her there..." He wheezed as he fought a losing battle for his life. "Go now. Go...quickly...before they..." And then he closed his eyes and was gone. There hadn't even been time for proper tears with the sound of dueled out mufflers floating on the horizon.

It was getting chilly as the sun set. Devon looked around the forest floor. There was plenty of kindling, but a fire was out of the question. They were out of food, but he dug in his pack for water and tried to get his mother to drink. She took one sip and shook her head. She pointed to Devon and whispered, "You," then drifted back into unconsciousness. The wound on her shoulder was wrapped in bloody gauze, and Devon wanted to change the dressing, but he had no clean bandages. He and his father had expected to explore that farmhouse and the town and see what supplies might have been left behind until they could find a doctor for her. The Marauders had found them first.

The smell of evergreens, sugar maples, and red cedars was refreshing, and for a moment he could almost imagine he was just on a hike. He thought back eight years to when he was sixteen, and his dad had taken him into these same Catskills to go horseback riding and then they had jet skied on Lake George. The trip was supposed to be his consolation prize for "winning" the Google Science Fair Competition on the national level, which came with a $50,000 award. After the protests that some half-breed kid like himself should never have been allowed to enter, he did not actually receive the prize money or the medal. The award was retracted entirely, and since then, things had gone from bad to worse. The only ones who could enter contests *or* have access to resorts of any kind now were the Marauders and the White Supremacists, known widely as the Whispies. They were also the new police. They were the *only* police.

Despite the dropping temperature, gnats and mosquitos were everywhere in the twilight, and Devon wished he had some bug spray. How was he supposed to find the Safe Place? Did it even exist? A part of him dismissed it as just a rumor, born of wishful thinking on the part of large segments of the surviving sane population. Dad had described it as a place of peace. A place where the Old Values still held. Where the color of your skin and the language you spoke and the tradition you practiced were not considered to be important. Only: Could you be honest? Would you be kind? Were you willing to work and contribute whatever skills you had?

Devon vaguely remembered that the United States used to profess these same principles. Before fair elections became impossible and always under question and the despots had moved into the White House. President Ganaffe, who had lost his second term in 2020, took back power four years later, and the Ganaffe clan had held it since. No one saw Ganaffe himself anymore, who would be in his late eighties by now, but someone was holding the reins of power in his name. And pure anarchy had ruled for the last five years.

Devon checked his pocket compass again as he stood up and brushed off his blue jeans. He wondered again how Dad knew in which direction to find the Safe Place, and why he trusted it to be more than a fantasy. But his parents had been privy to a lot of secrets of the resistance, secrets they had not shared with Devon. Better that way, he supposed, in case he'd been captured.

It was a little late to matter, but in the dying light, he surveyed the area for poison ivy; they had been lucky. He gulped down a third of the bottle of water, wanting to conserve it, but he was so thirsty. Mom still lay on the oversized wagon on top of their packs, which were filled with whatever Devon had been able to retrieve quickly from the SUV before he had sent it careening off a bluff, hoping the Marauders would assume they'd crashed. It had been a moment of impulse to take the cart with him when he left the farmhouse, but he never imagined how heavy it would be to drag it uphill with his mother *and* their belongings in it. Turning wearily, he started back up the mountain, a little more slowly this time, before he had to stop short.

Not ten yards away, a six-foot-tall black bear stood up on its back legs, facing them and blocking their path.

AUTHOR'S NOTE

I started writing this book with only three things in mind: the opening scene, an idea about using Devil's Breath in the plot, and an abiding frustration with the intractability I noticed in previously "reasonable" human beings, inspired by our current political atmosphere. I had no idea where it was going to go. It was not until I realized I could not solve the crises of the world in one book (and probably not in ten…) that I was able to bring it to closure. And then I wrote its sequel, Beyond the Pillars of Salt.

My purpose for this book is to ask people to think for themselves. For individuals to confront the possibility that in any given situation, the data fed to them by their friends, their political party, and their favorite media outlet may be incomplete, and may also, in fact, be opinion misrepresented as truth.

I understand that there is a distinct possibility that this novel will alienate many, the hard-core liberals and conservatives alike. It is really an attack on extremism in every form and represents my steadfast wish that neighbors and family, friends and fellow citizens, can find their way back to peaceful discourse.

Remember the time when we could disagree with each other politically without causing or taking "offense"?

***

My heartfelt thanks go out to my beta readers, Joyce Tisman and Maxine Cohen, for plodding through the unrefined version of this book. Your insights were invaluable. Special thanks go to my reviewers, Berry Fowler and Lynne Hinton, for taking time out of their busy lives to preview the finished manuscript at lightning speed and compose such humbling endorsements. It is deeply appreciated.

My cover designer, Joe Montgomery, always amazes me with his genius and skill, and I feel so blessed to have him create masterpieces for my novels.

To my developmental and copy editors, Erika Nein and Andrea Vanryken, thank you so much. And of course, many thanks also to Warren Publishing, who released the first edition. Special thanks go to the Very Indie Press for the second printing.

No work is produced in a vacuum. I am ever grateful for my family, friends, and colleagues who have allowed me to bounce ideas off them, even when I feared they would disagree with my politics, and who encouraged me when I wanted to throw in the towel. Special thanks to Dr. Steven Goldberg for unwavering support and friendship over the years, and to Ellen Gelerman, my fellow writer/comrade-in-arms and dear friend for nearly three decades.

ABOUT THE AUTHOR

Debra Blaine is a physician turned author. After thirty-plus years of practicing medicine, she wanted to contribute more to the healing of the spirit. The spirit of the individual and the spirit of the tzeitgeist, the global consciousness of our time. No small ambition, to be sure. So many are no longer open to listening to diverging points of view, but are manipulated by the schemes of powerful entities with their own agendas. How to reach people in a society which has become so fractured, that many even take pride in being rigid?

So, she writes fiction. Blaine hopes that if she can get her readers emotionally involved in her characters, she may make more of a lasting impression. And perhaps some will be inclined to be more tolerant when considering critical issues from the safer platform of entertainment, by hearing a story they might resonate with.

Dr. Blaine was born in New York City and grew up on Long Island, NY. She always had a passion for the humanities, and received her BA in the Plan II Honors Humanities Program at the University of Texas at Austin before attending Temple University for graduate studies in Comparative Religion. She ultimately changed paths, and matriculated at Baylor College of Medicine to earn her MD in 1987. She returned to New York for post-graduate training and practiced Family and Urgent Care medicine on Long Island and Queens for over thirty years.

She began writing novels in 2018 when she became frustrated and disillusioned with the changing focus of the medical profession, which now closely follows a business model seeking to optimize profit even at the expense of sacrificing health. Her first book, *CODE BLUE: The Other End of the Stethoscope* is a medical thriller that graphically exposes, in fictional form, the effects of corporate greed on the American healthcare system.

With our culture in America increasingly polarized and extremism now passing for the norm, Blaine was inspired to write this second thriller, *Undue Influences*. By postulating the intentional, chemical brainwashing of the American population by the two political parties, she hoped to create awareness and resistance to the practice of blindly following current fixated ideologies.

The sequel to *Undue Influences* is a dystopian fiction which takes place about ten years later. *Beyond the Pillars of Salt* is a representation of what our world might look like by the 2030's if we do not wake up and make fundamental changes. Not just to how we behave, but ultimately, to who we *are*. The warning is that if we do not learn to become better, more worthy human beings, we will engineer our own extinction.

The saga will continue as a science fiction series on the planet Meraki.

Blaine became a professional coach through FIA Coaching and works with clients to expand their paradigms and create a mindset that serves them, rather than following in the path of automatic life habits that may not. She is certified to train other coaches through this same organization.

In keeping with her new mission to present TRUTH in FICTION, the Very Indie Press was established so that Blaine can edit, format, and upload her books to distributors herself, cutting through the red tape of publishers who can take months to years. She has now added the service of guiding writers at every stage, including publication, to her coaching practice.

Dr. Blaine loves animals, nature, and being outdoors. She has a grown son who is also a physician, and she lives with her two rescue cats in Suffolk County, Long Island.

There is more information on her website, at Debra-Blaine.com.